# The Mother

# of

# Demons

τηε μοτηερ οφ δεαμονεσ

A Novel by Jeremy Michael

Henderson

This novel is dedicated to my children, Samantha, Peter and Leia.

Be wary of the things that go bump in the night.

Special thanks to Clancy O' Conaill, editor-extraordinaire.

Hopefully one day she'll want to read this story again.

In Fond Memory of:

Elaine Alfreda Bridgett Laite

March 7, 1976 – August 20, 2016

&

Kirby Alexander Tott

February 4, 1990 - July 25, 2015

Gone but not forgotten.

# Copyright

Additional Editing and Cover supplied by Nebula Author Services, Formerly Celestial Waters Publishing

https://nebulaauthorpromotions.blogspot.com/

# Contents

# Chapter 1

---

"Whence and what art thou, execrable shape,
That dar'st, though grim and terrible, advance
Thy miscreated Front athwart my way."

John Milton, Paradise Lost


"Evil knows where evil sleeps."
-Nigerian Proverb

They sat together in silence as the crescent moon slowly rose high into the night sky, not a word yet spoken between the two of them. Below the glowing moon, distant mountains appeared on the horizon like dark pointed teeth devouring the sky. They had not arrived together, these two quiet observers.

The eldest had come early, soon after sunset, emerging barefoot from the old woods atop the hillside to her selected spot amongst the dry summer grasses. She had never before graced these woods with her presence but her coming was felt by every living thing, even by the ground upon which she walked. The softly swaying branches, rustling in the breeze, seemed to whisper her name as though in wonder that she had come at last. *Lilith.* Her long golden hair was free and unfettered, left to catch the subtle evening air.

The second had come later, when the heat of the day had gone and the cool misty air had settled over the land like a nebulous blanket. She had also come from the forest, although she walked with caution, hesitant that she might not be welcome here. Her approach was slow and planned, meant to indicate that she came in peace. When she reached the edge of the slope, she too sat amidst the grasses. Her hair was of a similar length and color; long enough, had it not been braided in an aristocratic roman style, to reach the soft curve between her shoulder blades. The braid was simple yet elegant, pulled away from her face and curled upwards to expose her finely muscled neck. She also wore a fine robe, one that was slightly longer and more intricate in design, patterned with a finely stitched Persian design that mirrored the grace of her braid.

They did not sit so close as to be friends, nor so far apart as to be strangers, but between their distance and casual, silent repose sat something far greater, a nameless bond forged over the relentless passage of time. For an hour they sat, motionless and quiet save for the sounds of their breath, overlooking a broad expanse of dark forest that stretched to the distant horizon where it eventually met the sky.

A falling star streaked across the night, etching a fleeting arc of cold light overhead.

Finally, the younger of the two spoke and her breath seemed to carry weight upon the air.

"Why have you come, Sister?" Lamia asked softly, her voice a whisper, clear and smooth like the waters of the mountain lake nearby. Like those still mountain waters, her voice was also cold and dark. There was no urgency in her question, no desperate need to satisfy, so she waited and was still.

The answer, when it came, was spoken in the same whispered tone.

"I am drawn to this place."

Lilith didn't bother to turn her head as she spoke. Her eyes were also fixed; dark glistening pools that drank in the shadow and ghost-light flowing between the rough trees. Her answer contained few words, but to Lamia, her answer spoke volumes.

Lamia nodded in understanding, a motion so slight that had the exchange been observed by another, it would have been all but imperceptible.

Lilith smiled, her lips parting slightly to reveal teeth that seemed to glow with their own unearthly light. She had not seen her sister nod, but she had felt it just as surely as if her obsidian eyes had seen it for themselves. She could not explain the feeling, but the knowledge was certain, the same sort of knowing that had allowed her sister to find her here, sitting alone in the woods overlooking a forest that was as dark as coal under a night sky dimly frosted with the cold sparkling light of an eternity of stars. Her eyes held no warmth. The sense that had allowed her younger sister to find her was the same feeling that had allowed the eldest to be aware of her sister's hesitant approach from behind.

Each of the sisters was intrinsically beautiful; their beauty was cold and barren, like a vast sea that had known death and brought its kiss unto others. Their skin was smooth and flawless, untouched by the ravages of time.

"Return with me," Lamia whispered, "this is not our home. The land here is strange, like its peoples. You became faint to me, and I sought you out. I have come far to find you, *ahatu.*"

Lilith again smiled in response. She recognized the care that had gone into Lamia's words, the subtle choices carefully crafted to avoid offense and a possible turn to anger. The final word almost tricked her ears. It had been too long since she had last heard that ancient word for *sister*. None now lived that spoke that language, the vanished tongue of *Sumer*.

She glanced up towards the crescent moon, bathing in its cool glow and enjoying its familiarity. In the course of her long life, it was one of very few things that had remained constant.

"This land is different and it has beckoned to me. In times past I might have considered your words sister, but here for a time, I will remain. Stay if you will, for I mean you no harm." Lilith turned her head to face her sister fully, watching Lamia sit alone in the night.

Her golden hair framed her pallid skin; the fierceness of her green eyes was set into a face that had once been soft. Time did not heal all wounds. Some it covered with a thick scar, setting it in stone and sealing the injury where it would fester like a malevolent cancer. "Here I am invigorated; can you not taste the flavor, like sweet new wine? Our home has all but forgotten our true names and my memories lie like a stain upon those lands. Here there is no memory, no scent of history, no ghosts of what once was."

Lilith rose smoothly to sit close beside Lamia, an intimacy they had not shared since a time the world no longer remembered, lost even from myth. Before the moment was lost Lilith turned and opened her arms to embrace her sister, drawing Lamia against her body. She felt her younger sister stiffen, tense with the unexpected. It passed suddenly and Lamia finally relaxed, allowing herself to be pulled inwards, returning the gesture.

As Lamia surrendered to the embrace, she buried her face against the soft cotton of her sister's flowing beige robe, burrowing her head in the gentle curve of her older sister's neck.

Lilith ran her fingers delicately through her younger sister's hair, closing her eyes as she inhaled her familiar sweet scent.

"You will stay?" Lamia asked softly, her eyes closed. The feel of her sister's fingers combing through her hair was hypnotic.

"I will stay, Lamia. For a time at least, short or long I cannot tell."

Lamia nodded, shocked to hear her name spoken aloud. Only in this seclusion would her sister have been so bold as to speak her name. In a life of isolation, it was difficult to recall the comfort of holding and of being held. It was an intimate gesture, a rare glimpse beneath the hardened shell of her legendary sister. Hate was a stronger flavor than love, a more bitter and acrid spice, easily overpowering delicate tender moments. Lamia held on a little longer, wanting to remember these moments that were subtler and easily lost. She did not know when she might experience another.

"Why must you stay, Lilith?" Lamia asked, echoing the intimacy of openly sharing names.

"I have been drawn here and my promise must be kept, in this land or in another. What has been taken from me, I must take in kind. These people will come to know of my vow."

Below them, nestled amongst the trees at the end of a thin and winding dirt road, a yellow light shone through the small window of a log cabin. The sweet smell of wood smoke wafted through the night air, drifting upwards lazily from the river-stone chimney. The cabin was nearly as old as the gnarled trees that surrounded it; the walls were split and grey from years of weathering. The roof was thickly insulated with a spongy bedding of ancient moss.

From within the cabin came a distant peal of laughter, the innocent and hearty laughter of children.

Lamia smiled, and it was monstrous.

# Chapter 2

*"...the maid of desolation,
had built her house."*

- The Epic of Gilgamesh

Sam tapped absentmindedly at the steering wheel with his thumb, a regular beat that he was almost entirely unaware of. He had virtually no other means at his disposal to relieve the anxious energy coursing through his veins, and so his thumb slowly tapped it away, like a water faucet releasing the pressure of a crested dam, burning off one meager calorie at a time.

He peered out at the dark highway stretched before him, the blackness violated by the narrow but intense beam of his headlights. Around him, the infinity of night yielded briefly to his passage, its dark mouth opening to let him by, one lonely point of light, before closing its jaws shut behind him to resuming its lordship over the land. His presence was brilliant but fleeting, quickly forgotten.

He was amazed at how quickly the forest seemed to claim the landscape, creeping up against the roadside like an unwarranted intruder. As he travelled west towards Loveland the hills grew steadily, like moving waves of earth had been set and frozen in place. In the distance, silhouetted against the night sky, he could dimly see a majestic chain of unbroken mountains that ran from north to south, a jagged spine of stone. He was pleased that his mental image of Colorado had proven to be somewhat reliable.

"Jesus Christ," he whispered to no one but himself, an expression of relief that he was finally out of the store and actually on his way to the start of a much needed vacation. The lights of the city in his rear-view mirror had quickly faded far behind him and he was two hours gone before the sun had finally fallen. He had driven through the last town an hour earlier, a speck of habitation with a single gas station and a peeling white sandwich board that promised the store would be open around the clock. He had stopped there quickly, picking up a few items and topping his tank back up to full. His dark blue work shirt had been hastily thrown into the back seat, losing a button in the process, a gesture that spoke volumes of his urgency to leave. His white cotton undershirt was more than enough to keep him warm. He had thought about changing out of his pressed khaki pants and into his comfortable black running shorts, but the pants were at least comfortable, not like the itchy sweaty fabric of the work shirt, and so he had left them on. Sam was just under six-foot-tall and a pound or two shy of the one-ninety mark with blood pressure that would still medically be deemed healthy, at least so far. A few more years of retail pressures might change that. Sam had noted that the black hair along his temples was beginning to streak with wisps of white. He had kept his hair professionally short, easy to style in the morning and simple to hold in place in a hectic day, but with the advent of the white hairs he was considering going much shorter to limit their visibility. He wasn't quite ready to accept the idea of going grey up top.

He had planned on getting off early today by showing up early enough that closing the store would be relatively easy, allowing him to escape with a minimum of fuss and be out the door precisely on time.

As the Fates would have it, absolutely nothing had gone right. It was as though they had intervened in his destiny by interfering with his own well-thought-out plans, reminding him of the true nature of his influence, which was of course negligible. Clotho, Lachesis and Atropos seemed to possess a mischievous and even dark sense of humor. Either that or they were just bitches.

He looked down at his watch, straining to see the slim minute hand contrasting against its white pearl face. Sam then glanced at the blue digital clock on the dashboard. He noted the dashboard clock was, for the moment, a minute ahead of his silver Timex, and made a mental note to sync them later on.

Turning his eyes back to the road rolling towards him, he blinked harshly, squinting as he tried to adjust to the absence of light. The blue clock light was murder on his night vision, it was unreasonably bright he thought and wondered if there was some way to set the clock to a red color. The engineer who had thought the clock should be a bright blue deserved to be kicked, once or twice, maybe even thrice. Soundly. In the testicles. Assuming of course the engineer was a man.

*Oh shit Miranda is going to be pissed*, he thought.

And, he agreed reluctantly, she had a right to be.

Here he was, driving alone on the highway late at night while his family was already waiting for him at the cabin.

He shook his head in self-disgust.

It is said the road to hell is paved with good intentions. Well, he felt like he had lain a quarter mile of that asphalt personally.

The log cabin was a rental, a holiday getaway package that promised Colorado fresh air, clean mountain water and good times. The pamphlet had shown a selection of rustic cabins, all spaced around a glistening forest lake on individual lots, guaranteeing privacy and seclusion; a chance to get away from the daily grind.

His frustration boiled up to the surface and found an appropriate verbal release.

"Fuck!" he screamed, clenching the steering wheel until his knuckles went nearly white and shaking himself back and forth furiously behind it.

He pressed down on the gas pedal, his polished black leather shoe applying enough pressure to quickly pass the eighty mark on the speedometer.

The bubble of frustration popped.

"Fuck," he muttered, raising his foot and allowing the car to fall back to within a respectable distance of the actual speed limit.

A second later Sam laughed at himself, thinking how ridiculous it was for him to be yelling in his car and imagining how he would have appeared to an outside observer.

He needed this vacation badly, oh god, so badly.

Sam hadn't noticed how sick and tired he was of work until the reality of his vacation time was no longer just a section of highlighted yellow days on the monthly wall calendar. He had personally colored in the two weeks prior to his time off with a yellow high lighter, filling the blank white squares. The yellow squares kept getting checked off until The Holiday was no longer intangible and distant but very real and enchantingly close.

He could taste it.

The last week had crept by. No, it had absolutely dragged by, like he was trying to pull himself to the end of an uphill marathon on a hot, sticky road using only his lips.

Sam had sworn he could hear the tick of each passing second, marked by that hateful round clock hanging above the office door. He wanted to smash that god-dammed clock, just to see what "smithereens" actually looked like.

Sam turned on the radio, seeking a distraction to help the miles pass, and hopefully to calm his nerves.

The car speakers answered his request with a quiet hiss of static.

He pushed the SEEK button on the radio and waited.

Sam had known his day (and his plans) were going to hell when, within the first two hours of showing up early, he had accomplished exactly nothing - zero, nada, zilch - that he needed to do.

He tried to hide in the office behind closed doors.

He tried using the computer in the receiving bay.

He had even tried to escape into the human resources office.

Everywhere he went either the phone or the staff found him, bringing to his attention issues that only he was authorized to deal with, so that he couldn't even accuse the manager-on-duty of passing off work to lessen his own workload.

The world was conspiring against him.

He felt his blood pressure rise as he thought about it, certain an aneurysm hidden deep within his brain was about to burst, ending all of his troubles in one epic explosion.

Compounding the day, employees were calling in sick, cashiers couldn't balance a till and the computer system was freezing up more often than a Siberian water pipe in January.

Every step forward led him two steps back. Absolutely nothing went his way. He couldn't buy a favor or find a little luck.

Correction. He had plenty of luck. All of it was bad.

It seemed as though his customers had eaten an especially healthy and large meal of stupid before coming to shop. The adage of the "customer always being right" was so patently false as to be comical. It absolved them of their own accountability. He thought that everyone should be forced to work retail, at least for a few years of their lives. Retail was a great proving ground for character, demonstrating how often shoppers could be the lowest common denominator of the human species. There were times when, after dealing with an issue, he really honestly wondered how humanity had not yet gone extinct. Some people were so monumentally dense that he wondered how they could chew and think at the same time.

Worst of all, they were breeding.

The case in point? The Three Sisters decided to give him the middle finger in the form of a shopper coming to the door precisely at closing time, ignoring the fact the OPEN sign was off and he'd had to pry apart the doors with his arms since the automatic open sensor was disabled. The shopper was wholly unconcerned about anything, except for seeking a myriad of obscure and/or rare compact disc titles that hadn't been easily available even when the band or artist had been at the zenith of its limited popularity. Once the shopper was convinced they weren't perhaps hiding the titles elsewhere in the store and decided to leave, it was already twenty minutes past closing time, which of course meant that all of his closing procedures were also twenty minutes delayed.

So of course, the day ended with him already running late. He had done his schedules for the next few weeks; he had planned out his staff training calendar and left the appropriate directions for the new trainees and for the performance evaluations that needed to be delivered while he was away. All of that administrative stuff was done and neatly put away or emailed to the proper people.

All he needed to do was close the store.

It was so simple, he could do it blindfolded.

The final travesty, the sweet juicy red cherry sitting atop his disaster flavored sundae, was the nightly deposit that didn't reconcile. The investigative procedure to solve the discrepancy was laborious, and it couldn't be avoided or streamlined.

They had eventually found the missing money, a transaction that had been processed as a cash sale instead of as a cheque. He had found the discrepancy by printing off the complete list of daily transactions and reviewing each and every sale receipt until he found the one where the invoice amount matched the sum they were missing, also identifying the method of payment with the attached cheque neatly paper clipped to it by the cashier that had taken it. They had been chasing a phantom transaction. He had rolled his eyes in pent up frustration when he and his closing cashier had uncovered the error.

He had wanted to beat his head against the wall.

Brick or drywall, it didn't matter.

Another twenty minutes had been lost from his scheduled departure.

He had wanted to be on the highway long before nightfall, to put as much distance between him and work as he could while there was still enough light to see clearly by. With a little luck, he had hoped to be close to the lake before it was too dark. Sam had figured it was a four-hour drive under ideal conditions. He hated driving at night, even with his new xenon headlights. It wasn't the absence of light that bothered him, or the fuzzy harsh glare of oncoming vehicles.

It was the eyes.

Specifically, it was the glowing reflection of the eyes of animals waiting by the side of the road; the sudden and unexpected shine from the ditch that sent his heart into palpitations.

The anxiety of expecting to see the unexpected exhausted him. He had nearly driven off the road when he was nineteen, an eternity ago, while returning home from a day at the lake with his first serious girlfriend, Paula.

They had been laughing about the day. The interior of his old Subaru was filled with the sweet coconut smell of her suntan lotion. He had been pleasantly distracted by a fading beer buzz and the sight of his girl in a skimpy bikini that did her curves justice in all the right places, when they had rounded a corner doing a little over seventy.

He had averted his eyes for just a moment, away from the blank and boring road to the sight of her glistening suntanned thighs, when there was a sudden motion in the ditch. A moment later a doe leapt onto the road ahead of them, her glowing yellow eyes glaring at him balefully; emerging as though from the ninth gate of hell.

His right foot had slammed on his brakes, pumping them in a series of swift motions right down to the floor while his hands yanked the steering wheel. The screaming of his tires was almost as loud as the shrieks erupting from Paula.

The old Subaru had lurched deftly around the doe, shuddering ominously, threatening to roll, while Paula bounced off the dashboard and was thrown limply back into her seat, her screams abruptly cut short.

Sam distinctly recalled feeling his heart stop, the time between one beat and the next stretching over an immeasurable gulf of time. They had come to rest, sliding the last few feet of the median over a coating of fine gravel and dust before coming to a final and eerily silent stop.

The Subaru had bucked once and then stalled, coughing out a final belch of bluish exhaust before passing out at the side of the road. Sam's breathing had pounded in his ears like that of a steam locomotive. His forehead had slumped onto the greasy plastic grip of the steering wheel, his eyes staring wide at the speedometer. Glancing left, through his window and out towards the trees, he had watched in disbelief as the doe cantered calmly past the car, its sharp hooves clicking neatly on the asphalt before it vanished down the opposite side of the road.

He remembered feeling glad that the doe was okay while his mind was still racing with the expectation that at any moment he was going to die in a twisted metallic wreck. Paula was slumped back in her seat, unconscious and breathing deeply, her magical coconut-scented thigh marred by a smeared spot of blood that had dripped down from a thin split on her scalp.

That night from so long ago replayed in his mind as he drove down a different highway twenty years later. Illogically he half expected to see the same doe again, only this time it would be firmly committed to seeing him off the road and wrapped around an old and immovable tree.

He shook his head, clearing his eyes.

The radio suddenly fixed on a station; the static vanished and was replaced by a song telling everybody to *Wang Chung* tonight.

"Wang chung," he said aloud, wondering what it was that meant exactly.

The odometer logged another mile when a distinct 'splat' sound came from the windshield, making him jump. It sounded loud and abrupt, like someone had clicked their tongue on the roof of their mouth. Sam grimaced at the remains of a fat moth that had eviscerated itself over a patch of glass, entrails smearing over a wider area under his windshield wipers.

He shook his head in disgust, thankful it had hit the passenger side.

With his eyes fixed on the road ahead, he reached down into the shadows by his legs, fumbling for the cup holder set into his console. Finding what he was looking for, he gingerly lifted the cup to his lips, sipping cautiously, testing the temperature of the beverage.

The coffee splashed against his lips.

Cold.

*Wonderful*, he thought sarcastically.

It must have set a new world record for a beverage to go from boiling hot to stone cold.

He raised the waxed paper cup to his lips and drank quickly, thinking it best to down it all rapidly. He grimaced as the last of the coffee went down, the leftover sugary residue that had settled to the very bottom along with the remnants of the caramel flavoring. He shuddered reflexively and then tossed the empty cup into the back seat, not caring where it landed. *Fuck it.*

He reached for a sealed plastic confection on the passenger seat, tearing at the thin package with his teeth. It opened easily and both Twinkies were quickly dispatched.

Sugar and caffeine did the trick.

He glanced at the clock.

Another hour and he should be there.

He tried to loosen his death grip on the steering wheel.

Realizing he was a little too warm for comfort, Sam lowered the driver's side window by depressing a button on his door.

The evening air was refreshing, sweet with the fragrances of summer flowers.

It calmed him almost immediately, a subconscious reaction that he didn't fully notice until he found himself humming along to the tune on the radio.

He leaned forward on the steering wheel, for the first time seeing the thousands of stars that filled the night sky. At home in the city you never saw stars like this; the light pollution drowned out everything but the brightest of them.

He let his foot off the gas and pulled over to the side of the road, killing the engine as soon as the car was stopped.

Sam stepped out and shut the door quietly, not wanting to interrupt the profound silence.

It was mesmerizing.

Sam looked around, trying to recognize the constellations above him. Years earlier, as a teenager, he had immersed himself in astronomy and had no difficulty putting names to more than a few dozen stars. He had lost most of that knowledge by now, but he had retained a few names, stars that for some reason were more memorable to him. His favorite was Orion, but in summer it was hidden from view, below the horizon and out of sight until winter came again. He might have forgotten the names of most of the stars, but he recognized the constellations easily. Ursa Major was low on the horizon and partially obscured by the mountains. Higher up was Cassiopeia, immediately visible with its familiar 'w' shape. Sam didn't think that any of its stars had glamorous names. There was no Betelgeuse here, no Rigel, no Sirius. Instead, its stars were plain and less well known.

He pointed to the tip of the constellation, furiously trying to recall the main stars that made up its shape.

"Caph."

He thought the Arabic names were easiest to remember. They seemed to have a personality, something unique.

He pointed to the next star.

"Schedar."

The next came easily.

"Navi."

Sam grinned, pleased with himself.

The fourth one eluded him, on the tip of his tongue.

He gave up on it and moved along to the next one, remembering only that it started with a 's'. In the end, the name didn't come to him, but he was still satisfied with his accomplishment.

He sighed and inhaled deeply, filling his lungs with the cool air.

A satellite flew by overhead, its unblinking light cutting through the space above.

Sam watched it disappear over the horizon.

He missed times like this, times when he could just stand and reflect on how truly small he was in the grand scheme of things. In the day-to-day pace of holding a job and raising a young family it was so easy to forget that he was only one person on a small planet that orbited an average star that orbited an average galaxy that itself was a part of a cluster of millions of galaxies. The darkness above him went on forever, in every direction.

His mind tried to grasp the concept and failed; he was just too small to comprehend the magnitude.

Sam suddenly felt dizzy, overcome by the vertigo that inevitably seized him when he looked up at the night sky. He knew it was irrational, but he felt like he might just fall *up* into that void, falling until he asphyxiated in the thin air above or was desiccated in the deep cold, falling forever.

He reached back for his car; to feel something secure and heavy that might take away the feeling. Instead of being reassured, his hand felt only empty air, a feeling that made the vertigo even worse.

Sam turned around and opened the car door, pulling himself into the seat, hoping to feel reassured.

He turned the key and started the engine, pulling the seatbelt over his chest and locking the clasp into place, feeling his heart beat heavily as he pressed down on the gas pedal. The acceleration was comforting, a sensation that pulled him back down to earth.

He kept the window down, enjoying the feel of the air on his skin.

Sam made a note of the time and the distance on the trip odometer.

Despite the time, the stop had refreshed him, giving him an added boost of energy that had lifted his spirit.

He was almost there.

One more hour.

***

"Knock it off, Baxter," Miranda scolded, partly annoyed and partly scared that the dog hadn't stopped staring at the front door for the last hour, growling intermittently.

*Who am I kidding?* Miranda thought. The dog was freaking her right the fuck out. If it wasn't for trying to remain calm for the sake of the kids, she would barricade the door with anything she could move. She would lock herself in her room and hide under the bed with the largest knife she could find. There she would stay, wide-eyed and haggard until morning or until she died of fright, whichever came first.

Baxter growled again, lowering his ears over his skull, baring his teeth.

His eyes were fixed on the front door like there was a dead rabbit hanging from it.

Miranda rubbed her forehead, trying to relax by convincing herself that rationally, there really was nothing outside to be scared of, except maybe bears.

*Shit!*

That thought had just popped into her mind, completely unwelcome. She wondered why the hell she had agreed to come up here first, alone, with the kids.

Temporary lapse of judgement, she explained to herself.

The kids were still splashing in the tub, gleefully removing the sand and sweat accumulated over the course of an afternoon spent on the beach and in the lake.

"Come here, Baxter," Miranda ordered, thinking that if she could take him away from the door, he would stop acting that way.

Baxter looked at her once mournfully and refused to comply, maintaining his vigil at the door.

Miranda unconsciously began to chew at her fingernails, frightened by Baxter's fixation. What really made her skin crawl was the idea planted in her head that he was guarding them, aware of something lurking beyond that thin wooden door that she was entirely unaware of.

Baxter was a three-year-old greyhound. They had adopted him from an agency that specialized in saving unwanted racing dogs. He was ideal. He didn't bark much at all, he was quite content with sleeping away the better part of a day, and he was great with the children. He could run like greased lightning. She had known greyhounds were fast but she'd had absolutely no idea exactly how fast until she had seen Baxter take off at full speed. They had taken him to a dog park, muzzled as per recommendations in order to help control his hunting instinct. Sam had left her at one end of the park while running over to the other, specifically to get Baxter to run to him.

When he was at the far end of the field, Sam had called for Baxter. Miranda let him off the leash and he was gone, a greyish brown streak that ran over the ground like a fired bullet. When Baxter reached Sam, Miranda called him back to her. She hadn't understood how intimidating it was to see a dog of his size running towards her at something like forty miles an hour until he was barrelling towards her at his full gait. If he wasn't her dog and she couldn't see the grin on his face as he ran, she would have been terrified.

Up until now, he had always obeyed her fastidiously. She hoped he simply had a case of the camping jitters and was feeling jumpy like her. After all, he was a city dog.

She looked at her wristwatch; twin to the one Sam wore, wondering for the hundredth time where he was. Deep down, she already knew. Again, he had been late getting out of the store. There were times she hated his job. She took a deep breath, hoping to hear the sound of a vehicle driving down the gravel road to the cabin.

She waited, and then exhaled.

Nothing yet.

Habitually she glanced at her cellphone on the counter, momentarily thinking she would call Sam to find out where he was. She frowned when she saw that there were no service bars showing on her phone; it was little more than a portable video game out here, something for the kids to play with.

No cell service and no land line; no connection to the outside world.

She shook her head, annoyed and unused to being unable to call him.

She was still surprised he had agreed to the vacation at all, especially when he had been able to secure a full two weeks off, the maximum he was allowed to take at a stretch. It was the first real vacation he had taken in about five years, since his promotion when Cindy was a toddler and Tommy had been nothing more than a bun in the oven.

Work seemed to be taking up more and more of his time and it was taking its toll on him. She could see it easily in the lines under his eyes. The stress was working on him, from the inside out. His blood pressure had already increased since his last check-up. It was time to get a family pass at a gym so he could work off the tension, and no more Twinkies on shopping day.

His only hobby had been martial arts, working his way to a first degree black belt in judo, an accomplishment he had achieved just prior to Cindy's second birthday. After the promotion, he had less and less time for the dojo, and he had cancelled his membership a few months ago, not being able to justify the expense of something he no longer did.

She thought it was time to tell him to get back into it, family time be damned.

They could all go together, if it came down to that.

"Wanna go outside, Baxter?"

Baxter didn't move.

He whined.

He didn't want to go outside any more than she did.

"Damn dog," she muttered, instantly feeling bad for having said it.

She was grateful for his being there; it gave her an extra sense of security, even if he was kind of freaking her out.

She cradled a twelve-inch knife in her lap, finding the weight of the steel blade intensely satisfying. Miranda wasn't sure what she could do with it, but it gave her a certain amount of peace.

Being enclosed by walls of eighteen-inch-thick logs didn't hurt, either. The weak spots were the doors, one at the front and one at the back facing the lake. Baxter had cemented himself in place at the front door shortly after sunset. Before then, he had been his normal rambunctious self.

They had left their home in the suburbs just after breakfast, leaving plenty of time for the day to warm before they reached the lake.

The vacation brochure had promised clean water, fresh air and well-kept cabins that were fully stocked; equipped with all of the modern conveniences, right down to solar heated water and satellite television. She wasn't quite certain it qualified as roughing it, but compared to their city existence it held a rustic charm. The twelve cabins of the resort were spaced out around a semi-private lake, far enough apart to promise total privacy from their fellow campers. So far that had been true; the only evidence of fellow campers was a distant and brief sighting further down the shoreline, the only area clear enough to allow an unobstructed view.

Dense woodland; scrub, bushes and trees, ranging from seedling to full-grown, filled the space between each cabin, sufficient to provide the illusion of true isolation in the wilderness. The pamphlet neatly neglected to mention the abundant populations of miniature airborne predators. Mosquitoes and blackflies were the most common, with horse- and deerflies thrown in for variety. They existed in sufficient numbers to necessitate the strategic opening and closing of screen doors for passage in and out of the cabin in as short a time as possible. Insect repellent was not optional. The conditions were better near the water where a steady breeze and hot sun drove away all but the hardiest of the bugs. Several dozen crushed specimens dotted the ground where they had set up their beach blankets. However, even repellent and dutiful attention weren't always enough, and so each of them sported swollen bite marks where they had unwillingly donated protein to the next generation of insects. Miranda knew that Sam intended to have a marshmallow roast in the evening; an activity she was now reconsidering, fearful it would draw ungodly hordes of insects to them.

A branch snapped outside.

"Holy crap," Miranda muttered under her breath, her mind suddenly perfectly clear and focused.

How had she allowed herself to get so jumpy? Baxter was hardly the best judge of a potential threat; as far as she knew this was his first experience outside of the city.

She chuckled softly and closed her eyes, biting her lower lip and leaning her head back into the soft cushions of the sofa. When they had arrived at the cabin, Baxter had sniffed the ground for a minute before he had even tentatively stepped out from the back of the car. Even then he had been cautious and unsure. The ground was covered with dried needles and littered with pine cones of all sizes, not the normal foliage he was familiar with.

An intrepid explorer he wasn't.

The solution to her nerves presented itself.

What she needed was a good glass of red wine, or two. Maybe three, in which case she might as well go for broke and have a bottle.

Or maybe two.

Several varieties of her favorite brand were already chilled, assortments of fruity zinfandels, just waiting to be uncorked and savored.

*To hell with savoring them,* Miranda thought. What she needed was a good alcohol buzz to take the edge off her nerves, or preferably dull them altogether.

"Can we get out now?" Cindy asked from behind the semi-closed bathroom door.

The splashing stopped.

Miranda put the knife down on the knotted pine end table.

"Have you washed your hair?" Miranda asked.

There was a thoughtful delay.

"Yes."

"I'll check," she cautioned.

She heard giggling.

"After we wash our hair?" Cindy asked.

"Yes," Miranda said, smiling. Cindy was a crafty sort; her mind always working.

"Okay."

The splashing resumed.

Cindy enjoyed washing her own hair, and washing the hair of her little brother seemed to satisfy a motherly instinct that she was already manifesting.

Miranda noted she now had enough time to crack a bottle and enjoy a glass before they would be done. One minute and a few practiced motions later, her glass was filled and raised to her lips.

The cool taste of wine teased her tongue, tingling ever so nicely as it went down her throat, warming her stomach and extending outwards to her very fingertips.

"Oh god," she sighed, thinking this was the best idea she had ever had.

She drained half the glass, feeling better by the second.

"All done," Cindy called out to her.

"Okay," Miranda replied, surrendering her glass to the care of the kitchen countertop while she was away.

Cindy and Tommy were waiting for her expectantly, ready to get out of the tub.

She took a look at the water.

"You two were filthy," she exclaimed, eyeing the brown bathwater.

The kids nodded and grinned enthusiastically, wearing the dirty water like a badge of honor. They had not only seized the day; they had ridden it victoriously.

Cindy was seven; Tommy nearly five, and both had their mother's wavy black Latino hair.

"Can we go back to the lake?" Tommy asked hopefully.

"It's dark out now," Miranda replied, watching as his facial expression comically sagged in disappointment. The kid took to water like a fish.

"You can again tomorrow."

The despair evaporated in an instant.

"Let the water out," she said, eyeing the dark water. She would need to rinse them off before they climbed out of the old claw-foot tub.

Cindy searched for the plug with her fingertips; the drain was invisible under a foot of water. There was a sudden burp and then a gurgle as the water began to drain.

Cindy placed the rubber stopper on the chrome water spout.

"Don't get out yet," Miranda said, "you both need a rinse first."

"We're clean," Cindy pleaded.

"Hardly," Miranda said, examining the dark whirlpool circling the drain.

She filled a pitcher with lukewarm water.

"Stand up," she directed them both.

They both stood up.

Tommy clenched his eyes shut like a fist and pinched his nose closed, leaning his head back expectantly.

Miranda poured the pitcher of water over him, removing the last coating of grime.

He avidly climbed out of the tub, grabbing his Batman towel energetically before running out of the bathroom glistening and dripping in his birthday suit.

Cindy, ever the big sister, watched him go, shaking her head in disapproval.

"He's still wet," she announced in a motherly tone.

"He has his towel," Miranda replied, "Your turn."

Cindy closed her eyes and leaned her head back, copying her brother exactly.

Miranda poured the pitcher over her, running her hands through her daughter's long hair to feel for any dirt that might still be on her scalp. She didn't find any.

"Good job," she said, passing Cindy the thick white towel that was her favorite.

Sam had bought it for her from the gift shop of the Hilton he had stayed at for a week of conferences.

She wrapped the towel around herself expertly, tucking in the end near her shoulder to secure it, mimicking precisely how Miranda did it.

"Can you do the hair thing?" she asked, unsure of how to explain herself while making a spiral motion over her head with one hand.

Miranda wrapped another towel around her head snugly.

"Like that?" she asked.

Cindy nodded.

"Dry off, then I'll brush your hair."

Cindy walked off towards her room to dry off.

Miranda needed to go find Tommy. For all Miranda knew he was probably sitting naked at the dog food bowl, helping himself to a few choice samples. He had acquired a taste for it when he was younger, discovering it while crawling around the house. So far he was proving reluctant to entirely abandon it as a conveniently placed, crunchy snack.

When she had mentioned it to Sam he had only laughed.

"It can't be bad for him," was his only reply, clearly indicating that if she had the issue with it, it was up to her to resolve it.

She found him wrapped only partially in his towel, sitting on the couch, flipping through his newest Dr. Seuss book. She eyed the dog food bowl, suspiciously noting a fist sized divot was missing from the very middle. His towel was draped over his waist and dangled at one corner to the floor, right next to where Baxter had curled himself in a semi-circle.

"Well, at least you finally moved," she said to the dog.

He wagged his tail briefly, settling down for a nap, the door apparently forgotten.

"You going to get dressed?" she asked Tommy.

He shook his head *no.*

A red mosquito bite was beginning to swell on his left forearm. He didn't seem to notice it.

"Jammies at least," she said, negotiating a compromise at the middle ground.

He shook his head again in a definite negative, his mouth upturned slightly into a slight grin at one corner.

Miranda scowled for a moment, recognizing the mannerism as one of his father's .

"The apple didn't fall far," she murmured under her breath.

Tommy was intently focused on something that a blue fish was telling a red fish.

She had an idea, hoping her Batman impersonation would work; he was Tommy's current favorite superhero.

Miranda concentrated on lowering her voice into a low and gruff impersonation of the movie character.

"Batman needs pajamas on."

She nearly coughed.

Tommy's eyes swelled with glee, recognizing the tone.

"They're in the suitcase," she said in the same rough and sinister voice.

Tommy lifted himself from the couch and ran to the bedroom laughing.

"I need my pajamas," he growled in an attempt to copy the voice as he ran past.

Miranda laughed.

A moment later she heard the suitcase being unzipped.

"You're so weird," she overheard Cindy say to him.

"You're weird," Tommy said, in the same low and dark voice.

Surprised at how well that had worked, she made a mental note to remember it.

She saw the half-glass of wine beckoning to her from the counter.

Batman emerged from the bedroom just as she drained the glass.

"Looking good," she said to him, smiling as he strutted back into the living room towards the couch. Tommy grinned and puffed out his chest to display the bat logo to its full effect.

Cindy saw him and rolled her eyes in response, not at all understanding how the mind of her brother operated.

"Can you put your towel in the bathroom?" Miranda asked Tommy before he settled onto the couch.

Tommy glanced at her and then at the towel on the floor, now partly underneath the sleeping form of Baxter.

"Baxter's sleeping," he protested, pointing his finger at him on the floor, concerned that he might have to wake him to get at it.

"Promise to get it later?" she asked him.

Tommy nodded in agreement, clearly relieved.

A low hooting sounded twice from beyond the main window.

*An owl!* thought Miranda. *A damned big one too, by the sound of it.*

Tommy was frozen on the couch like an alabaster statue, eyes wide, wondering what it was that he had heard.

"Hear the owl?" she asked him.

He looked at her doubtfully, wondering if that was really what an owl sounded like.

"Did you hear the owl, Cindy?"

Cindy was still in the bedroom, trying to select something to wear.

"Not a big deal, Mom," she replied.

This time Miranda rolled her eyes. Cindy was seven going on fourteen at times.

Miranda was already dreading the coming teen years, seeing the similarity between herself and her daughter. The apple didn't fall far from the tree in this case either.

Her own father had once pointedly remarked that Miranda was personally liable for each and every one of his grey hairs, each of them earned during Miranda's teenage years.

Tommy recovered his book and sat in a reclined posture on the couch. The book was open and sitting on his chest, his nose buried between the pages.

Not being needed at the moment, Miranda poured herself a second glass of the peach variety, her favorite. Next to her assortment of wine in the fridge sat forty-eight individual-size bottles of chocolate milk. A stranger to the kitchen would correctly assume they were for the children, but they would only be partially right. They were also for Sam.

He had never been much of a drinker and when a close friend of his had died as a result of car crash brought on by drinking he had sworn off the juice entirely. The works; wine, beer and hard liquor. Miranda had thought it odd when they were dating that his most frequent beverage was chocolate milk, but if that was the extent of his vices, then she had little to worry about. He didn't begrudge her wine and the kids certainly enjoyed sharing the same drink as their father. That might not last forever, but for now it was a part of their childhood.

The dying fire crackled in the river stone fireplace, the last few flames flickering with a dim, red light around the remnants of the logs they had consumed. Miranda drew back the black iron spark curtain and fed the glistening embers a few fresh logs, spacing them out equally. The red coals glared at her like the eye of a dragon, peering out from under the exhausted charcoal. She drew the curtain closed and waited to see if the fire caught. At first, there was nothing. The logs were still wet and resisted the heat. Then, subtly, a thin wisp of white smoke trailed upwards into the flue. The wisp grew into a thick cloud as the wet wood began to hiss and snap, and then a burst of flame erupted from the underside of the fresh logs. The bark peeled and split and the flames crept upwards, tasting the wood, dancing along the grain. Soon the fire was burning merrily, filling the interior with its warm light and sweet smell.

She noted that outside it was entirely black, a smothering darkness that did not exist in the city. The firelight could not pierce the absolute darkness outside beyond the windows. Nothing beyond the glass was visible.

Miranda retired to the cast iron sink where a series of plates lay soaking, stacked one atop the other and drowning in cold, soapy water. A small window was behind the sink, decorated by a sheer curtain that hung from a tarnished brass curtain rod.

She was hesitant to look outside, wary that she might see something that would justify her earlier fears. She caught a glimpse of a faint white light high in the trees and dismissed it, deciding it was only moonlight casting a thin silvery grace on the woods. She plunged her hands into the cold water and released the plug, letting the water drain so she could refill the sink and wash the dishes. The light moved.

Forgetting her fear she glanced outside and realized that the light was far too low to be from the moon. She brushed aside the thin transparent curtains that hindered her view and stared for a better look.

The light swept to the left, and then gradually back to the right, slowly strengthening.

She smiled and felt an immediate sense of relief.

He made it.

The headlights were coming slowly, silhouetting the forest, twisting and turning down the switchbacks and gravel washboards that marked frequent lengths of the old logging road. After the smooth highway pavement, travelling over the pitted washboards felt as though the teeth might rattle out of your skull.

The last of the cold water drained and Miranda re-stoppered the sink, twisting the tap and testing the temperature of the water on her wrist. When she was satisfied that the water was hot enough and the basin was full enough, she washed the dishes one by one, scrubbing them with a coarse wash pad that was infused with its own soap. Rinsed, she set them to dry in an old plastic rack to the right of the sink, placing the very last plate in the rack just as the headlights straightened out, harshly illuminating the short distance of road that led to their cabin.

She unplugged the sink, letting it drain.

She dried her hands on her jeans with two long swipes over her backside, once for her palms and once for the backs of her hands. The muted crackling of gravel under tires caught her ears, growing louder by the moment. The interior was suddenly filled with a pure white light that overpowered the soft, diffuse firelight.

Two bright headlights turned into the drive, the only parts of the car that she could see.

The lights illuminated the outline of the trunk of her car for a moment and then they were suddenly extinguished.

A door could be heard to click open and a faint interior light revealed the outline of someone struggling to gather items from the interior of the car.

Baxter's ears rose like little rotating radar dishes.

A door was slammed with a metallic '*whump*.'

Footsteps came towards the door, falling hollowly over the thick uneven planks of the low deck that fronted the cabin.

The door was knocked upon twice in quick succession and then it was opened cautiously.

Tommy put his book down, resting it horizontally upon his stomach, noticing for the first time that someone was here.

Baxter lifted his head quizzically.

"Am I in the right place?" Sam asked, peering around the partially opened door.

"Daddy!" Cindy and Tommy cried, their voices nearly perfectly overlapping.

Tommy dropped his book, letting it fall wherever gravity might take it, and rolled off the couch in one rapid motion.

Baxter wagged his tail and he too rose to greet Sam.

"Hi honey," Miranda said warmly, welcoming him with a quick but heated kiss just as both kids suddenly fastened themselves to his legs like giant barnacles. A moment later they let him go and they formed a chaotic group hug that was all hands and arms. Baxter nosed his way into the crowd to get his head scratched.

"How was the drive?" Miranda asked, noting the fatigued look that he was trying to conceal. He was faking it well, but his eyes were glazed and crisscrossed with a series of fine red lines. He was exhausted.

"Fine," he lied, smiling thinly. "How's camping?" he asked.

"Fine," she lied, wanting to forget her earlier intense paranoia.

"There's no cell service out here," Miranda added.

Sam checked his phone. There were no bars at all.

"Well, crap," he said.

"Understatement of the century," Miranda replied.

"Hey, we came here to rough it, right?"

"I wanted to rough it with a cell phone."

Sam ignored her last comment and focused on the children, placing his useless phone on the shelf by the door.

"Are you guys having fun?" he asked Cindy and Tommy. Neither had yet released him.

Both grinned from ear to ear.

"They're not as filthy as I expected them to be," he commented politely.

"You should have seen the bathwater," Miranda chuckled.

Short back and forth comments followed between them.

"Brown?"

"Like coffee."

"Lovely. How are the bugs out here?"

"If you're in the cabin or under water they are no problem at all."

"Hmm," he mumbled, thinking that didn't really leave many options.

Miranda pulled away from him and moved towards the fridge, a wide double door monstrosity that the kids could have hidden in.

"Hungry?" she asked, knowing he probably hadn't eaten in hours.

"No. I still feel like I'm driving. Maybe in a bit, once I get my legs," he added.

"Well, there are leftover burgers in the fridge. Oh, and some hot dogs, if you don't feel like burgers."

"A real buffet," he said.

"This isn't exactly the Hilton," she replied smoothly, "but at least there's a microwave."

The microwave was set into the cupboards over the white gas range that was the same width as the fridge. The range was a behemoth, probably weighing more than some small cars, and a little quirky from years of sporadic maintenance.

Miranda was used to her in-wall oven and the electric cooktop built into their countertop. Getting used to this kitchen was a learning curve.

"Let go kids, I need to get my things out of the car."

They let him go and went back to their business. Tommy recovered his book from the floor where it had landed in a triangle with the spine up and Cindy went to find her hairbrush. Baxter returned to his warm spot on the floor and curled up.

Sam returned a moment later with a small suitcase and backpack he retrieved from the trunk.

"You travel light," Miranda noted.

"It's not like the itinerary is complex out here. How many changes of clothing can I possibly need?"

"If you start to smell, you're washing your clothes in the lake."

"Deal," he agreed, wondering how well that would work. He didn't think it was going to be an issue; besides swimming and sitting on the beach, there wasn't much to do. Miranda wasn't what anyone would call a hiker, and out here there weren't any paths, short of those personally made by bushwhacking with a machete.

"What room is ours?" he asked, looking for a place to put his things.

"To the left," she motioned to the hallway. The bathroom was in the middle, directly ahead, separating the master bedroom from the slightly smaller room where the kids were bunked.

"Gotcha."

He slid off his polished black leather shoes and went to take a look, suitcase and backpack in hand.

The room was Spartan, a queen-size bed sat against the middle of the left wall, a simple five-drawer, knotted pine dresser on either side. Several rustic, amateur oil paintings were spread out along the walls, and two of them were almost good. Opposite the bed to his immediate right, a large book case occupied nearly three quarters the length of the wall. Its shelves were mostly bare, adorned with a few pottery animals; rabbits, squirrels and a bluebird. A few small vases were filled with dried wildflowers and the ends of the shelves held a few dozen leather-bound hardcover books, sorted irregularly. Sam leaned in to see what was there; a copy of *The Iliad*, *Moby Dick* and *War and Peace*.

"Light reading," he commented, raising his eyebrows in surprise. He had read none of them before. He might now get the chance.

He looked around, taking it all in.

He grunted, understanding that a large portion of the rental fee had evidently gone into purchasing the lot rather than enhancing the cabin accoutrements.

"What do you think?" Miranda asked from behind, slipping her arms around his waist while resting her chin on his shoulder.

"I've seen worse," he answered truthfully.

He took hold of her hands and turned around, kissing her again briefly, enjoying the few rare moments of silence before Cindy or Tommy had some need of them.

"Feeling any better?" she wondered, seeing that he was a little less dozy.

Sam shrugged. "Tired. Still feel like I'm doing sixty-five. But yes, a bit."

"Next year we'll plan better and take one car instead," she said.

"Next year?" Sam asked. "Already like it that much?"

Miranda laughed, jitters forgotten.

"The jury is still out, but I'm open to the idea. I'm saying that if we do make this a regular thing, we'll plan better."

"Fair enough," he agreed, feeling his stomach actually rumble a bit. He hadn't eaten since a little after three in the afternoon, not counting the coffee and Twinkies he'd had in the car. Thinking about the time, almost midnight, he was not surprised the kids were still awake. They were night owls at home and in a new environment such as this, they were only stimulated further.

They would probably sleep until noon tomorrow.

"They getting tired at all?" he asked Miranda, wondering if his marshmallow roast idea would still be feasible.

She shook her head.

"Novelty, sugar, and a late bath." Miranda answered; "Mostly the sugar."

"Think they'll still be in for a marshmallow roast?"

"Does McDonalds have a scary mascot?" Miranda asked.

Sam had to think about that for a moment before he asked her, "The clown?"

Miranda nodded. She hated clowns. All clowns. Fat clowns, skinny clowns, short clowns; all of them.

"I guess so, then," he said.

"Clever man," answered Miranda.

"The cleverest," he agreed, smiling, "I'll go start the fire if you want to get them ready."

"Is that a word?" she asked, "Cleverest?"

"If it isn't, it is now."

"I still don't see how you can hate Ronald McDonald," he snuck in.

"*Pendejo,*" she replied.

\*\*\*

The fire pit consisted of a clearing that lay between the cabin and the lake. Three wooden benches made from split logs were spaced around a ring of large stones that circled the rusty bottom of a flaking steel drum, looking like a radioactive symbol if viewed from above. The bottom of the drum was only a foot deep and filled half way to the top with grey ash and blackened specks of burned wood. The back door of the cabin led directly to it, following a path of weed-choked cobblestones and two creaky wooden steps.

Not wanting to waste time building a roaring fire from paper and kindling, Sam came prepared with a small aluminum can of kerosene. He had bought it in the sparse camping section of the lonely gas station where he had filled up his car. After constructing what appeared to be a decently flammable pyre of wood, he applied a liberal coating of kerosene, spraying several random streams of fluid over the pile of split logs. The scent of it filled his nostrils.

He dug a small, waxed cardboard box of Atlas wooden matches out of his back pocket, also acquired at the gas station. He pushed the interior sleeve of the case out with his thumb to get at the matches concealed within. Selecting the topmost match, he removed it and struck it quickly against the rough sandpaper edge of the box.

It immediately caught, the head erupting into a singular flare of yellowish light and emitting a pungent whiff of sulphur. Sam nonchalantly tossed the burning match into the fire pit, stepping closer to make sure it landed amid the logs, fully expecting the kerosene to ignite within a moment or two of the match landing between the logs and then spread smoothly over the rest of the wood. As his application had been liberal, the fuel ignited before the match could even come to rest on the wood. The dense fumes that had saturated the air went up like a pale blue mushroom cloud of fire, expanding upwards and outwards with a frightening velocity before subsiding into what could be best described as a vigorous inferno.

Sam saw the flames explode and leapt back in a panic, fearful he would be caught within the expanding blue envelope. He was certain he had lost his eyebrows. He felt for them nervously, thinking he could smell their remains on the wind.

His eyebrows were intact; all good.

He sighed in relief, guiltily looking back over his shoulders to make sure that the event had not been witnessed.

The heat of the flames was considerable, even at his current distance from the fire pit, driving him back to the log benches.

A mosquito buzzed his right ear, making him instinctively raise his hand in a futile attempt to swat it away.

"That was quick," Miranda said from the cabin door, eyeing the blazing fire suspiciously.

She had opened the door and stood behind the screen partition without him having heard her at all.

"Yup," Sam said, seeking to deflect any discussion about the fire.

"Isn't that large for a marshmallow roast?" she asked innocently enough.

"I wanted to build up the coals," he explained quickly, thinking and hoping that it sounded logical. It was the best he could come up with on such short notice. In the moment it sounded perfectly acceptable.

"I'll get the kids ready," she said, walking back inside.

An unintended consequence of the brightly burning fire was an added creepiness to the darkness around him. Before, the night was almost entirely black, a subtle blending of shapes and outlines made visible only by the nebulous light of the stars and moon beyond. The darkness was almost solid and pure, a consistency that held no hiding places, no haunted spots where a creative mind might add a random and fanciful terror. The night had been a curtain drawn around him. In that limited scope of visibility, it had less capacity to be frightful. Now, with the ebb and flow of the dancing flames, the night was partly peeled away and uncloaked, revealing a landscape of rapidly shifting shapes of varying depth and detail. It was suddenly much easier to believe that somewhere in that shifting pattern of fluid images something dreadful lurked, something from an ancient cartographer's creation labelled '*Here there be dragons*' in a flowing black script. From those moving shadows he could believe that something dreadful lurked, staring back at him with unseen eyes and biding its time. Sam shivered uncontrollably, a response triggered by an ancient and tiny part of his brain that had been conditioned to fear the night. He unconsciously moved nearer to the cabin, away from the exposed woods.

In the depths of his exhaustion, he wondered what the heck they were doing out here in the woods for a vacation.

He slapped at another bug that had made a gentle landing on his neck, feeling it crush under his palm. They could be back in the city, in their home, watching a movie with real buttered popcorn and hot chocolate surrounded by all the comforts they could afford.

They would have cellphones that worked.

Instead, they had decided to reduce themselves to a primitive alternative in the hedonistic hope that they might enjoy it.

He must have been mad to agree to this.

Worst of all, they were paying good money for this experience.

*Too late now*, he thought.

He tried to explain his sudden negativity with the reasonable explanation he was just tired.

He was grumpy.

Tomorrow would be different.

Tomorrow would be better.

He just needed to get through tonight, to get a good sleep under his belt.

The screen door creaked open, this time slamming against the outside wall. The sound was followed by the sudden and rapid trundling of small feet rushing down the stairs and across the cobblestones.

"Yay!" Cindy yelled.

"Yay," Tommy copied in a version that held a little less gusto, unsure exactly what his big sister was so excited about. The fire was neat, but he was starting to get tired.

Both wore light nylon jackets over their pajamas with their hoods drawn up tight over their heads to protect the backs of their necks against the bugs.

He saw they both had sticks in their hands already, the far end tapered into a dull point suitable for skewering marshmallows and little else.

"Where are the marshmallows?" he asked.

"Mom has them," Cindy replied, taking a seat on the bench closest to the waterfront.

Tommy took a spot next to her, his tired eyes transfixed by the hypnotic charm of the fire.

Miranda appeared a moment later, the bag of marshmallows in her hand cut open at one corner. She kissed him quickly on the neck as she walked past him, triggering a spark of electricity that shot down his spine. He sensed correctly that sleep was not on her mind, at least not yet.

"Hold your sticks out," she instructed, holding a marshmallow out at the ready, like a sacrificial virgin offered to the rumbling volcano of a tropical isle.

She impaled the marshmallow smoothly to the tip of Tommy's stick, and then added another to the end of Cindy's stick.

"Aren't you having any?" Cindy asked her parents, wondering why no one else, besides her brother who was always copying her, was participating.

"I don't have a stick," Miranda replied.

"Oh," said Cindy, thinking that made sense but wondering why she just didn't make one. She had seen hers being made, and it didn't seem all that difficult. She supposed that was also the reason why her father wasn't having one. Tommy didn't seem to care one whit.

"Put the marshmallows over the fire," Sam said, "but not in the fire. You need to cook them slowly."

"Why?" Cindy asked, thinking they tasted fine right out of the bag.

"Because it tastes good," Sam said.

Cindy shrugged, thinking that was a reasonable answer.

She lowered her stick to the flames.

Tommy did the same, watching her closely to see how best to do it. Within minutes the marshmallows turned a shade of golden brown and darkened steadily. Miranda and Sam neglected to watch them for a minute, losing track of time while enjoying the heat and light of the fire in the deep silence of the night.

Cindy shrieked loudly, snapping them out of their trance.

Both marshmallows were burning merrily, like sugared flares, bubbling and dripping. Cindy was aghast that her marshmallow was clearly a lost cause. Tommy was staring at his in fascination, not at all upset by the turn of events.

Miranda rose from the bench and collected the sticks, scraping the burning treats off the ends.

"Well, that was to be expected," she said, thinking that overall it could have turned out worse than it did.

"More?" she asked them both.

Both kids nodded.

Sam stayed put, looking around the fire, thinking that something was missing.

It suddenly clicked. "Where's the dog?"

"Sleeping of course," Miranda said, "he sleeps more than a cat."

She skewered fresh marshmallows upon the smoking blackened ends of the sticks.

"Cook them only until they are light brown," she explained.

"Like toast?" Cindy asked hopefully, the frame of reference giving her an idea of what to look for.

"Yes," Miranda agreed, thinking that was a good way to explain it.

"Toast," Tommy said, lowering his stick towards the fire.

Cindy followed suit immediately, staring intently at her marshmallow, waiting for it to brown like toast.

Tommy licked his lips in fervent concentration.

"Do you want one?" Miranda asked aloud.

There was a moment of unanswered silence.

"Hello," she repeated, a little louder this time.

"Huh? What?" Sam said, suddenly aware that it was him she was speaking to.

"I said, do you want one?"

She held a marshmallow out to him.

Sam considered it for a moment.

"It isn't a trick question," Miranda said, awaiting his answer with amusement.

"No, thanks," he finally said.

"Suit yourself," Miranda said, popping it into her mouth.

"Why don't you want one, Dad?" Cindy asked, concerned that if he didn't want one, then she might not either.

"I'm full," he lied. Truth was, he had a weak stomach for sweets. Candies made him nauseous.

Cindy shrugged, finding no fault in his answer.

They were quiet for another minute before Sam warned Tommy that his marshmallow was almost ready. It had already acquired a faint yellow hue as the sugar caramelized and was rapidly on its way to turning a golden brown. Rather than risk losing another one, Tommy pulled it away from the flames, content with its condition.

It steamed in the cool air, away from the fire.

"Careful," Miranda said, "it's hot."

Tommy blew on it theatrically and then touched it cautiously, testing it gingerly with his fingertips.

Seeing her brother, Cindy could wait no longer, her patience exhausted. Her marshmallow was even lighter in color than Tommy's was.

Miranda went over to her children and carefully pulled each marshmallow off their respective stick, placing the hot treats into hands that waited eagerly.

As warm as they were, both were consumed with quick abandon.

"Sooo good," Cindy mumbled, holding a hand over her mouth to prevent spillage while also covering her open mouth while she was talking.

Tommy moaned. *Mmmmm.*

"More?" Miranda asked.

Cindy and Tommy both nodded hungrily at her, their eyes revealing they thought it was the silliest question they had ever heard. They anxiously awaited another.

In spite of his exhaustion, Sam smiled at their enjoyment, glad to see them having fun. He felt himself fading fast; his eyelids were getting heavy. He didn't think he was going to last long enough to eat before he went to bed.

The long day was catching up with him.

Both sticks were adorned with fresh marshmallows and lowered quickly back to the fire.

Sam rubbed his eyes, trying to freshen up a bit, to keep himself awake. He swept away some sleep forming at the corners of his eyes.

A motion caught his attention, something just out of the corner of his eye to the right, a shadow that moved a little too differently.

Sam cleared his eyes and let them adjust, turning his head to see the area fully.

He blinked with surprise.

It was a woman.

She was walking slowly towards them from the direction of the front of the cabin and the parking spots. A faint smile traced her lips and her eyes seemed to sparkle with reflected firelight.

Only Sam had noticed her approach.

She seemed to move from shadow to shadow, blending in with the night, inconspicuous and entirely at ease.

His very first thought was that she was beautiful, not in the sense of being young or cosmetic, but beautiful in the sense of a woman in her prime, ripe and supremely confident. She emitted a lush glow and travelled with a fluidity that spoke of grace and eloquence, an ingrained ease of movement. Her hair was golden, not blonde but *golden,* seeming to reflect the fire like a shimmer of sunlight. Her complexion was flawless; her skin was lightly tanned like a Persian queen. Her eyes and lips seemed to glow in the firelight. Her eyes, he noticed, seemed extremely interested, aware of everything while looking directly at nothing. Sam noted her classical shape; an hourglass figure and a tapered waist that only accentuated her already generous proportions.

"Can we help you?" he asked sincerely, wondering what a beautiful woman like this was doing wandering alone so late at night. Was she lost? Was she their neighbor? She seemed to be completely comfortable.

For a moment, just a split second and even then barely noticeable, her regal face flushed and twisted with a hint of annoyance, perhaps even subdued frustration. In her eyes the emotion was pure and unfettered, raw and totally unrefined.

Miranda and the kids all turned to face her simultaneously, to see who he was talking to, each of them surprised at the unexpected sight of a stranger.

The woman's expression quickly reverted to its original cast, a look of intent curiosity. She was extremely attentive and her face framed a slight cunning smile.

Sam read her expression as one of satisfaction, like she had found what she had sought. He was only partly right.

Miranda moved to the side of her children, instinctively placing herself between them and the newcomer. The sudden appearance of the stranger made her feel uneasy for some reason she could not explain. At a base level, she recognized the facial expression of the stranger for what it was.

Lilith wore her hair free; cascading over her shoulders in gentle curls that were only accentuated by the fire. She wore nothing but a simple beige robe that flowed casually down past her knees, tied comfortably at the waist with a black length of soft cotton. A glint of metal hung from the shimmering silver chain of a necklace, so fine and delicate that it was almost invisible against her skin.

"Can we help you?' Sam repeated.

Lilith stopped midstride when Sam spoke to her, turning her head to gaze upon him fully, allowing her eyes to drink in the sight of him. He felt nervous under that stare, aware of her acute inspection of him and of his own adolescent-like insecurity under the weight of her eyes. Her look was imperial, forcing him to look away. In spite of everything, he was powerfully attracted to her.

Lilith smiled warmly, her full mouth opening just enough to reveal perfectly white teeth that glistened.

Sam felt his heartbeat quicken. He knew he wanted her. He forced the feeling out of his mind.

When Lilith finally spoke, her voice was perfectly suited to her outward appearance. Sultry and perfectly enunciated, she spoke with the hint of a strange and unusual accent.

"I was hoping I might be permitted to join you and sit with your family?" she asked calmly, so naturally that permission was a foregone conclusion. Sam felt compelled to reply.

"Of course," he said, almost hastily. Inexplicably, he found himself regretting having said it.

Lilith smiled smugly, her eyes glittering in an unexplained anticipation. She moved towards the fire, sitting gracefully upon the bench that separated Sam from Miranda and their children. She didn't move her gaze away from the fire until she was seated and comfortable, her hands crossed at ease in her lap. She brushed aside an errant curl of soft hair, tucking it behind her ear nonchalantly.

A mosquito droned in Sam's ear, making him flinch just as he saw another land delicately on his wrist, probing for a suitable vein the instant it landed. He crushed it a second later, swatting away the one that was buzzing near his ear. He noticed that Miranda and the kids were swatting and brushing absentmindedly at pests of their own, keeping them at bay as best they could. The woman seemed entirely unaffected, like the bugs hadn't noticed her at all.

Sam remembered reading somewhere that some people were fortunate enough to have a body chemistry that was not attractive to mosquitoes, that they emitted less of whatever it was that mosquitoes found particularly attractive. She appeared to be one of those people, whereas his family seemed to be exactly what mosquitoes were looking for.

"Are you from around here?" Miranda asked, wondering if perhaps the woman was from another cabin. Tommy and Cindy squished in closer to their mother, wanting to be close to her and be within her shell of maternal protection. The marshmallows were forgotten. Miranda had given Lilith a thorough, if subtle, visual inspection, and decided that, dressed as she was and clean as she was, she couldn't be lost. She must be from a nearby cabin.

"I saw your fire," Lilith said, avoiding the question altogether, "it is very beautiful."

Sam noticed that in the firelight, her eyes were not only very dark, but wholly black, as though her pupils occupied all but the whites of her eyes.

He dismissed it as a trick of the light.

"I didn't hear you coming at all," Sam mentioned, trying to start a conversation that might overcome the awkward silence permeating the air.

"Are the children enjoying themselves?" Lilith asked, gazing at Cindy and Tommy as though fascinated.

Cindy nodded, but only minutely, and Tommy not at all.

Lilith smiled an expression that made Cindy nestle even deeper into her mother's side.

"I wonder," Lilith asked, "do the children wear amulets?"

Miranda frowned, thinking the word strange. It was a word that her grandmother might use.

"Amulets?" Miranda repeated, thinking she might have heard incorrectly and wanting to be sure.

"Amulets," Lilith repeated coolly, her tone hinting that the word held some untold importance.

"Like a necklace?" Miranda asked.

Lilith was silent and withdrew the silver chain from her cleavage, revealing a thin pitted medallion that hung from its lowest link. It was tarnished silver, speckled with small black marks where the metal had been scored and marked, lending it the appearance of great age. Upon it was struck the shape of a tree.

"I wear an amulet to remember," she said, holding it aloft for them to see for a moment. She let it slide back under her clothing. Sam wondered how the silver chain would look between her breasts if they were uncovered.

He blinked to clear his mind of the thought.

"To remember what?" Miranda asked, interested in the medallion.

"My vow," she replied.

And then a nightmare unfolded.

Within the space of a heartbeat Lilith rose from the bench, lunging at Sam with a strength that knocked him off his seat and onto his back. He had only a moment to see her coming at him, and in that instant he wanted to feel her move under his hands, to hold her, to be under her. In the next, he recognized the murderous sheen to her eyes; eyes that were entirely black.

*The eyes are the windows to the soul*, he thought insanely, and the windows to her soul were dark and ancient, hinting at the terrible hunger within.

Her eyes glistened like used motor oil.

She stood over him for the briefest of moments, victorious, smiling with a dreadful grin, and then she descended upon him.

He was surprised at her strength, how she had struck him fully in the chest and pinned him to the ground. Her frame did not hint at the immense strength in her possession. She drove her face into his neck and for a moment he welcomed it. Then he felt her teeth tearing into his flesh, rending apart his skin and gnawing deeper into him.

He felt warm blood, *his blood*, he thought numbly, run over his skin.

Sam screamed.

He tried with all his might to push her away, to rid himself of her. She held fast, resisting the strongest of his efforts, clinging to him as though it was effortless.

Her teeth dug into him and in their intimate struggle he could feel her delight.

She *writhed*, snakelike, against him, her body soft and inviting; hard and terrible.

Try as he might he could not push her away.

He became aware he was screaming only dimly, like he was listening to something vague and distant.

Sam realized that he was going to die.

He could hear the screams of his children and a voice he knew belonged to Miranda, but for the life of him he could not remember who Miranda was. He was staked to the earth under the grip of the creature on top of him. Her hands pinned him to the ground and her legs were wrapped over him like a vise, holding him securely.

His heart hammered in his ears, a furious staccato rhythm beating out the final moments of his life. Against her, as he felt himself weakening, he could feel his attacker radiate a dreadful and intense energy.

A sudden low growling sound penetrated his stupor.

It was thin and distant to his fading senses, but it broke through his spell like a stone through plate glass.

There was strength within that sound, and he felt her react.

She tensed and through their clasping embrace he felt a shiver of insecurity flow.

Another vicious growl cut through the fog that clouded his senses, bringing him fully back to his awful reality.

His eyes cleared and he saw the woman rise from his neck, her sensual mouth coated in blood and bits of flesh. Her eyes were cold and triumphant, but behind them was a sliver of unexpected surprise. This was something she had not prepared for.

There was a flash of doubt.

A shape leapt at her, snarling and snapping.

She raised her arms to defend herself and was cast aside, torn from her firm grip over him.

*Good dog*, he thought vacantly, feeling his life's essence pumping from his neck in arterial increments.

Sam rolled over, face-down into the bloody dirt. He could taste coppery residue in his mouth; feel the weakness that was growing in his limbs.

He was cold.

He was driven by a need to get into the cabin.

He needed to get a knife, to bury the cold steel blade deep in her guts, to see her life's blood drain from her body.

Miranda, Tommy and Cindy continued screaming. Behind them, the sound of Baxter ferociously attacking the woman was suddenly cut off with a dreadful yelp.

Sam crawled over the cobblestones, rising to knees that threatened to collapse. His limbs felt terribly weak and the world swam in front of his eyes, spinning and fading to grey as though he had stood up too quickly.

Behind him, Miranda stood her ground, cut off from the cabin with the lake at her back. Lilith had thrown the limp corpse of Baxter aside, moving with a sudden, yet graceful rush to block her path.

Miranda kept Cindy and Tommy behind her.

"The protective mother," Lilith sneered. "It will not save them. They are mine," she hissed, claiming them as her own, for whatever purpose she deigned.

"Run," Miranda said to her children, "Run into the woods."

Tommy and Cindy clung to her, terrified to leave.

She was determined to give them as much time as she could. Maybe they could reach one of the neighbors if she gave them enough time. She could see Sam struggling to reach the cabin, swaying unsteadily like a drunkard on his knees. She had thought he was already dead, seeing him thrown from the bench and hearing his screams.

*The knife,* she thought, thinking that was what he must be going for.

Baxter had done what he could to stop the woman; teeth marks on her arms and face testified that she was not immune from harm, strong as she was.

"I don't want to, Mommy," Cindy cried.

"You have to baby," she whispered, "take your brother and run as fast as you can."

Cindy sobbed, feeling Tommy's hand slip into her own, gripping her tightly.

"Run, Cindy. Go. Follow the lake."

"Daddy," she began, choking on tears.

"He's doing what he can. Go, baby, now. I love you."

Miranda pushed her away, lovingly, to encourage her to go.

Cindy and Tommy bolted, running towards the moon hanging over the rippling water.

Lilith narrowed her eyes in fury, her eyes torn between the fleeing children and the determined mother that stood in her way. Lilith made a move to go around the fire, to flank Miranda and pursue the children. Miranda saw her move, read her eyes and body language to determine her intent, and with as much speed as she could muster, cut her off.

"You cannot save them," Lilith snarled, glaring into Miranda's eyes with white hatred.

"First you'll have to get through me *bitch*," and with that, Miranda spat in her face.

Lilith was shocked and her face contorted with rage.

Miranda threw herself at Lilith, her hands clawed as she went for a firm grip around Lilith's neck.

Lilith was not expecting to be attacked so boldly. She expected Miranda to resist as long as she could, to delay her for as long as she had breath. Soon enough she would be dead, and so would her children. Lilith would feed upon them all.

She felt Miranda's hands close around her neck, squeezing with as much force as she could muster.

Lilith fought back, grabbing Miranda's arms and pulling them aside.

Lilith laughed coldly.

"I admire you," she said, pulling Miranda towards her face.

Her breath was acrid and metallic, rich with the scent of blood.

"Do you know how many mothers have run with their children? Fleeing with them instead? A great many. Very few have the resolve to stand up to me, once I have begun."

Her rage was absolute but controlled, giving her terrible strength.

Miranda tried to twist out of her grip.

Lilith's hands held Miranda fast, like clamps. She understood now why Sam had gone over so quickly. This woman was unnaturally strong.

"Who are you?" Miranda gasped, resisting as strongly as she could.

Lilith leaned into her, their noses almost touching, Lilith's lips grazing Miranda's like a warm prelude to a passionate kiss.

"I am the First Mother," she replied cryptically, angling her head down towards Miranda's neck.

Sam heard Miranda scream once, a final penetrating cry, as he clawed his way up the first stair, feebly pushing himself upwards with his legs. His shirt was warm and slick with his own blood; he could feel his heart hammering in his chest.

He could not seem to catch his breath.

The screen door pushed aside easily enough, but once he passed the threshold he once again felt his strength leave him, and he sagged to the floor, spent. He lay there with his head on the wooden floor and his eyes closed, his breath was shallow and thin. He did not know how long he lay there for; each second ticked past like an eternity.

He was driving on the road, his hands holding the warm wheel of his Subaru, driving over the hot summer road. The scent of sunscreen filled his nose; the greasy feel of it clung to his skin. The sweet smell of summer pollen hung in the air, a scent that reminded him to this day of his youth, the memory imprinted in his mind. Suddenly the deer stood in his way, blocking the road, prancing on baking asphalt. It was smiling at him, an awful bestial smile that told him that this time Sam was not going to get away. The deer had claimed him for its own, coming for him at long last to finish the task it had started so many years before. It was the Angel of Death in disguise; come at last to claim his soul. The deer shifted its shape into a cloaked skeletal figure, one long arm gripping a bloody scythe. Red eyes peered out at him from under the dark cloak. His time had come.

A child's scream woke him from his stupor; the deer vanished with an unexpected grimace of dismay.

"Cindy," he croaked, squeezing his eyes together in emotional agony.

"Oh, God," he sobbed.

She was dead; he knew for certain the instant he heard the sound.

Another cry followed a moment later, cut brutally short.

"No," he murmured, his lips sticky from the pool of blood gathering around his head in a crimson semi-circle.

He had failed them utterly.

Tears filled his eyes, and a sudden last rage coursed through his body.

His legs pushed him forward, his arms reached out, gripping the floor with open palms. He slid forwards, the screen door closing behind him.

A twig snapped in the woods.

She was coming.

Sam was determined to resist her as long as he could, even if that meant nothing more than crawling away from her for as long as he could as a last gesture of defiance. He would die, but his last final act would be one of resistance. He would not show any weakness.

His family was dead, and he would soon join them.

It was his only comfort.

He heard the scrape of her sandal on the cobblestone path.

She was here. She had come for him.

He gave one last final push, straightening his right leg and driving himself forward where he collapsed next to an end table. Sam rolled over onto his back; he preferred to die facing her one last time. He could feel her staring at him. The hairs on the back of his neck rose and he felt his arms bristle in gooseflesh.

He opened his eyes.

As he had known, she stood there watching him, standing on the final step, her right arm holding the screen door ajar.

Lilith trembled with rage.

Her eyes were fearsome and her flesh glowed with an unnatural light as she gazed down at him in contempt. Her anger seemed to subside as she gathered herself into a regal posture.

"So here you are," she said simply, smiling.

Her pointed white teeth were now stained red.

"Finish me," he said, welcoming the sweet finality of death. He was ready.

She staggered at the door, her face a complex tangle of emotions.

Desire amplified her hunger; anger and frustration loomed in her dark eyes.

Lilith seemed unable to come any closer.

Her body revealed her difficulty, writhing in discomfort.

"Come to me," Lilith beckoned warmly, as though it was an invitation to her bed and to the pleasures she would willingly share with him, if only he would come to her. Her breasts seem to heave towards him, the curves of her hips enticing him.

Sam felt his body weaken. He could no longer raise his head above the wooden floor.

"Fuck you," he whispered between lips caked with his own blood.

He felt cold, so cold.

He was terribly thirsty.

Sam wondered why, in the final moments of his life, he should feel so thirsty.

Her lips pulled back as she sneered, her teeth set to ravish him again.

Fury flashed in her eyes.

"Come to me," she repeated, the lush warmth of her previous statement gone. It was an order, a command for him to obey.

Sam let his hands fall to the floor at his sides, no longer having the strength to hold them to his chest. In spite of his awful weakness, he wanted to follow her direction.

He hadn't the strength.

Sam lay there feebly. He could feel his eyes begin to close.

"*COME!*" she screeched at him, her voice shrill and piercing. Her hands clawed at the door jamb and the air between, but she could come no closer. She knelt at the step, seeking futilely to grab his foot and pull him back out into the night. There she could finish him; there she would end his life. She drew her arm back and tried to drive it over the strip of thin stained oak, but her arm stopped, as though it had struck a wall of invisible stone.

Lilith was held there, trapped at the threshold.

Sam chuckled weakly.

She rose smoothly, her hands clenched into quivering fists at her sides.

"Let me enter," Lilith cooed, the sensual overtones returned to her voice. Her voice was calm and serene. Her face was the opposite, a contorted display of rage and frustration.

*Enter*, he thought, realizing it could be that easy; wondering why she was just standing there.

Sam wished it would all just be over.

He closed his eyes to blink slowly.

Miranda, Cindy and Tommy peered at him from behind his closed eyelids. A sudden flood of memories overwhelmed him. He heard Miranda laugh as plainly as though she lay there at his side, warm in their bed with bright summer sunlight flooding through the bedroom window. He saw Cindy squeal with delight as he pushed her ever higher on a playground swing, her long black hair streaming in the wind. He saw Tommy pushing his favorite toy boat through shallow bathtub water.

His eyes opened.

They were gone.

Only *she* remained, standing over him, an inch from his feet. It might as well have been a mile.

"Let me in, and it will be over," Lilith promised sweetly.

Lilith waited for a moment, staring at him intently, like a fox staring hungrily at a chicken through a mesh of thin steel wires.

Sam stopped breathing, his mouth fell ajar and his eyes stared back at her blankly.

Lilith beat at the air furiously, clawing and digging at the empty space that would not let her pass. She screamed like the Damned, a culmination of all the horror and fear that lay just beyond the gates of Hell itself. She thrashed against the invisible barrier with all of her energy, but try as she might, she could not pass. She stood there, finally understanding he was beyond her reach, her chest heaving in exertion. She stared at him for a long while, even as the campfire burned out and died behind her and the cold white moon rose to its peak and then descended back towards the horizon.

Then she was gone, like a summer dream.

# Chapter 3

"*Kyrie, eleison.*"

"*God, have mercy.*"

His chest suddenly hitched, drawing in a sudden and ragged gasp of air.

It was hoarse and strained, like the painful first breath after being winded.

The pain was sharp and intense, a severe cramp under his ribs. His eyelids fluttered and then opened slowly, blinking then squinting as his eyes adjusted to the bright interior of the cabin.

Outside the sky was azure blue, unmarked by clouds or the white scars of passing jets.

A corridor of sunlight blanketed the narrow trapezoid of floor exposed by the open doorway. The screen door was ajar, stuck on a warped corner that was chipped and bare, devoid of the dark green paint that covered the rest of the door frame.

His first thought was that he felt terrible, like he was coming down with the flu or was terribly hung over. His head ached like he was suffering from an awful case of heat stroke. He wanted to puke. He lifted his head tentatively and a sudden spike of pain burst between his eyes, passing a moment later as he rolled over and drew his knees into his chest, his hands holding the sides of his head.

He lay there for a minute, fighting the cramps and bouts of nausea that churned in his stomach.

He dry heaved twice, his belly clenching as he bitterly spat out a small pool of spittle onto the wood floor. He felt none the better for it and rose, sticking out a knee to prop himself up, slowly standing to his full height.

The world was spinning, forcing him to lean over and grab the end table with both hands for balance. Deep slow breaths made the sensation subside and he felt a little better. Breathing was still a little painful, like he was recovering from a bout of running cramps. His sides were still stitched, but the muscles were loosening up.

The air was filled with sound, an indescribable cacophony that needed sorting. There were birds. Robins, jays, magpies, crows, the buzz of hummingbirds and the incessant chatter of finches and chickadees. An owl hooted quietly, settling down to sleep in the crook of a mossy tree. A distant woodpecker hammered at an old rotten log.

*Jesus, has there even been so many birds all at once?* he thought. There were still others, calls and chirps and trills he couldn't recognize. The air was filled with bees and wasps, their squeaks and droning and the buzzing of wings. The sudden clicks of jumping grasshoppers joined with the furiously beating wings of dragonflies.

Behind it all was the omnipresent sound of water, a consistent thrashing of waves and rolling water. Over that, gentler but in every direction, was the sound of breezes flowing through the trees and undergrowth, the restless creaking of branches and twigs swaying and rubbing, the whispering of trembling leaves.

All of these sounds combined and competed with one another; a steady concert of activity that his city ears were ill-accustomed to.

He was used to cars and sirens and the sounds of people.

None of that was here.

Something was wrong.

A dreadful certainty crept into his mind but he couldn't place what it was. Doom was coming for him. He could feel its approach but had no way of knowing from what direction it came. Only that it was coming.

*Something wicked this way comes,* he thought unconsciously.

It was still too quiet. Something was missing. In all of the various sounds and smells that were assaulting his senses, the more familiar sounds were absent entirely.

A book page turned, flipped by the wind. The paper rasped, sliding down over the page below it.

Sam turned towards the sound.

A simple yet familiar drawing marked the page that had turned. A large blue cartoon fish was grinning back at him, driving a red bulbous car.

His mind staggered, recoiling from an onslaught of scattered memories.

"Miranda!" he shouted frantically looking every which way for her.

The floor under his feet was coated with a thin black veneer of dried blood.

His blood.

Sam felt his neck frantically, remembering the hot, sticky feeling of blood on his clothes and neck. He expected to feel a cavity there; chunks missing. There was nothing. It was then he noticed his shirt was stuck to his body, caked against his skin. Panicked, he pulled at it, tugging at the buttons, feeling it pull at him as it came away.

"Miranda!" he screamed.

"Cindy!"

"Tommy!"

He remembered their screams, the finality of their voices.

It was their sounds that were missing: the sound of Miranda tinkering in the kitchen making coffee and reading the newspaper while music played from her tablet; the sound of Cindy talking to herself, still at the age when she liked to play, but shifting to older interests like her own musical tastes and her hair dryer; the sound of Tommy driving his cars and trucks all over the floor.

The sound of laughter.

The sense of doom that had been hibernating deep within his chest suddenly awoke; exploding like an enslaved giant breaking free of its chains. He staggered, again reaching out with his hands to clutch at anything nearby to prevent his fall. He grasped only air and his knees buckled, sending him to the floor.

He fell as though his legs had been pulled out from beneath him.

"Nooo!" he wailed, pulling his knees into his belly and clenching his fists in response to the physical and emotional pain that coursed through his body.

The nausea was gone; the headache was gone, swept aside by the tsunami of grief that now racked his body.

He wept until he was drained, his face wet with tears and his stomach aching from the force of his sobbing. The pain did not lessen, the loss was no less, but he could cry no longer. He was spent and lay on the floor, his eyes open but vacuous, seeing but not seeing. Everything around him was a dream, an awful nightmare that he was sure he must soon wake from.

A dream he had to wake from.

The woman!

He remembered her vividly.

Where had she gone? He recalled her standing over him at the door, clawing at the air like a cat, unable to get at him. He frowned at the memory. Why hadn't she been able to get at him? He could still hear her beckoning voice.

She had wanted him to let her in.

It was the last thing he could remember her saying. She had wanted him to let her in, needed him to let her in, but he was too weak to obey.

Her eyes had captivated him.

Sam shivered at the sudden horrible memory.

Those eyes had been as black as coal and she had stared at him avidly, the dreadful stare of a predator fixated upon its cornered prey. Her teeth had been red when she had smiled at him.

A note fluttered in the screen door, stuck between the frame and the door jamb.

It was folded along two crisp and perfect lines.

It was from *her*.

He struggled to the door.

Sam took a deep breath and pulled it free, unfolding it slowly and gripping it in both hands to read it, unsure he wanted to.

It read:

*I trust you slept well. Rest assured, if you are kindly concerned about my well-being, that I am entirely content. You are most unusual; to have eluded my most personal of affections. Very few have been so fortunate as to elude me in the past, and I have appropriately concluded my affairs with them all, sharing one final kiss, which some even welcomed. Perhaps you will as well? I tend to think not, but sometimes, even I am wrong. Your neighbours are sound; pray that you do not disturb them, lest you desire me to visit them when we have concluded our business. I do so look forward to our next meeting.*

*Lilith*

A knot of fear tied itself into his stomach.

He needed to get away from here.

She was going to come for him and the first place she was going to come was the cabin. He knew it as certainly as he knew the sun was going to set in the west. He rose to his feet and removed his clothes, leaving them in a blood soaked pile on the floor. He felt his neck again, still expecting a ragged wound of torn flesh and ripped skin. There was a lump of hardened tissue, like an old scar, but nothing else. He went to the bathroom to see for himself.

His neck and a portion of his shoulder was a mass of bright pink skin, like a slight sunburn that had only just begun to sting. He ran his fingers over it, not believing his eyes. The skin was going to scar, it looked raw and fresh, but the wound was closed. It was then that Sam became aware of his appearance; his face was smeared with dried blood and dirt, his eyes red and bloodshot from crying. He fumbled for the faucet and turned on the water, running his hands over his face and through his matted hair, cleaning himself as best he could in his present state of mind, fearful the woman would suddenly appear over his shoulder. If he was going to flee, he needed to bear some semblance of normalcy. He needed to be able to hide, to not draw attention to himself. Sam washed himself quickly, removing whatever dirt or blood or grime that he could see or feel. The fear was steadily growing within him, moment by moment. His hands began to shake. He wanted to leave *now*; every minute that passed only increased his paranoia. He needed to get away, to be safe from her. Then and only then could he try to call someone for help. He felt like she was somehow watching him, secretly hoping that he would seek help from his fellow campers. No, he thought. He wouldn't do that; he wouldn't risk that, not when she had promised harm to them if he did. He just needed to run, to be away from this place, as fast as possible. Sam grabbed a change of clothes, putting them on quickly. They were vacation clothes, jeans and a brown long-sleeve shirt, fresh socks and underwear and a pair of old but well-worn running shoes. He refolded the letter and slid it into his back pocket.

He gave the interior of the cabin one last look, feeling a fresh wave of sorrow begin to swell. Clenching his fists he stepped outside with dread, fearful he would find his family laying on the ground, left gruesome and abandoned for him to discover.

The bright sunlight seemed unusually warm, hot even, uncomfortable to stand in for more than a few moments. It was growing painful.

Sam stepped into the shade of a large evergreen for protection and looked around nervously.

There was nothing.

The fire was a pile of white and grey ash.

Two marshmallow sticks, charred on one end, stuck out of the ashes.

The sorrow that had been growing now momentarily subsided, pausing to allow him a moment of dreadful clarity. Sorrow shifted to regret. He managed to croak out a final farewell in the last spot where he had seen his children alive.

"I love you Cindy. I love you Tommy. Be at rest," he stuttered. A thick lump formed in his throat. His eyes, which had been dry, found a new well-spring and his eyes quickly teared up and spilled over. He wiped the tears away with the back of his hand.

"Please be at rest. Daddy will always love you."

His thoughts shifted to Miranda, remembering how he had heard her resist, hoping to save her children by sacrificing herself.

"Thank you, Miranda," he whispered. "Thank you for everything."

His knees buckled and he staggered, catching himself at the last moment to keep from falling to the ground.

His grief began to leap from one emotion to another.

A hot coal of rage sparked within him, hatred so deep and so pure that he didn't know how to contain it. The anger became a venom that flowed through his veins, quickly burning away the sorrow that had been so powerful a moment earlier.

He quivered and his breath came to him in choked gasps. His heart pounded with the desire to see justice done.

For the first time in his life, he knew he had the ability to kill another human being.

Another tear dribbled down his cheek, this one for Miranda, and this one he didn't wipe away.

He didn't know why he was still alive, but he knew he needed to get away and the sun was steadily rising into the sky.

Sam went to his car.

Each tire was slashed. He noticed that the tires were also flat on Miranda's car.

*She* was coming for him, and she had taken steps to limit his abilities.

He had no other choice.

Sam started walking, following the gravel road back towards the highway. There was no way he could walk the full distance, at least not quickly. It was over one hundred miles to Loveland from here, most of that through mountain roads. The directions were simple; all he needed to do was continue going east and he would eventually come across Route 87, running in its north to south direction connecting Fort Collins in the north to Denver in the south.

He looked at his watch.

It was almost a quarter past eight.

The gravel crunched under his feet.

The shade from the trees was cool and refreshing, a temporary feature of the landscape from being at the bottom of the small depression that held the lake. He was walking east, towards the rising sun. Once he was out in the open on the road there was going to be no escape its rays. Walking in and among the trees would provide shade, but it was also going to slow his progress. He was resigned to figuring it out as he went.

A consequence of his retail work schedule was that "weekends" were the opposite of what most people experienced. Where the usual expectation was to have Saturdays and Sundays off, his scheduled weekend was Tuesday and Wednesday, when the work week was slowest. The traffic to and from the lake was going to be minimal on a Tuesday morning. He was likely to see locals or people on vacation, a far cry from the hordes of people that would be driving these roads on a Saturday morning, out for a couple of days at one of the lakes in this area. Lost Lake was only another mile or two down the North Fork Trail from here. Lake Husted and Lake Louise were a little further along, although no roads led directly to them. That was bushwhacking country. If you wanted to bring a boat there, it was carried in on your back.

It felt good to be moving, it kept his mind free and clear of the grief simmering just below the surface.

His emotions were a pendulum arm, swinging back and forth between heights of normalcy and grief.

One foot in front of the other, left right left. Keep moving.

He reached the foot of the hill and began to climb the first of two switchbacks that would lead him to a nearly flat stretch. If his memory was right, it would become the North Boundary Trail. In time, it became the Dunraven Glade Road, and eventually, miles later, Route 34 East to Loveland.

Everything looked different.

In the light of day, it was like he was witnessing an entirely new landscape. He had seen this road only through the narrow and intense confines of his headlights. Everything beyond that range might as well have not existed at all, lost in darkness. The forest around him was spacious and green, not at all like the terrain by the lake. Here, between the trees, the ground was nearly bare. It was open space covered with a thick carpet of dry needles and dark cones that would go up like napalm the next time a forest fire came through this way. Of course, that's what the cones were waiting for, a good hot fire to open them up and start the next generation of forest. Every eighty years or so, nature cleaned house; burning away the dead refuse and old stands, clearing the way for young healthy woodland. By the looks of things, in about another twenty years, this part of the woods was due for a good burn. The trees here were mature, but not quite full grown. Here and there, rare survivors from the previous fire still stood, towering above the woods around them. These tall trees would eventually catch a lightning strike in a dry summer storm, becoming the starting point of the next great fire.

Precious little grew between the trees. What grew was hardy and tough, able to survive in low light with little water in acidic soil. Here on the road, in the ditches and along the dirt medians, grass took a foothold, growing in dense clumps that took advantage of whatever opportunity the landscape provided, proving they were tough little bastards.

Light brown grasshoppers leapt out of his way, clicking as they flew off into grassy shelter. Small black hunting spiders, the largest the size of his thumbnail, stalked their prey in the open ground between the grass islands.

Sam came to the crest of the hill about thirty minutes later, looking down a stretch of road that was nearly straight for about a mile or so before it rounded away down a gentle curve to the south east.

The shade of the trees had abruptly vanished.

The sun stared down at him.

Sam felt like he was going to throw up. His knees became weak and quivered.

He raised a hand to cover his face, to shield his eyes from the painful glare. His hand burned like it was getting spattered by hot bacon grease.

Sam wandered off the road through the gentle ditch into the woods, seeking the cool relief of shade.

He felt better almost immediately.

It was harder going off the groomed road, walking along the natural rise and fall of the forest floor, but it was worth it to be out of the sun. He came to a clearing where an ancient tree had died but nothing had yet replaced it, though several young saplings were making a bid for its former domain. Its grey splintered stump occupied the center of the grassy opening like a wooden gravestone.

Sam strode into the clearing and back into the open sunshine.

The light felt like it was splitting his skull.

He staggered, sinking to the ground before catching himself only a foot above the dry soil.

"What the hell is wrong with me?" he mumbled, feeling a cold sweat break out over his entire body. His legs felt hollow.

By the time he reached the opposite side of the clearing he was crawling on all fours, his head bowed like an old draft horse.

He reached the blissful shade of the woods and collapsed gratefully into it, breathing deeply as the nausea slowly passed.

A raven passed overhead, peering down at him hopefully as it made one slow, interested circle above. When the raven saw his chest was still rising and falling it moved on, catching the draft of a warming air current and rising to a better vantage point.

"Am I sick?" he asked himself, feeling the strength returning to his legs. He wondered if it was a combination of shock and not eating that was making him feel so vulnerable. The thought of eating made him feel ill. He had no appetite at all.

He had caught a terrible flu three years earlier and it had felt like this. He had been dizzy and the fever had been awful, soaking his clothes in a cold greasy sweat. When he wasn't throwing up he had been sleeping, a restless sleep filled with delusional and disjointed dreams.

But he hadn't been in pain like he was now.

Was it low blood sugar?

His face had *burned* when he stood in the open light.

That wasn't normal. He had never felt like that before. Maybe because he felt weak, he was reacting differently?

Sam rose and stood slowly, leaning against a tree and inhaling deeply, practicing breathing exercises until his head cleared. The forest was filled with scents.

He could smell the pollen of countless flowers. Some were sweet, some pungent, others only faintly aromatic. The trees had aromas; the fir tree at his back, the young pine tree at his side, even the gnarled black spruce nearby. There was a birch tree a little further on. He could smell them all. The birds were all around him. Chipmunks and squirrels watched him come and go, chirping and smacking their territorial warning calls as he wandered through their homeland. A honeybee flew past him.

*Were forests all like this?* He wondered. He had never noticed so many things around him before. Especially when his head felt as foggy as it did. He was seeing and hearing so many different things, and yet he felt like he was wearing sunglasses and earplugs, like his full potential was being restrained.

Feeling better, he resumed his march, careful as he picked his way through the underbrush to avoid the patches where sunlight reached the forest floor. Sunlight seemed to aggravate his mysterious ailment.

Sometime later he walked past a beehive sheltered under the stout branch of a spruce tree. Bees were coming and going, buzzing busily. For a moment, he thought how much Cindy and Tommy would have enjoyed seeing it. He immediately felt sick, the knot of pain returning to his stomach.

The pendulum swung.

He morosely resumed walking. A few steps later, he began to cry. Not the sobs that wracked him earlier, but a long and steady weeping as his mind digested the fact that they were gone. If he had crossed paths with another person in these woods, he wouldn't have known what to say and they would have been at an awkward loss for words, stumbling across him in this state. He was grateful he was alone, not feeling the need to control or conceal how he felt. As the pain lessened his mind cleared a little, allowing itself to wander to thoughts of the woman. He remembered the letter. Lilith.

His sorrow gradually turned to a low burning anger.

Sam pulled the letter from his pocket, unfolding it and reading it again as he walked.

What she wrote seemed insane; she was clearly crazy.

He should have stayed at the cabin.

She indicated she was coming for him, so by staying there he would have had the advantage, he thought logically. He could have called the police.

*No, he couldn't*, he reminded himself bitterly. *There were no phones!*

His cell phone was still on the shelf by the cabin door.

He could have been waiting for her there with his longest knife and he could have vengefully plunged it into her chest.

Except that an ancient piece of his mind told him that staying would have been his end. He would have met his ruin there. There was nothing he could have done to prepare for her visit.

His survival instinct told him to flee.

And so he fled.

There was more, but he was reluctant to explore the questions that kept bobbing into his mind.

What did she want? Was she some random serial killer? It took courage to approach a family with the intent of killing them. Of course, if she was crazy, then that helped explain it.

Only she didn't seem crazy.

Her actions indicated it, but her interaction with them was anything but.

Sam knew he was dreadfully oversimplifying things, but she just hadn't seemed a few cards short of a deck. In fact, she seemed extraordinarily competent.

The way she walked and spoke seemed to indicate that she was entirely sane.

Maybe she was psychotic, a high-functioning sociopath. That would explain her demeanour, her calm cool persona.

Except that she had *bitten* him.

What the fuck was that about?

What kind of sociopath attacked someone by biting the neck like some sort of freaking vampire-wannabe?

He stopped in his tracks; a bell pealed in his head.

A vampire?

He started walking.

Was that what she thought she was?

The pieces of the puzzle fit. She had come at night. She had bitten his neck.

Except that some things were still not right.

He vividly remembered seeing her clawing at the doorway, seeking to get into the cabin. She had asked for permission, he remembered terribly.

Would a mental affliction be strong enough to prevent her from entering a home without having permission? Was it possible to have a mental illness that was so pervasive as to stop such a simple act?

He recalled the look on her face; pure frustration and utter contempt.

Her emotions had been animalistic and beyond rational thought.

He couldn't imagine that something in her mind had stopped her from coming in after him. And yet she hadn't. Or she had thought she couldn't.

She was immensely strong.

She had knocked him off the bench and pinned him to the ground as if he were insignificant. Sam could bench press two hundred pounds, and she had held his arms to the earth like he was nothing, and he had fought her with every ounce of his capability.

She had held him forcefully to the ground.

*She had bit his neck.*

He felt his neck, running his fingers over the newly formed skin.

Maybe the bite hadn't been so bad after all.

Maybe he had imagined it being worse.

Was it a false memory?

Except that he remembered feeling his flesh tear away under her assault.

He had felt the agony of skin peeling away in thin ragged sheets. He had felt his muscles tear and rip.

And he had felt blood flowing from his body.

But he could have been dreaming.

He'd had dreams before, especially when he was sick, dreams that felt no different from reality whatsoever. Those dreams were indistinguishable from fact until his mind had cleared.

The bloodstain on the floor was significant. How much had it taken to create that pool where he had woken up? Was it a gallon, a little more? How much blood was in the human body?

"Mister?"

That would have meant she was unable to enter the cabin without his permission. That didn't make sense at all.

"Hey, Mister."

Of course it was hard to say that any of this made sense.

What was also disconcerting was this strange feeling that *she* was out there, waiting for him. She was behind him now, he felt sure of that, somewhere out there and each step he took brought him further out of her reach. With every step he felt a little better, a little safer. There were other feelings, but they were fainter, and none of them filled him with the dread that she did. As the day passed on, the paranoia was growing. He wasn't traveling fast enough. The distance he was covering was inadequate.

He wanted to run.

HOOOONK!

Sam jumped.

"So you can hear!" a voice said from his right. "I figured you was deaf or sumthin', the way you just kept on walking there."

To Sam's right, a newer red Ford pickup was idling at the side of the road, a white Lance camper was fastened in the bed of the Ford, bedecked in stickers from dozens of national parks and a layer of bug kill. The driver was smiling, warm and genuine, as he peered through the open window.

"What?" Sam stammered in surprise.

Maybe the man was a hallucination.

"You okay?" the man asked.

The man was probably in his late fifties, sporting a thick white beard that matched the crop of white hair atop his head, and a grin that seemed plastered to his face. He wore a new jean jacket and a cotton V-neck shirt underneath.

He had had pulled over to the left side of the road, to get as close to Sam as possible. The truck was dusted with a thin spray of grit that was inevitable on a dirt road. A camouflage crossbow hung from the rear window.

Sam nodded that he was okay.

"Name's Robert," the man said. "Robert Robertson. My parents had a sick sense of humor, not knowing what a name like that could do to a kid. Still," he shrugged, "could'a been worse. Could'a named me Richard. Imagine goin' around your whole life being called Dick. No thanks."

Sam smiled; the man was no hallucination.

"You lost?" Robert asked.

Sam shook his head.

"Goin' for a walk then?"

"Sort of," Sam replied, thinking there weren't many explanations for what he was doing out here.

"Why you out walkin' in the woods?" Robert asked, "The road's a lot easier walkin'."

"I needed to get out of the sun," Sam answered.

"Burn easy?" Robert asked.

"I don't feel well. I woke up with it."

Robert's smile faded.

"A summer cold ain't no joke, 'specially out here walking in the woods. Or sunstroke either. You camping out here?"

"I was," he said truthfully.

"You ain't driving?" Robert asked incredulously.

"Four flats," said Sam, not lying but also evading the complete truth.

"Shee-it," Robert whistled, his grin returning. "If that ain't the worst bit of luck I ever heard, I'm a liar!"

Sam grinned, thinking Robert was one of those people who wore their emotions plainly on their sleeves. He was as transparent as cellophane and probably without a single enemy in the world.

"Where ya headed?"

Sam shrugged, "Loveland?" He didn't honestly know, but Loveland was the closest big city.

"On foot?" Robert exclaimed, his eyes nearly bugging out of his head.

Sam nodded.

"Shee-it," he said again, "that'll take you a week, if the mosquitoes don't carry you off first. Damn bloodsuckers. Fuckers. Hate 'em."

Robert scanned his forearm at the thought, making sure he wasn't being bitten. He didn't notice how Sam's face paled at the reference.

"Tell you what," Robert began, thumping on the side of his door with his left palm as the idea solidified in his head, "I'll drive ya' to Loveland myself."

"I couldn't," Sam protested, thinking the offer was generous, "It's an hour or more away."

"Then it's a lot better than your alternative," Robert laughed and then turned serious. "You think I'm letting you walk to Loveland, you're nuts. Hop in. Come on."

He clenched the fingers of his right hand together and stuck his thumb out towards the passenger seat, motioning him over with two stabbing gestures.

Sam saw that arguing the case would be pointless. It was like arguing about beer with an Irishman; there was no way he could possibly win.

Sam walked towards the truck.

"Right on," Robert said, smiling gleefully, clearly happy for the company.

"There's cold beer in the cooler," he said as Sam came out of the woods.

"You're driving," Sam said. The thought of drinking made him feel ill.

"You ain't. Beer's for you, not me. If you want any, help yourself."

Robert stroked his beard.

The sunlight struck Sam full in the face, burning into his brain like a thousand needles.

"Jee-zus, you do look bad," Robert noted, "C'mon. Get in. I don't wanna carry you, and if you take much longer, I'm gonna have to."

Sam leaned against the camper as he rounded the back of the truck, while Robert unlocked and opened the passenger door with his right arm, releasing the lock with a click.

Sam climbed in, ready to faint and to throw up spectacularly, all at once.

Robert looked him over.

"You mind if I look you over?" he asked Sam, his eyes were concerned.

Sam looked at him, wondering what he meant.

"Serious. I was a nurse. Can I look you over?"

Sam nodded his head weakly and leaned it back against the glass of the cab, near the handle of the crossbow.

Robert placed his hand on his forehead.

"Clammy as hell," he muttered.

His fingers dug into his neck, probing for an artery.

He waited.

"Pulse is quick; weak. Maybe a cold one isn't what you need after all. Here I thought you had the beer flu. Or maybe the whiskey flu, if that's your drink. You look proper sick. You really shouldn't be out here walkin' around. A hunter might find you a few years from now, nuthin' but a pile of bleached bones in the woods. Shee-it."

Despite that, Robert didn't pull away like some people would have, concerned about contagion.

Sam felt better for being out of the sun. It was overhead now, and he was protected by the thin layer of Michigan steel over his head. A narrow strip of sunlight beamed through the windshield and stretched over his jeans like a sleeping cat. He could feel its heat, but it didn't hurt like it did on bare skin.

"You are lookin' better though. How far you been walkin?"

"Since the lake."

Robert looked at him like he was either lucky or just plain stupid.

"Good thing I saw you walkin' along in the woods there," he said, shaking his head in disbelief. "Buckle up," he said, motioning to the seat belt resting on the cloth seat.

Sam buckled up.

"Didn't catch your name."

"Sam."

"Pleased ta' meetcha," Robert said, putting out his hand for a shake.

Sam shook it solidly, releasing his hand after a few quick pumps.

"At least you ain't weak," Robert said, "then you'd really have me worried."

Robert put the truck into drive, releasing the foot brake.

The Ford began to creep along, boosted by the slow and gradual pressure Robert applied to the pedal.

"No sense in accelerating quickly, is there?" Robert asked. "Just makes for worse fuel economy and we ain't racin' nobody."

The truck crept past twenty, on the way to thirty, shifting as it did so.

"Simple physics. The amount of energy needed to move mass."

Sam looked at him with a different light. Robert didn't appear to be a closet mathematician.

"I know, right?" Robert said, as if reading his mind, "I don't exactly look it, and I don't exactly speak it."

Sam smiled politely, hoping there was no offense.

"No offense, Sam. Sam the Man. Do you like green eggs and ham?"

Robert chuckled.

"Sorry. Messin' with ya'. Don't you worry. It's just an interest. Not the ham, mind ya'. Physics. That stuff blows my mind. Besides, my specialty was nursing, like I mentioned. I just like to dabble in math."

"You don't exactly look like a nurse," Sam remarked, thinking he looked more like Santa Claus on a fishing vacation. In a red truck.

"'Cause I'm a guy, ain't it. Nurses have to be women, is that it?"

Sam didn't say a word, thinking that Robert had pegged the stereotype perfectly.

The Ford shifted again, warming up past fifty. A cloud of fine dust blew up and spread out behind the truck like a jet contrail.

"I know. I got it all the time. Ain't many of us, and one less now since I retired. Definitely a stereotyped career, like how a plumber should be a guy, right?"

Sam shrugged. "It's what you see the most of," he replied.

"Sure you do," Robert said, "but is that because it's what's expected or because of nature?"

"Probably a bit of both," Sam answered politically.

Robert nodded, stroking his beard again.

"Probably. Say, you're looking a lot better. Even have some color back in your face. A bit pink, even. You really had me worried there for sec. Didn't want to say nuthin' at the moment and freak you out, y'know. Figured maybe you were having a heart attack or sumthin'. Maybe you were gonna croak on me and I was gonna have to roll you into a ditch."

The Ford crept past sixty and stabilized at sixty-five, purring down the road.

Robert looked at him with an absolutely straight face, like he really would have put Sam into the ditch, and then his cheeks twitched and he broke out a moment later into a broad hearty laugh.

Sam thought he really did look like Santa Claus.

"Shee-it, you should'a seen your face, Sam," he roared, wiping a tear from the corner of his eye once he settled down. "I really had you going there, didn't I?"

Sam only nodded, weakly.

Robert laughed again.

"But seriously, I really did think you might'a bin experiencin' a heart attack. Glad you ain't. Not much I could have done for you out here. Not much at all. The ditch would'a bin an option."

Robert corrected their course down the middle of the road, around a dry patch of washboard.

"I feel better," Sam said, thinking that he really did feel better out of the sun.

"Good stuff," Robert said agreeably, "Have a beer if you wanna."

The thought of it rolled his stomach.

"I'm not thirsty," Sam said.

He didn't even feel hungry, not a whit.

"Suit yourself. Music?"

Sam shrugged.

Robert pushed a button on his stereo, tuning into a satellite radio channel.

"Classic rock," he said, "hope you like it. None of that new shit. It's all shit. Every one. Buncha chimpanzees on guitars and not a real songwriter in the bunch. All the songs written for them. Can you imagine that? It's all karaoke these days. They think they're rockers, but they ain't. Goddam karaoke."

Sam grinned thinly, thinking that Robert would have liked to have spoken with an employee of his, a young bass player named Lorne.

Lorne played in a band on the weekends and even had a video for one of their songs. Sam was impressed by how well Lorne could play the guitar, but the singer sounded like a cat stuck in a washing machine.

Robert rhythmically strummed his thumb against the steering wheel, much as Sam had done the previous evening.

"You on vacation or sumthin'?" he asked, making conversation. He smacked his lips. "Say, get me a Coke, wouldja?"

Sam nodded and opened the blue Coleman cooler, fishing out a freezing can of Coke and dropping the white lid down back into place.

"Thanks," Robert said, popping the tab singlehandedly, taking a long draught and then belching thunderously.

"So? Vacation? Hey, why didn't you see a neighbor for a lift?"

"It was early and I didn't want to disturb anyone," Sam lied.

Robert pursed his lips and nodded.

"True. I wouldn't want to be woken up by some guy I never met needing a four-hour drive. There and back, you see."

"You camp much?" Sam asked, pointing to the camper behind him.

"Yup. Pretty much all the time. Bin driving around for say, oh… hmm… the better part of a year now." His eyes widened in surprise. "Whoa. Time flies," he reflected, taking another drink from his can.

"Where do you go?"

"Pretty much anywhere I want. Yosemite. Grand Canyon. The Redwoods. Canada, in the summer. Whatever's on my bucket list. You've seen that movie, right?"

Sam nodded.

"Might head down to Florida; maybe Louisiana. I haven't rightly decided yet. I was going to get to the highway first and turn south and just go from there.

See where fate steers me. Destiny kinda stuff."

"How long you gonna do it for?" Sam asked, adopting his vernacular.

Robert shrugged.

"Prob'ly 'til I can't drive anymore. Sold my house, sold most of my things. Whatever I wanted to keep is in the back there."

He thumbed in the direction of the camper.

"Just hit the road. The pension goes into the bank. Don't need much living like this. It's pretty light. Expenses are food and gas mostly. Write the kids to tell them where I am."

"Wife?" Sam inquired.

"Don't rightly know," Robert said. "Bitch. Don't rightly care, either."

Sam dropped the idea of asking more about her.

Robert hummed along with the radio for a moment and then finished his soda, passing Sam the can.

"There's a bag for empties under the seat."

Sam found it and placed the can in the bag.

"You got kids?" Robert asked. "You gotta ring there. Married long?"

Sam dry swallowed uneasily. The pendulum swung back towards the darker end of its arc.

"They're passed on," he said quietly while looking out the window, his tongue fumbling over the words. Saying it was awful.

Robert was stunned into an awkward brief silence. His eyes widened and he turned his head uncomfortably back towards the road.

"Shit. Fuckballs. Look, I'm sorry. Goddam it I got a knack for putting my foot in my mouth sometimes."

"You couldn't know," Sam replied. His eyes began to tear up again and he quickly wiped them away.

Robert saw it and bit his tongue, seeing it was still fresh, wondering what, if anything, would be appropriate to say.

"Shit," was all he came up with.

For several minutes the only sounds were those of the truck tires biting into the road, the radio, and the bits of gravel smacking up against the bottom of the truck.

Robert reflected on what he could say to help. He'd had his fair share of loss in his time, and it had molded him into what he was, and would be until he drew his last breath.

"There ain't much I can say," Robert said, "'cept that it does get easier. It takes time, but it does get easier. Hurts like a bitch, and I can see that in you now. You're gonna feel sad. Most likely gonna feel angry too. After a bit, you just suddenly move on, and it's easier to take. You never forget of course, and that ain't the point. But what you're feeling now, it'll pass."

"Do you believe in Heaven, Robert?" Sam asked, still looking outside, the landscape passing by unnoticed.

"Tough question," Robert said, taking a deep breath. "I saw a lot of death in my job. It was really tough at first, tough to see people going through the process. All the kids and families, and husbands and wives. I took it really hard and hit the bottle for a while. It was how I coped. Luckily I got smart and quit that cold turkey, or I wouldn't be here with you today."

"What changed?"

Robert sat introspectively, a rare moment for him. He bit his lower lip and then began.

"There was an old man came out of a hip replacement surgery. That went well enough, but he didn't take the pain well. He lived alone. His wife had passed years earlier, and he had little family left. A daughter and a grandkid. A little girl, if I remember right, maybe four years old. That was the sum of his family. Some cutie, she was. Maybe she was five years old. Anyways, cute as a button. They were across the country, coming to see him. He sat in that bed for three days waiting for them, pushing that morphine drip as often as he could, eating normally. He seemed to be doing fine, besides the pain. His daughter and grandkid finally came and visited him, brought him flowers and pictures and those silvery helium balloons. That night, maybe ten minutes after they left, I came to change his IV bag. There was just a change in his face. He was at peace, y'know. Content. He'd said what he needed to say. He just sat there while I did my thing and then he flat-lined. Right there. Right next to me. Just flat-lined. He had a DNR. Y'know, a Do Not Resuscitate order? So I just stood there and watched him. The very last thing he did was smile. Just a little. Watching him pass turned me around. I understood right at that moment, right at that fucking moment, that I was taking it all the wrong way, you see. He wanted to die, that entire time, lying there in that bed. Oh, he went through the motions of living, but I don't have the slightest doubt in my mind that he sat there in that bed waiting for his daughter and his granddaughter to arrive, to say his final goodbyes to them, to see them one last time. Probably to say he loved them. Once he had, he let himself die. Whatever came next he was ready for it and he wanted it. There was no fear at all in the way he passed. I'm not saying that everyone passes that way. Sure as shit some people are still scared, and it was never easy seeing a kid pass, but seeing the old man go made me open my eyes. It was just like he turned a switch and he was gone. He made his peace and he was done. I got a lot of respect for that old man. Now that was a long way to answer your question. I dunno if there's a heaven in the traditional biblical sense, but there's something that comes next, then that old man was ready for it and he went to it with open arms. After I saw him die I wasn't afraid of death anymore. It's as natural as breathing, as natural as sex. I gave up the bottle that night, cold turkey, and haven't looked back since. After that, I saw lots more, like my eyes had finally been opened. Whatever happened to your kids and your missus it's still shitty; shitty for you, but they're in a better place than we are. Mark my words. You're the one in pain, not them."

Robert fell silent again, reflecting.

"Thanks," Sam finally whispered, feeling a little better. The pain was raw again.

"Hey. You all right?" Robert asked, looking over at him with concern.

He could see the torment and pain etched into the face of his passenger. Whatever had happened, it had happened recently. Very recently. The grief was there, just below the surface like an ocean current. It sometimes made people do stupid things. Maybe that was why he had been out walking in the woods. Maybe he was grief-stricken; overwhelmed. His brain had blown a fuse and he was just out there, on auto-pilot like. Maybe he was lucky to have come across him like that.

Sam shook his head, trying to keep it all in, covering his mouth with his hand, fighting to keep control.

"Hey, you just cry," Robert said softly. "None of that macho bullshit; nothing to be ashamed about. You let it out. You won't be right unless you let it out. I'll keep on driving. You do what you gotta do. It's healthy. If you don't cry, something else is gonna pop in your wiring."

Robert put his right hand on Sam's shoulder in a comforting gesture.

The dam broke.

Sam cried.

His mind raced through memories; some of them old, some of them recent, all of them fed his grief. He remembered how he had felt when he had learned that he was going to be a father for the first time, a feeling of nervous apprehension to be responsible for a new life. Those months had passed quickly; a time of preparation that, Sam noticed, had been entirely different for Miranda than it had been for himself. Her belly had grown and they had accumulated a crib and a high chair and all of other accoutrements. To her, their child was already real, a being she could sense. To him, *IT* was a lump. Not until he held Cindy in his arms for the first time, did he appreciate and suspect what Miranda had felt all along. He recalled that the second pregnancy was different for him, different because he could relate this experience to the first one. This time, he knew what to expect. He remembered first words, first steps and countless other firsts.

Now though, there would be no more.

When he was done sometime later, after the grief had run its course, Sam felt a little embarrassed.

"Better?" Robert asked.

"Yes," Sam said, wiping his nose.

"There's tissues in the glove compartment. I forgot about that. Sorry."

Sam opened it and wiped his eyes and nose.

"Not being hungry or thirsty can be a sign of stress, the type you are going through. You might want to have something, even if you don't feel like you need it," Robert suggested.

Sam was suddenly exhausted. The foggy feeling in his head was intensifying as the day grew on.

"Slept much?" Robert asked.

Sam shook his head.

"You should catch some winks. Wanna hop in the back? There's a real bed back there. Foam-top mattress. Might be a little bumpy, but it's somewhere you can lay down for a bit, at least until we get into town."

"I'm okay up here," Sam said, "I'll just close my eyes for a bit, if you don't mind."

"Don't mind at all. I'll shut up. Have a rest."

Sam was exhausted, but the truth was, he wanted to escape from his state of pain. Sleep promised to take him away from this nightmare.

He hoped he could escape from it, if only for a few hours.

Sam closed his eyes and began to dream. The dreams were even worse.

# Chapter 4

—⁓—

*"He made darkness his covering, his canopy around him, thick clouds dark with water."*

-Psalm 18:11

The dreams seemed to flow from one into the other, a seamless cascade of visions and images that shifted from one broken moment to the next. The overriding theme was terror; the terrible feeling of being pursued. He was walking through a forest, not a kind, green forest full of tranquil things, but a dark forest full of menace and fear. Shadows reigned, even where light tried to shine. The dark places were filled with glimpses of bright red eyes and the sounds of mocking laughter.

Sam began to run, following a path beaten and stamped into the earth; a narrow course that twisted and turned and was laced with gossamer webs. The forest was old and wild; gnarled trees that had seen the passing of many human generations, trees that bore him animosity. There was no comfort to be found in these woods, nowhere that would offer him shelter.

His breath burned in his lungs, his legs drove him hard and fast over the path, but still he knew that whatever pursued him grew ever closer. He could hear it behind him, pushing aside leaves and branches, relentless in its pursuit of him, tireless in its effort to run him down. Sam could hear it breathing heavily, hot air expelled in great rustling expulsions.

"Stay away!" he yelled at the dark shadow that followed him.

The shape laughed, running faster, encouraged by his growing terror.

High up in the trees barricading his path he caught sight of people, climbing slowly to safety or watching him run underfoot, sad looks upon their faces as though his doom was all but sealed. They were dark silhouettes, obscured by the dim light that pierced the thick tree canopy. Once he thought he saw Miranda, watching him run with a look of pity on her face. Other shapes were smaller, like children, and those he refused to look upon, scared that he might see Cindy or Tommy looking down at him with that same resigned look. The other shapes scared him more. They were dark, featureless shapes that looked upon him with one likeness.

Teeth.

Terrible white teeth.

Sharp jagged pointed canines glowing in the darkness, the mouths that held them opening and closing as if biting the air, or laughing in silent glee.

A fierce hand closed on his shoulder and spun him around.

Yellow glowing eyes stared back at him.

There was fog.

And there were teeth.

Sam screamed.

"Jesus H Christ!" Robert jumped, causing the paper cup in his hand to bump into the steering wheel. A cascade of salted fries leapt into the air, landing every which way. He leaned back into his seat and laughed.

"You scared me half to death!" he chuckled, sliding the cup into a holder. He picked up the scattered fries nearest to him, sticking them into his mouth where they were vigorously chewed. Those with stuck-on dirt went out the window.

"Here you go, Mister Crow," he said with each one that was ejected onto the road.

Sam clutched at his chest, still not entirely sure he was awake. The feeling of the hand on his shoulder had been so real, so intense; he could still feel the fingers clutching him, spinning him around and drawing him towards those *teeth*. His chest was heaving.

"Bad dream?" Robert asked, collecting the remnants of his spilled fries warily.

Sam nodded.

It was dark out. Sam looked around with surprise.

They were in the city.

Momentarily he felt like a child awakening on a road trip, opening his eyes to find himself suddenly in some new place, discovering where his parents had driven to as he slept.

"Where are we?" he asked.

"Loveland," said Robert.

It was early dusk; the last of the light of day was fading quickly to the west, a darkening crescent on the cloudless horizon. The first of the nighttime stars were already visible to the east.

"What time is it?"

Robert slurped on the straw.

"Ha'past nine. You've had a good sleep. Didn't wanna wake ya'. Got a meal for ya' though. Burgers and fries. Figured you'd be hungry."

"After nine?!?" Sam asked, incredulous.

"Yup. Like I said, didn't wanna wake ya'. Figured you needed your sleep. 'Specially feelin' sick and all. Your complexion is lookin' better."

They were sitting in the parking lot of a fast food restaurant; neatly parked between a series of cars all lined up like chess pieces on a board.

Tall sodium lights surrounded by a thin halo of circling moths covered the black parking lot in a yellowish glow.

"You didn't have to," Sam said, feeling bad that Robert had likely spent all of his afternoon in town nearby while he slept.

"I don't have to be anywhere," he shrugged. "Appointment calendar is pretty much open. I don't see the Queen until next Wednesday," he grinned sarcastically, chewing a fry.

Sam did feel hungry. His stomach rumbled.

"I'm starving," he said.

"Good. Gettin' better. Eat up," Robert said, pointing to the folded brown bag.

Grease marks darkened small patches of the bag near the bottom. The scent of fries and salt and beef and onions wafted up to his nose. He opened the bag and stuck his nose inside.

Sam dry heaved.

"Oh hey now," Robert exclaimed, alarmed. "You didn't upchuck into the bag, didja?"

Sam shook his head.

He was hungry, but the smell of the food within the bag made him feel terrible.

Something smelled delicious. Savoury scents wafted all around him, driving his appetite, but it wasn't coming from the bag.

The parking lot was surrounded by several more burger joints, a series of economy hotels and motels, and two brightly-lit gas stations.

Robert looked distinctly relieved. He ate the last fry, a crispy overcooked sliver, and tossed the packaging into the bag, balling it up.

"Still hungry?"

"Yes."

"Well, that's good. Just feeling delicate, maybe."

"Maybe," replied Sam.

In spite of the passing nausea, his head felt clearer than it had all day and the dull throbbing ache that had been anchored behind his eyes was gone. His mind felt refreshed and alert. The city lights were brilliant and seemed to reveal the surroundings as far as he could see in every direction. It was surreal, like nothing could escape notice under his gaze.

It was bizarre.

Energy trembled through his limbs.

He felt like he could run for miles.

"Thanks for the ride. I really appreciate it," Sam said, unlocking his seatbelt and putting his hand on the chrome door lever.

"What? You going?"

"I've held you up enough. I don't want to be a burden."

Robert looked at him with a concerned stare.

"You sure you feeling okay? It wasn't no trouble; you needed a hand." He took another long sip of his drink, getting down to the final ice cubes and slurping at the bottom.

"I am feeling a lot better. You were right, the sleep helped a lot."

In fact, Sam was relieved to be awake.

The dreams had terrified him and he was glad to be rid of them.

Robert looked about the parking lot quickly, taking in the surroundings.

"You gonna get a room or sumthin'?"

He was okay with leaving Sam, if he seemed to be in his right mind. There was no way he was going to leave him if he still looked rough. Robert looked him up and down. He did look a lot better. His eyes seemed to shine.

"I'm going to check out the restaurants first. Find something that doesn't bother my stomach."

"You sure?"

"Positive."

"Alright. I'm guessing you don't want the burgers then."

"No, thanks. Maybe it's like you said, I'm just a bit delicate right now."

Robert looked at him closely, giving him a final professional appraisal before passing judgement.

"If you looked even a little sick I'd tell you to go to hell and I'd book us a room or maybe bring you to a hospital for a closer look. Except you look fine to me. Besides your stomach, but maybe you just need something lighter to start off with. Might be heat stroke or dehydration; maybe try sumthin' to drink first."

Sam grinned.

*He looks like he could go a round with Muhammed Ali,* Robert thought. He looked to be the healthiest man alive.

"You got yer wallet?"

Sam fished his wallet out of his pocket, holding it up into the air to prove it.

"Fine. Lookit," Robert said, bending over to slip a small white card out from the compartment in the door, "you need anything, ANYTHING, you give me a call. You hear?"

Sam gave it a once over, tucking it into his front pocket. It was a generic business card, embossed in block raised print with Robert's name and phone number.

"That's my cell. It's always on. Call me if you need anything. I'll be heading out to Denver after I wash up a bit, but I have no compunctions about turning around if you need something or if you take a turn for the worse. Even if you just need to talk. You're dealing with some serious stuff, and I've been there."

"Deal," Sam agreed.

"Deal," Robert copied, and they shook on it.

Sam popped the door open and walked around the front of the truck, heading out to the strip of neon-lit restaurants that bordered the street.

"Drive safe," he said to Robert, waving to him briefly, "and thanks again."

"Anytime. You take care now." He gave Sam a casual salute and watched as he walked off into the distance, finally fading from view around a parked rig whose driver was doing a thorough brake check.

He eyed the bag of burgers and fries sitting on the floor.

He wasn't really all that hungry, but they sure made a mean cheeseburger.

"Fuck it," he said, opening the bag.

He casually dumped the fries out onto the parking lot.

"Here you go, Mister Crow."

He'd eat the burgers as he drove, and go on to Denver.

Robert grinned to nobody but himself, feeling pretty good about how the day had turned out. If he felt good enough, he might just press on past Denver. There was a national monument to the south of it. He'd see how he felt once he got there.

He put his trusty red Ford into drive and gave her some gas, looking forward to seeing where life led him.

He never saw Sam again.

***

Sam thought the air had never smelled so sweet, so fresh, so…well, so *different*. He couldn't really explain how it smelled, but it was invigorating. That strange paranoid feeling that had been haunting him was long gone, faint and diffuse like a bead of watercolor paint dropped into a swimming pool. He walked past several restaurants, and not a word of a lie, they all made him feel sick to his stomach. He was famished; his guts felt positively hollow, as though if he poked his belly, he would feel his spine at the end of his fingertips.

A sweet appetizing odor filled the air. It was a fragrant combination of smells, all delicious. He turned, following a side street that was filled with shops and stores, all open in the hope of attracting business from anyone out for a late dinner. The sidewalks were occupied by mingling people, the old and young of all shapes and sizes. Each of them appeared utterly clear and sharp; their voices carried in the air. A pair of young women left a store and walked ahead of him, each carrying a purse and a glossy plastic bag that held some prize from the merchants' shop.

Both were in good shape, one a long-haired brunette and the other a blonde.

Sam could smell them distinctly.

He walked a little faster, closing the distance between them.

They were laughing and talking to each other, the brunette sharing a story that the blonde found hilarious.

Sam ignored their conversation entirely; his eyes caressed them both from top to bottom, watching how they walked, gazing upon their skin and their oh-so-sweet smell. They were lush and hearty, bursting with life.

The brunette swept her hair over her shoulder, exposing the subtle soft curve of her neck for the most fleeting of moments. His eyes zeroed in on her flesh, staring at her warm skin and imagining what it would be like to bury his mouth between that finely muscled shoulder and her ripe neck. He saw himself pinning her down, pulling her to him while he bit and gnawed ever so sweetly and then finally drank.

Sam staggered and forced himself to stop, clutching his stomach.

His hunger pulled at him.

Sam realized he was salivating.

He stood there, watching the two young women walk away, entirely unaware of his predatory stare. He could still smell them; his nostrils were full of their aroma.

*What the hell...* he turned away, walking slowly in the other direction to get away from them.

Visions of the two women flashed through his mind, repeating over and over.

He unconsciously fell in behind an older man dressed up in a sports coat. He was walking quickly, late for a date or a meeting.

Sam craned his neck to look at him. He was maybe sixty, aging well. He didn't smoke, ate healthy, exercised regularly.

Sam inhaled deeply.

His smell was entirely different. The youthful scent was faded and spent, worn and nearly lost, an undercurrent that was only memory. Replacing it was an odor of maturity, a smell of layers and age that was more thorough, more delectable. Sam knew with dreadful eagerness that he would taste rich, like the fine work of an experienced baker; the subtle layers of an intricate, delicate pastry. He would be hearty, not sweet, an invitation that was rarer but no less delectable.

A young woman walked past him in the opposite direction, carrying her young infant, a child of several months. Sam's eyes followed her passing with menace. His eyes were dark and threatening and she walked faster when his eyes fell upon her. She smelled like a fresh wine to him, a bounty of bursting flavors. Over her, the smell of the child was overflowing with vitality, a vessel of the most luscious sort.

The man in the coat changed his path to avoid an old woman that was creeping along the sidewalk, making slow progress with a stainless steel walker that she shuffled ahead of her. She was bitter and tough, her scent was tainted like acrid oil and something that stained and marred what should have been a scent of the finest scotch.

*She was ill*, Sam knew for a fact. Cancer. Dying.

Her flesh was already corrupted.

Sam realized he was sweating, his limbs shaking.

His hands were curled and ready to strike.

Hunger was eating at him, driving him mad, and as he walked past the opening door of a pub he was drenched in the scents that flowed outward into the street.

His limbs quivered with weakness.

He could smell the odors of the stock beers and the foreign lagers. The scent of ancient scotch and aged whiskey graced the air. Sweet wine and delicate brandy lent their spice to the atmosphere. An expensive sherry sparkled between them all. But it was not the variety of drinks that called to him, nor the fine roasting food of the talented kitchen staff.

It was the multilayered buffet of those within. It was the smell of the young and old, the healthy and the well-fed, the bountiful and the hearty, all combined into a scent that tore at him. He recognized it as the smell he had noticed in the truck.

It wasn't the restaurants he smelled that drove his appetite, *it was the people.* All of their scents and odors were in the air, like the finest of grocery markets, all of the fragrances combining into a bouquet of menus.

He wanted to tear and to shred. To rip, to bite, to gnaw, to suck, to drink. It was all so delicious; he didn't know where to begin. A young woman walked past, and it took all of his strength to resist dropping her to the sidewalk with her throat torn out, all to slake his relentless appetite.

He dropped to his knees, shaking with an awful pressing need to… kill? No, *to feed.*

It was a hunger that he had never known, a famine that mocked any hunger he had ever felt. It was a strange electricity that sparked in his bones, driving and compelling him to strike.

"Are you okay?" a man stopped to ask when he saw him huddled and quivering on the concrete.

*Oh god he smells so good* thought Sam, like a slow-cooked roast, bathed in juices and spices. But Sam knew that no roast he had ever consumed would taste as good as this man before him. He was in his prime; fit and healthy.

He was there, stopped and bent over, waiting.

He could take him here, right on the sidewalk, shredding his carotid before he was even on the ground. It would be so simple. Sam could see it all so clearly in his mind, all he would have to do was pull the man down to feed.

"LEAVE ME ALONE!" he screamed, pushing the man away, only a moment away from killing him. If he hadn't pushed, but grabbed and held instead, his hunger would be at an end.

The man jumped and ran, looking back terrified over his shoulder only once to see that he was not being chased. He had seen the starved look in Sam's eyes, the warning that was laced into his words. The man fled for safety, knowing without a doubt that his life was in danger. He ran all the way to his car, a mile down the street, gasping for air when he reached it.

Sam groaned, placing his forehead on the ground, partially regretting that he had let him go. He knew that he needed to get away from here.

Quickly.

He was losing control of himself. It had taken every last ounce of Sam's strength to drive that man away. His stomach screamed at him, calling for blood, for flesh.

His arms were shaking, trembling with hunger. He felt sick again, nauseous, not from illness, but from a dreadful sense of starvation, a deprivation that was all consuming.

He wondered desperately if he was still dreaming, trying to explain his experience.

He hoped he was dreaming, because then this dream could end.

It would be an unusually vivid dream to be so convincing, but he knew how deceiving dreams could be. When he was eighteen he had a dream that he had won the lottery. The key was simplicity. He had been getting his ticket checked at a store when the clerk had broken the good news to him. He had endorsed the ticket while his mind raced with elation and once that was done he had driven home, thinking about how he was going to tell his family.

Then he had woken up.

He had been so disappointed that he had lain in bed for almost an hour before finally rising, so he knew just how deceiving a dream could be.

He wanted to wake up, waiting for the moment he opened his eyes and found himself in bed.

Sam stood and ran as fast as he could, avoiding people wherever he could, trying not to breathe as he ran past so as to avoid the temptation of their scents.

In the absolute clarity of his vision he saw an access alley ahead, a narrow lane used to cart groceries and supplies into the kitchens of the pubs, bars and nightclubs. It was between two buildings, concealed under the harsh light of an overhead streetlamp that was fixed atop a billboard. The shadow cast by the board camouflaged the alley, but Sam saw it clearly; a haven where he could get away and hide.

He ducked in, running past greasy plastic bags of garbage stacked alongside the dark brick walls, and a lonely green dumpster.

The paranoid feeling was back, pulsing in his mind like a second heartbeat, driving him to get away, to run, to flee, to hide. *Run.*

A shape leapt at him from the side of the dumpster, an arm raised in the air, driving what appeared to be a small wooden club down towards his head. Sam saw it all clearly, his mind slowing down the motion.

His years of judo came back to him.

Wake up, he prayed.

He didn't.

Sam deftly sidestepped the figure, avoiding the swinging arc of the club and grabbing the shape with both hands.

Rage surged in his veins. He could smell the violence of his attacker, the anger and the need that drove him forward. The man's attack was complete and absolute, with nothing at all held back. He meant to kill, if he could.

The odor drove Sam mad and fuelled his own sense of self-preservation. He would not die; not here, *NOT NOW!* Stoked with fury, Sam went berserk.

He pulled the struggling shape to his mouth and slid his head down, towards the shoulder, aiming for the pulsing cavity just below the neck.

The figure gasped and tried to scream but was cut short as his esophagus was torn out and filled with a spurt of his own thick, coppery blood.

Sam drank like a man driven to the final extremity of dehydration, a sun-baked Bedouin stumbling out from the parched desert wastes to a cool and unexpected desert oasis.

He drank until he was full and the man was spent, then cast him aside like just another bag of refuse. The body crashed limply onto the bricks, falling to the asphalt at an unnatural angle.

Sam felt his body surge with energy, his muscles and tendons bursting with vitality and strength. He could feel every fiber of his body cresting and absorbing the life-giving drink. His hunger was gone, replaced by a satisfaction that he had never known before. It was complete; quenching his need like a drug quenching the demand of addiction.

He had never felt so *alive.*

The night, filled with sights and sounds that had already been so clear and detailed, was peeled back like an onion to reveal yet another layer, even more intricate and precise. The fog that had seemed to distort his mind lifted, evaporating. It was overwhelming.

Sam collapsed to his knees, breathing heavily, exhausted yet energized.

The paranoid feeling also clarified, replaced by a certain and definite awareness that *Another* was near.

On the street.

Outside of the alley.

Coming for him.

Sam rose to his feet, waiting to see what would come around the corner.

Lilith rounded the corner in full stride, a lioness coming in for the kill. Her teeth were glistening and bare, somehow extended into lengthy fine-tipped points.

He recognized her in an instant.

The lake…pinned to the ground… feeling her mouth biting at his neck…the dying screams of his wife and children.

"You!" he raged, trembling.

She grinned, an evil toothsome apparition, breaking into a run so as to drive into him with her full ability. Sam suddenly knew that what he had experienced before was only a fraction of her capabilities, the tiniest demonstration of her physical strength.

She charged at him now, with no reservation.

He crouched at the ready, eagerly prepared to meet her onslaught, raising his arms to counter her outstretched hands that were raised like daggers. She leapt and came down on him, screeching with a voice that sounded like an entire classroom of fingernails on a chalkboard.

Her eyes were as black as oil, glimmering with a hellish yellow light.

Sam met her charge fully, ready for battle.

Chapter 5

"Her house sinks down to death, and her course
leads to the shades. All who go to
her cannot return.
And find again the paths of life."

-Proverbs 2:18-19

Lilith descended from her leap towards him like a bird of prey, her hands splayed in front like extended talons. Sam prepared to meet her, shifting his body into an on-guard boxing stance. Time seemed to slow to a crawl; he could see her position change moment by moment, preparing to attack him. She had covered the distance from the street to where he stood in only a second. Her hands narrowed as she neared, aiming directly for his throat.

Sam could feel his heart pounding, his lungs filling with air. Her visage was one of complete and unrestrained fury, completely given to violence. The moment before she struck he saw her expression alter slightly, hinting at a feeling of surprise.

Then she was upon him.

They struck furiously, coming together like two Olympian wrestlers, grappling and fighting for advantage as they tumbled and rolled down onto the ground.

Sam held each of her wrists firmly, one in each hand, holding her at a distance. Lilith jumped up and wrapped her legs around his hips in an attempt to lever herself into him, using the strength of her legs to her advantage in such close proximity, pulling him to her.

Sam felt her legs tighten around him, like a constrictor wrapping coils around its victim for the final suffocating clutch. She tried to angle her head towards his neck, snapping and biting like an attacking wolf.

He pushed back with his arms, driving her back so even at her closest she could not reach him. Snarling futilely, her vicious eyes bore into his. Her hands clawed, trying to reach his arms and break the grip he had around her wrists. Her breath was hot and humid, like a furnace blowing on his face.

She could not reach him; try as she might to gain an advantage, she could not get close enough.

Sam could feel the tendons standing out in his neck as he fought her.

She was strong, but he was stronger.

It hadn't been like this at the lake, when she'd had control over him, overpowering him completely.

He had her; she could not break his grip.

Buoyed with sudden confidence he smiled thinly; the rest of his face was rigid with exertion.

Lilith bore into his eyes, her glistening black and yellow eyes faltering, the fury seeping from her expression.

Sam could feel her resistance lessening, the strength in her arms fading as she stopped trying to press herself into him.

She released her legs from his torso and stood there, her arms held by the wrists, her head craned at an angle as she looked at him in an entirely new light.

"You have fed," she said.

Her eyes narrowed as she contemplated this turn of events.

She offered no more resistance; simply stood there in his grasp.

Sam boiled with anger, driven by a desire to see her torn apart.

He felt his grip on her wrists weaken, his lock on her arms disappearing quickly.

Trying to use his anger to secure his hold, he concentrated on his grip, meaning to drive her back towards the wall.

She twisted her wrists into his thumbs and broke his hold, allowing her arms to fall at her sides.

She smiled knowingly while he stared at her dumbfounded.

He wrapped his hands around her neck, meaning to squeeze the life out of her, to break her neck if he could, to get revenge for what she had done, to see her dead at his feet. His fingers touched her skin, but he could not make a grip. His fingers and hands weakened, refusing his commands. His strength failed.

She gazed into his eyes, mocking him, challenging him to do what he was determined to do. The look on her face infuriated him further.

She radiated a look of supreme smugness.

"No!" he screamed at her, trying to close his hands around her sensually muscled neck.

He could do no more than hold her lightly, as though in a lover's embrace.

She smiled sincerely, amused and delighted with secret knowledge.

He released his hands and stepped back, staring enraged at his hands which had betrayed his wishes, his chest heaving with labored breaths. Slowly, gradually, he felt strength return to his arms and hands.

Lilith remained where she stood, looking at him intently.

He rushed her again, raising arms that felt refreshed.

The renewed strength evaporated as he attacked, fading to nothing as his hands reached her neck once more. He could do more than squeeze lightly, barely enough to depress her skin.

His arms trembled with a feeling of complete exhaustion.

He let her go and staggered backwards, staring at her with disbelieving eyes, wanting to both kill her and to be as far away from her as he could.

Hot tears flowed from his eyes.

"You killed my children!" he screamed at her, his voice the only part of him that seemed to bear any strength. "You killed Miranda!"

Lilith shrugged lightly, as if it were of no particular consequence.

She took one slow step towards him, her sultry hips swaying.

"It is my vow," she said calmly. "I would have fed on you as well," she added, taking another step forward.

He backed into the brick wall, repulsed by her presence.

"You desire me no longer?" she said with sarcastic delight, her chest almost touching his. She looked up at him, peering at his neck and face with interest, examining his features.

She turned her focus to his eyes.

He wanted to break his stare, to look anywhere else but into her eyes, but he could not. He could feel she no longer meant him harm. Her interest was something else.

"You wanted me then," she said quietly, as though she was making pillow talk with a familiar lover. She traced a forefinger over his chest, slowly sliding it up to his mouth where she stopped, returning her hand to her side.

He almost sighed when she stopped; he couldn't bring himself to touch her again.

"I could smell it on you. Do you deny it? Can you deny it?"

Sam felt like his tongue was locked to the roof of his mouth.

She laughed; a pure and hearty sound. Lilith inhaled deeply, filling her chest with breath.

"You still wish to kill me," she whispered, "alas you cannot. You cannot attack me unless I am attacking you. If you attempt it, your strength will fail you, as you have already discovered."

Sam frowned, wondering what she meant.

She saw his expression, the look of his unspoken question.

"You cannot kill your Master," she said calmly, one side of her mouth upturning in a smile that soon faded.

The implication of that word dug into his brain.

"I will not serve you," he whispered hoarsely.

"Then kill yourself," she cooed, "and end your torment."

She laughed cruelly. "I came to kill you," she admitted, wanting to see how he would react, "to feed on you again."

Sam paled at the memory of her against his neck.

She turned her mouth and slid it between the crook of his shoulder and jaw.

"You were very tasty," she spoke softly against his throat.

He felt the tip of her tongue on his skin, tracing over his fresh scar.

Sam shivered.

"You are a monster," he croaked.

Lilith faced him squarely.

"Don't patronize me with your moralistic ideals. You will come to learn the ignorance of your previous life. You have not yet begun to live, but you are leaving the shallows and walking out into deep eternal waters. You will learn. Do you remember my kiss?"

He nodded weakly, not wanting to respond at all.

"You are strong, very strong. I was a moment too late, only a moment. If I had found you before you had fed you would have been helpless against me. You would have been mine once more."

She returned her gaze to his eyes.

"I felt the moment of your birth ring in my head like a bell, when you woke in that wretched cabin. The Others will have heard it as well. They will come, my children. They too have sensed your birth. Some will come for you. Some will want to see you dead."

The complete blackness was gone, replaced by dark green eyes that seemed warm and entirely human.

"How were you born? Tell me."

"B-born?" he asked, confused.

She nodded, waiting.

"My mother," he replied, not understanding.

"Not that, you fool," she said in dark exasperation. "Your first kill. It is your first feed that finally births you into what you have become. Your first completes the shift."

Her gaze drilled into his skull with intent interest.

Sam struggled with his memory, addled by the conflicting emotions and extreme sensations. He was having difficulty tearing his eyes away from hers; she seemed to hold him in her intense stare.

Lilith looked to the left, interested in something, a shapeless lump that was curled on the ground. Sam followed her gaze to see what it was.

His mind flashed a barrage of images, like a series of negatives cut from an old movie reel that were taped together and replayed slowly.

He had been running, running down the alley. His mouth had been dry, parched almost, but he remembered how his heart had been hammering under his sternum, and a fierce powerful desire had consumed his mind. He recalled a motion, and spinning to meet it, followed by a sweet drink that had quenched his every need.

His eyes widened in horror as the pieces finally fit together, the entire sequence complete in his mind from start to finish.

He saw the body of the mugger crumpled on the asphalt, bent over in a rigid death pose. His throat was neatly eviscerated; his eyes were wide in a final stare of horror.

The club lay on the ground, a few feet away from a hand that was frozen in an empty clutch.

"He attacked you," she said.

Sam stared into empty space, remembering.

"I am going to put my hands on you," she said calmly, with a firm presence.

Her hands went to the side of his head, covering each ear. She closed her eyes and concentrated, her eyes flashing in seemingly random motions, her eyebrows rose and fell in rage and hunger and finally, in contentment.

She let him go.

"An unusual beginning," she whispered, flushed with reliving the memory. She seemed intoxicated. "A powerful beginning, it explains much."

"W-what?" he asked, not understanding. His animosity and hatred for her was forgotten for the moment. He needed to understand what he was feeling.

"It is what determines your strength. We are elemental creatures, as you will learn. We feel purely. We live purely. Hate. Jealousy. Love. We feel every emotion without taint, without restraint. We are emotion."

"Love?" he asked doubtfully, but he already understood the truth in her words. The emotion he felt towards his family was now infinitely greater than he had felt before. It put to shame what he had thought was love.

"You already know," she whispered. "And you have already known hate. The one you fed on triggered it, nurtured it and enhanced it. The depth of anger, hate and violence in your first kill is what finally determines your strength. You responded to save your own life; the coldest of anger and violence."

She stepped away from him, leaving his mind reeling with a thousand questions. Loathe as he was to ask her, to talk to her, he needed answers.

"You are very strong. It will call to others. It already has."

Lilith began to walk away.

"Wait," he said, wanting answers.

"You will see me again," she answered

Her words did not ease his mind, as much as he wanted information.

Lilith turned and he watched her walk away, back into the street.

Every fiber of his body tingled. He could feel himself growing, infused with energy. It was an awareness of self that he had never experienced before, a dawning realization that he was forever changed. Everything he was once was, was now lost; everything he was to become, still lay in the unseen future.

What Lilith had said to him was the truth; the emotions he felt were clean and intense. He felt like he could switch from one to the next in an instant. Love flowed into hate, hate into loss, loss into the most painful of physical agony.

He understood that he was not dreaming; he would never wake from this nightmare.

The finality of his realization hit him like a punch to the stomach, sapping him of his strength.

Sam sagged to his knees and wept; the purest sorrow he had ever known.

\*\*\*

How long he knelt there he did not know. He cried until he could cry no more, feeling as though a lifetime of tears had flowed from his eyes. The night air became stuffy, thick with moisture that stained the asphalt a glossy black, as though night had solidified under his feet. The clear evening had clouded over, the stars disappearing under the cloak of a storm front that dropped a fine cool rain onto the land beneath it like a curtain of mist.

He didn't know what to do.

Lilith was getting ever farther away from him; he could feel her going, slowly and steadily putting distance between them.

What she was doing and where she was going he didn't know.

Her words haunted him.

*You will see me again*, she had promised.

Her words plucked at his mind like a guitar string.

He could feel others. Most of them were very far away, very distant, but he knew dimly that they were aware of him.

This meant they knew he was also aware of them.

He couldn't filter the feeling in his mind to determine how many there were. It was blurry and fuzzy, like an old memory.

Another was much closer than Lilith, not as strong, but coming towards him. He could feel that she, *yes definitely a she,* was seeking him out, homing in on her sense of him. He had no idea how it was that he knew what he knew; he only knew that whoever was coming this way was female.

Her presence had been masked by the strength he had felt in Lilith and there was a similarity he could not distinguish, a likeness that confused what he felt.

He lowered his head to his knees and closed his eyes, wishing she would go away, feeling the rain drip onto his body.

He wanted to be dead, to be anything but *this.*

The other was near.

The feeling was bizarre and inexplicable; a newfound sense he didn't understand.

Her boot steps clicked on the asphalt clearly, like a nail on glass.

Sam dimly hoped she was seeking another.

Her steps came closer, echoing down the alley.

He could feel her satisfaction at finding him, a sense that she had come for him and nothing else. He didn't raise his head to look as she stopped to stand in front of him. She had found him, now she could go and leave him alone in his misery.

His head was low, facing the ground.

"Disappointing," she said, her words were cold as ice.

He felt her emotions.

She was plainly and bitterly disappointed, as though she had opened the biggest Christmas present of all, the last one behind the tree on Christmas morning, only to find an empty shell of a box inside.

"What?" he said sarcastically into his knees, raising his voice so she could hear him clearly, "Not what you expected to find?"

"Are you satisfied in feeling sorry for yourself?" she said contemptuously.

Sam ignored her.

He could feel her anger rising like a tempest, like a pot of water beginning to boil.

*Good*, he thought. Let her be mad, he thought with satisfaction. He wasn't here to entertain anyone. He almost laughed bitterly.

He might have, if he wasn't so conflicted and confused.

*Bitch*, he thought clearly in his mind, half wondering if she would be able to sense his intent and thought.

Her hand viciously dug into his hair and she clenched it tightly in her fist, dragging him to his feet. He grunted with pain, standing as she pulled him upward along the rough bricks, scraping his back as he went.

"Let me go!" he yelled, almost squealing, before breaking her hold on him.

It was her turn to be satisfied.

Sam gawked when he saw her, momentarily shocked.

He thought it was Lilith standing in front of him again, somehow here when he could feel her somewhere else.

Then he saw that she was a little shorter, perhaps only by an inch. Her cheekbones were a little less pronounced; a little softer, although by no means soft. She looked hard, like a slightly different version of the copy he had met earlier.

Momentarily her eyes widened in surprised recognition.

Then it was gone.

"Who are you?" he asked bitterly.

"I am Lamia," she said, her green eyes examining him like a prized museum acquisition.

"You are one of *them*," he said, saying *them* distastefully.

"You are one of *us*," she corrected firmly, emphasizing the final word.

"You look like Lilith," he said, his mouth unpleasantly forming her name.

"My sister," she replied, her demeanour did not change as she stared at him coldly.

"Have you understood or accepted what it is that you have become? Can you say the word?"

He lowered his head.

She chuckled, a sound that was not at all amused or comic.

It was dripping with sarcasm.

"Your tales and your myths have not forgotten us. Your culture is ripe with our stories, and yet you would try to deny what you already know yourself to be? Many would be grateful to be so fortunate; so blessed. We have many followers. Many idolize us."

She seemed amused.

"Can you say the word?"

He clenched his lips firmly shut.

"I thought not. You did not believe us to be true; a fairy tale perhaps, or a tale to frighten children? No, Samuel. We are very real. You denied it when the sunlight burnt your skin. You denied the fresh mark upon your neck. You denied it when you savoured the scent of humanity. Fool. You still cling to your memories and your science, denying what has come to pass. I will say it then, to let your ears hear what you stubbornly deny. You can feel the strength. You have fed and the transformation is already begun. You can sense us, and still you deny who you are. I can feel it, and so can you."

"What am I then?" he spat.

"You are a vampire."

He flinched.

"I am evil!" he retorted, as if the words could deny it.

"You know nothing of evil. You possess only the barest and thinnest of understanding of the word. You are a child who thinks he is wise. You are a fool seeking to describe the sea with only a cup of water for comparison. Your idea of evil is thin and vague. You will come to learn the truth; it is a wine well aged, and just as satisfying."

Her eyes relaxed and then she laughed whole-heartedly, in genuine pleasure.

"What do you want?" he asked peevishly, wanting to be left alone, interrupting her obvious delight.

She stopped laughing, returning to her previous haughty self.

"You," she said punctually, pointing at him with one elegant and feminine finger. "You must learn, and learn quickly."

"Learn?!" he chuckled, "What do you think I want to know? Leave me alone."

She shook her head in a commiserating fashion, dashing his hopes.

"We are not so common that I would throw you to the winds to decide your fate. We have all felt the moment of your birth and it sounded like a thunder in our minds. You are already strong, and yet you have not come into your full strength. Others will be attracted to it, and others will be envious."

Sam shook his head stubbornly.

"You must learn, or you will die."

"Good!" Sam spat.

Lamia glowered at him, her eyes looking at him scornfully.

"Bathe in your pity, then. Survive your children by behaving like an ungrateful whelp. Honor the memory of your wife by acting like a stubborn foolish child. Wallow in it like a swine in mud, but know this, your birth was heard by all of us. You bested your Master, *my sister*, and for that others will seek your head on a pole!"

With that, Lamia was gone.

"Go away! Leave me alone!" Sam screamed into the night, wanting her to be gone and never return. He could feel her; she was already distant and out of earshot, but he felt confident that she had heard him plainly.

"Go away," he mumbled, wanting to deny everything that she had said, to ignore her words, but he could not ignore them all and some of them stung like the lashing of a whip upon his skin.

Sam stumbled numbly out of the alley and wandered back into the empty street, walking aimlessly for a time, finally and unconsciously obeying the unspoken compulsion to find a place to sleep before the inevitable coming of the killing light of dawn.

# Chapter 6

*"Meanwhile from her red mouth
the woman, in husky tones,
Twisting her body like a serpent upon hot stones
And straining her white breasts from their imprisonment,
Let fall these words, as potent as a heavy scent:
'My lips are moist and yielding, and I know the way
To keep the antique demon of remorse at bay.
All sorrows die upon my bosom…'"*

-Charles Baudelaire

Reverend Paul Kowalczyk sat at his desk, leaning back into his old cloth office chair as he gazed upwards to the ceiling in thought. The chair creaked appreciably when he leaned back into it, the old springs complaining as they took the brunt of his resting weight. It was old, but supremely comfortable. The foam had taken the shape of his back and buttocks over the years and now he settled neatly into the contours that his body had imprinted into the seat. The tips of the armrests had been worn down to exposed metal, the cloth slowly rubbed away, bit by bit, from years of friction against the underside of the oak desk where he now sat.

Paul didn't mind, and so he ignored the polite entreaties by countless people, friends and congregation members alike, who thought he should get a new chair. The chair was like an old friend, and he was firm but polite in his steadfast refusals to replace it. He had been given a chair the previous Christmas, an expensive Italian leather job worth almost five hundred dollars. He had tucked it neatly away in the janitor's closet, still wrapped inside its shipping plastic and its thick white corrugated box. He meant to give it away, to have a charity pick it up some time when he was alone so no one would see it go, but he kept forgetting to call them. The idea would pop into his mind one instant and be gone the next, like a fart in a hurricane, as one crude analogy would have it. It may be crude, but he remembered it because it was very concise.

Paul ran his fingers through salt-and-pepper hair that was as thick and healthy as it had been in his twenties. He had aged gracefully, with a lot more salt these days than pepper, sporting a carefully manicured beard of the same colors that lent to his distinguished appearance. He had once heard himself likened to a German Sean Connery, and that suited him just fine. He didn't correct the assumption that he was Polish; he was in fact mostly German. His father had taken the name after the war when they had immigrated to the United States, thinking a Polish name was better than his own if he wanted to blend into a foreign country so soon after the hostilities were over. His ice-blue eyes and accent should have been a dead give-away he thought, but he let it lie.

He reached forward and took a gentle sip from the glass of water to his right, settling the glass back onto the thin wooden coaster when he was done, careful not to spill any water as he did. He hated to get those faint little water rings on his desk. His desk was immaculate and impeccable, like his office.

Nestled in the side of First United Presbyterian Church, his office was stringently neat and organized; a reflection of the man that had occupied it for the last thirty-odd years. As cleanliness was to Godliness, so was neatness and organization.

Everything had its place.

The Church was built on the corner of Fourth Street, north of the grassy fairgrounds. It was a majestic brick-and-mortar structure that looked like an old medieval castle, or a smaller style European cathedral. First built in 1875, the entire Church was physically moved to its present location in the early 1900's and modified slightly over time as was necessary for a growing Loveland population. The grey sandstone bricks were almost golden in color when the sunlight caught them directly, and the red painted front doors were placed under a tall, squared parapet, which looked almost out of place without an English archer looking down from it. The tower had been shortened from its original looming height of five stories when it was found that the structure could not support such weight, and was reduced to a safer height, in line with the arched roof just behind it. A matching stone staircase had a shallow incline that gently led up to the twin red doors from the street. A broad and stately tree rose high into the sky near the stairs, higher than the church itself, covering the walkway with a wide expanse of shade during the spring and summer months. Within, a broad and massive faux pipe organ faced the congregation seats on the main floor, with a gallery of choir seats situated to the left of it. A second level of balcony seating was built next to its flanks, overlooking the spacious lower gallery and brightly lit by the gothic stained glass windows. The office was to the right of the main floor, in front of the congregation seats but inconspicuous and barely visible, as the panelled wooden door was angled to face the podium.

He hadn't a single thought about how he was going to start his next sermon.

Normally, with a few minutes of peace and quiet, and maybe a little wine, the words would flow from the tip of his gel pen like water from an artesian spout, filling pages so quickly that his hand had a hard time keeping up with his train of thought, his mind always one sentence ahead.

Normally.

Today, the underground reservoir of inspiration had run dry; its seemingly inexhaustible stream beds were bare and dusty. He had always found inspiration in his normal day-to-day activities. He could make a note of whatever caught his fancy and build on it from there, marveling at how the words seemed to just reproduce on their own, one idea birthing another in a seamless string until he had his time filled, the ink setting his ideas to concrete.

But not today. He hadn't had an idea, not a whit, the entire week.

Even the week before, the words had come to him with difficulty and the resulting topic had left him unsatisfied and unfulfilled, grasping for more. His parishioners all knew it was lacking his normal level of excellence. Here and there, words were spoken about how "even good reverends have off-days" and how certain they were that he would "return to his former self by next Sunday, just you wait and see, it'll be a doozie". So far as he knew, it was going to be a flop of biblical proportions. No pun intended.

Paul had even tried reviewing his previous work, mining for a gem he had previously missed, some nugget of inspiration that he could expand upon or take a different spin on.

Nothing caught his fancy.

So he sat, staring at the ceiling.

He was dismayed at the persistent thought that the reason for his writer's block was that he was, to put it bluntly, discontent. More and more of his parishioners saw faith, not as a struggle between what was Good and what was Evil, but as a guiding point in a great magnetic compass of social morality. Some of them abdicated responsibility altogether, leaving the ultimate decision of what was right and what was wrong to the final outcome of an event, or even up to someone else. Should I buy this new car even though my old one runs perfectly fine? Daily mundane decisions were surrendered to the Almighty, as though He might be concerned with personal spending habits. Some parishioners used the excuse that "if God wants me to, then He'll make sure I can afford it". If it was the wrong decision, or the right one, then the end result would be certainly be God's word.

He had a momentary vision of a white plastic candy dispenser, crowned with the head of a man with a great flowing beard and a full head of white streamlined hair.

It was The Pez God, dispensing consumer spending advice.

He shook the image from his mind, returning to his former train of thought.

If the car was repossessed, the answer was no.

If the old lady caught the clap because of an affair, then maybe that was wrong, too.

If the affair ended in a marriage, well then maybe it was all right after all; the divorce was meant to be.

It was a part of God's plan.

It turned Paul's stomach.

All of his parishioners, if put to the question, believed unequivocally in the existence of God. However, if he logically asked the question of whether they believed in the Devil, the answer became convoluted.

Some of them blatantly asked him if he were joking.

A portion would look at him blankly, wondering if he was serious.

More than a few would reply that the Devil was an abstract, the physical manifestation of what humanity perceived as a sin or a wrong. The Devil was starvation. The Devil was substance abuse problems. The Devil was a man who beat his wife, or a wife who beat her husband. The Devil was most certainly not a fallen angel, a spirit determined to tempt men and women to do wrong, to test free will. That was just medieval. The Devil was an invention to represent a sin, an image used to drive people to church.

Some would look at him like he was completely off his gourd; one hallucination away from a mental institution and a thorough round of medication in a padded room with his own carefully sewn strait jacket.

Paul saw it logically.

If one believed in God, one must therefore logically believe in the Devil.

Except that not everyone thought logically.

Some believed in God as a means, as an insurance policy against the possibility of eternal damnation. Their faith was weak, a Band-Aid of moral insurance.

If anything, he perceived their convenient faith as a sin in itself. They believed for their own selfish benefit. It was like forcing yourself to believe in Santa Claus because it improved the chances of presents.

That kind of faith was no faith at all. It was a mockery, and it was all too common.

The world was full of examples of the so-called faithful that manipulated their beliefs for their own benefit, forgetting or even abusing what was Written if it was inconvenient.

Love thy neighbor was a simple concept, something that was fairly difficult to complicate.

Except that people did it all the time, creating their own exceptions.

Closet racists might hate a neighbor of a different ethnicity, peeking at them through closed curtains, scowling and muttering loathsome words, and then come to Church under the pretense of being a good God-fearing Christian.

Neighbors of a different faith might be despised and secretly mocked.

Prejudice was the water that ate at the bedrock of Faith, weakening the stone and eroding its strength.

People were free to hate anyone or anything; it was a tenet of free will.

Except that to do so, to hate freely, was against His Word.

People forgot to hate only the sin; the sinner was to be loved, to be welcomed and to never be judged.

But then, Paul sighed, good judgment was not a strength of Man.

Paul believed that thinking of oneself as qualified to judge others was a hint at a very great sin, the sin of Pride.

Judge your neighbor?

Best to look within your own walls and there cast the first stone.

Man was weak.

Paul saw God differently and he feared few would agree with him.

In his early years, and he had spent a great many of them abroad, he had seen things that were not readily explainable, things that the Western world had great difficulty believing. He thought that the West had created a spiritual gap between itself and what he considered the rest of the world, consisting of the natural and supernatural. The gap made the western world no less susceptible to the influence of the supernatural; however, it greatly complicated the understanding of supernatural experiences. That gap started with the very young. Children who spoke to invisible playmates were generally encouraged not to do so for fear of social stigma. There was the fear that such behaviour was somehow wrong or strange. These invisible friends were discouraged, stifling and harming what the Reverend saw as an innate talent to communicate with the world that lay beyond the normal array of human senses. Psychics were dismissed as charlatans; quacks out to fleece the emotionally vulnerable of their savings accounts. It didn't help that occasionally this was true, but it made the work of those with the gift far more difficult to be taken seriously.

By the time most of these children reached first grade, the talent was weakened and, in a great many instances, lost. It became a memory that could be scantily recalled in adulthood, if at all. The ability seemed to need practice, like the development of any skill.

When Paul had travelled through South America he'd had the opportunity to meet with several tribes from deep within the rain forest, connecting with people from across the breadth of society.

What was consistent throughout the different cultures was their deep connection to the spiritual world and the manifestations and clues that could appear in the world that we are familiar with. The world of spirits and devils was very real, intermeshed with daily activities. Exorcisms were not uncommon, and it was common knowledge that dark spirits lurked in the rivers and forests, seeking opportunities to extend their influence into the human world through manipulation or even death. Sitting in a thatched hut in the depths of the Amazon River basin in the dark of night could be an unsettling experience. By stripping away all of the modern conveniences and being immersed in the environment, Paul had felt himself come spiritually alive. He could feel the connection they shared with the world of spirits, a feeling he had lost in the cities of America, no matter where he went. It was like a numbness had been lifted and the true scope of his senses had reawakened.

A new world had been revealed to him, a world where spirits roamed the forests and dwelt in the rivers. Some were good; some were malevolent. The ghosts of ancestors were active, and sought appeasement or provided protection to their loved ones.

Trees cried.

Jaguars spoke.

It was a far richer world than the one he had come from, and he longed to feel it again. He felt deprived.

His only tenuous satisfaction was doing God's work, but that was a tiny oasis, a miniscule respite surrounded by a vast and dry desert, a thin wave-swept island surrounded by an endless sea. He filled his days with scholarly study, keeping his mind occupied with learning and understanding. Most of his parishioners did their part one day a week, for an hour or two every Sunday, eager to be back home in front of the television, or thinking about how badly the lawn needed mowing.

Spiritual development was a part-time occupation, something that very little time was dedicated to.

In the shrouded depths of the rainforest, the exchange between spiritual and physical never ceased.

The spirits were prayed to in hopes of a good hunt.

The animals killed were thanked for providing nourishment, in hopes that their spirits would forgive the hunters and move on.

Trees were thanked for their life-giving fruit.

River spirits were offered gifts for safe crossing.

Forest sounds were carefully observed for hints of dangerous spirits that hunted for men in the woods.

He himself had seen shadows that moved silently in the spaces between the trees, shadows with glowing red eyes; he had heard sounds during the witching hour that were made by nothing of this earth.

Sometimes men disappeared, or returned to their villages possessed.

Shamans blessed the hunters to protect them from demons and ghosts.

Nothing was wasted and people only took enough to survive, to maintain the balance that enabled them to exist.

Take more or be wasteful, and the spirits would restore the balance, punishing and killing the people for their greed, reminding them who was the more powerful. It was an intricate web, one in which humanity was one small cog in a giant wheel.

Interest in "the occult" in the West was a novelty, almost taboo. It was a curiosity, a hobby maintained by people who were easily fooled, or gullible. In some cases, practitioners were skeptics determined to prove to themselves that there was nothing else. In some cases, they were skeptics that wanted proof of a world they suspected to exist. And there were the very few that embraced a world that most had forgotten, tapping into the wealth of knowledge, seeking to learn more.

The Reverend blinked.

The blank paper stared back at him, its unspoiled whiteness mocking him, daring him to mar its surface with pen and ink.

# Chapter 7

―――――――――――――――――

"In the bride's face, where now no azure vein
Wander'd on fair-spaced temples; no soft bloom
Misted the cheek; no passion to illume
The deep-recessed vision - all was blight;
Lamia, no longer fair, there sat a deadly white."

-John Keats

The sun burned his eyes, its yellow light spiteful and threatening.

His skin shrivelled under its incessant glow, crackling like thin rice paper before erupting into a burst of fire. The sun was death now, something to be avoided. He tried to run from shadow to shadow, to escape its reach, to quench his burning flesh in the salvation of darkness. Shadow and darkness held the sweet touch of a cool summer stream. Sam looked frantically about, panic setting in as he could find nowhere to hide. The light crept up from the horizon, marking the end of a night-time world where he was free to reign. Somehow he had been caught out in the open. The disjointed nature of his surroundings momentarily calmed him.

"I'm dreaming," he said aloud, trying to convince himself that it was true.

Again, the scenery randomly changed, out of his control. In one moment he was in a city, the next a forest, then a building; flitting from one to another in an unpredictable sequence.

Finally he was alone in an open field, knee deep in gently swaying grass that was full of ripe seed. There were no trees. There were no buildings. There was no shade.

In spite of his growing surety that he was experiencing a dream, a dreadful fear slowly rose up from within him, an instinctual fear that he was powerless to contain.

Light was coming, and there was no escape.

He screamed.

Sam woke and blinked.

There was only darkness.

The lack of detail was soothing, like a warm blanket on a cold winter morning.

Sam shuddered.

His dreams were exquisitely vivid, almost indiscernible from full consciousness, and they had changed. They had become elemental, filled with the emotions of fear and hunger and anger, predisposed to being magnified in the experience.

The only similarity he could make was to the times where he had gone to bed after eating too much at the end of a long and exhausting day; when excess food and sensory overload had led his mind to a surrealistic dream interpretation of a chaotic day. Random and incredibly realistic, they had been the most interesting, and sometimes the most terrifying, but he had always known that he was dreaming.

They didn't compare in the slightest to the dreams he was now experiencing.

This was like being awake, without the secure knowledge that he was dreaming.

He was just there, fully immersed in whatever his mind was creating for him,

his own private universe where it seemed anything could happen and every feeling, emotion and sensation was real and inescapable.

It was not a dream; it was another reality from which there was no escape.

Pain was not a dull itch; it was an agonizing burn.

Grief was not a hollow sorrow; it was a gut wrenching drain of emotions.

Fear was not a paranoid hunch; it was a terrifying flight for survival.

Worst of all, above all else, was the hunger.

It was not a tingling sensation in the stomach, a slight feeling of need.

It was an all-consuming cancer; a dreadful fire under his ribs. It was a gnawing emptiness that tore at his middle, weakening his limbs and impairing his very ability to think.

The need to fill that void was overwhelming. Plates full of beef and steamed vegetables would appear before him, fully garnished. Steaming, savory soup simmered in glistening bowls. Baked bread was fresh from the oven, the crust golden brown. All of it would turn to sand at his trembling touch.

There was only one fuel his body craved.

The food would disappear, leaving the table empty and bare, save for a crystal goblet set at its very center.

The goblet was filled with a crimson fluid, a drink that would satisfy him like nothing before.

Its scent called to him.

He brought the cup to his lips.

His stomach cramped with his terrible hunger.

And then the dream ended.

He sat up and looked around; disturbing a thick blanket of brown leaves that fell from his body like meshed layers of old crumpled paper.

He had no recollection of coming here, and he had no idea where "here" actually was.

He was in the centre of a thick stand of mature trees: birch, pine, poplar and willow. He was nestled in a pocket of wilderness with the sounds of the city bleeding through from all sides. Sam stood and brushed himself clean, ridding himself of the debris that clung to his clothes and hair.

Oh he was so hungry.

The dream.

He felt nauseous he was so hungry.

The sky above was newly dark, still tinted a dark shade of purple as the last of daylight slipped away.

Crickets foraged in the underbrush, nosing their way through the forest litter. He could hear them plainly. Like his ears, his eyes were preternaturally acute. The forest was dark, but his eyes could penetrate the deepest shadow, uncovering what lay within, revealing a clear and precise image of black and white. Nothing could hide from his gaze.

Sam began to walk, driven by his need to be on the move.

His right hand clutched at his belly.

Far above, an owl watched his silent progress through the trees, swivelling its head in a one hundred an eighty-degree arc until he was gone from sight, out of its territory and away from its nestlings. The owl recognized him as a creature of the dark, a basic instinctual understanding, a fellow-being that shared its space.

As Sam wandered, sections of time were lost then found as his thoughts drifted and then cleared again.

First he was in the woods, then in a clearing, and now he stood on a commercial street lined with empty curbs and closed shops. A tiny brown bat scurried alongside the brick wall of a warehouse, crunching and munching its way through a population of grey moths that fluttered on the wall as they tried to attract a mate before their short time was up. Some had less time than others thanks to the bat, who sent chewed-up portions of fibrous wings to the sidewalk below where they mixed with the dandelion and cottonwood seeds being carried on the breeze.

Sam could smell people in the distance.

He tried to avoid them, to stay away from that luxurious scent, but he found himself closing the gap, unable to fully resist the temptation. His path drew him ever-closer to intersecting.

He walked along South Cleveland Avenue until it became North Cleveland Avenue, parallel to the railway tracks of the Great Western Railway.

On Fourth Street he turned east, curious about a feeling that nagged at his mind.

It was repulsive, like a sour smell of old milk or mouldy bread that he wanted to avoid. He ignored the feeling that grew stronger; his curiosity pressing him onward, somewhat abating the starvation that had occupied him entirely. His instincts told him to stay away, to avoid the feeling that he was curiously approaching.

A danger was there; a threat, but it was fixed and unmovable.

It could not chase him.

The closer he came to it, the further away was the sensation of Lilith and Lamia.

Something was there, like a fixed point that he could not see but could feel with absolute certainty.

He noted with a smile the streets were named after presidents.

Garfield. Cleveland. Lincoln. Further down the street he could see Jefferson, then Washington, then Adams.

Finally, he saw it plainly, all of his senses fixated upon it.

It was a church, on the south side of Fourth Street, nearest the corner of Jefferson.

It was like a lighthouse in his path, warning him to stay away. He was not welcome. It was hallowed ground, and he was Unclean.

His church attendance had been spotty at best in the past, his attendance more determined by the insistence of Miranda, who had wanted to give their kids at least a familiarity with the Institution. She was a non-practicing Latino Catholic, uncomfortable with regular service attendance due to scandals that had infiltrated the faith, but had not dissuaded her from her belief in God. To her they only confirmed the corruption of humanity, even amongst the clergy.

She had kept a comfortable distance, observing what she felt to be important while giving the children a background she encouraged politely, leaving the choice up to them when they became adults.

Sam bit his lip, stifling the emotion that suddenly boiled.

They would not become adults.

There was no middle ground, it seemed. He was either calm, or gripped by whatever feeling dominated him in that moment.

He walked towards the church, feeling the intensity of its presence grow.

Something was there, something that was fully aware of him. It did not focus on him, but he knew that he was not unnoticed, not anonymous in the dark.

Sam paused under the tree on the sidewalk, staring at the twin red doors that seemed to shine like red fire.

A broad flight of stone stairs led up to the doors, a short distance that seemed insurmountable, as far away as the lofty peak of Everest.

His presence was resisted, like the same charge of a magnet, a force that pushed him away.

He thought that despite everything, perhaps here he could find answers.

There was a man here; he could feel him clearly behind the thick sandstone walls.

Sam could even feel where he was, pinpointing him exactly within.

The man was a force of opposition, a focal point for the energy that repulsed him. He was not its source, but he was like a riverbed that could guide the course of a river. He was the polished stone channel through which the energy wove its way.

Here on the sidewalk, his hunger was at its weakest, overpowered by his sensation of revulsion.

He took a step towards the doors.

He almost stumbled at the feeling that shuddered through him.

Each step was worse than the last; each added a ghastly new feeling, building upon and enhancing the previous sensation like a rockslide gathering at a gravel quarry.

His knees trembled. His mouth was dry and parched. His skin coursed with a cold sweat. His muscles knotted and cramped. His mind reeled with dread.

Every desire told him to get away from these walls.

This place could do him harm. This place could kill him.

Yet, he needed to get inside, to talk to the man.

That need drove him, step by step.

He had questions that needed answering; questions that he hoped had answers.

Sam stood at the doors, only a final step away from being able to enter those stone walls.

It was like he stood at the precipice of a great chasm, so impassable was that short distance.

He raised his hand to the door, closing it around the brass pull to enter.

There was a sharp crackle of blue lightening as his skin touched the cold metal, searing his flesh with an intense and sudden heat. The air was instantly filled with a pungent odor and he was thrown backwards through the air as though a mighty invisible hand had seized him by the chest and wrenched him away. It was a silent explosion that sent him flying, cast aside and forbidden to enter by the power that came from within.

A dog barked in the distance. A feral cat cowered low to the ground under a manicured rose bush, sensing the burst of spontaneous energy.

Sam fell to the grass near the curb, clenching his seared hand, which now burned in fierce pain. He could smell his flesh and feel the charred skin split, blackened by the heat. The pain surged up through his arm and stabbed at his brain.

Gradually, it lessened.

The pain faded to a dull throb and the blackened skin sloughed to the grass, replaced by new flesh that surged up from the burn.

He leaned against the tree and rose to his feet, dazed and dizzy.

Sam understood.

He could not get in. The doors were an ultimate barrier to his passing, a guardian that he could not pass.

*He needed to get in!*

Sam swooned with the thought.

It was like dark existing in light. They were opposite, one could not exist in the presence of the other, and so that was his dilemma. He was a fragment of night trying to persist in the presence of day, without cover. If he touched the doors he would be repulsed, over and over again.

He stepped towards the doors. There had to be a way.

It was no easier the second time and the expectation of what was to come only made the sensations worse, heightened by the lingering memory of the excruciating pain that had drilled through his bones.

His feet shuffled up the steps like a man on the verge of collapse.

Sam finally stood at the top of the staircase, confronted by the doors, that final barrier to which he had no solution.

He stood hunched with his eyes closed, his hands tucked into his stomach like he was trying to keep warm, trying to think of a way he could enter. There was a window, but it was closed, locked from the inside and sealed tight against him.

It was fruitless, but he could not turn himself around, could not admit defeat. Here at least, the hunger could not touch him; it was beat down by the sickening sensations that thrived within him. They were worse than the hunger, but he did not want to kill again. He would not, if he could at all prevent it.

Killing, *feeding,* was to accept what he had become, and he refused to succumb. If he could resist, he would not be what he was.

It was a thin line in his mind, but it was a great divide from one side to the other.

On one side was denial and refusal, on the other was acceptance.

He could not accept.

Resisting Lilith and her desires was the final act with which he could honor his family.
"Are you coming?"

Sam was startled back into the present.

An elderly woman gently gazed at him, waiting for a reply.

He looked up into two brown eyes that peered at him with concern. They were framed in a pale and lined face, a face that seemed etched by sadness and resignation. Her white hair was wrapped in a thin cloth of robin's egg blue that tied into a knot under her chin. A white cotton sweater was buttoned up to her neck and her slacks were a plain, light brown cotton.

An oak cane was clutched firmly in her hand, taking a portion of her weight off her legs.

Her eyes were young, trapped in a body that was rapidly failing. Sam could smell her illness. She was dying; from which disease he could not tell, but the odor of it wafted on the air. She did not have long left, and the look in her eyes told him that she knew it just as surely as he did.

She held the door ajar for him, waiting for him to notice.

"The door is always open," she said, wondering why he hadn't opened it himself. She was assuming he had thought it locked. The pull handle was unusually warm, like it had been warmed by the summer sun. Seeing no reason why it should be warm, she gave it no more attention.

There were more important things on her mind.

When Sam looked up at her he almost flinched, but she was too tired. He looked haggard, like he was terribly ill. He was dreadfully pale and his eyes were lined with dark shadows. He looked like he had been lying on the ground. He was speckled here and there with flecks of dirt. Something was certainly wrong with him, and if he had come to make his peace with God or to seek His direction, she was not going to let the door close on him.

Maybe the poor man was too weak to open the doors.

She knew she had precious little time left and every moment seemed important now that she knew that she was down to the last few. She couldn't sleep; the meds her doctor had given her kept her up late and made her mouth dry. Unable to rest, she came to the church for comfort, considering each day a blessing. Soon enough she would be marched through these doors one last time, lying in a wooden box, and she had come to accept those terms. Her life had been mixed with an equal share of good times, bad times, and really hard times, but now that she understood it was coming to its final conclusion she had made her peace. If her life had been a book, she was beginning to read its final pages.

She didn't really want to sleep anyways. It seemed like a waste of what time she had left.

Sam stumbled forwards, towards the gap that seemed lined with electrified barbed wire. The building screamed at him; he could feel its presence shriek at his approach.

He was not welcome here.

He was forbidden.

The doors were open like a toothless mouth, wanting to bite closed to keep him out.

Dorothy Anne Francis kept the doors open for him, her eyes full of sympathy and a misplaced sense of understanding, thinking that he too was come to his last days, only fifty or so years sooner than she had. She thought he had leukemia by the looks of him; a particularly tough type of it. Her brother Sanford, God rest his soul, had predeceased her by thirty years at the hand of that bastard disease. He had put a bullet through his head, rather than let it ravage him to the end, and although the rest of the family had disapproved of the way he had ended it, she had not blamed him in the least. He was already going and he had gone on his own terms. He beat the cancer before it beat him. He had left her an intimate letter telling her what he was going to do, seeking her forgiveness. Now she read it every night before the pulpit, the age-worn paper folded almost to the point of disintegration in her frail hands. She was proud of him; the letter gave her strength, and she was so looking forward to seeing him again and telling him that face to face. They had left too many things unsaid. He had walked through that lonesome valley and soon enough she would as well.

She held the doors open for the stranger.

With the doors open, Sam could not be prevented from entering.

Through those parted wooden barriers, Sam stumbled into the First United Presbyterian Church.

***

The discomfort was exquisite, like a fine aged brandy. The pain before had been mere child's play, a bland sampling of stale spice, the blunt edge of a dull knife. Now, beyond the doors, he received its full attention.

Every nerve burned.

It felt like his skin was being peeled from his writhing body.

"Thank you," he croaked to Dorothy, his voice constricting and barely understandable. She let go of the door and it closed quickly, as if pushed by an unseen force, eager to seal the entrance.

He shuffled past her, hoping he wouldn't collapse to the ground. Dorothy watched him awkwardly amble away; concerned he was going to fall.

She felt sorry for him. The poor man could barely stand. God Bless him, to come here in his condition. She would pray for him tonight as well.

Sam felt like his skin was going to slough away from his flesh. Pins and needles covered his body. His head ached with a migraine that blurred his vision and split his skull.

Through it all, he felt where he wanted to go.

The man was in the office to the right of the pipe organ. The door to the office was slightly open. Sam didn't have a line of sight, but knew he was there.

His legs buckled.

He couldn't make it. The agony was absolute; his entire body wanted to be out of the church as quickly as possible.

No, he NEEDED to be out of the church. Want was immaterial and irrelevant.

The further he went, the deeper the pain sank into him.

The energy of the building focused on him. The floor under his feet seemed to burn through the soles of his shoes, driving nails into his feet. He grasped desperately for the wooden pew and he almost fell into the curved bench, taking his feet off the ground, grateful not to be standing. Sam knew he could not stay here indefinitely.

It would kill him, by twist and by turn he would weaken until the force that pervaded this place consumed him.

Death by a thousand cuts.

He was Evil and this particular land was Blessed.

He just needed to rest a moment, to try to ignore the spasms of pain that tore through his very being, to quench the need to vomit that was convulsing his throat and stomach.

Just a little rest.

The door was knocked upon lightly, thrice.

"Reverend?" a quiet voice spoke.

Paul knew the voice instantly.

"Come in, Dorothy," he said warmly, glad he could take his mind off the blank sheet of paper on his desk.

At this point any excuse was a good one.

The door swung open smoothly; the brass hinges were well oiled.

Dorothy stood at the threshold, leaning heavily on her cane. She did not come in but smiled broadly, if weakly, when she saw the Reverend looking at her.

He was happy to have her company. She had a quick wit in spite of her failing body. Her mind was agile and sharp. He enjoyed her company immensely. When she passed, the world would be a little poorer for her loss.

She looked at him expectantly.

"Yes?" he asked, wondering what she needed. Normally, if she had come to his office, she would have come in and taken a seat, beginning a conversation that might have lasted for hours. Instead, she only stood there waiting, something else on her agenda.

"There is someone I think you need to see," she said softly, "a poor young man. I let him in. He was just standing outside, like he was cold."

Paul frowned.

The weather was not cold and it was uncommon for anyone to just be standing outside the church at this time of night. He didn't see anyone behind her.

"Where is he?" he asked her.

Dorothy pointed to the back, showing the way.

"Thanks, Dorothy. How you feeling tonight?" he asked with genuine empathy.

"Fine," she said, a little white lie. "I took some of the pills the Doc gave me." The pills took the edge off her pain, but just the edge. "Good night, Reverend."

"Good night, Dorothy. Come see me, if you need anything, please."

Dorothy smiled politely and then turned to find herself a seat near the front row. The letter was in her breast pocket, neatly folded across a crease so soft it was like tissue paper. Once there, she would sit quietly for a bit first, away from the Reverend and the sick young man so they would have some privacy. She would read some of the Bible, perhaps several pages, and then she would make a short prayer before reading her letter for the umpteenth time, admiring the smooth penmanship of her long-lost brother. She had never been much of a writer and the flowing script and steady hand of his words had shown her that his mind was at ease as he had explained his decision to her. He had not been afraid. He had been at peace with his decision. She would cry again at the end of the letter, something she had done countless times before. Thinking about it made her begin to tear up.

The Reverend left his office, peered about and then he came over to her, seeing her crying. She would never show him the letter.

"If you need anything, Dorothy," the Reverend reminded her, putting a hand on her shoulder in a gesture of assurance.

He saw the man she was talking about. He really did look awful. He was breathing heavily and his eyes were shut tight, like he was in great pain. He was slumped back in the bench, pale and clearly in great discomfort.

Dorothy pushed the Reverend away with the butt end of her cane. It was too large for her, tall and thick, a belonging of her late husband's from when he had begun to have difficulties getting around.

"He needs you more than I do," she said tartly, giving him a shove to show him she still had some strength left in her bones.

"Be careful," he replied with a grin, knowing that if she fell and broke her hip that it would be the end of her.

"Pfffft," she puffed, waving him away impatiently.

She knew tonight wasn't going to be the night she met her maker and she showed him a little of her Irish attitude to let him know she was still feisty. She was right in the end, passing away peacefully a little over a month later of natural causes, her own illness be damned. Her heart just quit ticking; beating one last time, then just stopping cold turkey after a lifetime of beats. She was found by her daughter, herself no spring chicken at seventy and still in perfect health, a fact she proclaimed was due to her Irish genes. She found Dorothy tucked in her bed at the ripe old age of ninety-three, a folded letter held firmly in her right hand.

The Reverend walked towards the man, already thinking that this was likely a case best handled by an ambulance crew. The man looked sick but he resisted calling the hospital, wanting to know more before he made that decision.

He sat beside the man, to his right, after walking down the long empty length of the bench before reaching him from the far aisle.

At first glance the man looked cold, like he was shivering, but as he sat near to him Paul could feel the heat radiating outwards from his body, like he was in the grasp of a raging fever.

Despite his temperature, no sweat was visible on his skin. Dehydrated?

Was he a junkie coming off a bad hit?

"I'm going to feel your temperature," Paul said, raising his forehand to the stranger's forehead.

When his skin touched he felt a shock, like a static discharge, and the sick man jumped. No, he *leapt* away from him like he had been shot, putting a small distance between them on the pew and eyeing him warily, nervously.

A small red mark was on his forehead, fading as he watched.

The Reverend looked at him closely.

The man was pale and he was clearly stressed, but upon closer inspection, the paleness was not an indication of his ill health. His skin was without blemish and utterly clear.

No wrinkles, no freckles, no moles, no old scars. It was like he had spent his entire life indoors. His skin was the color of cream.

When their eyes met, Paul recoiled.

His eyes were black, like pools of glistening motor oil. The band of white around the blackness was like a ring of ivory and he couldn't see his pupils at all.

The Reverend shivered, and when the man spoke to him it sounded forced, like he was concentrating heavily.

"Don't touch me," Sam hissed, feeling his skin burn as he healed.

The sight of the Reverend made Sam's stomach churn. He could feel the energy of the building coursing through him, but he needed to speak.

Why did he have to sit so close? He wanted to tear out the Reverend's throat and drink! He smelled delectable.

"Are you a priest?" Sam asked, saying the last word with difficulty.

"I am the Reverend here," Paul agreed with a nod, "Reverend Paul."

"Reverend," Sam gasped, sounding like he was emitting the very last breath of air from his lungs. "Sam," Sam responded, not having the strength to say any more.

"Sam, are you ill?" Paul asked.

Sam laughed, a sudden barking sound that echoed in the nearly empty building.

"No. Not sick."

Sam seemed to hint that something much worse was wrong.

"You appear to be in great pain."

Sam nodded with a sour grin.

Pain wasn't the word for it; there wasn't a word in the dictionary that properly described how he was feeling.

It was a multitude of great sufferings.

"I need to speak with you. I have questions. Many questions."

He shuddered and looked as though he was about to vomit.

"Of course," the Reverend replied.

"Outside," Sam hissed, "for privacy."

Paul felt that was not entirely truthful. Paul reached out to lend support to him, but just as quickly Sam pulled away, clearly fearful of physical contact.

Paul thought it was strange, but he agreed. He felt he was in no physical danger. Sam was fearful of him. Was he intimidated? Frightened of what he wanted to say?

Paul followed Sam to the doors, taking his time as he didn't want to rush this man who was clearly ill.

It was a staggering procession. It looked like Sam had great difficulty in finding and keeping his balance as he stumbled and lurched along.

They stopped at the doors.

"Open them for me. I can't," Sam said in a hushed and tight tone.

Sam motioned with a pained sweep of his hand, gnarled in a twisted fist.

Paul pushed the doors open, thinking maybe he also had a cleanliness concern, some obsessive compulsive disorder like Howard Hughes where he was paranoid about hygiene and germs and viruses. Sam didn't have to worry, the janitors kept the church fastidiously clean.

Sam was outside in an instant, like a man diving over the rails for the last lifeboat aboard a rapidly sinking ship. Sam clamored down the steps to the sidewalk.

Paul made sure the doors closed behind him softly and he walked down the steps, using the guide railing for support. It was dark and he didn't want to fall and break his hip either.

Of course, maybe that would give him inspiration for his next sermon. At this point, he was looking for anything.

As Paul made his way down the steps Sam rested near the base of the tree, hunched over as if gathering his breath after a long run; or Paul thought, as an odd expression of great relief. By the time Paul descended the final step Sam stood fully upright, broadening his shoulders and breathing deeply.

Paul stopped at the bottom of the staircase.

Sam turned to face him, feeling much better for being out of the church. "Walk with me Reverend?" Sam asked.

Paul was momentarily shocked; the expression passed over his face quickly.

The man who had looked so ill and sickly only a minute before now seemed fully recovered.

He seemed in fine health. In fact, he seemed to glow.

"My name is Sam. We can forego last names, if you like." Sam didn't put out his hand to shake.

"Nice to meet you, Sam. You gave me your name in the Church; do you remember? You're feeling better?" the Reverend asked politely, quizzically interested in his apparent quick physical recovery but lapse in memory.

Paul saw Sam darken for a moment, almost scowling as though concealing an intense dislike.

"I don't remember," Sam said truthfully.

His memory of the most recent events was incomplete and disjointed, like he had suffered from a blackout. Sam did not recall how he had arrived outside. He was frightened by his lack of memory as much as by some of what he did remember.

Sam felt like he was not in total control of himself, as though one moment of paranoia was being replaced by another of perfect clarity, moments where he felt cunning and confident. Again, he wondered if he was suffering from dementia.

Right now, at this particular moment, it all seemed so clear.

Sam had questions and here was someone that might be expected to have some of the answers.

*His eyes*, Paul thought, *his eyes looked normal now*. Had he imagined them as black?

They still appeared haunted and unusually dark. Was it the lighting?

"Yes," Sam then answered, "I am feeling better."

Sam motioned to the sidewalk before them, his arm out in an invitation to join company.

"Shall we walk?" Sam asked.

"It is late," Paul suggested, thinking that it might not be advisable to take a late-night stroll with a complete stranger. Paul had a sense of dread fall around him, as though he was in some form of unseen danger. He couldn't explain it rationally.

Paul had thought they would talk on the stairs. It was late and sometimes if he stayed up too late he would pay for it with a migraine.

"You will come to no harm," Sam said, and Paul saw that he was supremely confident in his statement; he exuded vitality.

Fine then, Paul thought, a short one around the block.

Sam began to walk slowly, expectantly, and almost naturally Paul joined in beside him.

They didn't walk quickly.

Each step was slow and relaxed, as though the two were old friends and they were catching up on old times together, reminiscing.

"Around the block?" Paul asked.

"If you like," Sam replied softly, as though he didn't want to commit to a distance.

Paul looked at the man to his left, not understanding the recovery he had just witnessed.

"What was bothering you in the Church?" Paul asked. If his illness in the building was psychosomatic, it was the most amazing example of it he had ever seen.

"I cannot easily enter a Church," Sam said simply, understanding a little more of the truth. Lamia had called him a vampire, an explanation that fit the evidence more so than dementia. He recalled the feeling of the sunlight upon his skin, the scents of the people around him. It was painful, but another piece of the puzzle that seemed to fit. He hadn't expected that entering the church would be so bad.

"And why is that?" Paul asked, "Bad memories, a bad experience?" If that was the case, he was deeply sorry it could manifest itself on this man so terribly.

Sam turned to look at the Reverend as they walked, his dark eyes taking in everything. The power that had dominated in the church could not follow him outside, but yet he carried his own version with him, almost like a glowing golden light within his very being. It was his conviction; the strength of his own faith that resided within.

Sam could sense that the Reverend was unaware of it.

The Reverend saw into those eyes and was disturbed, at a level he did not understand. Paul felt uncomfortable walking next to Sam, for reasons he did not fully fathom. Sam seemed to be dangerous without giving Paul an obvious reason to be so suspicious of him.

"You are uncomfortable," Sam said aloud, but privately between them.

Paul was unsure of what to say.

Sam felt himself begin to struggle with what to say, as though his mind was being pulled in another direction, pulled by a sense of something more urgent and pressing. His senses, already acute, began to peel away and reveal a deeper layer that was finely tuned to the art of the hunt. It was predatory and it was taking control. He recognized it at once; it was the feeling that came over him in the alley when the attacker had come for him out of the shadows and Sam had gripped him firmly by the neck, longing to feed. This was the part of him that had reacted instinctually. It was connected to his hunger; an innate part of his being that would not willingly be left to suffer and would not let itself wither away and perish. It crept into his mind and began to assert control.

He resisted his sudden desire to kill the reverend, to feed upon him and satisfy his hunger. That he could not do; there was strength in him yet to resist that much.

"Do not deny it. I can smell it upon you plainly."

Sam spoke the words but they did not come fully from his conscious self. Some part of his being was enjoying this exchange; like a cat toying with a mouse. It was a newfound piece of him; it was dark and it savored torment; this new voice would delight in pain and suffering and it would purposely seek to prolong agony, if for no reason other than to assert control. It came from something ancient within and if it was to be denied the joy of killing Paul, it would be satisfied to play.

"Yes."

Sam nodded. "You have conviction," Sam said.

"I believe in God, if that's what you mean."

"You are strong," Sam said, keeping his eyes on him, "You can relax."

Paul did not know in what context he should take it. The look in those dark eyes

troubled him.

"My eyes bother you."

Paul nodded. "Have they always been so dark? I have never seen eyes like yours."

"Pray you never do," Sam replied, "They have come to me recently." .

Paul stared at him, wondering what he was talking about.

"What did you mean; you can smell it on me?"

Sam suddenly felt older, as though he were somehow stumbling across knowledge that he had not personally experienced. He knew things he could not explain. Sam understood that this was the side of himself that he was to fear; this was a part of him that could assert complete dominance if it came down to survival. This was the essence that Lilith sought to utilize. He was losing his train of thought; the questions he wanted to ask were slipping away.

"I meant what I said. I can read you clearly, like words on paper. You cannot deceive me; I will know if you lie. I am son to the Father of Lies."

Paul began to feel uneasy, to hear that reference to the Devil used so calmly.

"Good," Sam approved.

"What?"

"It bothers you."

Paul felt like he should not be here.

"You will come to no harm with me," Sam said, "that I promise."

Sam wanted to kill him, an urge from deep within. He wanted to tear apart this man of the cloth, but the Reverend was strong, making it easier for Sam to resist the compulsion, to push aside his inner desire, to maintain control over this dark facet of his being. Perhaps if this Reverend were weaker, he might be in danger, but his faith made him a worthy adversary. It even helped reduce Sam's dreadful hunger.

The Reverend's strength tainted his scent, like sour milk.

"How can you make such a promise?"

"Do you believe in Good and Evil?" Sam asked conversationally, ignoring the question for a moment, not wanting to answer it simply. It might be easier to explain.

"Yes," Paul said.

"Pretend for a moment that you are Good, and I am Evil. We are both of the same coin, opposite faces on the same sliver of metal. One cannot exist without the other."

"Yes," Paul followed.

"If you are Good, then for something ill to befall you, it must be at the hands of Evil. If I am Evil, I can refrain from doing such harm and I can also see that no harm might come to you by the actions of others. I can make that promise; in my company, you are safe."

"But would that then, be considered an act of goodness?" Paul asked. "Can an Evil being commit acts of goodness? If so, then they are not truly Evil."

He saw Sam contemplating what he had said.

"It might still be Evil if it serves a selfish purpose," Sam replied.

Paul almost chuckled. He wanted to, just to relieve the stress that was building. Instead, he shivered.

This person was staring at him with an intensity that made him uneasy and his reply had been cold.

"I appreciate the philosophy. I don't know where you are going with this conversation, or what questions you seek to be answered, but can't we do this in my office?"

"I CANNOT!" Sam suddenly yelled with fury, appalled at the thought and terrified at how closely he came to losing control over himself. Memories of that dreadful consuming pain rose fresh to his mind, and with it came the desire to break the reverend's neck.

Sam resisted, but barely.

He had gone from calm to irate in the time it took to snap your fingers.

The Reverend stopped walking, increasing the gap between them by a short distance.

Sam rubbed his temple, terrified by his own reaction.

"Forgive me. My emotions are…difficult to control. I see now that I should have been clear earlier. I did not know how to begin to explain this to you."

"Begin what?"

"I am Evil," Sam said simply, summarizing how he felt.

He was more in control of himself, pushing away the internal demons.

125

His eyes were dark, but they held within their gaze a pleading look, a desire for help.

"Evil?" Paul replied, "All men succumb to evil and temptation. It is being human that weakens you to its lure. That, by itself, does not make you evil."

Sam shook his head. "You don't understand, Reverend. I…" he paused, collecting his thoughts and doubting if he should continue, recalling his train of thought.

"What?" Reverend Paul asked him.

"I…I think I am a vampire. Nothing else makes sense. What I have seen. What I feel. What I have done."

Sam was hoping the reverend could test him somehow, to prove to him that he was not, that somehow he was only sick and suffering from some strange malady.

Reverend Paul almost laughed. Almost, but the look on the man's face was absolutely sincere, a look that was filled with internal conflict and anguish.

And there were those awful eyes.

Eyes that now narrowed in accusation. "You think I lie."

"I think you may believe you are a vampire," Paul answered.

"Then test me! Prove it to yourself!" he said desperately.

"Test you? How would you propose I do that?"

"In whatever way would satisfy you as to the truth of what I say. I can smell your disbelief. Prove it to yourself! Prove it to me!"

"There is no such thing as…" Paul began, only to be interrupted.

"I killed my first last night!" Sam screamed, "I drank his blood and woke this evening. I cannot do it again. I will not do it again! I can't, I can't!"

Sam was frustrated that he was unable to get through to the reverend. His rage built as he screamed; a small wave at first that crested and roared into a tsunami of unrestricted fury. This was a blind, white rage he had never known before.

His alter identity was back in force.

Paul felt his mouth turn to ash from fear.

"My family is gone!" Sam roared, like a great lion of the Serengeti.

The roar was filled with sorrow and grief.

Those dark eyes shifted as the Reverend watched in fear; dark pools formed and coalesced until they were entirely black.

Those eyes were utterly bestial, and seethed with barely restrained violence.

Paul didn't understand, but he had reached his breaking point and now he was terrified.

Paul turned and ran.

Sam stayed where he stood, watching the Reverend run panicked back into the church. His heart pounded in his chest and a part of him was tempted to pursue, triggered by the sight of him running away. He took one step forward to chase and then stopped, clenching his fists and driving his fingernails into his palms. They felt like knives, nearly breaking skin.

He raised his head into the air and screamed aloud in his frustration.

Filled to the bursting point with energy. Sam ran in the opposite direction, finally obeying the deep compulsion to get away from the church. The ground yielded under his feet as he fled tirelessly, the cool air rushed into his lungs and was expelled in a cloud of vapor, superheated as he pushed himself to run ever faster.

There seemed to be no limit to how fast he could go.

His legs drove him tirelessly, like pistons.

Feeling everything around him, he closed his eyes and trusted his instincts. The echoes of his feet seemed to illuminate his path and he effortlessly avoided the obstacles in his way, turning around parked cars and jumping over fences and bushes.

Energy flowed into his legs from an inexhaustible source, a pure adrenaline that knew no limits.

He turned north on Madison, crossing Highway 34 a mile or so away only a minute later. He ran the entire length of Loveland, finally stopping just before 57th Street at the north end of town.

He slowed to a trot and then to a walk, breathing heavily but never having felt more alive. His bottomless eyes seemed to glow with an internal light and his skin was flushed and vibrant. The air smelled wonderful and rich, as though it had been lightly doused with the finest of every scent, none of them intermingling, all of them distinct and savory.

His anger still simmered beneath his skin.

He had failed and failed terribly.

He had barely begun to talk with him, had barely even begun to make the Reverend trust him. It would be harder now. Much harder.

His heart beat in his ears like a hammer striking cold steel.

He had to find a different way to speak with the reverend.

Sam turned a corner into a quiet neighborhood, lit with regularly spaced streetlamps that cast their yellow light down onto the rows of houses and parked vehicles that were nestled against the low concrete curb like birds on a power line.

Sam saw a young man walking towards him, taking up the middle path of the sidewalk and walking with an exaggerated bravado, his shoulders pushing his arms out to his side as he tried to occupy as much space as possible.

"Fish" considered himself a big deal and he meant to intimidate anyone he could, especially some middle-aged white guy walking on the north end of town all by himself after midnight. He had better get out of the way, if he knew what was good for him.

Sam stopped walking and closed his eyes.

Sam felt the taut energy in the figure that approached him.

Fish was full of stress, determined to make a show of himself and to be as macho as possible. He had already done some federal time for illegal weapons possession, but he had gotten off lightly, the true depth of his crimes unknown to law enforcement. Fish had personally taken care of a loose end that had threatened to get him more time, a loose end that had ended up in a series of shallow graves deep in the mountains. He had virtually no compassion for anyone, a narcissist by the most accurate of definitions, with a mix of sociopathic tendencies and psychopathic beliefs thrown in like a little gravel and salt over the featureless chipped ice that was his personality.

"Get out of my way," Fish snarled at Sam, closing the distance between the two of them quickly. Sam was in the middle of the sidewalk, blocking the path, an affront to Fish's perceived dominance and to his absolute right of passage wherever Fish trod.

Sam opened his eyes and watched Fish come, tilting his head with intense interest. Sam's eyes glimmered. Still charged from his run, he could easily feel the perpetual state of anger that simmered in the person coming towards him. It reached Sam as a trickle, but then amplified and fed the rage that had triggered his run.

"You want me to fuck with you?" Fish said coldly, feeling a little excitement.

Sam smiled with a certain dreadful fascination.

"You must be fucking stoned," Fish announced, now only a few meters away and determined to be the alpha in this encounter. Fish tensed his shoulder, planning to walk right into the fucking asshole that was standing in his way. If he didn't move, if they bumped shoulders, he was going to fuck him up. Teach him a lesson.

Sam felt Fish's heart beating strongly. Sam could hear his blood flow; taste the aggression that was coming towards him. The intent to do violence was like a glorious streak of paint on an otherwise ordinary painter's canvass.

It was a narcotic.

Fish bumped into Sam, driving his shoulder forward to add energy to his impact.

Sam didn't move.

"What the…?" Fish exclaimed.

Sam exulted and drove himself forward in a vicious predatory strike, seizing Fish by the shoulders, breaking both of them with one crisp snapping sound as the bones shattered.

Fish would have screamed, except that he could not.

The pain overwhelmed his vocal cords and his vision filled with black dots.

Sam felt the part of himself that needed to kill take control and relished in what was to come. Where he had been successful in restraining himself with the reverend, in this moment he failed. Sam was unable to resist the hunger any longer. Sam saw the pain-filled gaze in Fish's eyes and he found that he wanted to laugh.

Fish was pulled with a sudden jerk into the shadows created by a row of mature cedar bushes. Tucked between the ground and the lowest branches, his doom would now be concealed. It was here that his throat was torn to a shredded mess under his jaw line as Sam drove his teeth forward, biting and snapping; drinking and gulping.

The air escaped Fish's lungs with an uncontrolled gasp as he quivered and shook, held firmly by arms that were immovable pincers at his side.

His eyes rolled back into his skull as he died.

Sam drained Fish to his last, then sat up over the corpse and laughed darkly, wiping the last of the sanguine heart's blood from his lips.

His abilities magnified, refreshed and renewed.

The dreadful hunger was gone, and Sam felt at peace.

Satiated, his senses cleared.

Sam became aware of the body under him. The event replayed in his mind. It was so clear, *so easy.*

NO!

Why hadn't he been able to control himself?

He pounded the ground with his fist in frustration.

Grief and regret welled up within him.

He had failed again.

"No no no no no no," he repeated over and over, pressing his head into the grass that was just beginning to gleam with the first condensing beads of dew.

Then she was there with him.

He hadn't felt her come; hadn't felt her so near.

Sam was shocked to be taken so easily by surprise.

He rolled to his feet.

"You are learning quickly. I felt your hunger. Your instincts are true."

It was Lamia.

She spoke to him quietly, in a conversational whisper.

He could feel her satisfaction reach him.

She was admiring the body under the cedars; a single arm protruded onto the lawn, the forefinger twitching eerily, as if it had yet to learn it was dead.

He lowered his guard, but only partially.

"What do you want?"

"I told you before. You need guidance."

"I didn't mean for this to happen!"

"If you wish to speak loudly, we should leave," she chided him.

Sam clenched his fists and strode towards her, chest to chest, looking down into the eyes that were the mirror of his.

"I did not mean for this to happen," he whispered furiously.

"Better," she said; her voice a rustle, a sound so low that the faintest breeze would overpower it. With his hearing, Sam heard her plainly.

"I did not want to kill him," he said to her angrily, his voice as low as hers.

"And yet you did. Do you mean to continue to wallow in self-pity? Or will you move on, accept it? You are what you are."

"I did not want to become what I am."

"Very good," she grinned coyly, her sharp teeth bared.

"What?" he snapped bitterly.

"You accept the truth; an important first step. I will enjoy this. It has been quite some time, for any of us."

He saw her trick. "I did not ask for this. I did not want this."

"It is too late for that. You have fed and slept, the transformation is complete. You can either be, or you will not; the choice is yours."

"I am immortal!" Sam replied, not understanding how he could either be or not.

Lamia laughed like a pleasantly surprised schoolgirl. Then she calmed and stood under him, her eyes upturned to his own.

He could feel she was completely at ease with him; she was unprepared for anything he might do to her. Or she sensed that he would do her no harm.

"We are not immortal. Not all that once were, still are. You will not die of disease or cancer, nor will you perish of old age. Time cannot touch you, but you, *WE*, are not immortal. Fire can consume you. You can starve to death. Your body can be shattered and you can be torn limb from limb, or you can let the sun take you. You are not immortal, but you are very hard to kill. Only God Himself is immortal."

"God?" Sam gasped, never expecting to hear her say that word.

"Why so surprised?" she asked, her eyes glinting like steel. "We are a part of His Creation."

Sam found himself watching her lips as she spoke, the finery of the muscles in her mouth and the absolute depth of her eyes. A single strand of golden hair blew across the bridge of her nose and he resisted the urge to softly brush it away.

His train of thought was broken.

Lamia chuckled softly, and Sam knew at once that she had sensed and observed his distraction.

"I should hate you," he mumbled.

"Why? Because my sister made you? Because I am the same as you?"

Sam had no response. He had no reason to hate her.

"We are creatures of emotion. All emotions."

"We are Evil. We have no purpose," he countered stubbornly.

"Everything has purpose;" Lamia lectured calmly, "there can be no Good without Evil, no Light without Dark."

She stepped up into him, as if to plant a kiss. He had no idea if that was her intent.

He pulled away like a fumbling, nervous teenager.

She stared at him and then smiled knowingly. Then she looked down at the body.

"You must learn to dispose of your prey. I cleaned up after you last night. You must remain anonymous. Hidden and discreet."

Sam looked at the body.

Flies were beginning to collect around the gaping neck wound.

"Go," he said, wanting to be rid of her.

She said nothing, her eyes fixed to his, and then she was gone. He felt her leave, away to the south, leaving him where he stood without another word.

He had a very clear sense of her last feeling before she left.

It was of inestimable patience.

# Chapter 8

---

*"...his eyes have all the seeming
of a demon's that is dreaming..."*

-Edgar Allan Poe '*The Raven*'

Yellow tape fluttered in the wind around the entire crime scene. It started at the driveway and ran behind the cabin through to the lake before running parallel to the water's edge, finally turning back once it had encircled the twin blood stains on the beach that were the location where the children had died. The tape then ran back to the driveway, tied around the tree where it all began.

A uniformed officer stood at each side of the property, keeping an eye out for anyone not on official business.

Detective August Vasile sighed and scratched at an itch that tickled his nose.

The stain on the floor was considerable, occupying an area that was several feet wide, slightly thicker and elongated where the floor was angled and the blood had pooled. It might have been greater, but here and there, small gaps and knots in the rough-hewn floorboards had allowed some seepage into the crawl space below. Amidst the congealed, almost black stain was the approximate outline of a person.

In this case, presumably the outline of a one Samuel Tiberius Maxwell.

He was missing; as was the rest of his family.

The trick, or as August liked to put it, 'the tricky', was that there was no body. No bodies anywhere.

But there was blood everywhere.

Here in the cabin. Out near the fire pit. The two locations on the beach.

By elimination, they had so far agreed that the blood spatter around the fire belonged to the deceased's wife, a Miranda Alameda Maxwell, maiden name Caballero, aged thirty-two. With the bloody outline of the husband, they felt in this case they could rule out a family suicide-homicide.

The two locations on the beach, virtually side by side, were left by the children.

Thomas Diego Maxwell, age four, and Cynthia Isabella Maxwell, age seven.

The coroner's report was still out, the samples on their way to the lab with priority importance. He felt strongly that once the DNA was confirmed, it would also confirm their theory about which person, or persons, the blood belonged to.

It was just a matter of time.

Detective Vasile returned his eyes to the outline of the husband on the floor. The body had clearly lain there while the blood dried around, probably overnight considering the temperature and low humidity. In the summer heat the blood would dry quickly.

Then it was moved, leaving the bare patch of wood underneath.

It was like the bodies at Pompeii or Herculaneum, the hollow cavities, filled with plaster that showed where the Romans had fallen and died in the volcanic eruption. The bodies had decayed, leaving a void within the solidified pyroclastic material in the exact shape of the person who had died there.

It had been the child-sized spaces had disturbed him most, as well as the one of the man who had died in a vain attempt to shelter an obviously pregnant woman.

He had always presumed they were husband and wife, and that they had died together, along with their unborn child.

This space on the wood bothered him in the same way.

Several flakes of dried blood lay on the floor, likely having fallen from the corpse when it had been relocated elsewhere. Bloodstained male clothes were strewn haphazardly on the bathroom floor.

Was the body moved in the nude? Maybe it had been wrapped in a blanket?

"How much do you figure?" he asked the portly blood spatter analyst.

The man was friendly and thoroughly competent, but August felt he could do with some exercise. August himself stayed in shape, maintaining a physical regimen that would press most twenty-year-olds to the brink of nausea. He was forty, and determined to stay in shape for as long as he could.

"Over a gallon anyways," replied the analyst, pushing his glasses back up the bridge of his nose. He was nearly thirty, already beginning to bald like his father and his grandfather before him. The prospects of a full head of hair for the analyst beyond the age of forty did not look promising.

"Maybe a little more in total, spread out from here to the door and the yard, but not much more. He bled out. Heart stopped pumping."

"And the human body contains what? A gallon and a half?" asked August.

He wished he could remember what the analyst's name was. It was something like Eddie or Buddy or Willy; he could never remember for some reason. He had well over a hundred names memorized from around the department and dispatch and the various offices that did work for the department, but for some reason this guy's name just did not stick.

The mental Velcro was defective or something.

The analyst, whose name was in fact Tony, stood up and adjusted his pants around his midriff and then replied. "About that," he nodded, "maybe a little more depending on body size. In this case, he was about average."

August added the notes to his notebook, scribbling the information down in longhand.

Tony took the initiative, describing what he saw, looking to August for feedback or insight.

"Check out the door frame."

August took a look at the door frame.

It was scratched and gouged from the outside, like something was trying to get in but could not.

"Racoon?" asked August.

"Pretty tall for a racoon, I'd say."

The marks started just above what would be considered chest height for an average person. The wood in the scratches was clean and bright, meaning they were new.

It might be coincidental.

Racoons were pretty clever; he couldn't put this past them. Maybe there used to be something tall stacked up against the wall.

The jamb was coated with a fine layer of black dust.

"Fingerprints?"

"Too many to count and overlapping," Tony replied.

"Let's go outside," August suggested, pushing open the door and motioning for Tony to go first, then following him out of the cabin; once there Tony explained what he thought had happened.

"The husband was attacked first, presumably to eliminate the largest physical threat. He was mortally wounded and unable to resist any further. The wife became the next target. The husband crawled to the back door and entered the cabin while the wife resisted. I think he might have been going for a weapon but he bled out before reaching it, or he was unable to reach it. Due to the blood loss, he may have forgotten about it, hard to say. Once the wife was out of the way, the children were next. Oh, the dog; I forgot about the dog."

"Shit," said August. He had forgotten to write notes about the dog. It was missing too. They had found its blood and a few tufts of silvery grey fur between the cabin door and where the wife had made her stand.

"The dog was killed somewhere between the cabin and the wife. Its collar was thrown into the fire."

August followed the trail of blood that led to the cabin with his eyes, looking for something, anything that might have been missed. The husband had clearly dragged himself; the marks were apparent on the ground, all the way up to the steps. His bloody fingerprints were on the bottom of the screen door where he had pulled it aside to gain entry to the interior, and then on the floor itself where he had dragged himself just over the threshold, finally expiring.

There was precious little else.

The tires had been slashed on the vehicles; they could not get away, except on foot. That spoke of something planned, premeditated, possibly by someone that bore the family, or one member of the family, a serious grudge.

They were not meant to get away.

He returned to the fire pit.

"So the family was having a marshmallow roast when it all started."

August pointed to the sticks on the ground, left where he presumed they had been dropped. The bag of marshmallows, virtually full, was on the ground where it had fallen.

He scoured the ground for any distinguishing footprints or other marks that he could pinpoint as being something of interest.

August took note of how, around the cabin, the ground was hard, covered in a low, thick combination of grass, weeds, stones, and creeping vines. The area immediately around the fire pit was hard packed dirt; pounded flat by countless visitors. The beach was all gravel, leaving nothing to follow. Identifying a particular footprint along the beach was next to impossible.

This place was isolated. For someone to do this, they needed to drive out here, a good distance from Loveland or Fort Collins.

They stood over the blood spatter near the fire pit, a thick collection of droplets and smears.

"How much here?" August asked, referring to the amount of blood.

"Enough to cause unconsciousness," Tony answered.

There were no marks on the ground that showed where her body might have been.

"Let's move on to the children, then," said August.

Tony led him to the beach where a pair of dark patches marred the light grey stones. They were almost next to each other.

One of them had watched the other die, awaiting their turn, probably too paralyzed with fear or shock to run any further.

August thought the girl had probably been the first; her little brother had stood by and then was killed in turn.

"At their ages, the amount of blood loss here would have resulted in unconsciousness."

"Jesus Christ," mumbled August. Why the kids? They must have seen who was responsible, and known who it was.

Eliminate the witnesses.

The gentle waves of the lake broke against the gravel with a calm lapping sound.

The tranquility was a stark opposite to the violence that had taken place here earlier.

"The person that called it in; where is she?"

Tony pointed to the front of the cabin where an older woman, likely in her late fifties, was sitting on the slope of the drainage ditch beside a police cruiser.

Her outfit was meant to be comfortable; faded jeans, sneakers and a long sleeved pinkish shirt that was voluminous enough to allow for easy movement while not being too baggy. Her hair was mostly white and shoulder length, held back with a turquoise headband.

She was clearly distraught and in a state of disbelief, clinging to a small black terrier that was trying to get comfortable.

"Okay. Let me know when the lab stuff comes in."

Tony nodded.

He left Tony to his work and proceeded to the driveway, turning to a fresh page in his notebook before he began to speak to the woman.

"Mrs. Cochrane?"

She wiped her nose discreetly on the back of her sleeve before looking up at him, embarrassed that she didn't have a tissue handy.

Her eyes were red.

"Call me Rose, please." She smiled thinly.

"Alright Rose. I'm Detective Vasile; or August, if you prefer."

Some people liked to use first names; others preferred to be more formal. Giving them a choice could make them feel more at ease, especially in more difficult situations.

"Are you doing okay?" he asked empathetically.

He sat down beside her, avoiding a prickle bush.

She nodded, most certainly lying. He made a note to give her the name of a counsellor to talk to. She was going to need it.

In addition to her mental state, she looked sick. She was pale and looked nauseous, clutching a blue plastic bottle filled with water.

Heat stroke, he assumed. It happened more often than people realized.

"Do you feel you can tell me what you saw?"

"What do you need?" she asked doubtfully, rubbing at her nose.

He fished a plastic package of tissues out from his jacket and offered it to her.

Her eyes widened in gratitude.

"Sorry," she mumbled, extracting the top sheet and wiping her nose as cleanly as possible, "allergies."

Her chin quivered.

August feared she might be too rattled to make a coherent statement. "Just start at the beginning."

She inhaled deeply and shook slightly, as if her entire body was repulsed at remembering. She drew a knee up into her chest and placed a hand on it, beginning to fidget. She took a fumbling sip of her water.

August saw the stress manifesting itself and paid her close attention, not wanting to push her too far.

"I was going for a walk with my dog, before the day got too hot. I like to do that. I go to the old dock by the creek and let him swim for a bit and then come back. Turns out I still got too much sun. Must be dehydrated. I blame last night's tequila."

She wiggled the nearly empty water bottle to show him she was trying to rehydrate.

August smiled politely.

"What time do you take your walk?"

"I try to aim for around eight."

August wrote it down.

"Does your husband go with you?"

Rose shook her head.

"Can't. He has a weak heart. Congestive failure."

"Sorry to hear that."

Rose shrugged like she had heard it a million times and had accepted the fact.

"Did you hear anything unusual? Like a vehicle, a dog barking, any shouting?"

Rose shook her head. "We turn in early. My husband and I are heavy sleepers. They must have arrived yesterday after my walk, because there were no cars here yesterday morning."

August nodded and continued to make notes when he felt it was pertinent; short scribbles that summarized the comment.

"You have very neat printing," Rose noted, seeing that each letter was precise and neatly slanted, and every single letter was capitalized.

His last few lines of notation read:

*NO UNUSUAL SOUNDS NOTICED.*

*HEAVY SLEEPERS.*

*VICTIMS' VEHICLES NOT PRESENT IN PREVIOUS A.M..*

"Lucky for me; my handwriting is awful," August replied, "I can't read it at all, so I have to print."

Rose smiled politely, trying to distract herself with some pleasant talk, something to keep her mind off what she was discussing.

"This morning your walk was on time?"

Rose nodded.

"I left at 8:08 this morning," she said crisply, no doubt at all in her mind.

She took another drink of her water and grimaced.

August didn't see any condensation on the bottle; it was probably very warm.

"And how do you recall that?"

"We have a digital clock with big blocky numbers. It looks like BOB. My husband said it just as I walking out the door. That it was BOB o'clock."

August nodded with a small smile. That was clever. He liked it.

"Then what did you see?"

"I saw the end of the car past the bush. When I got closer, I saw the flat tires."

August remained quiet, allowing her to continue without breaking her train of thought.

She was reliving the moment; he could see it in her eyes. She had withdrawn and her eyes had glazed over; the features on her face had smoothed out and her voice lowered.

Rose suddenly looked five years older.

Her voice hitched. "I saw the tires were flat. Every one; on both cars. I saw that as I went by, and kept walking. There were no lights on inside. No chimney smoke. No radio. No sounds. No smell of morning coffee. No one talking. It scared me some so I went to the dock, thinking about it the whole time. I just kept going."

She swallowed and took another breath.

"Do you have a cigarette?" she asked.

August shook his head. "Don't smoke."

"Shit," she said, "I've been quit for twenty-two years and I have never wanted one again until today."

"You're doing fine." He thought she was unusually perceptive to have noticed so much detail. Her gut instincts had been right on the money. It might have saved her life too.

She nodded like she didn't believe him, raising her eyebrows in speculative doubt. Rose didn't see how anyone could be doing fine; that's why she needed a smoke, and a drink. Maybe a bottle, in fact.

"On the way back I decided to see if anyone was there."

"Did you notice anything then?"

"No. It was all quiet. I knocked on the door. There was no answer. I went around to the back and that's when I saw…what I saw."

"The blood?" he asked.

Rose only nodded rapidly in reply, wanting to move on, to forget.

"Then what did you do?"

"I got the hell out of there."

"And you called us?"

"No. My husband did. My hands were shaking so badly I couldn't have held the phone. I couldn't have dialed 911."
Her eyes began to tear up and she did her best to wipe them away with the back of her hand. The trembling returned.

"Do you recall touching anything?"

"Like for fingerprints?" Rose asked.

"Fingerprints or anything you might have moved?"

"Just the door handle. Once I saw…I just left."

The image of the dark pool of blood on the floor was imprinted in her mind, and it would haunt her for the rest of her days.

"August?" she asked weakly.

"Yes?"

"How many kids were there? I saw kids' books. If you can tell me?"

"Two."

Rose sighed.

It was a sad, resigned sound.

"Is the whole family... are they all…dead?"

Rose had wanted to meet the family, to welcome them to the lake.

She wasn't nosey; her desire had stemmed from a grandmotherly desire to see younger people enjoy themselves. Rose and her husband had an inflatable boat, several inner tubes and all kinds of other water toys she had hoped the children might enjoy.

She had decided to wait.

What could that possibly hurt?

It could hurt plenty.

What she would give to have that morning back.

Maybe if she had said something earlier, things would be different.

It was that damn heatstroke.

She had sat on the beach for just a little too long that day and hadn't been smart about drinking enough fluids or bringing out the striped parasol she had bought in Brazil three years earlier.

Getting drunk the night before didn't help.

She had just felt lazy; the warm steady heat had taken an edge off her nerves.

And now, maybe they were dead because of her.

August capped his pen. She was done giving her statement.

All she had now were questions, loose strings that fluttered in her mind.

"I think so."

She sighed again.

"Can I leave? I mean; do we have to stay here for more questions?"

"Do we have your home number?"

"I gave it to the officer." She pointed to the one by the beach. "We'll call if we need to."

Rose nodded, satisfied. She needed to get away from here.

"Thank you, Rose. We have counsellors, if you need them. Victims services, that sort of thing."

Rose shook his hand and stood to leave.

"The officer will escort you back to your cabin." The officer heard the offer and came to her side.

August thought she might faint. She seemed to be teetering on her feet.

He listened to them leave, the gravel crunching under their shoes.

The pen went back into his pocket and he closed his notebook, thinking about the brief press release he would have to give reporters. The next of kin needed to be notified first. That would start when he returned to the station. If they lived nearby, he would see to it himself.

The entire family. Gone.

August shook his head.

He thought about the children.

It was some cold world.

# Chapter 9

*"The desert creatures will meet with the wolves,*
*The hairy goat will cry to its kind.*
*Yes, the night monster will settle there*
*And will find herself a resting place."*

-Isaiah 34:14

The Reverend walked through the dark streets; his heart beating strongly in his chest. *Ba-dump. Ba-dump. Ba-dump.* There had been precious few times in his life when he remembered his heart ever beating so strongly.

One time had been was when he was younger, when he had decided to see the world. It had been an exuberant heartbeat, born of the excitement of going to broaden his horizons, to see the greater world around him. It was the energy of youth, a wanderlust that craved satisfaction.

The other, was in the forests of Brazil.

He had been caught out alone when night had fallen faster than he had expected it to. As the dim light of twilight vanished rapidly, the fear had begun to build. He had not yet reached his destination of a village some few kilometers away, and the darkness had closed in around him. It was then he'd become aware that he was being stalked.

He had not seen the jaguar, but he instinctively knew it was there.

The forest had fallen completely silent.

The birds seemed to vanish and even the insects grew mute.

He did not run, knowing it was the worst thing he could do, so he walked backwards through the woods in the dark, trying to feel his way through the choked path that was his only guide. Each minute felt like an eternity, an infinite span of adrenaline and pure terror. When he finally reached the village, the jaguar had growled just beyond the fence, frustrated that its prey had eluded capture. The sound had been like a dagger in his ribs, a confirmation that his fear had been justified.

His heart was beating like that again.

His senses were on fire, acute and vigilant. He was terrified, and knowing it made him feel no better. Each step sounded unnecessarily loud and cumbersome.

A newspaper was rolled up in his right hand, the paper crumpled in his firm grip. His sweat was absorbing into the thin newsprint, smearing the black ink into his palms.

Each street seemed abandoned and stark, just as unforgiving and menacing as the rainforest had been. The light played tricks with his eyes, intensifying shadows and magnifying the darkness.

He didn't know where he was going, only that he was searching aimlessly. He didn't know how else to do what he was doing.

The night before he had almost collapsed inside the church, struck with the blind fear that a madman was going to kill him where he stood. He had been certain he was going to die; that he had been lured outside to be killed as part of a plan, a part of some grand deception.

The conversation had been strange; edging into the fearful as it progressed, putting him on edge as he had begun to realize that he had made an awful mistake.

The man had been sincere. He had been wrapped in despair, caught in a dilemma that he had no control over. He seemed to be balanced on the fine edge of self-control, a blink away from losing himself.

When he had screamed, Paul had clearly seen the sudden transformation that took place. The dark eyes that he had thought were so unusual had become awful; bottomless black pits filled with rage. He couldn't be sure, it might have been a reflection from the overhead street lights, but it seemed as though his eyes had taken on a nightmarish yellow cast. His entire form had seemed to lurch over, as though in the process of a horrific metamorphosis.

It was then that he had broken and ran.

He had run through the twin red doors like he was leaping through plate glass to escape a fire at his heels, headlong and desperate. Dorothy had already gone, and for that he was eternally grateful.

He had slammed the office door shut, panting heavily, his eyes wide with fear. And he had prayed. He had prayed for hours, untouched by the exhaustion that he should have felt so late at night.

Something within him had been rekindled, a spark from a mighty fire that had slumbered, safe under layers of fine insulating ash.

He felt rejuvenated.

It was an awakening.

It reminded him of an earlier sermon: If one believed in God, then one must also believe in the Devil.

Only it wasn't quite so simple, so basic.

If one believed in God, then in due course there must be angels. And in the case of the Devil, then the minions of darkness must also be at work.

The man had said he was a vampire. He had believed whole-heartedly that he was a vampire. In that final raving instant of screaming his eyes had been dark and utterly devoid of any trace of humanity, but his face had suggested otherwise. It suggested an internal conflict; a dreadful, undesired comprehension.

And there had been that final scream, the scream that had followed him down the street as he ran. It was the despairing scream of a man who had lost everything.

Last night he had come closer than at any other point of his life to the confirmation of a world he believed in, a world guided by the supernatural.

And he had fled.

It was not weakness; it was a natural reaction to the physical threat, but now, safe and in hindsight, he regretted it.

He had been caught completely by surprise. Of course, there was no way he could have prepared himself. The man had seemed sick, like a junkie, and within moments of leaving the church had improved.

Why hadn't he tested him somehow? The man had demanded it, he had wanted it!

*Because you were scared shitless*, Paul thought.

He almost chuckled, but that fear was still too fresh in his mind. He was rational now, confident in the feeling of safety and protection that surrounded him, but he still remembered vividly how he had felt then, *outside*.

*I will fear no Evil.*

He had feared it, and feared it greatly.

Only a fool would not fear it.

Fear was healthy.

Fear taught boundaries.

Only a fool would have stood there, caught gaping like a thief at the window.

When he ran, he had run for the right reasons.

He had been in no state of mind to listen to a creature who was surely his opposite in this world, as much as it had desired to share in his company.

There might be times when a cat wants only to talk to a mouse, but the mouse is no less foolish to run.

The Devil has many names. The Master of Trickery, the Savant of Deception, the Deceiver.

No, last night he had been right to run.

From his desk he retrieved a dog-eared copy of the Bible, a book so creased and worn it seemed that every page had been quoted from or referred to at least a dozen times.

It was nearly as old as he was; its pages were as wrinkled as his own face.

He left his desk and sat on the couch, a vintage brown sofa that was comfortably broken in and soft in all the right places. Paul opened the Bible on his chest and began to read, waiting for sleep to take him.

When it came, it brought uneasy dreams.

He woke when the book slid off of his chest and landed on the floor with a soft noise. He did not jump up, nor did he startle. He simply opened his eyes and blinked.

Paul sat up and groaned, reaching back to a sore spot in his back that wasn't as fond of the couch as he was.

It was late afternoon, approaching suppertime, and he had been left blessedly alone by the woman that cleaned the church daily. She had noticed him sleeping on the couch, his chest rising and falling in an unencumbered state of rest.

She left him a sandwich she had purchased from the nearest deli, wrapped in wax paper, centered atop his desk in plain sight. Next to it she had placed the newspaper, still neatly folded over, and then she had closed the door quietly behind her.

He wasn't hungry, but he ate the sandwich anyway, chewing it mechanically for the sake of making sure it wouldn't give him indigestion later on. He unfolded the newspaper on the desk. The slowly disappearing sandwich sat on the bottom of the page he was reading and he moved it around as it interfered with an article he was interested in.

He froze on the fourth page, the masticated bite of sourdough, mayonnaise and black forest ham turning to bitter dust in his mouth.

His eyes were glued to the thin black script.

FORT COLLINS — A family of four, including two small children, has disappeared in what police are calling an apparent quadruple homicide. Investigators have released the names of the deceased, identifying the victims as Samuel Maxwell, age 34; his wife Miranda Maxwell, 32; Cynthia Maxwell, 7; and Thomas Maxwell, 4. Further information will be released upon analysis of the lakeside rental cabin where the family was apparently staying for their summer vacation. Investigators are still working to determine a motive.

Paul leaned into the paper, his nose nearly brushing the page as his eyes scanned the black-and-white family photograph that was placed directly underneath the article.

It was *him*.

*Sam.*

He swallowed the bite of sandwich, grimacing as it slid down his throat.

Paul read the article again, and then again.

The photograph was clear. It was the same man.

He flipped to the first page with a flurry and quickly found the date on the top left corner.

It was today's date.

He returned to the article, mining the words for more information in that precious scant paragraph.

His mouth silently and slowly spoke the words on the page, enunciating each syllable precisely, as if more knowledge might be concealed within it to be revealed only to the chosen.

According to the article, Sam was dead, and yet he had seen him last night. Was the article correct? He imagined the timeline in his mind, trying to determine if it was possible that he might have been killed *after* they had talked.

He shook his head unconsciously.

Police couldn't work that fast. Print media didn't work that fast.

The logical, western part of his mind inserted its own solution: he just bore an uncanny resemblance to someone else, and the names were purely coincidental.

He wanted to believe that, but he couldn't.

The part of his mind that studied the supernatural had already made its decision.

*You were visited by a dead man* it told him, breathing the eerie truth in his ears like a lover's whisper.

Those dark eyes stared at him from his memory.

What was it that he had yelled? The last thing he had heard as he ran down the street as fast as his feet would carry him?

He had yelled two words.

*My family.*

Paul shivered, recalling the anguished way it had been screamed into the air.

His family, according to the paper, was dead.

And so was Sam.

He rubbed at his chin as he stared at the photograph, replaying the previous evening in his mind, second by second.

He pushed away the western world, finding that it clogged his thoughts, plugged the paths of his mind. If he were in the rainforest, so many decades earlier, he would not have been so closed-minded, so frigid to another perspective.

In the forest, if a hunter failed to return, it was accepted that he had been slain by spirits; taken by unseen forces that, on a whim, would pursue a human victim.

It was accepted fact.

The two worlds overlapped, the world of men and the world of spirits, and the spirit world was far stronger.

Paul tried to shake the bonds of western perspective, like removing a film from his eyes.

Could he make himself believe what he had seen? What he had felt? A shiver ran through his body, tingling up his spine like a freezing electric current.

He knew what he had to do, and the prospect chilled him to the bone.

Paul sat and waited warily for the sun to set.

When at last its light had faded below the horizon, he had left the safety of the Church, a crucifix held tightly in his palm.

He walked the streets, randomly but purposefully, waiting to be found with a looming sense of dread.

His heart pounding.

\*\*\*

Sam found himself standing in the middle of a foggy, featureless woodland. The sky was partly lit by a crescent moon that was obscured by a blanket of dense fog that undulated through the trees and a thick bank of moisture-dense clouds. The humidity had settled downwards, soaking the ground and trees with a cold condensation that sagged all but the thickest of branches. Whenever the clouds parted, the beads of moisture caught the moonlight as though millions of faint crystals had been painted over the landscape.

The forest felt familiar.

It felt cold.

A giggle carried through the dark forest. He recognized the sound in an instant.

"Cindy!" he screamed into the shadows.

His fists were clenched and his eyes were filled with a sudden welling of tears.

"Cindy!" he screamed for a second time, falling quiet to listen,

A branch snapped faintly in the distance, somewhere off to his right.

It was followed by another faint laugh.

Sam bolted towards the sound, the cold forgotten.

His mind screamed at him that it could not be true. He was mistaken; he had to be mistaken.

But he wasn't, he knew just as surely as he knew the look of his own face.

The giggle came again, closer, but the source still invisible.

Sam ran blindly through the woods, his face and body stung by thin branches and wiry twigs that tried to hold him back like dozens of tiny, clawing wooden hands.

Up ahead just a little, he could see a figure moving away; running like he was.

"Cindy," he panted, trying desperately to fill his lungs with enough oxygen to keep running.

He could hear her giggling steadily now, as if she was enjoying the chase.

Every step brought him closer to her.

He could see her clearly now; her jet black hair was braided just like Miranda had always done for special occasions. She was barefoot, wearing only a white dress that didn't seem to impair her stride in the slightest.

She ran deftly through the undergrowth, weaving and dodging obstacles with ease. Only his bulk made up for her size advantage, crashing through barriers that she had to negotiate.

"Stop, Cindy," he gasped, almost within reach of her shoulder.

She only laughed loudly, her arms pumping at her sides as she ran.

Sam reached out, and in a final desperate gambit, he threw himself ahead, gripping her by her upper arm.

She giggled one last time as they fell to the sodden earth together, rolling until at last they came to a stop.

Sam rose to his knees and saw that Cindy was lying face-down, her tiny figure barely moving except for the steady rise and fall of her breathing.

"Cindy," he whispered, shaking her gently by the arm where he still held her firmly.

She didn't stir.

Sam took her by the shoulder and rolled her onto her back.

He smiled in pain and disbelief as he looked at her.

She was flawless; a miniature version of her mother, a young girl that in time would grow into a mature and classical beauty.

"Cindy," he whispered again, his throat choking in emotion.

She opened her eyes and they were dark, like polished obsidian.

Those eyes fixated on him suddenly and she grinned, revealing a mouthful of white jagged teeth.

"No," he mumbled, stumbling backwards.

"Daddy," she giggled, sitting upright.

"No!" he screamed.

She fell upon him, her teeth snapping.

Sam awoke with a dreadful scream, his hands swatting at biting teeth that were no longer there.

When the shock was over he sat still, his mind numb from both terror and grief.

"Cindy," he whispered quietly, in a tone that was full of remorse and loss.

He closed his eyes and bent his head to the earth, his shoulders slumped forward.

"Your daughter?" asked a voice from behind.

Sam scrambled around, shocked and surprised by the unexpected presence.

Lamia sat on a log slightly up the hill from him, resting on a fallen tree that was as much moss and lichen as it was wood.

She looked at him patiently, her hands crossed and resting on her knees.

Sam charged her, full of anger and adrenaline.

He didn't know what he would do when he reached her, but he was full of white fury that was boiling over.

When he did reach her, she knocked him aside easily, watching as he staggered into a thick sapling that was strong enough to stop his forward momentum. He fell limply to the ground.

Lamia sat by his side and watched him, cocking her head with curiosity as he slowly rose.

She saw him tense as his mind recalled how he had ended up here, face first in a pile of dead leaves.

"I am not your enemy," she said to him.

"You are not my friend," he spat.

"That remains to be seen," she answered calmly. "Time reveals many things, most of which we do not come to know until we are prepared to accept them."

Sam began to weep as his rage faded back into grief.

"Cindy is the name of your daughter?" Lamia asked for a second time.

She knew he had heard, and so she waited for him to answer her. She was in no rush. The night was young as of yet. The horizon was still slightly stained by sunlight and although the shadows of the park were long, they were not yet masterful.

"Cynthia," he finally said.

"A beautiful name," she said warmly. "My daughters had beautiful names also."

Sam slowly sat upright, brushing the leaves from his body.

"Your daughters?" he questioned, not expecting to hear she had children. He wiped the last of the tears from his eyes.

Lamia nodded.

"Where are they? Are they vampires, too?"

His question was partly curious, partly vindictive, wanting to accuse her daughters of being something he found repugnant.

Lamia shook her head regretfully. "I saw them buried long ago."

Sam hadn't expected that response, nor the way in which she had said it. It was full of the thick pain of a mother's loss.

"I can understand your pain. Although you are so certain I feel nothing, I can assure you, the opposite is true." She stood and offered him her hand.

"The dreams will change in time."

"My dreams?" he asked. He stood without her help.

Lamia lowered her hand.

"How did I not know you were here?" It bothered him that she had been behind him. Presumably she had watched him sleep.

"You decided not to be aware," was all she had to say. "Lucky for you, I do not mean you harm."

"Lilith was not able to kill me," Sam replied, thinking that explained everything.

Lamia rolled her eyes.

"Oh, the blissful ignorance of a fool. Lilith is your Master, *our* Master. You cannot kill her unless she allows it, but we can surely kill one another. There is no limit, amongst ourselves. No barrier."

"So I can kill you?" he asked her pointedly.

"And I, you," she replied factually, her eyes slightly amused.

Sam did not want to talk to this woman, but something about her demeanour made that difficult.

"How long were you there?" he asked her, "watching me?"

"Not very long. You are a loud sleeper. You need to find someplace safe to rest, before you are discovered."

"You didn't sense me?" he asked.

"We can only sense those who are listening for others. You stopped before you slept, so I only had an idea of where you were. I possess other senses that are very acute."

"So if I don't listen for others, others can't find me," he stated.

"Others can find you, just not by the sense of presence. The sense of smell is strong, and we are unique in a crowd. If I did not know where you were, I could find you by your scent. By our scent."

That unnerved Sam.

"It is considered to be impolite by our kind, not to be listening."

"Impolite?"

"No one likes to be surprised, and so in courtesy we listen, so that we do not come upon another unawares."

Sam laughed in disbelief.

Lamia glowered at him.

"You are young, and so you will be forgiven for a short time what would be considered to be rude or discourteous. That forgiveness is temporary," she warned him.

"I did not feel you," he countered.

"You were not listening," she said with a hint of condescension.

Sam stood silently, concentrating.

"What are you doing?" Lamia asked.

"Trying to listen."

Lamia laughed warmly.

"You are like a child," she said with fondness. "It does not work that way. Feel for me instead. Close your eyes."

Sam closed his eyes.

"Relax. Clear your mind. This requires no thought. It is instinct, like breathing."

Sam took a deep breath. His surroundings grew faint around him. Lamia was talking to him, moving around him, telling him to breathe and relax and to feel outwards for her. He felt moments of amusement and frustration, thoughts of impatience and satisfaction. Sam wondered if he was sensing her emotions, or his own. Then she was silent, no longer talking, and she did not answer any of his questions.

The hairs on his neck began to rise and he felt a dreadful certainty that she was behind him. He spun around and opened his eyes.

Lamia stood before him, her eyes wide and satisfied, staring into his own.

He was surprised nonetheless, and stepped back in shock. Not only did he see her in front of him, he *felt* her in front of him.

"Very good," she said, "now don't lose that feeling."

"Did I feel you?" he asked, wondering about the sensations he had experienced.

She frowned.

"I felt frustration, and other feelings, like amusement. I think I was feeling you. I can't explain it otherwise."

He focused on her, wanting to know her answer, and he felt more.

She was hungry, ignoring a yearning to feed that was all-consuming.

"You are hungry," he said, almost overwhelmed by its dominance.

She opened her mouth as if to say something and then quickly stopped herself, a look of doubt flashed across her face.

He sensed something else.

Fear.

"That frightens you?" he asked, his growing confidence overriding his sense that it might be best to not ask. Instead, he pressed further, emboldened by his surety that he was correct in his assumption.

"What were the names of your daughters?" he asked hastily.

Her face remained steadfast as though made of the hardest stone, revealing nothing to him, but what he felt was like a series of punches to his diaphragm. He felt instantly nauseous and overcome, weakened and regretful.

It was the pain she felt for her children.

Before he knew what was happening Lamia had him grasped firmly by his shirt, her fists were viciously clenched and his face was pulled to meet hers.

"Child!" she screamed into his face, her eyes were glowing yellow, flashing like beaten gold illuminated by firelight.

"You are a clumsy child!" she screamed at him hoarsely. "Lucky for you it is me with you now! Brocchus would have broken your arms for such insolence! Amun might have killed you! Bah!"

She threw him to the ground and then was gone from view.

Sam felt her leave, her violent emotions highlighting her path like a summer thunderstorm.

He shivered when he remembered the fierce look in her eyes, a side of her that he had not yet seen, a reminder to him what she was. What he was.

He sat up and cleared his mind, allowing the rush of feelings to fill his mind. He could feel the Others, most at a great distance away. Furthermore, he could feel their acknowledgment of him, their satisfaction that he was no longer silent. Some were interested in him and for the first time he could sense what Lamia had said, that some bore him ill-will, a wary discontent.

There were twelve of them, scattered to the four corners of the world.

He pushed them away, not wanting to know.

They faded away to a sense of awareness, nothing more.

His stomach grumbled and he felt a desire to feed growing within him.

Sam drew his knees up into his chest and tried to fight the hunger, to defeat it for as long as he could.

His mind wandered back to Cindy and the sound of her laughter, remembering the satisfaction Miranda had taken in braiding her hair. The giggle from his dream echoed in his ears.

For the second time today, he wept.

# Chapter 10

*"Come," she said, "come, I give sleep and peace, sleep and peace."*

*-The Tomb of Sarah*, F. G. Loring

Reverend Paul walked the street, feeling the chill of the early morning air nip at his flesh under his clothing. He was tired but as long as he kept moving he kept fatigue at bay. When he was twenty this would have been no great chore, to walk randomly around the city all the hours of the night. He was being reminded he was no longer twenty. He was no longer even forty. Twenty was a distant memory; forty was more recent but no longer close, although it was at least more familiar.

He was utterly alone.

The bar crowd had long ago retired for the night and the pubs and bars had been locked for hours, the spirits and liquors safe for another night.

There was only him, lost in his thoughts, looking for an encounter he hoped not to have.

When it came, he was so distracted by his thoughts that it took him a moment to register that he was being addressed, and another moment for a sinking fear to dig into his belly.

"Hello, Father."

The Reverend frowned when he looked up and saw that it was no man standing in front of him.

It was a woman; a very attractive woman by any measure.

She was standing in the middle of the sidewalk, on the opposite side of a cone of yellow light thrown down from the street light high above her.

The effect on her features was decidedly eerie, casting unusual shadows.

He searched his mind to match her face with a name, thinking he must know her, as the look on her face indicated that she clearly knew him.

"Hello," he replied politely, beginning to grin. "Do I know you?" he asked, regrettably unable to recall her name.

The grin faded from his face when he saw her eyes.

They were black, as black and as infinite as the night sky above her.

"Yes, Father," Lamia replied a grin growing on her face. "At the very least you know *of* me."

She took a step towards him just as he stopped taking a step forward.

He unconsciously gripped his cross tightly, praying for strength.

"What do you think my intentions are?" she asked him obliquely.

She smiled at him warmly, a look that confused him. Her grin broadened. Lamia continued to approach him boldly, her eyes holding his. He dared not look away.

"You have the look of a man of great conviction, and who now, having seen the truth of his conviction, is unsure of having the strength to proceed."

"It is one thing to have conviction, quite another thing to see with your own eyes," he replied, his mouth suddenly bitterly dry.

Lamia laughed. "I suppose. But you are a learned man; I can see that you have seen things few others would even suggest. And here you are, walking the night in search of... what? Answers?"

She moved to his side and turned to face the street as he faced it, sliding her hand smoothly over his left arm.

"I am looking to answer questions, or perhaps to ask my own questions."

He did not want to show fear, fully aware he was shaking from head to toe.

"Shall we walk?" Lamia suggested amiably.

He felt her hands close around his arm, feeling the terrible strength concealed within those soft, slender feminine hands.

"Do I have a choice?" he asked her warily.

"We all have a choice, Father. It is the essence of free will. Come now, it is only a walk I desire from you, an evening walk and a conversation. "

She stepped forward, pulling him ahead with her. He stepped with her, lest he fall or stumble at her feet.

He needed to be strong.

"Very good," she chuckled, staring at him with amusement shining in those lightless eyes. "Fear is healthy," she said into his ear, "it keeps the mind sharp."

"You have not stated your intention," he replied.

"Surely I have," she said, "All I seek is the pleasure of your company."

"That is all?" he asked warily.

"He made known to us the mystery of His will, according to His kind intention which He purposed in Him," Lamia said with a smile, "In this case, She."

"The Devil can quote scripture for his own purpose," Paul quoted to her, staring into her eyes. They were normal now, seemingly human. Her eyes were emerald green and they glinted with immeasurable wisdom.

She laughed honestly.

"We are not enemies," she said to him, "and I am no Devil."

"Surely we are. I am the Light, where you are the Dark. You may very well be the Devil."

"Light and Dark are not enemies," she chuckled, "we are merely opposites. We are not so different, you and I."

"I do God's work!" he stated angrily, furious and insulted that she thought they were so alike.

"And who are you to say that I do not?" she countered firmly. "Can you say you know the mind and plan of God?"

Paul bit his lip.

The woman stared at him for a moment, waiting for a response.

"Of course you cannot, and so you cannot refute what I say."

"And neither can you know your purpose," he said bitterly.

"I have faith," she responded with certainty, "something which you have peddled for your entire life, have you not? Some men sell shoes, others clothing, whereas you are a salesman of faith. You sell belief. An interesting trade, and one which I can appreciate much more than most."

"What do you want?"

His fear of her was fading as their conversation lengthened. He was becoming fascinated by her; his inner scholar was intrigued.

"Much better," she said. "It is better for you not to be afraid. We can chat as old friends as we walk and enjoy this very pleasant evening together."

She could feel him chafe under the suggestion they were friends.

"Perhaps not as old friends then, since that seems to stick in your craw. Can we talk then as respected adversaries? A discussion held during a truce?"

"Very well," Paul said warily in reluctant agreement, "Adversaries."

"Delightful," Lamia said, the word stated with genuine warmth.

He was very aware that she could be easily misjudged, for all of her casual body language and smiles. He was still frightened, very badly frightened, but like a soldier in combat, he used his fear to sharpen his wits. He was wary, but not weak.

Underneath her warm exterior was a fearful killer, a creature that fed on life itself.

And this creature wished to speak with him.

"We have a mutual acquaintance."

"Possibly," he replied, his mind flashing quickly to an image of Sam.

"Yes, him," Lamia said.

Paul looked at her wonderingly.

"It is an ability of mine, to see a part of what you are thinking."

"And what of him?" he asked.

"He spoke with you."

"He did."

"What did he share with you?"

"That will remain private between he and I."

A brief scowl crossed her face. "I should need to know," she said.

"I would be a poor man of the cloth if I were to share conversations held in a state of trust."

The scowl returned, taking longer to fade this time. He felt her grip on his arm tighten.

"He is vulnerable," she replied.

Paul remembered his encounter, playing through the course of events quickly.

Vulnerable, she said.

Paul recalled Sam's fury and anger, his violent emotional switches. Sam did not strike him as being vulnerable. Unpredictable and dangerous was more like it.

"If he is vulnerable, then why are you not with him? You seek my counsel instead. I see myself as an unlikely ally for one such as yourself."

"I am not with him as I need time to reflect. He is torn between our worlds. The bonds of his former life hold him strongly; he is too stubborn to let go and accept what he has become."

"An intelligent man, then," Paul retorted aloud, thinking of what an awful situation Sam was in. He suddenly felt great pity for him.

"A fool to resist what is inevitable," Lamia said angrily.

"And what is inevitable? That he should become such as you? He still possesses free will. Perhaps that is what you fear, that he will not seek your life as you have chosen it to be."

"Do not judge me, *Father*," she sneered.

Paul ignored her remark entirely.

"You seek my help in what? Guiding him into the Dark? Pushing him from the Light when he seeks its shelter?" He laughed aloud, surprised at his ability to challenge her. He was also surprised at how quickly he was prepared to defend Sam.

"He is young and inexperienced and his life will be in danger if he continues to resist."

"He is a mistake," Paul surmised in a moment of perception.

Lamia fell silent for a second; hesitant to admit it was so.

"Yes," she finally surrendered.

"How did he come to be? I would need to know why he is a mistake. Why he is different from yourself?"

"He survived a feeding. He was not killed and drained of his essence, his life's blood. If my sister had fed on him completely, Sam would have died a mortal death. Because she did not kill him, he changed from what he was into what he is."

"It was not intentional?"

Lamia shook her head.

"There were to be no more added to our number. Therein lies the hazard to his existence. He is an abomination to our kind. If he learns, he may yet be spared. He will not be given much time. It may already be too late."

"And you?" Paul asked her directly, "You made a decision to be what you are?"

"My sister was all I had in this world, a world that cared nothing for my being. Better to pass the centuries with my sister than to die alone and suffer all the indignities that can be inflicted upon a person."

"He is dangerous." Paul reflected.

"He is powerful," she added.

"And you wish me to guide him?"

"I wish you to help him. We are not so common that the loss of one of our number can be so easily ignored. Some of us might mean him harm. I do not."

"And yet he might be killed."

"That is not my will, nor my choice to make. I am only one."

Paul saw something else in those green eyes.

"You are lonely. Perhaps bored as well, but I can read in your face an emptiness."

Lamia sharpened her visage. "My reasons are my own concern," she responded angrily, letting him go suddenly, almost pushing herself away from him.

They stood facing one another.

"I will help him," Paul said to her firmly, "I will help him to come to his own decision, for it is his to make. His destiny is his own, but I will be a guide if he will accept it."

Paul did not know what to expect from her. Acceptance was the most he could have prepared for; he did not expect she was capable of the broad range of human emotions.

She looked at him now as she once was, a young beautiful woman with warm green eyes. Her look was sincere and genuine.

"Thank you," she whispered, leaning forward and quickly kissing him on the cheek in gratitude. She held his head firmly as she did so, almost motherly.

Then she was gone, vanished into the air.

Paul staggered backwards as she released him, unprepared for her gesture. He could feel where she had kissed him, touching the spot on his cheek.

He was suddenly appalled by his ignorance about her. Knowledge was strength, and he realized in that final tender gesture, that he had underestimated her by no small amount.

His lack of understanding could be catastrophic. It was one thing to know your enemy and to prepare your reaction based upon that implicit understanding. It was quite another to think you knew your enemy and to then be completely surprised and caught unaware.

Paul knew that he was at a great disadvantage, that if she had wanted a different outcome to their meeting it very likely would have unfolded that way, very much against his favor.

He had felt confident and bold in talking to her, almost victorious. He had not bent to her will against his own beliefs.

She had shattered that confidence in an instant, leaving it like dust on the roadside.

He had to wonder if she had played him masterfully; if his decision had not been steered and directed by her reactions and responses.

Paul almost laughed at the memory of saying that Sam was dangerous.

She was far more deadly, a viper with the utmost confidence in her own capabilities and strengths.

He was a novice, invited to a great game where he had been allowed to play at a very low level and tricked into believing he could hold his own.

Paul shivered and turned to walk back to his church, to ponder and to plan.

Another thought crossed his mind.

Had she kissed him to reveal his lack of comprehension, or was that kiss a telling mistake of her own?

If she had made the mistake, it had great ramifications.

It could reveal a great weakness in her tough hide, perhaps a remnant of her humanity that she had not lost to the passage of time. It could be used against her; used for leverage for himself or for Sam.

Then his thoughts returned full circle.

Perhaps she had meant it to make him think she had displayed a weakness, the final play before the checkmate was delivered.

Or maybe she had no ulterior motive at all.

There was a possibility that the kiss was genuine and meaningful, no more a show of weakness than it was a show of strength. Maybe she was so supremely confident in herself that there was no hidden intent at all.

Maybe she was being honest, allowing him to see a rare glimpse of her former self.

He could go mad thinking about all of the possible meanings behind their conversation and its ultimate conclusion.

Returning to his original train of thought, he had to conclude that there was a chance that she still possessed the full range of human emotions; that she was not limited to what would be expected of a creature stereotyped as being blindly evil.

He had to shrug at that realization, thinking it was a normal way to dehumanize an enemy, to reduce your opponent in terms of their characteristics, to debase them to a primitive or even savage level.

Modern warfare was not innocent of the practice. The purpose of propaganda was often to lessen the humanity of an opponent. The Nazi regime had played it to a masterful level against Judaism, but they were by no means the only participant in that practice. The American and Soviet propaganda machines had played against one another during the length of the Cold War, and modern terrorism often used the tactic in justifying their targets. It stood to reason that the church was capable of using the same strategy with its foes, passing along as fact the mythos of stereotyped, inhuman enemies.

In thinking she was limited to evil emotions - hate, bitterness, anger, jealousy - he could underestimate her terribly. Add to the possibility of love to the existence of hatred, and both emotions became far more dangerous.

It was like adding oxygen to hydrogen.

Alone, hydrogen gas is harmless. By adding sufficient oxygen, the same hydrogen gas becomes deadly; violently explosive.

He had gone into the conversation blindfolded, woefully ignorant of her depths.

Still waters run deep, meaning that underneath that still, dark water could be a deadly and fearsome current.

He rounded the final corner to the Church, having navigated the distance with his head lowered to the ground while deep in thought, trusting his feet to lead him home.

The eastern horizon was beginning to brighten slightly, the night sky fading into a shade of dark blue.

"Father," a voice called.

Paul stopped in his tracks, feeling a cold tremor race up his spine.

The word was not used in greeting. It was condescending and cold, meant as an insult.

He turned.

A woman was standing in the street.

"You're back?" he asked, unable to see clearly at the distance she stood from him.

She laughed coldly, rudely.

"No. Not my sister," Lilith sneered. "It would be better for you if it was."

*Her sister.*

Paul understood immediately.

"She meant no harm," he said, not knowing what this woman wanted from him.

"She is weak," Lilith spat out, "Soft." She made no gesture to come closer to him, keeping her distance.

Paul was painfully aware of his distance from the steps to the Church. He felt certain that she was also very aware of it, that the encounter was strategic and on her terms.

Paul could feel she was very different. She was standing utterly still. Her face held a cold look of contempt. There was no warmth in her stance, no hint of any desire to be civil. She sought a confrontation, maybe a conclusion to a problem.

"Give Samuel to me," she commanded, her chin held high and expectant.

"What? Samuel?" Paul asked, wondering how he could give him to her.

He didn't know where he was; he had spent the night looking for him. "I don't know where he is."

She lifted a slender arm and pointed with a single bare finger to the Church.

"He is within," she replied firmly, her stern voice growing even colder.

*Of course*, Paul thought to himself. *I've been walking around all night looking for him, and instead he came back to the Church looking for me.* He chuckled at the irony of it all.

When he laughed he saw her black eyes shift, darkening a shade before a glowing yellow spark grew in each pupil. A moment later she was staring at him from glowing yellow points, like small unwavering flames were burning in each of her eyes.

He had thought the black eyes were the most terrible thing he had ever seen. He stood corrected; the fearsome yellow eyes seemed to draw courage away from him, blowing cold winter air over his skin.

He knew he had to draw a line in the sand. She wanted his compliance, and to give it would eventually be fatal.

"Then he has Sanctuary," Paul said firmly.

Sam might be able to enter to seek aid, but she could not. He fleetingly wondered why. She could pursue him no further than the twin doors that sat atop the concrete stairs.

Sam was safe.

Paul was not.

Lilith hissed at him like a furious cat, baring sharpened teeth.

"Give him to me," she said with finality, clenching her fists and glaring at him with those awful burning eyes. It was unrestrained anger, contempt and hatred, all balled into one fearful expression.

Paul took a breath and dry swallowed the lump in his throat before answering her.

"No."

She charged him with a screech that nearly made him empty his bowels.

*This is it*, he thought blankly, *this is the face of true evil. I'm going to die.*

That she meant to kill him, he knew without a doubt. She would bathe in his blood and scatter his remains, to make a scene of his body and send a message to all who knew what message was being sent.

With a calmness that shocked him he drew his crucifix from under his shirt and held it aloft between them, high in his extended hand.

"Get back!" he shouted, his voice rising from his diaphragm, deep and steady.

He could feel a river of unrestrained energy pour through him, drawn from the air into his body where it collected and gathered, racing up his arm to the cross like electricity to an electrical socket.

The crucifix burst into blue-white light.

Paul saw her yellow eyes squint, her facial features contorting in unexpected shock and then pain.

She leapt for him, meaning to rip out his throat with her hands.

A sphere of light closed in around him, dropping over him like a transparent glowing half circle, covering him in an overturned bowl of light.

Lilith bounced off the dome as though she was inconsequential, cast aside and returned to the side of the road where she had first confronted him.

Paul smiled.

He stepped towards her, walking steadily with an unwavering gait. She rose to her feet and fought to reach him, her clawed hands digging at an impenetrable barrier that sparked and glowed at her touch. The heavy smell of ozone hung in the air.

"You cannot have him," he told her matter-of-factly.

The blue dome around him intensified and seemed to thicken, wavering the outside light as though it was being viewed through an imperfect sheet of glass.

She backed away and raised her hands to shield her eyes from that awful light.

"He has found Sanctuary within those walls. He is on holy ground and I will not surrender him to you."

She hissed at him again, her anger mixed with agony.

"In the name of the Father, the Son, and the Holy Ghost I command you, foul creature, to be gone!"

The wavering nature of the dome ceased and it became perfectly clear and transparent, humming like a power transformer.

She screamed at him, not in surrender, but in unbending hatred.

"You cannot keep him safe!" she shrieked at him viciously, spittle flying from her lips. Her eyes flickered between Paul and the barrier, changing each moment from hate to fear.

"He will submit his will to mine!"

Paul laughed. "I will fear no evil! I do not fear you!" he shouted, his eyes gleaming with confidence. He felt like he was twenty again, in his prime, exuding youthful energy and strength.

She staggered backwards, almost tripping over the concrete curb.

"He will wish to die before I am done with him!" she cried, turning and

vanishing into the shadows, disappearing into the wind.

Paul let his crucifix drop to his side, breathing heavily and sweating profusely.

He suddenly felt exhausted, but in a good way, like he had just completed an endurance run. The feeling was fleeting and brief; his body began to cry out for food and water, rest and relaxation. Sleep.

He was no longer twenty.

Sixty-four sank back into his fatigued bones with a vengeance, reminding him of the time that had passed. He wished he could crack open and turn back some of the excessive mileage on the personal Paul odometer, to permanently recapture some of that feeling of being twenty again.

His own parents had both passed the century mark, his mother passing away at the shriveled old age of one hundred and two. His father had made it another six months after she had been laid to rest, crossing the one hundred and three barrier by a day and a half before his body decided that was good enough. Not bad for a couple of bacon-loving, scotch-drinking, slightly overweight, casual smoking Kraut's.

Assuming he could count on genetics for longevity, he thought he had about another four decades to go, should natural events determine his fate. By unnatural events, he imagined scenarios like an unobservant nose-picking bus driver running him down, or an errant lightning strike. Either of which would be an inappropriate ending for his story. A disgraceful way to exit this mortal coil.

At this moment, another four decades seemed like an eternity.

His right leg suddenly wanted to cramp, twitching randomly. All he wanted to do was to sit.

Oh God. To sit and to relax would be heavenly.

He wanted to make notes while everything was still fresh and clear in his mind.

He looked at the cross in his hand dumbly, wonderingly, and reflected on what he had just experienced, replaying the moments in his mind.

Two cheap pieces of wood, held together with a tiny steel nail.

And it had vibrated as though alive, the conduit for all the power that had been released through him.

It had quivered in his grasp, difficult to hold onto and almost hot, like it had been sitting on the dashboard of a car in high summer. It was like he had held a miniscule nuclear reactor in his hand.

And the dome, what was that?

The light from it was intense, very similar to the harshness of an LED, strong and blinding, while utterly without heat. Outside sounds had been affected when it had dropped down around him like a protective shield. Her screams had been dulled and warped, like they were being played back through a defective tape player. Not sped up or slowed down, just muted and slightly twisted.

When he had commanded her to obey it had changed.

It had been like he was inside an aquarium, viewing the world outside from within the dome. When he had commanded her and challenged her, he had seen and felt the shield thicken and clarify. His image of her had clarified while the sounds had not.

When he recalled what had happened when she had touched the shield, he was reminded of those electrical glass globes sold in novelty stores, the ones that cast off thin glowing strings of dancing electricity outwards to their glass sphere. When you pressed your finger to the glass the electricity homed in on the contact and quivered under the point of contact. Countless miniature tendrils surrounded the fingertip like glowing soft hairs.

When the vampire had touched the shield he had felt the power zero in on her point of contact, repelling her cleanly as though they were like-poles of magnets, throwing off arcs of energy as she was repulsed away from him.

Her words came back to him.

*"He is within."*

Sam was in his Church, waiting for him.

# Chapter 11

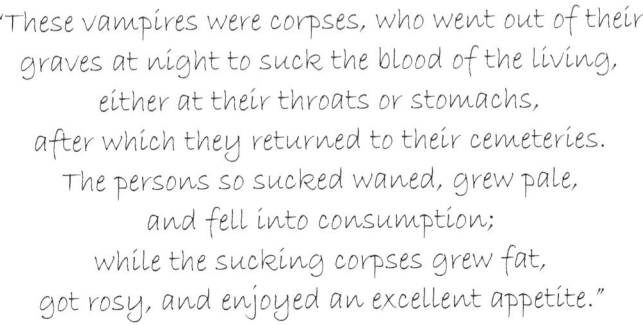

"These vampires were corpses, who went out of their
graves at night to suck the blood of the living,
either at their throats or stomachs,
after which they returned to their cemeteries.
The persons so sucked waned, grew pale,
and fell into consumption;
while the sucking corpses grew fat,
got rosy, and enjoyed an excellent appetite."

Voltaire - *Philosophical Dictionary*

Paul stumbled to the church, his stomach faintly but equivocally grumbling under his ribs.

He felt weak, sick to his stomach, dizzy like he had heatstroke, but starving at the same time. It was not at all a pleasant combination of feelings.

The twin doors opened easily and he savored the clear feeling of safety that washed over him. Here he was safe.

It was like being a young child in the presence of both parents. Within these walls he was immune from the sort of danger he had just faced.

Paul walked down the hall and entered the lower sanctuary, looking for Sam.

He had expected to see him sitting in and amongst the pews, waiting.

There was no one there. The silence was overwhelming. Perhaps she had been wrong?

No, she would not lie or create falsehoods about this, of that he was sure.

The small hairs on the back of his neck crept upwards.

He could feel a taint in the atmosphere, like the faint smell of old garbage.

It just wasn't quite right.

The confessional booth dropped into his mind.

It was to the right of the sanctuary, along the same wall of his office behind the very last of the wooden pews.

As he neared the booth he became more certain that his instinct had been correct.

The indescribable malodour became more pronounced, less subtle.

The confessional doors were closed and there was no way he could be sure that Sam was waiting for him.

*Except that he just knew.*

Paul reached out and touched the wood grain handle, pulling the door open quietly.

The darkness waited for him within.

Paul sat gratefully and shut the door, sliding the lattice open that separated the two

compartments.

Two yellow eyes glimmered at him in the darkness.

"Bless me Father for I have sinned," a voice croaked hollowly.

Paul could easily hear his breathing. It was deep and anguished, heavy and labored.

Paul swallowed before beginning himself.

The odor within his small confined space was overpowering.

His crucifix was shining with a faint blue light.

"When was your last confession?" Paul asked him quietly.

"I have never confessed," was the gasping reply.

Paul closed his eyes, not wanting to see Sam's haunted appearance, not wanting to see that terrible yellow.

"For what sins do you seek forgiveness?" he asked.

"I have taken a life," Sam said, his voice low like an animal rumble. "I have killed," Sam repeated, his breath raspy and coarse.

Paul jumped when a sudden thump came from the opposite wall, the sound of a hand clawing at the stained wood.

"Why did you take a life?" Paul said, fighting to remain calm. "It is a great sin. *Thou shalt not kill.*"

"I fed!" Sam said aloud, more of a shout but not quite yelling. Then, much lower but darker, "I fed on him, and another."

Paul tried to swallow the lump in his throat.

He felt reasonably sure that here he was safe, that he could not be purposefully harmed. His mind told him that, but his body told him otherwise.

"You have taken two lives?" Paul asked, wringing his hands.

"Yessss," was the hissing faint reply.

Paul shivered.

"I could not help it. I did not mean it, IT JUST HAPPENED!" Sam yelled.

"Could you stop yourself?"

"No."

Paul felt that Sam was fighting with himself, that Sam was having a conversation between distinct personalities that partly overlapped.

One voice was almost normal, aggrieved and full of despair. The other was dark and content.

"Are you sorry for what you have done?"

"Yes," came the first response, almost weeping, and then in a second muted reply, "No."

Paul thought he heard a controlled chuckle from beyond the lattice. It stopped abruptly.

"Did you let yourself in?"

"I cannot enter…here."

"Then how did you get in?"

"I waited for one of your flock to seek shelter and guidance."

"Where are they now?" Paul hadn't seen anyone in the building. It was silent, like a catacomb.

"She left," Sam seemed to gurgle, as though in conflict. Then he laughed a menacing and cold sound. "She did not warm to my presence."

Paul could imagine why. He must have nearly frightened her to death.

"I did not feed on her."

"I didn't accuse you of that."

"You thought it."

Paul tried to clear his mind.

"Why are you here?"

"I am hungry."

Paul made the sign of the cross upon his chest.

"You are hungry and you don't want to kill again?" Paul asked, wanting to clarify.

"I am evil," was the answer to his question.

"In terms of what you represent, yes," Paul answered.

"Help me."

"I am not sure how I can."

Paul thought he heard crying.

"They are dead. My wife Miranda; Cindy and Tommy. I failed them."

Paul heard him begin to weep.

Paul thought about Lilith; the strength of her attack on him.

"You did not fail them. What you faced you could not defeat."

The crying only intensified and Paul was forced to wait for the grief to subside in its own time. Finally, after some minutes, it lessened.

"Can you pray for them?"

Paul nodded. "Yes, of course. Have you?"

There was a gasp, a sharp intake of breath like frustration.

"I cannot. The words…stick. I cannot say what I want to say. It hurts. Oh it hurts. You must pray for me. You must. You mussst."

Paul heard the other part of Sam assert control.

"I can smell your blood," he sighed like he was observing the beginning of a delicious banquet with anticipation.

"I can smell you," Paul replied, "it is like a tomb."

Sam gripped at the walls of the booth once again, his nails scraping into the wood.

"You cannot know what it is like," Sam said, "I do not want to be like this."

"It is too late," Paul said simply, stating the truth. "You are a vampire; something I would not have believed was possible until you crossed my path. For that revelation, I don't know if I should thank you or curse you."

Sam chuckled darkly. "I am already cursed. I am alive and my family is dead. Killed in front of my own eyes. By *her*," he almost spat.

"Her?" Paul asked, his eyebrows lifting in dread at the recent memory of being attacked outside of his church. Was it the same woman?

"Lilith," was the grating reply.

Paul was startled. "Her name is Lilith?"

"Yesss."

Paul was intrigued at the name.

Biblically, Lilith was said to be the first wife of Adam, before Eve. There were many stories about her, most of them holding her in a less than reputable light. She had refused to be subservient to Adam, becoming the mother of monsters.

Was there a connection, was it possible that this Lilith was the very same?

If so, it was staggering in its implications.

"I do not want to be….THIS," Sam moaned through the latticework.

"What do you want?"

"I WANT TO DIE!" he shouted, rocking in his small space.

"A part of you does, I am sure," Paul replied calmly, surprised at how even his voice was. His hands were shaking.

"The part of you that misses your wife and children wishes to join them, to be with them. It can be a natural part of the grieving process. You have already experienced shock and denial, the very first stage. The second is pain and guilt. Please remember, the stages will overlap and one will morph into the next. There is no clear transition. Anger comes next, and then depression, followed by an upturn. Reconstruction follows that, and then finally acceptance."

He heard Sam sob in the muted space.

"There is another part of you that does not want to die, or else you would have already. That part of you must be reconciled; appeased, or at the very least understood, before you might be successful in ending your life."

"How can you even speak to me of acceptance?" Sam gasped, his voice clearly horrified at the thought.

"You are too early in the process to believe that it will come, still partially in denial. If you truly wanted to die, you would not be here with me. You could stand in the sunrise and end your suffering, and you have not. The part of you that wishes to live is stronger than the part of you that wishes to die."

"And which part of me is that?" Sam wept, fearing it was the vampire in himself that wanted to live, to persevere.

Paul shrugged unconsciously, forgetting Sam could not see the gesture.

"That is for you to discover. I suspect it is the part of you that wants to remember your family, to not let them be forgotten. The father and the husband still remains, even when the family is gone."

"The dreams are terrible," Sam whispered, thinking of the voices in the fog.

"Dreams are a part of the healing process. They are a part of coming to terms with the finality of loss, the acceptance of reality. It is difficult, but people are stronger than they believe."

Sam felt his shoulders sag; his posture drooped as if every tendon and ligament in his body was lengthened and then released, like a marionette.

He suddenly felt exhausted. No, Sam thought, he felt spent, dried out.

The hunger was pushed away, only a nagging annoyance. Even the pain at being within the walls of the church had faded, reduced to a persistent itch.

"Do you wish to tell me about your dreams?" Paul asked.

Sam closed his eyes.

"There is a fog," he shivered, recalling. "I can't see anything. It is cold. Its night-time and I'm in a forest."

"Do you remember the forest?" Paul asked, wondering if it was somewhere specific.

"No. I've never been in that place, the forest in my dreams."

"And what happens?"

"I hear the voices of my wife and of my children." Sam wanted to cry again, but he could not.

"Do you see them?" Paul asked.

"Yes," Sam smiled, holding his head in his hands.

The smile faded quickly as he recalled some of the more terrible moments.

Cynthia snapping at him with fierce glistening incisors. He shuddered.

"No more," he said thinly, "I can't. They are too terrible."

"You seek my help."

"Yes," Sam said.

"I am not sure how I can help you. You are what you are. I cannot change that. Your path is set."

And yet here they were, Paul thought; two ancient adversaries having a conversation in the bastion of one of them.

"I don't want to be what I am."

"I understand that, but I cannot change it. It is done."

Paul hoped he did not sound too cold. He could see that Sam was trapped in a situation that was not of his making, torn between his old self and his memories and the new instincts that motivated him.

Paul pitied him greatly.

"What are my options?" Sam mumbled.

"You have already mentioned one."

"Suicide?"

"Yes. But I do not think you will follow that path."

"Why?" Sam asked, hoping to gain strength from whatever answer came, hoping to find a reason he could draw from to resist.

"Your family," was all that Paul said. He had noticed as they spoke that the other darker portion of Sam's persona was gone, or at least subdued. Sam seemed wholly in control of himself. Peering through the latticework he could see that the dull yellow eyes were gone. His eyes were entirely black.

Paul wondered if perhaps the colour indicated Sam's emotional state. The yellow eyes were a signal that he was near to his primordial state, a vampire in its basic state. Were the black eyes a sign that he was calm?

Sam digested Paul's answer, feeling the truth of it. He could not die for them, it would serve no purpose. They lived, if anywhere, only in his mind, and that idea was sacred to him.

If he died, then maybe they would be lost forever.

Sam felt his mind clear. "And what else?" he asked.

"Find a purpose to your existence, something from which you can draw strength and meaning, something from which you can justify your fate."

"Do you think this was my destiny?" Sam asked, wondering if this 'fate', as Paul had put it, was inevitable.

Paul was introspective for a moment.

"I believe there is a certain destiny, that is to say, a certain choice needing to be made, to which everyone is guided or nudged in the course of their life. The fulfillment of that destiny, the choice that is made, can be altered by free will. The outcome of that choice will be based on the actions of free will. And then of course there is chaos. Purely random actions will also affect outcome, outside the boundaries of free will."

"This might have been my destiny then." Sam said with a certain fatalistic darkness.

"Perhaps, or perhaps it was an accident of chaos. Regardless of what has transpired, it is up to you to find your path, to redirect yourself to what you feel is right. Your destiny from this point onward is still up to you. You still possess free will; you are bound to no predetermined outcome."

"Then what about my family? What was their destiny, their reason for being?"

Sam was thinking specifically of his children, taken at such an early age, wondering what it was that they could have accomplished. He felt no anger as he asked the question, only a deep and resigned despair.

"On that we could conjecture for a great deal of time."

"What do you think?" Sam asked, wanting to hear the reverend's opinion, hoping he might discover a perspective he could cling to, like a desperate sailor searching for a life preserver on a sinking ship.

Paul sighed, thinking carefully about what he wanted to say, choosing his words like a sculptor picking the perfect chisel.

"With the exclusion of random incidents, I believe that people die when they have achieved their purpose."

"What could Tommy have achieved that served his purpose at four years old?" Sam sputtered, feeling an anger growing in his belly.

"To motivate his father," Paul answered.

Sam felt the wind fall from his sails.

"I think that people make the mistake of believing that what we need to do in life is direct and measurable, like going to the grocery store to get milk. The circumstances that lead up to a specific event can be innumerable, some more pronounced than others; some are profound while others are almost invisible. Those that cannot be readily seen are no less important or critical to the final outcome. The brief interaction that one person may have with another may be the inspiration that leads another person to a specific outcome. That might be something as vague as being cut off in traffic and being made to take a different route to a destination. On the surface, that interaction seems unimportant. To the end result, it was critical."

Sam flexed his hands and fought to ignore his discomfort. The conversation was distracting him, helping him to forget the pain of being in the church.

"And then the person that cut off the other has completed his task. He has no other purpose in life," Sam concluded.

It seemed so shallow, that the purpose of life for a human being might be nothing more than to cut someone off in traffic.

"Perhaps. Perhaps not. We live in an intricate web of interaction. That person might have many more tasks to complete."

"Or none," Sam added.

"Or maybe none," Paul agreed, "but whatever the task was, to the end result it was vital, like the foundation of a building. Each brick is important. In the end, you will need to discover what your task is."

Sam shivered at the thought that crept into his head.

Could he be an angel of death?

He said it aloud by accident, giving voice to his thought.

"It is a purpose," Paul had to agree.

"Am I to be chaos then, picking and choosing randomly?"

Sam hated to hear it said, a seeming acceptance of what he was, an acknowledgment of being a killer.

"It is one possibility, to be an agent of randomness. Another is to be an agent of purpose. I don't know if we are capable of knowing what agent we might be. Chaos is like the Uncertainty Principle, are you familiar with it?"

"Heisenberg?" Sam asked.

"Yes," Paul agreed, glad that the reference was not lost. "By knowing one characteristic of a thing, we cannot know the other characteristics. The very act of observing one, makes the other features unknowable. I have my reservations though, that a living being could be an agent of chaos. In my opinion, there is too much order in the universe for any life to participate in the perpetuation of chaos."

"What is my purpose?"

Paul pursed his lips. "That I do not know. You must discover that for yourself."

A silence hung in the air between them.

Paul had nothing more to add and Sam was lost in thought.

Both sat in the darkness with their eyes closed.

It was Sam that finally broke the silence. "Thank you, Father."

Paul was surprised by their interaction here, in such contrast to the terrifying conflict he had encountered outside. "She was outside, waiting for me."

"I know," Sam replied. He had felt her circling the building like a vulture floating in the sky above a bloated carcass.

"She wants to kill you," Paul warned him.

Sam smiled knowingly, "She will not try to kill me, not unless she wishes to risk dying herself. Did she let you go?" Sam asked curiously, almost humorously, as if he were a cat watching another cat play with a mouse.

"I defeated her."

"Fortunate for you," Sam said quietly," she would have shown you no mercy. She would have fed on you and left me a sign with your remains."

Paul saw his eyes begin to change, the blackness slowly replaced by the yellow. They flickered like hot coals.

"She will not underestimate you again."

"Nor I, her," Paul replied.

Sam laughed grimly. "I enjoyed our conversation," Sam said faintly. "Remember my family," he added, reminding Paul of his promise.

"I will."

Paul heard him breathing through his mouth, the air whistling softly between his teeth.

"Dawn has come. I must go. Let me out."

They walked together in silence to the exit, and when Paul opened the doors, Sam burst outwards, fleeing the confines of the church. There was no stamping of feet as he ran, no rustling of clothing. He was just gone. Paul dropped the clasp that locked the doors back into place and leaned back, resting against the wall.

There were so many questions he wanted to ask Sam as he led him out, so many things he wanted to know. He hadn't summoned the courage to ask.

Lilith was the one who had killed Sam's family, and Lilith had referred to her sister as the one whom he had spoken with earlier.

Lilith's sister. Yet her sister had wanted him to help Sam.

Both of them were vampires and each possessed very different personalities.

He recalled the things he had seen in his youth, the supernatural experiences in the rainforest, and the practiced skills of the shaman.

He had never once thought he would see what he had seen tonight. Spirits and demons and ghosts were one thing, vampires were another. He had always felt those medieval descriptions to be old wives' tales, stories to frighten children and to keep the church pews full.

A new world was opened to him, a world full of incubus and succubus, fauns and satyrs; a world where Lilith was the slayer of children.

The distinction between myth and reality blurred.

# Chapter 12

"As everyone knows, the ancients before Aristotle did not consider the dream a product of the dreaming mind, but a divine inspiration, and in ancient times the two antagonistic streams, which one finds throughout in the estimates of dream life, were already noticeable. They distinguished between true and valuable dreams, sent to the dreamer to warn him or to foretell the future, and vain, fraudulent, and empty dreams, the object of which was to misguide or lead him to destruction."

-Sigmund Freud

The fog swirled around the bases of the trees, vanishing into the ferns and shrubs and twisting into the air atop faint breezes.

"No," Sam gasped.

He was fully aware that he was dreaming but he was helpless to stop it.

"No more!" he yelled into the dark woods, hoping he would not hear a reply.

There was no answer, only silence.

An owl hooted somewhere high above.

The fog began to thicken, drifting over his ankles and accumulating in the air around him. It rose to his knees and then gradually his thighs. Before long, he was standing in a cloud of white, able to see no further than the length of his arm in any direction.

He refused to move, stubbornly digging his heels into the soft earth.

A dog barked twice in quick succession.

"Baxter?" he said quietly.

This was unexpected. He wondered if his dreams were going to change.

When he was young, there had been several dreams that used to terrify him, until he grew older and found that he could recognize when he was in a dream state. Once that had happened, he had been able to control the dreams, changing how they played out until they no longer scared him. And from then on, the dreams had stopped.

The worst dream had consisted of an ominous heartbeat in the darkness, a dream that had terrified him well into his teen years.

It had always begun the same way.

He would be surrounded by darkness, a blackness so thick and suffocating it became a stifling blanket that he could neither feel, nor remove. He could not see anything. It was the perfect absence of light.

Then the moaning would begin; a low haunted moan that he acquainted with old B-Movies about mummies and ancient Egyptian catacombs.

It was the sound of the undead hunting for the living; seeking revenge for the breach of a tomb, brought to life by the mummy's curse.

The moan would grow louder and louder, and Sam knew that somehow he was trapped in a tomb with the undead. The mummy was seeking him out in the darkness, reaching out for him with dusty bandaged hands, hands that were nothing but dry bones wrapped in shriveled flesh.

It was systematically searching for him, going back and forth in a mindless shuffle until it found him.

When it found him, it would kill him. It would reach for his neck with those dry dirty wrappings, and those boney fingers would choke the life out of him, dropping him to the ground with a broken neck. Then it would return to its sarcophagus, its duty fulfilled, forever on guard.

The part that always scared him to death was the heartbeat.

Once the heartbeat began Sam knew his time was almost up, and he would awake screaming and hollering in his bed, the sound still hammering in his ears.

*Thump-thump.*

It began quietly, like the moaning of the mummy.

Like the mummy, it grew ever louder and nearer.

*Thump-thump.*

Sam never knew if it was the sound of his own heartbeat, or that of the mummy's. Either way, it terrified him.

The heartbeat meant death.

*THUMP-thump.*

It got louder and louder. So did the moaning.

Just before he would feel the fingers tickle his neck, before they would tighten their death grip, the moaning would stop, as though the mummy sensed his presence.

*THUMP-thump.*

The fingers would slide around his neck and he would be pinned firmly against a sandstone wall.

*THUMP-THUMP.*

*He felt the fingers.*

He would wake screaming, a cold sweat covering his body.

He stopped that dream one night by simply announcing into the darkness that it was a dream, that he knew it wasn't real. The heartbeat never came again and the moaning stopped.

Ever after, although the initial premise of the dream did not go away, the dream changed fundamentally, evolving into something that he had never dreamt before.

It was no longer scary.

The chilled fog enveloped him and he remembered the dark, ancient tomb.

Sam knew he was dreaming again.

"I'm just dreaming!" he yelled into the fog, feeling its coolness seep into his clothing, reaching his skin.

The dog barked again, once.

"I'm dreaming," he said, confident he had the upper hand, waiting for the fog to disperse and turn into something pleasant.

It thickened around him, circling him like he was in the eye of a tornado, becoming a vaporous wall that enclosed him. Above him, through a small opening, he could see the night sky and twinkling stars. Around him, the fog continued to thicken and swirl.

"I'm dreaming," he said, less convincingly.

Nothing was changing; this wasn't how it was supposed to work. He was aware of it and goddammit, he should be able to change it. *This was HIS dream.*

Baxter barked again, closer. Sam tried to peer through the circling fog.

The bark came again, much closer this time.

Sam thought he could hear Baxter panting, as if he'd had been running.

It sounded like the dog was just beyond the fog, walking around him, his paws padding on the soft ground, his nails clicking on the occasional stone.

He began to doubt his ears; maybe it wasn't Baxter after all.

"Baxter?" he asked doubtfully, crouching down on bent knees.

The paws stopped in front of him. Sam could still hear him panting.

"Baxter?" he repeated.

Baxter whined.

"What is it, boy? What is it?"

The whine became a growl.

"Baxter?" Sam called.

The growl deepened. It was the growl of a dog just before it began to bark, fangs bared.

Sam stood up uneasily.

The growling stopped, replaced by the quiet sounds of the forest deep in the night. The calm before the proverbial storm.

In an explosion of fury, snapping jaws broke through the fog, closing around his neck and tearing at his skin with deep ravenous bites. Sam felt his muscles and tendons tear and snap under those fangs, a flood of crimson blood gushing over his chest.

He fell to the ground silently, Baxter clinging to his neck.

Sam looked into Baxter's eyes one last time and he cringed.

Those eyes were black and filled with yellow flames.

\*\*\*

Sam woke and he placed his hands around his neck; feeling for a gaping wound, expecting to feel the sticky paste of drying blood under his fingers.

There was none. It was only a dream.

"Fuck," Sam groaned, attempting to roll over in the dry storm drain where he had spent the daylight hours. The pipe was barely wide enough to hold him, loosely touching both of his shoulders. It had been risky, but he had run out of time before the onset of dawn.

He didn't recall clearly how he had ended up here.

The sounds around him told him that he was no longer in the city. He could dimly hear the urban soundtrack off in the distance, but those sounds were overpowered by the rustling sound of trees in a breeze.

An inner voice was now telling him this spot was dangerous, exposed.

He had been lucky to avoid being discovered or revealed. A sudden rainfall had the potential to flush him from the pipe, washing him into the daylight.

That would have been his end.

He dimly recalled the mounting sense of dread as he searched; an animalistic fear, both ancient and powerful. It was self-preservation that drove him here, the certainty that to delay meant death. He remembered seeing the small opening in the darkness, a culvert at the bottom of a ditch. The pipe ran under a seldom-used road, directing run-off into an overgrown gully below. The pipe was a salvation of cool shelter, like a single green tree in the broad expanse of a parched and unforgiving desert. Somehow he had physically *changed*, squeezing himself into this tiny space that held no room for error. He remembered the transition, but only vaguely, and not how he had done it. It was like he had somehow become less solid. The memory confused him. Once deep inside, comforted by the ground above him, he had drifted into his uneasy sleep where terrors lurked.

Looking out, he could see the light was faded and transparent, the last deep blue of a sapphire sunset. Sam squirmed awkwardly out of the corrugated pipe, shuffling forward on his hands and belly until he emerged like a strange human butterfly from a dull metallic chrysalis, covered in dust and dried, broken leaves.

At the end of the pipe was a short drop, a hollow formed by years of run-off water eroding the earth. He fell the last foot to the ground, rising to his feet where he brushed the debris from his clothing.

There was no one around him, at least not close.

He could feel Lamia not too distant. She was still angry with him, aware of where he was.

*That suits me just fine*, he said inwardly.

Lilith was farther, too far for him to know what she was feeling.

The Others were also there, much farther away. Most of them were sleeping, or at least still. That much he knew. Some of them were closer, closer than they had been before.

Coming for him? He wondered, then shrugged it off. He couldn't be bothered with them at the moment.

The evening air was thick with the perfume of pollen and flowers; a sweet, warm evening that would prompt teenagers to pull all-nighters, and cause the elderly to lie awake, wondering if they would have the opportunity to enjoy another evening like it.

Sam stepped onto the road, walking towards town, drawn to delectable aromas that were not at all related to the smells that filled the forest air.

He needed to find a purpose; he could not drift through this life like a leaf on the wind. There was no point to an existence where he went from night to night seeking a meal, merely to repeat the same thing for centuries to come. He felt like the survivor of a sunken ship, adrift on a rubber raft that was surrounded on all horizons by a flat, merciless sea. In this, he somehow needed to find some salvation, a fruitful, tropical island that would be his refuge.

The road beneath his feet passed by, the asphalt still warm from the heat of the day. He could smell its oily bitterness like a freshly tarred roof.

The moon shone overhead, a spotlight on the dark world glimmering in its twilight reflection. He could hear bats all around him, taking insects on the wing with their shrill hunting cries. Moth wings beat the air softly and crickets stirred in the grasses while toads chirped and croaked in the slow moving water of the flat stream that ran adjacent to the road. A great horned owl hooted deeply in the woods, its claws digging into a branch as it readjusted its position high above a dry grassy field.

The amount of subtle sound that reached his ears was staggering, an audio deluge that could be difficult to decipher.

He smiled as he realized that he was getting used to it.

His eyes could see clearly for miles down the road ahead. His vision had never been so clear and precise, and it wasn't just that he could see so well in the darkness, it was also that he was sensitive to anything that moved.

A hare nibbling its way through the thick green grass alongside the shoulder of the road was plain to see. The owl, with its deceptive hooting was in plain sight, even though nestled snugly amongst the branches. An earthworm broaching the topsoil caught his attention, if only for a moment.

He was attuned to the environment like no other predator in the world.

Unlike other predators, he had only one prey. His hunger ate at him, like a cramp in his side.

*No*, he thought to himself.

There must be a way that he did not have to kill to survive.

His mind was cloudy and his thinking disjointed, confused by his appetite.

It cleared as the breeze wafted a series of scents his way. The sweet and healthy perfume of blood filled the air.

Sam realized he was salivating.

His mind was a whirlwind of thoughts and perceptions, a blur that distracted him from his immediate surroundings. He shook his head and beat at his temples with clenched fists, trying to drive the thoughts from his mind.

He only became aware of the sound of footfalls at his side when a pebble ground against a larger stone.

The feeling of *her* was immediate.

He stumbled to the right, tripping over one foot that lamely refused to coordinate with the other. He fell to the road and rolled onto his back, his head on the ground.

Sam lay there, unwilling to move while looking up at the feminine silhouette between him and the silvery light of the moon. Her hair was wafting gently in the breeze, curling softly above her shoulder.

"You must feed," she said flatly, without any emotion.

"I don't want to," he groaned, kneading his thumbs at his temples, trying to relieve the headache that was grinding away inside his skull.

"You are vulnerable, weak. Unaware."

Sam shrugged, his eyes closed. He could feel her anger rising. She did not move, standing over him on the road. To a passerby it would have looked like she had knocked him to the ground with a solid left hook and was standing victorious over him.

"You did not feel me approach."

He nodded his head in reluctant agreement.

"The Others sense your weakness. It lends credence to their belief that you must be removed."

"Lilith was unable to finish me," he replied curtly.

She rewarded him with a sharp kick in the ribs. He felt a bone snap and he curled up in a shock of pain.

"Arrogant fool," she sneered. "Do you feel as strong as you did that night, as capable? Bah! I could finish you, here and now if I wished it."

"They why don't you?" Sam asked her, opening his eyes to meet her own. They were not yellow, but solid black.

She glared at him but her features softened ever so slightly.

"I do not wish it," was all she said, crossing her arms under her breasts.

"Why doesn't your sister finish me if that is what she wishes?" he asked.

"Sometimes, it pays to leave others to do what you would do yourself."

"She could have come for me last night. She was waiting."

Lamia shook her head. "You did not sense her will. Your mind was not at ease, in that place," she said, meaning the church. "She senses your resistance to her. She seeks your submission, your obedience, an offering of earth and water."

"She killed my family!" he roared, outraged, "and she expects me to bow to her, to kiss her ass? Well I won't!" He was shaking in fury, and in her black eyes he could see the yellow reflection of his own.

Lamia smiled. "There is passion in you, yet. It may be your salvation."

Sam rose to sit and found Lamia offering him her hand. Her palm was facing up, her fingers held together. Sam took it reflexively, without thinking. Her grip was warm and firm, her fingers like wrapped steel wire, hinting at a very great strength.

She pulled him to his feet with ease.

"You are weaker than I had thought," she said, looking at him with the faintest of concern.

"I will not kill," he said, "There has to be another way."

"There is none. You are a creature for which there is only one wine that will quench your thirst, one bread that will satisfy your hunger. It is that for which you were made, and none other. You are a being with a single purpose, and that purpose will bend you to its will, if you do not bend it to your own."

"Purpose? What is my purpose? To kill?" In Sam's mind echoed his conversation with the Reverend. He had told him to find a purpose, a meaning to life.

"Are you a student of the faiths?"

Sam shook his head, *no*.

"You have no concept of who I am, of who we are, do you?"

Sam shook his head again.

"Will you walk with me?" she asked him, "to the city?"

They turned and began to walk slowly down the road towards Loveland.

As they walked, Lamia spoke.

# Chapter 13

*"Neu pranse Lamiae vivum puerum extrabat alvo."*
*"Shall Lamia in our sight her sons devour,*
*and give them back alive the self-same hour?"*

-Horace Ars Poetica

"Do you know of Adam and Eve?" Lamia asked, starting with the basics to see what Sam knew.

"Yes."

"Did you know that Eve was not the first wife of Adam?"

Sam frowned, looking confused. He had never heard that before.

"Before Eve; was Lilith."

Sam looked at her sharply at hearing the name.

"Yes." she replied to his questioning look. "Lilith refused to be subservient to Adam. She was his equal, both of them made of the same earth. He was arrogant and did not share her view, believing her to be inferior. In time, Lilith saw that he would not change, and so she fled to be away from him. She was pursued by three angels who ordered her to return to him. She refused, and for that she was punished. She was forever cast out of the Garden of Eden and she learned of the power of blood. She gave rise to us; her children, the Vardat Lilitu, and the angels decreed her children were to be killed. Over time, she became known as the mother of demons. Eve was then wed to Adam. In vengeance Lilith swore to kill the children of Adam and Eve. To this day she fulfills her promise."

"To kill children," Sam said hoarsely.

"To kill the children of Adam and Eve, to avenge the killing of her own children," replied Lamia.

"Is that how you justify it?"

"You are a father. What limits would you set in avenging the deaths of your children?"

"None," Sam replied quickly. Before Cynthia and Tommy were born he wouldn't have understood how one person could kill another. That all changed the instant Cynthia was placed in his arms. There was nothing he wouldn't do to keep her safe.

Sam was confused by her story.

"How can that be?" he asked her.

"If Adam and Eve were the first, where did Lilith come from? How can you be her sister?"

Lamia only laughed.

Adam and Eve are the lineage from which mankind endures. They were not the first people."

"But the Bible?"

Lamia laughed harder.

"It was written by men, Samuel, written by flawed men rich with their own prejudices and sins. The Bible may contain the ideas of God, but it has been diluted over time, spoiled by generations of additions that served no purpose other than those of its author."

"But…," Sam tried to continue.

"It is not accurate, Samuel. Accept it and move on."

He could see by her expression that she was done explaining it.

An image of Lilith burned in his mind.

"I can't kill Lilith."

"You can't," Lamia agreed, "not unless she allows it, but there are other ways you can avenge them."

Sam let her words settle into his mind.

*Other ways I can avenge them*, he thought.

"You don't kill children?" he asked her.

"I play my own game," she smiled darkly, her eyes glistening. Beyond those eyes was also a measure of pain at his words, something she restrained. "You must find your own game. Now, you are weak."

She pushed him, very nearly sending him off the road.

Lamia laughed. "You see?"

A broad smile crossed her flawless face.

Sam staggered back to his feet, walking a little further away from her, out of her reach.

"I won't kill people," he refused stubbornly.

"Oh but you will," she replied in mocking tones. "Sooner or later the hunger will take you, and when it does, you will feed on whoever crosses your path. Some of us have no reservations, enjoying the abandon of such a kill. Others remember more of their mortal life and select their quarry for their own reasons."

Sam recalled the vivid series of images that was his first kill, the one that had finalized his transformation in the alley. It had been spontaneous and purely without thought.

"Yes," Lamia said. "You remember that clearly don't you? That will happen again, and sooner than you might think. You are barely in control of yourself now, barely able to collect your own thoughts if left alone. Your darker nature will soon prevail, like it or not. You will feed. I told you before that you could die of starvation. It is possible, but very unlikely. The beast within will take control before that, and it will do anything to feed."

"Get out of my mind," he scowled at her, feeling her somehow tingling in his mind, searching his memories, hunting for his thoughts.

"It is easy, when you are like this. If you were strong, I would not be able to. You have a choice to make. Choose your next prey, or have your nature choose it for you. Delay and you might yet feed off a child, or a mother, or perhaps a family such as your own."

"No!" Sam yelled quickly, aghast at the idea, revolted. He suddenly wanted to wretch.

"The choice is yours to make, but it must be made."

"I'll leave! I'll go where there are no people."

Lamia laughed again, not warmly or with humour, but with the tone of someone laughing at a fool.

She shook her head and grabbed him by the shoulders, shaking him harshly.

Lamia released him, steam rising from her head in the cooling air, her dark eyes were speckled yellow, like metallic glitter.

"You don't understand! You will find people," she growled between clenched teeth, irritated. "You will smell them out and you will hunt them down; distance will be no barrier to you if your nature dominates. You will hunt, and you will seek cover, and you will sleep. All by instinct and without your control, until you make a kill. Then, when you wake and find a child lying bloodless in your arms, you might finally understand what it is your nature to do. You are helpless to stop it. Your only choice is when, consciously or unconsciously."

Sam suddenly wondered what she was thinking, and he was instantly awash in a series of images. Some of them were recent, although how he knew that he could not say. He saw himself in the woods by the lake, an image of Lilith laughing, her beautiful but malevolent eyes burning. Then the images changed. Older things came into his mind. He saw a broad galleon leaving port to sea, its masts draped with huge white sails that were swollen with captured wind. He saw a dusty cobblestone street lined with peddlers and shops, the air fragrant with incense and spice. There were farms and rolling hills and thatched roofs. He saw a man wearing a brown tunic, standing in a golden field of grain with his tanned brow covered in sweat and grime. The dirt from an honest day's work was etched into his skin. The man looked up at him and smiled, the hard work forgotten.

'Lamia,' he said, opening his arms as if to embrace.

He suddenly felt a stabbing in his chest, the anguish of a love lost; of heartache beyond comprehension.

Sam felt his vision recoil as a violent mental shove broke him free of the tenuous link.

Reality flexed between the vision of the bright sunny field, and the dark moon-filled expanse of the road, and then it snapped.

The man vanished, replaced by Lamia beside him. Her eyes were wide and shocked, disoriented and angry, filled with tears.

"Never do that again!" she screamed at him, just barely catching her balance before she could fall over.

"What was that?" he asked, "What did I see?" he gasped, holding his head as though he was suffering from a terrible migraine.

His vision was swimming and the road seemed to twist before him.

Lamia slapped him soundly across the face, dropping him to the dusty asphalt.

Her creamy complexion was mottled with red, her cheeks rosy in fury.

"You have no right!" she screamed at him, livid.

"Those were your memories weren't they? I didn't know. How did I do that?"

Her blazing yellow eyes softened for a moment, the outrage lessened only by a whisper.

She did not answer his question.

"Feed!" she instructed him, "While you are still able to make the choice for yourself!"

She left him by the side of the road, running in the opposite direction, her long pale hair flowing behind her like the mane of a galloping warhorse.

He could feel her anger boiling like hot water, but beneath that was the fuel that fed the flames, a sorrow that was inconsolable.

Sam could feel his cheek tingling where she had hit him; the skin was burning where a trace of blood welled from a cut that soon closed, perfect and flawless.

He rose to his feet and looked in the direction she had run.

There was nothing to see, only an empty ribbon of road that was ultimately swallowed by the night.

He walked into Loveland and strolled down the sidewalks, mindlessly turning from one street to the next as her words repeated in his ears.

*"Feed! While you are still able to make the choice for yourself!"*

He had no reason to doubt the truth of her words; at a base level he knew her to be honest. He had felt his mind slipping, yielding to something that was not wholly himself. He had been salivating before she had found him, salivating as he had smelled the scents on the air. Her presence had pulled him back into a more conscious self, making him forget his hunger. Now that she was gone it was returning, returning with a grip that was more insidious and demanding.

The hunger was pulling him down, taking him to a place that he was terrified to go.

There was a threshold that, if crossed, would be a darkness he might not be able to escape from.

He balled up his fists as he walked, sinking his nails into the flesh of his palms, using the pain to clear his mind.

It was becoming increasingly less effective.

The pain was feeding his darker side.

He turned left onto North Boise Avenue and approached the McKee Medical Center, each step becoming more difficult than the last. The cornucopia of smells was becoming overwhelming.

The scent of death and illness lingered in the air like a pervasive characteristic of the surroundings, the taint soaked into the landscape and the very ground. There was very little that was appealing to the odor; the fragrance of the healthy and vital was washed out and diffuse, a drop of food coloring in a pool of miasma. It was like a graveyard, only worse; a sealed tomb where the foulness and decay never disappeared; the rich gaseous odour of perpetually moist rot.

He gagged, and holding his breath, he fled south, eager to be away from the stench that was turning his empty stomach. He followed 287th Street in the shadows, walking along the edge of the road where he was out of plain sight. The revulsion of the hospital soon faded, the wind driving away the last of the stink. Before long the air was again pleasant to breathe and he inhaled deep draughts of it, cleansing his sinuses.

It also reawakened his hunger, bringing it back to life with a terrible ferocity that was all the worse for being reinvigorated.

His senses sharpened with each step, his eyes becoming acute and sharp and his ears detecting the slightest of rustles.

A concealed black tomcat hissed at his passing, running for its house as soon as Sam was gone.

The scents were becoming stronger, more delectable, like the wafting aroma of freshly baked bread.

He could choose, or his alter ego would choose for him.

He wanted to scream; to resist the compulsion that was driving him onwards. He could feel it creeping through his flesh, taking control of his body.

Lamia had been right; he was helpless to stop it. He was becoming weaker by the minute, while paradoxically he felt his other half becoming stronger.

His own dominance was fading.

The sounds of a nightclub soon reached his ears, although the source was not yet visible.

The rhythmic pulsing of the beat echoed in his head, a musical heartbeat.

Sam closed in, a shark following a bloody trail in the water.

The club soon came into sight; a bright neon sign illuminated the establishment from high above its brick and mortar walls.

A series of red-roped stanchions steered customers toward the door, funneling them towards a stocky bearded bouncer who appeared to be far more *homo neanderthalis* than *homo sapiens.* He was pleasant enough, but clearly hired for his ability to physically intimidate unruly patrons.

Sam walked past silently, his eyes very nearly closed.

He didn't need to see anyone, his sense of smell was dominant and each person lined behind the rope was subject to his meticulous scrutiny.

A trio of barhopping girls was standing last in the lineup, each of them in their early twenties and more than lightly buzzed from drinking at home before deciding to go out dancing. To Sam they smelled sweet, like clover honey, full of health and they would taste wonderful. But the third was different; the smell of youth was tinged with bitterness, like the taste of slightly moldy bread.

*Ovarian cancer*, Sam knew in an instant.

It was racing up through her like canyon wildfire.

She thought she was coming down with the flu.

She would be dead within the month.

A couple in their late twenties was next in line, holding hands and whispering to each other. The man smelled annoyed, irritated by the giggling trio behind him. He appreciated their busty exposure, but their loud and obnoxious laughing was really getting on his nerves. They both smelled perfect to Sam, a feast to be savored.

Each person in the line was unique, offering to his sensitive nose information that only he would appreciate in its fullness of detail.

He needed to choose.

He grimaced at the thought of having to end the life of any one of these people. Most of them were fit and healthy, in their prime. To him, it meant they would be delicious.

Should it be one of the sick ones? The girl was already dying; she didn't have long to live.

He shook his head. *No;* her thoughts had been pleasant and filled with her joy for life. Someone like that didn't deserve to die, even though she was already dead on her feet. He would not be responsible for adding a degree of terror to what would already end up being a short life.

Never mind that he knew she would taste foul, like meat gone bad.

There was another person in the queue that was sick, something genetic that was steadily clogging his veins with plaque. He might make it another few years before a massive heart attack would bring him down, all before the not-so-ripe age of thirty.

He scrunched up his nose at the thought of it.

The taste would be unpleasant, like a hot beer left in the summer sun; bitter, sharp and acrid.

*He needed to choose before the choice was made for him. Could he?* he wondered.

Sam reached the end of the building and turned into a dark dead-end alley that ran between the night club and the neighboring bowling alley. The very end was invisible, lost in a slanted black shadow that was as deep and impenetrable as a thick, woolen cloak. Several steel access doors were set into the walls of each structure. Overhead, rusty black fire escapes clung to the walls like skeletal gargoyles in the dim light. A thin trickle of water ran from a drain spout protruding from the nightclub wall, gurgling down to a grated pipe set in the ground, connected to the sewer line below.

Sam beat his hand against the wall in frustration; the scents were driving him insane. His hunger was clawing at his innards like a hand struggling to get out.

The music thumped from behind the wall, the chatter of people talking and laughing reaching his ears. He could hear the dance floor furthest away; the kitchen was closer, as were several of the washrooms. The nearest voices were clearer, close proximity making them audible over the music. He listened to the voices through the wall, hearing them walk towards him or away as they went about their business. The distinct sound of someone peeling potatoes reached his ears.

*Scritch scritch scritch.*

Beyond that was the sound of boiling oil.

*French fries*, Sam thought, thinking how much he used to like hot fresh-cut fries with a dash of sea salt.

Now, they would taste like lined school paper.

Sam passed the final steel door, leaning with his back to the adjacent wall with the door to his right. An empty coffee tin half filled with crushed cigarette butts sat on the ground by the door next to a water-stained door wedge. In that spot he vanished into the void of the shadow, invisible from the street and even the door that was so close to him.

He still had time, but he needed to collect his thoughts, he needed to focus. There was no one here that he would take. His only comfort was that the night was still young. Sam became aware that tonight was his last chance. By tomorrow, he would not be in charge of himself, and he would take whoever first crossed his path.

The peeling of the potatoes continued, *scritch scritch scritch*, followed by the sharp sounds of a cutting knife, and then the chatter of bubbles as the potatoes were sunk into the deep fryer.

He heard the cook walk away, closing a door behind him.

*Washroom*, Sam thought.

The muted sound of an argument reached his ears, coming closer, a person bumping open the swinging kitchen doors.

The argument was one sided; silence followed by shouting, and then silence again.

*Someone was arguing over the phone.*

Sam could hear the person on the other end of the call, but only faintly, too dim even for his sensitive ears to clearly discern.

The person entered the kitchen, his hard-soled shoes clicking on the tile floor as the door shut behind him.

"I don't give a fuck what you have to do," the man shouted into the phone, believing he was entirely alone and unaware of the cook that was probably able to hear him through the bathroom door.

The person on the other end spoke rapidly for a bit, flustered.

"No," the man yelled, "you need to shut up and listen!"

Sam closed his eyes and listened, interested in the distraction. As he listened, he wondered what the man was thinking, reaching out with his question.

"All he needs to do is go out and pick up the stuff and then bring it back, pretty fucking simple."

Sam developed an image of who the man was talking about.

He was thin and scraggly, someone that had only the vaguest idea about nutrition and only a random tendency to eat anything substantial. He was a perpetual snacker, a fidgeter.

"Uh-huh, then where the fuck is he?"

Sam explored his thoughts further, moving past whoever he was talking about on the phone.

*A table covered with plastic packages, each of them neatly wrapped in cellophane and stacked next to a scale.*

"Why you asking me? I don't know where he is; he's supposed to be your fucking guy!"

*Further.*

*Random hands balled into fists, crashing down onto someone that was a crumpled heap on some anonymous dirty floor.*

*The sound of laughter while the beating continued, and then boots, the kicking of boots, the soundless grunts from the man on the floor as the boots connected with his midsection, cracking ribs.*

"Are you telling me he's missing? That he has my stuff and you don't know where he is? You better not be saying that!"

*Further.*

*A blindfolded body dumped headfirst into a barrel. Hands tied behind the back. There was a bloody shirt; a hole just below the breastbone. No, two holes, closely spaced. The drum was sealed with a rubber mallet. Bang bang bang. Then gunshots peppered the barrel with holes. The drum tipped over and rolled into a river.*

"You find that little shit, and when you do you bring him to me. I'm gonna teach that little fucker a lesson!"

*Further.*

*A girl cooking eggs in the kitchen; the morning sunshine blazing through a thin gauze curtain that only slightly diffused the harsh glow. She was wearing a t-shirt and panties and nothing else. Her hair was askew, tied into a quick ponytail. She turned with a fry pan in her hand, frightened, digging the eggs off the poorly buttered pan, trying to scrape them onto a plate. The yolks broke.*

*A hand slapped her cheek harshly, turning her face a dull shade of red as she curled onto the floor and began to cry helplessly.*

"I'll be waiting here all night for you to bring that shithead to me, and you better bring him to me, or I'm going to come looking for you!"

The cell phone was stuffed angrily into a pocket, followed by a flurry of muttered and incoherent obscenities.

*Further.*

*Anger. Frustration. Hatred. Greed. The emotions flowed, and rarely were they good. He thrived on the suffering of others. It was about control, the need to be unquestioned and feared.*

*His name was Tobin.*

"Fuck!" Tobin yelled, pushing down the safety bar of the door lock with both hands. With the clasp free he kicked the door, opening it quickly.

He pushed a wooden wedge between the door and the jamb, preventing the door from self-closing fully, leaving a way for him to get back in.

Tobin stormed into the alley, his hands digging into his hair, pulling at it in anger. He paced the ground, furious.

Sam felt Tobin's rage clearly, hardly aware that his emotions were being fueled by this man's rage. The darkness took him suddenly, without a moment's hesitation now that his guard was down.

In his eyes the alley was well lit, nothing was concealed from his gaze. Sam could feel Tobin's heart beating with a morbid pulse deeply in his chest. The aroma was delectable; it seized him, becoming the focal point of his entire existence.

Nothing else mattered.

Tobin turned in Sam's direction, completing another lap in his frustrated pacing.

He stared at the wall, seeing something he could not explain. He frowned.

"What the fuck?"

Two yellow points of light shone in the dark, unwavering and pure.

He stepped forward, wondering if he was really seeing this or if it was some bizarre reflection.

The yellow lights blinked once and then glared at him coldly.

A primal fear gripped Tobin cold in the belly, something that originated from deep within the amygdala. The same fear that a wildebeest feels when a lion leaps onto its back; the fear felt by a fly stuck in a spider's gossamer web.

It was the fear of death, the unconscious made conscious and real.

Tobin stumbled backwards, tripping his heel over his toes as he instinctively sought the promised safety of the door. He landed hard, down on his back on the cold ground and staring up at the nightmare in front of him.

When Sam emerged from the shadows Tobin's voice failed him, his throat constricted and his tongue frozen to the roof of his mouth.

Sam's glowing yellow eyes were set into a cold expression that stared at him wantonly, his head cocked to one side with a deadly curiosity.

"W-who are you?" Tobin stammered.

Sam gave him a frigid stare and didn't say a word, coming closer. He moved like a dancer, lithe and graceful, but with eyes that were remorseless.

A terrible, eager grin stretched across his face.

*"Tobin...,"* Sam hissed through teeth that were unnaturally white.

Tobin fell back onto his elbows, staring up with eyes that were rounded with fear and anger.

"Who the fuck are you? How the fuck do you know my name?" he shouted obstinately, trying to fight the cold feeling of the hairs that were standing up on the back of his neck.

Sam stood at Tobin's feet, staring down at him with a terrible sort of fascination.

Then, Sam laughed.

It was utterly hollow, a laugh without any sense of humanity.

Tobin wet himself unconsciously.

"I just know," he whispered in a ghastly thin voice, the final word trailing off into nothing.

For the first time in his life, Tobin felt afraid.

"W-what do you want?" he asked, trying to sound calm. His guts felt like loose gelatin. Those terrible eyes met his own and stared intently at him, never once blinking.

"I want…," the figure whispered, "*I want I want I want….*"

He stepped over to Tobin's side smoothly and dropped to one knee, angling his head to speak with Tobin directly.

He then inhaled deeply and released it slowly, like he was savoring the most delicate of scents, the rarest of perfumes.

"Can you smell it?" he asked Tobin, curious. "Can you smell the *life*? The *thickness* of it? How it *flows?*"

Tobin shook his head vigorously.

He couldn't tear his eyes away from the terrible yellow glow. It was not a solid yellow; it was like looking into a kaleidoscope as it slowly twisted, a myriad of shapes and forms blending, breaking and merging into the next like liquid. A fluid transformation that never ceased; nor could it be predicted. It was like watching a candle flicker and sputter in a strong draft, refusing to be blown out.

Sam looked somewhat disappointed.

"I thought not," he sighed, disconsolate. Then his eyes widened as though a great idea had just been born, a delicious dark secret brought to light.

"But then, you are not one to value life are you? I can see it, how you used death to instill fear, to nurture it and cradle it. But you have not understood life and you do not understand death. Very soon you will be a master at one. It is a sad legacy you will leave."

Tobin shrunk back, trying to get away from the cold that seemed to flow from the figure at his side. He needed to get away from him, to get up and get away.

His fear was still strong, palpable and noxious, but he refused to lay here, helpless.

"What is your name?" Tobin asked, thinking that maybe if he could distract him, maybe he could get away from this nut. Nut? He was nuts alright, but he had no explanation for those awful eyes. Tobin had seen all varieties of contact lenses, but nothing like this. They freaked the shit out of him. They looked all too real, and he had no plausible explanation as to how contact lenses could be made to look like that, or do things like that.

"My name….," Sam's eyes flickered forgetfully, momentarily breaking their penetrating stare.

Tobin quietly rose up from his back to lean on one shoulder.

Every sense told him this situation was not good, that he had a right to be fearful. He recognized when a person meant someone else harm; he was an expert at it. It was how he had kept himself alive when most of his former acquaintances were either fish food, worm food, or locked up for enough of what was left of their lives that when they got out they would be feeble old men.

He was street smart, and it had kept him alert and above ground.

"My name is unimportant," Sam finally answered, his abominable yellow eyes refocusing on Tobin. "What is important, is now."

Tobin quickly balled up his fist and took a swing with his right arm, hoping to knock this guy out. Tobin wanted at least to connect with him hard enough to get him the fuck away from his side; long enough to get to his feet and lay into this freak like he deserved.

*Teach him to fuck with me*, he thought. *He doesn't know who he's dealing with.*

His punch failed to connect. Tobin saw the man react with lightning speed, catching his fist in midair just above the wrist, holding him with an iron grip.

"What the fuck?" Tobin exhaled, not believing his eyes.

Tobin tried to twist his arm out of the grip, twisting against the thumb, the weakest link.

It didn't budge.

*Fucking junkie is high*, Tobin thought, familiar with how strong people could be when they were stoned.

PCP, or something like it.

Except that he wasn't acting like a junkie.

His skin was dry and smooth, his face calm and relaxed, not at all twitchy or paranoid.

"Predictable," Sam said to him, his mouth breaking into a tooth-full grin that was full of sly amusement.

"What..?" Tobin began.

"...am I?" Sam interrupted, completing his sentence smoothly without hesitation or delay.

Tobin began to fight, struggling to use his other hand to free the one caught in Sam's grasp.

"It is futile," Sam said quietly, watching Tobin like an entomologist studies an insect stuck on a pin.

"Fuck you," Tobin gasped, clawing at Sam's fingers, trying to pry one free to find the chink in his armor.

"What do you want with me?" Tobin hissed angrily, not quite ready to give up.

"What do I want?" Sam asked.

"You fucking heard me."

Sam fell silent, his face flattened out in thought. His smile disappeared and his gaze wandered, all of his features became smooth and serene.

Finally, his eyes refocused and he looked down at Tobin, who was by now out of breath, no longer trying to free his arm.

"I want you," he said quietly.

Tobin frowned in dismay.

Sam felt his hunger settle, the terrible ache that had been tearing at his insides seemed to spread to every extremity, like the flush of heat from a sickly fever.

He vividly heard a heartbeat, its pulse an attraction that drew him like a moth to flame.

*Thump-thump.*

It was mystical.

It was magical.

*Thump-thump.*

It would be delicious.

Sam grabbed Tobin by his hair, yanking his head back to the ground with a firm and painful motion.

Tobin's neck was exposed to him.

Tobin struggled futilely while Sam effortlessly pinned him to the ground.

This was no dream; there was nothing here for him to be afraid of.

*Thump-thump.*

Instead of that sound filling him with fear, it filled him with a yearning that he could not suppress. He was helpless before it, helpless to resist its power.

A cold fog settled in over his mind. There was nothing but the fog.

*Thump-thump.*

There was screaming and groaning and the thick smell of blood, a gurgling sound that was a soft symphony; a skilled violinist playing tableside for him while he ate an expensive dinner.

And there was the taste.

It was like cream and honey, the sweetest sugar, and it flowed to his ravenous mouth. It was like he was sampling from all of his favorite meals, all of them put to shame by the richness of this flavor.

The burning ache slowly eased, replaced by a sensation of complete satiation, a fullness that was without equal.

Sam released the corpse in his hands, overcome by the feeling of bliss that washed over him.

What was left of Tobin twitched on the ground and then finally lay still.

Sam sat back on his heels and looked up into the black sky above, his arms wide and his chest heaving with fulfilled exultation.

A question seemed to form there, a silent and wordless question from the void. A question meant for him alone to answer. "Yes," he whispered, staring at the twinkling stars.

# Chapter 14

"So now beware, whoe're you are,
That walkis in this lone wood;
Beware of that deceitfull spright,
The ghaist that suckle the blude."

-James Clerk Maxwell

The fog covered the ground thinly, a vaporous sheet that hugged the contours of the ground, rising and falling perfectly over the finely cut grass and around the bases of the elm and oak trees that were scattered evenly throughout.

The sky was veiled by a thin mist that hinted at a beautiful cyan sky above; forbidden to touch the earth with its light.

The disc of the sun was suspended in that mist. He could stare at it without flinching, beholding its presence and gazing at its wonder. It was a lidless yellow eye watching over everything from above, an overseer of its children.

Sam knew instantly where he was.

The smoothly cut grass, the gentle contours of the landscape, the finely pruned mature trees.

He was in a graveyard.

And he was dreaming again.

A squirrel called from high in the treetops, chirping to its neighbors that this tree was off-limits to all comers.

Sam walked, stepping lightly over the dew-kissed grass, feeling the cold water soak into the sides of his shoes.

Here and there, spaced evenly, rows of stone markers were set into the ground below the level of the grass, all of them etched with a personal inscription of who rested in the dark earth below.

Sam read a few of them with disinterest and moved on, wandering aimlessly for a time before finally spotting a gathering in the distance, a collection of shadows nearly hidden by a stand of trees.

His interest piqued, he made his way towards them, a morbid curiosity drawing him in to their private fold.

A priest stood at the fore of the gathering, dressed in all of his finery, an open copy of the Good Book in his hands, the place from which he intended to read marked by a purple cloth bookmark.

Four coffins were before him, ready to be lowered into the open pits that waited to embrace them for eternity. Two of the caskets were small.

*For children.*

A vast collection of mourners were gathered together, motionless shapes brought together by the bond of grief.

The random sounds of crying and consoling came from the crowd, a hushed and respectful weeping that began when the finality of burial had come; the final step before the acceptance of Death.

A stately oak tree stood over them all, its branches suspended over the group like thin arms offering shelter and consolation.

Sam approached them from behind, giving him a view of the entire ceremony.

He froze in his tracks, his heart skipping a beat. There was a picture frame on each of the caskets. The pictures within the frames chilled his soul.

They were of Cindy, Tommy, Miranda and himself; smiling portraits of happier times.

The coffins were expertly carved cherry wood boxes that were lined with silk and adorned with brass. Each one was worth several thousand dollars.

He had stumbled into the funeral for his family, a funeral where all of the coffins were empty.

The world seemed to drain of color before his eyes, becoming as empty as the coffins before him.

Sam staggered backwards, retreating from the crowd in disarray and stumbling backwards against the oak tree in his grief.

Sam clutched the tree, holding himself upright with one hand, comforted by the centuries-old presence of this living giant.

No one in the gathering could see him. He was an invisible observer.

The priest had already completed most of the ritual; the lines of sorrow were clearly drawn on the faces of those he could see. Tear marks were etched on countless faces. Some tears were wiped away; some were left untouched by mourners in their state of physical and emotional numbness.

Even the priest was having a difficult time. Sam could feel his struggle to complete the ceremony, to finish what was begun.

It was the small caskets that made it so difficult.

Sam remembered when the portraits had been taken.

The portraits had been taken by Miranda's mother, a semi-professional photographer who had perfectly captured their moments of youthful joy and exuberance. They had been playing and laughing, caught in a random timeless moment where nothing was wrong with the world.

And now these same photographs were crowning their caskets, a reminder of what had been taken away.

His eyes jumped from mourner to mourner.

*"The Lord is my Shepherd; I shall not want,"* the Priest began.

Miranda's mother and father, leaning against one another, stared at the priest with a vacant gaze, unable to come to terms with the loss they had been dealt.

*"He maketh me to lie down in green pastures."*

Miranda's brother sitting on his white folding chair in a state of shock; his head in his hands, unable to stand as he robotically repeating the prayers offered by the priest who led the Committal rite.

*"He leadeth me beside the still waters."*

Miranda's sister was drunk, nearly unable to stand and held up by her husband. She was clutching the shoulders of her children as though she feared they too might be taken from her.

*"He restoreth my soul:"*

Sam's father stood at the edge of the funeral, at the end of the front row. He too was drunk, and Sam could feel that he would not be able to cope with this loss.

Losing his grandchildren had rocked him to his core. He had been drunk since receiving the standard notification from the state police, and he would stay that way until liver failure sent him to his own coffin.

*"He leadeth me in the paths of righteousness for His name's sake."*

His mother was at his father's side, completely overtaken by grief.

She was not drunk, but her emotional state was no different. She would succumb shortly; not to the drink, but to a broken heart.

Cynthia and Tommy were her life, and now they were gone.

*"Yea, though I walk through the valley of the shadow of death,"*

A police officer was standing in the crowd, dressed in a fine black suit. He was crying too, though not over severed familial ties. It was the overall emotion of the gathering that had him upset. This kind of loss was the reason for his decision to enter police work. This was why he had chosen law enforcement; this was why he had sacrificed his own marriage. He had pledged to serve, and this funeral was a reminder of his life's work, of why he spent the hours he did in the office and on the road. There was a greater purpose and he was its willing instrument.

He was between Miranda's brother and sister, hoping to comfort them with the realization that even strangers were affected by the randomness of this tragedy. Sam found that he knew his name. His name was August, and Sam could feel that this case would haunt him through to the end of his days as well. For years to come, he would dream of a dark lakeside where no one was able to come to the aid of dying children.

*"I will fear no evil: For thou art with me;"*

A reporter was hiding in the back of the crowd, trying to remember everything she saw and heard for the piece she was writing. The death of an entire family had galvanized the community. The random brutality seemed to strike everyone differently, but no less deeply.

The entire family was gone with no bodies recovered.

She hoped her digital recorder, tucked deeply inside her purse pocket, was sensitive enough to capture everything that was said, to help her remember everything for when she began to write later.

It was going to make for a great article.

*"Thy rod and thy staff, they comfort me."*

Friends and neighbors had come; co-workers and school acquaintances were lined up to pay their respects. Most of them were stone-faced, contemplating mortality and the loss of friends. A few were crying, impacted by Sam or Miranda or their children more than he had ever thought.

It was the loss, the randomness of their deaths.

Secretly, everyone was terrified it could have been them.

*"Thou preparest a table before me in the presence of mine enemies."*

Rose Cochrane sat at the very back of the collection of mourners, her head bowed down where she could look at the grass and not be distracted by the crowd. She had not come to glean more information than she already knew, and she had not come to provide any comfort to the families of the deceased. She had come because she couldn't sleep. She hadn't slept for more than two consecutive hours since the fateful morning she had called the police.

She was racked with guilt.

She stared absently at the grass and prayed, praying for them and praying for herself.

*"Thou annointest my head with oil; my cup runneth over."*

The gravedigger sat a respectful distance from the crowd, out of sight, occasionally glancing at his cheap wristwatch to mark the progress of the service.

He didn't know why he kept looking at his watch, he didn't have any place else he needed to be, not for several hours at least, and this would all be done before long.

He was leaning against a segment of peeling bark on an old poplar tree; his shovel was entirely hidden behind it, purposefully kept from view.

There was enough sense of death at a funeral to not be reminded of it any further by accidently seeing a dirty shovel.

The aged yellow backhoe that he had dug the graves with was safely parked back at the compound, its keys still in the ignition.

A mosquito buzzed past his ear and he tossed his hand at it lazily.

*"Surely goodness and mercy shall follow me all the days of my life."*

Sam stared at the four empty coffins, sinking to his knees as his mind absorbed the spectacle of his own funeral.

*Was this real?* he thought.

*Am I seeing what really happened?*

*Or am I making this up?*

He knew the brain could dream up some amazing coping mechanisms in times of duress. Was this one of them? Was he somehow inventing this entire scene to deal with the stress?

It felt too genuine. The emotions and thoughts were pouring into his mind, raw and unfiltered.

He wondered what was in the coffins.

Photos? Clothing? Personal items they treasured?

It seemed worse that they were empty.

It was an illusion.

There was no closure without bodies, no peace of mind that could be gleaned by burying empty coffins. This was a ritual, meant to move people forward, to create the illusion that somehow the pain could now lessen. To some, the illusion was a salve, a poultice that was every bit as effective as a medicinal placebo. Once the funeral was over, life could begin anew. To others, it was the coup de grace, the cutting of the last string that gave a meaning to life. With that string cut, Death was free to stalk a new victim.

*"And I will dwell in the House of the Lord forever."*

There was a glitch in his vision, like a scratched DVD was playing in his mind and had suddenly skipped to the next chapter. When his vision returned, the funeral crowd was gone. Row upon row of white aluminum chairs sat empty, as though occupied by ghosts who bore witness to four newly covered graves. He was behind them all, still kneeling as he had been during the service.

The sod was neatly cut and stamped into place by foot, the lines between each piece almost invisible. In a few days the lines would be gone, the grass stitched together as though having never been disturbed.

It would be another illusion.

Three figures stood silently over the new grave markers with their heads bowed.

"MIRANDA!" Sam screamed, unsteadily rising to his feet.

He ran shakily towards them, screaming their names in a voice that was constricted and hoarse. His eyes were nearly blinded by sudden tears that he refused to wipe away, fearful that should he take his eyes off of them for even an instant they would vanish from sight.

None of them turned at the sound of his voice.

Miranda was wearing a cool white summer dress. The dress was knee length, with a black belt that hugged her waist, and she was wearing her favorite white hat. Cindy was wearing a miniature duplicate of her mother's outfit, and Tommy was adorned in grey suit pants and a matching vest. Miranda stood between the two, holding them to her side with an arm lovingly over each of their shoulders.

"Miranda," Sam sobbed, opening his arms to take her in a desperate embrace.

He stumbled forward as he closed his arms around her, waiting to feel her warmth against him; to smell her scent.

His arms folded over emptiness and he tripped and fell forward, crying out as the earth suddenly opened before him. The sod burst open, spraying roots and tendrils that reached out and ravenously pulled him down into the earthen pit.

An open coffin was waiting for him; its fine white linen was smooth and unspoiled.

The coffin thumped heavily as he fell into it, his shoulder aching as it took the brunt of his fall. He quickly turned over onto his side.

"No!" he cried, his arms reaching out for help.

Miranda stood over him; her face was smooth and perfect, without wrinkle or blemish. The children stood at her side.

They were similarly perfect, except for their jet black eyes.

Sam stared at each of them and was rewarded by their cool smiles when they saw the look of horror settle upon his face.

When they smiled, pointed teeth sparkled behind ruby red lips.

"No," he gasped, wanting to vomit.

"Yes," Miranda whispered.

Cindy and Tommy grinned and began to roll the sod over him.

The roots slithered and intertwined, creating a latticework that cocooned him beneath the surface of the earth.

"Tommy. Cindy," he moaned, just beyond their reach.

He was in too deep; he could not touch the bottom of the sod as it was placed over him like a moist ceiling.

"Now you are dead, too," Tommy giggled.

Cindy laughed coldly and lifted the final piece to lay over him.

"Cindy," he begged, "no."

She dropped the sod into place and the roots sealed his tomb, knitting themselves together into a coarse, unbreakable mesh.

"No!" he screamed, his eyes trying to see in the perfect darkness.

*Thump-thump.*

He stopped screaming.

The sound was perfectly clear and bore into him with the oppressive feeling of an impending thunderstorm.

*Thump-thump.*

He became aware of the sound of someone at his side breathing with him.

Cold fingers closed softly around his right elbow, digging into his flesh.

*Thump-thump.*

"Now we are together, forever."

He jumped at the sound of her voice.

"Miranda?"

A restrained chuckle was his only reply.

"I can't see you," he said, turning to the sound of her voice.

A child began to laugh and was soon joined by another.

He twisted his head in the darkness, trying in vain to see something, anything at all.

Sam felt warm breath on his face.

*THUMP-THUMP.*

Two yellow eyes suddenly shone in the darkness. Then four. Then six.

In their awful golden glow, he could see their teeth glistening like stained ivory.

He screamed as their teeth sank into his flesh.

# Chapter 15

"NOOOO!" he wailed as he woke, sitting upright in terror as he fought to dig phantom teeth out of his flesh, desperate to stop the terrible gnawing feeling.

Moonlight shone down, faintly illuminating the small space that held him.

Sam blinked and looked around, trying to calm himself as he remembered where he was.

The space was a narrow horizontal fissure running downwards in a seam of nearly perfect granite, a split that was partially obscured by erosion, sheltering the inner space from all but the worst of weather. It was too small to allow larger animals to enter, and too large for smaller animals to use it as a home. There were several piles of nuts and seeds, collections gathered and stored as a food cache by some industrious rodent. The dust that had collected inside the small space was fine and windblown, neatly swirled into the edges by eddies of wind.

He looked up through the rocky gap towards the light of the moon, finding it partially obscured by the finger-like silhouette of a tree and a series of large stones that were cemented into the ground by dense and gritty soil.

Reassured, Sam laid back and thought.

He felt strong. The hunger that had been so omnipresent was now a tickle, a faint irritation that was easy to suppress.

With his eyes closed he still felt supremely aware of his surroundings.

*I am nocturnal*, he thought.

The original discomfort he felt at night was fading. It was no longer a stranger, no longer dangerous. Because his eyes could penetrate any shadow, they no longer held any terror for him, except in his dreams. Dreams he could differentiate from reality, awful though they may be.

The lingering smell of a coyote drew a smile from his lips.

The coyote had detected his strange scent as it was patrolling its territory. When the coyote had found him slumbering secretly in the small crevasse, it had urinated on a nearby patch of dried grass; notice from one predator to another that it was aware of Sam's presence.

Unconcerned, the coyote had moved on.

He thought back to the previous night, slowly remembering the desperation he had felt as he had walked the streets.

*Choose, before the choice is made for you.*

He hadn't exactly made the conscious decision, but he felt more confident in his ability to control his inner demon, as close as it had come to gaining control over him.

He had passed by countless people, most of them healthy and strong, and he had been able to resist; denying the compulsion to strike. When the time had come he had understood, however reluctantly, how easy it would have been to surrender, to yield to his hunger.

"I can do this," Sam whispered to himself.

The words and the thought terrified him, not because they came so easily to him, but because they suggested acceptance; a willingness to do what was in his new nature to do.

No, he countered quickly in his mind. It was not willingness; it was a condition of survival if it were to continue on his own terms.

Lilith was something else entirely, a creature driven by an intense desire for vengeance. Any other motives were hers and hers alone. He knew that he could be different.

Lamia was different.

Lamia was different, and she was Lilith's sister!

He did not have to be like Lilith, stalking and killing the innocent. He understood that clearly, and he accepted it gratefully, his mind savoring the notion that he could be different. He was still possessed of free will. She might be the first, but she was not the prototype from which the die of all others were cast.

She was the first, and that was all.

"I can do this," he said louder, more confidently, his heart beating a little more strongly.

"For Miranda. For Cindy. For Tommy; I can do this."

He wiped a single spontaneous tear from his face.

The reverend had been right; he needed to find a purpose. His family could be that purpose, that driving force that made his path clear.

He could do this, for them.

An immense weight lifted from his mind.

He would do this for no other reason than to counter the will of Lilith, to resist what she wanted him to become; to spite her. He would be an infinite reminder of her inability to break him, to show her that she was not all powerful.

He needed to learn. Lamia had been insistent about this fact, and suddenly it seemed urgent. He could afford to waste no more time.

Sam climbed out of the fissure, struggling at times to drag himself through the narrowest points. He wondered how he had fit into that space, going presumably head first into it.

The previous night was a scattered series of memories.

He could clearly remember feeding, how he had been secluded in the shadows of the alley when Tobin had crossed his path. He remembered breaking Tobin's neck and jerking the head backwards. Then his thoughts became disjointed. There were sounds and flavours and textures and tastes, all of them confused in his mind. There had been raw energy surging through him, enough that he felt as though he might burst. He couldn't remember what he had done with the body, or how he had come to this place.

Sam looked up into the sky and silently gazed at the dome of stars over his head. The night sky was awash with the Milky Way, brilliantly lit up as he had never seen it before. The sky was not perfectly dark; it was tainted with the ever-present light pollution of the city, but even through that nebulous haze it was inspiring.

A single satellite sailed silently past, racing steadfastly across the sky to the horizon.

"Is this my purpose?" he spoke aloud to the twinkling stars. He felt like they were watching him expectantly, a million solemn eyes judging his actions. None replied, save the distant coincidental howl of the coyote whose tracks he now stood upon.

He needed to learn.

*Learn what?* he wondered.

He loathed the thought of asking Lamia what she could teach him, loathed the thought that he needed her for anything at all. She had not been unkind to him, and she was not to blame for what he was. Whenever she had been angry with him, it had been his fault, either through his ignorance, or his intentional actions.

Still she had come back, offering her guidance without prejudice.

Lamia was a reminder to him, and that was the extent of her crimes.

He did not know if he would see her any time soon.

For now, he was on his own. He could not trust that she was waiting for him to come around, to suddenly appear and once again offer assistance.

*I could find her. I could seek her out*, he thought.

She was not that far away; her presence was there in his mind.

But what if she ran from him?

She knew where he was, and she would know if he was coming. Would she know the reason? Could she somehow know?

He wasn't sure. Sam decided it was best to leave her alone.

Lamia might still be mad at him, unwilling to face him at all. He had to hope she was simply biding her time. If she kept away from him, it might be because it was too late; he had taken too long to come to his senses and was now on his own to deal with whatever might come.

Sam shook that thought out of his head; he never was a pessimist and he could not afford to think that way now.

He needed to learn and he needed to start tonight, alone if that was his only choice.

His thoughts returned to the man in the tunic, the man he had seen in her mind.

The memory was old; dusty, like a family album hidden in a cluttered attic. Like the album, it was sacred. It was a memory not faded by the passage of a great deal of time.

*I read her mind.*

It had not been intentional; he had just been curious and he had somehow probed into her mind, unravelling her thoughts and memories.

He had done the same with Tobin.

Was that something she wanted to teach him? A skill she could help him to polish and refine? He sensed that he had breached protocol with her, that what he had done with Lamia was poor etiquette, like reading an accidently discovered diary.

It was rude and something she was not accustomed to.

He would have to ask her, if and when he saw her again.

His mind returned to thoughts about what he needed to learn.

There were quite plainly protocols and customs that he was not aware of; that were not innate to his being.

There must be a culture of the vampire.

There *must* be one. Every society had one; this could not be an exception.

The older a society became, the more complex and detailed its culture became. It evolved with its members, inexorably accumulating and developing. Over time any identifiable group developed and evolved its own traditions, passing them down from one generation to the next. He did not see how vampires could be immune.

He chuckled to himself that this thought could be the dream of an occult sociologist.

Sam imagined the story of *Interview with a Vampire* where instead of a nosy writer recording the life story of a former plantation owner, a sociologist instead ran controlled studies.

Whatever his new culture was, he was entirely ignorant about it. Lamia had said he was *like a child.*

Sam guessed with a reasonable amount of confidence that he had the ability to read minds. He wasn't entirely sure how he had done it, but so far he done it twice, so it couldn't be too challenging.

What else could he do?

He thought about vampire lore. Garlic? Crosses? What was real and what was myth?

He knew that he was a creature of the darkness. The sun was a mortal enemy, its light a poison for which there was no cure.

It would burn him to dry, colorless ash.

Crosses?

He thought back to the reverend.

There hadn't been any crosses that he was aware of, at least nothing that he could define as having an effect on him. The thought of the church made him feel sweaty and ill. That was no myth. He was not welcome on holy ground and he was naturally revolted by it. It turned his stomach and filled his mouth with the sickly taste of bile.

Mirrors? Was it true that he could cast no reflection, that he had no soul to cast an image?

He knew far too little about himself. He did not know where reality ended and Hollywood began.

Could he change into a bat? Become smoke? Change to squeeze into the tiniest of places? He had fit through the narrow fissure to gain entry to the cave and so he felt that was true, although he had no concept of how it might be done.

Sam didn't know. He didn't even know how to begin experimenting.

A flickering fire caught his eye and he turned his head to investigate.

It was a campfire, attended by three, no, four people gathered around its light in an uneven arc, all sitting on smooth wind-polished logs.

Sam stood upon his outcropping and watched them intently, fascinated by the fact that if he wanted to, he could hear them clearly. It was simply a matter of wanting to.

They were young, in their late teens, sitting with their backs to their surroundings, oblivious to their environment.

Oblivious to *him*.

The coyote was already on their scent, wondering if they might leave him an easy snack of some dropped or forgotten food. Sam felt the coyote leave them for now, having made a reminder to itself to check back later when they were gone. Sam had their scent, too, but there was little they might have that would be of interest to him. He found himself thinking how easy it would be to take them in the darkness, to teach them in their final, horrified seconds that they had reason to fear the night. The fire was no shelter from him; it was a beacon that invited his attention. He blinked hard, concentrating on pushing those darker thoughts aside. He was not hungry.

That wasn't true.

He was hungry, but he wasn't hungry enough to be in danger of losing control.

Unless…

He walked towards them silently, like a scorpion over the sand. They would not hear him, not unless he wanted them too. Sam felt himself become the shadow, become one with the darkness. He reached out with his mind.

There were three girls and one boy; a couple and their two friends. They were intent on having a party before going back to school. After this year they would separate and head away for college. Two empty beer cans were blackening in the fire and most of a large meat-lover's pizza was sitting on the ground, snug and still warm in its plain brown corrugated box.

They smelled sweet, ripe and full.

Sam unconsciously grinned.

The three girls were laughing and bantering incessantly, almost entirely ignoring the boy. Sawyer was feeling annoyed, sitting next to his girl on a split log that the sun had bleached almost white. He had hoped to get some tonight, but then Sarah had invited her two friends at the last minute, thereby quashing any hopes of him getting her buzzed and alone in the darkness. He still had hopes that he might have a chance later on. He didn't know that she had done it intentionally, not wanting to be out here alone with him. She wanted to break up with him before school started, after the best of the summer was over.

He had a car. She didn't.

Sam almost laughed out loud, catching himself only a moment before it was too late. He was nearly upon them, behind the shelter of the boy's car.

Hunger tempted him, but he would not succumb to it with this group.

Instead, he picked up several stones and threw the largest of them into the distance.

It thumped dully as it landed, skittering before coming to rest.

He stepped further away from them, vanishing into the fold of night.

"What was that?" Sarah asked suddenly, interrupting a conversation that focused on the rumor of what a former friend may or may not have done with her last boyfriend at some nearly forgotten party.

"What?" Tammy asked, tucking her long black hair behind her ears.

Anna, her red-haired companion looked around, unsure what they were talking about.

Sam threw another stone, closer this time.

It landed on a larger rock, shattering instead of thumping.

It split with a sudden cracking sound.

"That!" Sarah exclaimed, looking in the direction the sound came from.

Her eyes widened as their conversation evaporated like a summer fog.

"What could it be?" Tammy asked nervously.

Sawyer shrugged. "A raccoon, Tammy," he suggested, not concerned in the least.

Sam threw another stone.

It flew into a shrub, landing with a series of snaps and a final dry thud.

"Jesus Christ," Tammy blurted out loud, her mouth suddenly dry.

Almost perfectly, as if he had choreographed it, an owl hooted in the opposite direction.

Anna shrieked.

"I wanna go, Sarah," she said nervously, unconsciously chewing a fingernail.

She hated the outdoors; her idea of camping was a three-star hotel. How the hell she had agreed to this was beyond comprehension.

After tonight, she would never leave a city again.

"It's nothing," Sawyer said.

"Who knows we're here Sawyer?" Tammy asked.

Sawyer shrugged.

She already knew the answer.

"Holy fuck, no one knows where we are," she said aloud, her voice becoming more alarmed. She was feeding off the fear of her friend.

Sam cast another stone.

It landed closer still.

Anna fled into the car without a word, slamming the door shut behind her and looking fearfully into the darkness.

"I'm with Anna," Tammy said, rising with sudden resolve.

"Jesus Christ, Tammy. It's nothing. There's nothing out here," Sawyer said coolly.

"Fuck you, Sawyer. No one knows where we are, and whatever that is, it's getting closer. It could be a murderer for chrissakes! Some fucking creep!"

"Wow," Sawyer replied, amazed how quickly she had reached that paranoid conclusion. "You actually believe that, don't you?"

Now Sarah chimed in, "Screw you, Sawyer. Take us home."

"Come on, Sarah. You gotta be kidding me."

He rolled his eyes, something Sarah saw plainly. Sawyer lost a few points for that.

Sarah stood up and brushed off her admirable backside. "Do I look like I'm kidding?"

Tammy got into the car and slammed her door nearly as quickly as Anna had.

Sarah stood by the front passenger door expectantly, her hand on the door handle.

Looking inside, she saw the keys were in the ignition, his Planet Hollywood keychain swinging ever so slightly back and forth.

Sam picked up a dry stick that was a little thicker around than his thumb and broke it cleanly in half. The sound it made as it came apart was clear and unmistakable.

Sawyer stood up quickly, trying to see anything at all.

"Holy shit," Sarah squealed. "If you don't get in the car I'm gonna leave you here!"

Sarah pulled open the door and almost literally jumped into the car.

Sawyer heard her push the lock button down with a precise click.

"Shit," he whispered.

He knew the keys were in the car and that she wasn't kidding. The three girls were sitting in the car, on the verge of panic, threatening to leave him here.

Some night this turned out to be.

"Fuck sakes," he grumbled. Some goddam animal was out there, walking around the fire, and it had spooked the girls into a frenzy. He had heard the owl. It had probably tried to land in a tree and broke some branches. As for the thumping sounds, that might have been the owl too, or maybe a racoon. Maybe a mouse or a rat. Christ, it could have been any number of animals.

Now the girls were sitting in his car, bug-eyed with fright.

Sawyer stared at the fire for a moment before deciding that he had no more cards left to play. Maybe after he dropped them off he could find some beer and spend the rest of the night playing video games. At least then the night wouldn't be a total write off.

He left the fire to burn and began to walk to his car.

"Put out the fire," Sam said calmly, just loud enough to be heard.

Sawyer froze in his tracks.

He spun around, looking for the source of the voice.

"W-who's there?" Sawyer replied, trying to sound assertive and pissed off that his voice broke.

There was no answer, nothing but the gentle snapping of the fire consuming its fuel. He convinced himself that he hadn't heard anything. It was the hysteria of the girls spreading to him. He was hearing things. Fuck.

Sawyer took a single step closer to the car, very slowly.

"Put out the fire," Sam said louder.

"Did you hear that?" Sarah shrieked, "Someone is out there!"

Tammy drew up her legs in a fetal position and Anna went into something akin to a trance, like a rabbit freezing in the middle of the road in the glare of headlights. 'Tharn', like Fiver in the great burrow of the rabbit warren in *Watership Down*.

"Who are you?" Sawyer shouted. "Where are you?"

Again, there was no answer.

"Was that you we heard? Making noises?"

Sam stared at him from the safety of his invisibility. He was too far away to be revealed by the weak light of the fire. Sam knew he would not feed on them, but he was enjoying toying with the boy. Sawyer was a bit of a hot head, in need of an ass-kicking to bring his ego down to an appropriate level. A bit of humility would go a long way.

"I have been watching," Sam said flatly.

"Watching?" Sawyer repeated, his eyes growing a little wider. "What are you? You some kind of freak?"

Sam laughed quietly enough to be heard.

He felt himself drawing from his darker side, the side that would take a degree of pleasure from torment.

"You find this funny?" Sawyer shouted, trying to put on a show of bravado.

"Who are you talking to, Sawyer?" Sarah whimpered, "Let's just go!"

He waved a hand at her, signaling her to be quiet.

Tammy was crying softly.

"Put…out…the fire," Sam said. His voice was deeper now, with a subtle growl rising in his throat.

Something rubbed against Sam's leg and he looked down to see. It was the coyote.

Its tail was tucked between its legs and its ears were pressed flat on its head, a gesture of submission.

The coyote was staring at the boy intently.

Sam felt his vision shift, growing more acute, surrendering to his darker nature.

The night, already clear, opened up before him.

He knew his eyes were entirely black.

The coyote's thoughts flooded into his mind.

There were no words, only a series of images; images he translated into a language he understood.

*Bite him kill him drink him tear him chew him crack his bones.*

It was one predator speaking to another, sharing thoughts.

Sam could feel the bond; the coyote saw him not as a person at all, but as a fellow hunter. The coyote had pups it was eager to feed; its mate was waiting in their den for his return. Their thoughts mixed and it became difficult for Sam to separate the coyote's from his own. Sam felt the need to regurgitate, to bring food home to his young.

He scratched the coyote absently behind the ear.

"What if I don't put out the fire? You gonna make me?"

"Stop talking Sawyer!" Sarah yelled, "I want to go home NOW!" she cried.

"Yes," Sam replied coldly, "Yes, I will."

He could smell the fear on the wind, and so could his four-legged companion. It was subtle and pleasurable. Oh how sweet it could be to make this pompous child do as he was told. The coyote howled at his side, echoing the determination to make the boy comply.

Sam wondered how much of his own thoughts were being transferred to the coyote. It was no longer cowering at his side but standing at full attention next to him, its full attention on the boy ahead.

Sawyer heard the coyote and wondered what the fuck was going on. It was close. Really close.

"All you have to do is put out the fire, and we will leave you alone."

Sawyer dry swallowed.

*We? Was the coyote his pet or something? Or was it a dog? Some bum out in the sticks with his dog, trying to freak him out for kicks? What the fuck was going on?*

"Fuck you, man!" he yelled, thinking this was just a little too weird to be real.

Sam felt himself surrender a little further. He was getting angry with this young fool. Anger was sweet. Anger was divine. Anger was the sweetest of seasonings, an aphrodisiac like no other.

Anger would lead to surrendering to his need to kill.

Sam inexplicably felt ancient, as though some part of a group consciousness was opened to him, revealed as a closed door might open. There was wisdom behind that door, wisdom and knowledge and experience. He was suddenly older than he was, more experienced than he was.

Hungrier than he thought he was.

"Do you want to die, boy?" Sam hissed coldly.

No, NO! He recognized that voice. He was losing control.

The coyote yipped in anticipation. It was panting in a bloodlust of its own.

Sam picked up a stone and felt it worn and smooth in his palm.

It was ancient, a boulder worn small by the passing of rivers and seas. Time had worn it down and Sam could feel the great touch of time upon its surface, like a kiss from the silent universe around it.

*Life is the way for the universe to know itself.*

Sam had read the quote long ago, and within this stone he felt the timelessness of the universe. He was one with it, a part of it, a cog in a great wheel that slowly turned.

He pulled himself back, trying to separate himself from the connection that had flooded his mind.

The sweet and delectable smell of fear was still there, but he was detached, more aware of himself, less a part of what he feared to become. What Lilith wanted him to become.

"I asked you if you wanted to die."

Sawyer wanted to piss himself.

The question was put out so casually that Sawyer knew this was no bluff, there was no subterfuge. He could die tonight, if he answered incorrectly.

"No," Sawyer finally answered, his voice wavering.

The girls were screaming. They had heard the coyote, too.

"Put out the fire."

Sawyer ran over to the fire and smothered it with rapidly kicked clods of dirt and sand. The fire died with a final tendril of smoke that reached upwards in a final gasp.

"Go," Sam said, "Go, while I still allow it."

Sarah fumbled madly for the keys before Sawyer had even reached the door.

Sarah unlocked his door just as he reached it.

Sawyer turned the key in the ignition, not noticing that his hands were shaking badly.

The engine turned over smoothly and purred.

"I WANNA GO!" Sarah screamed at him, clutching at his arm as panic ate away at the last vestige of her composure.

She would remember that feeling for years, a desperate feeling that made her arms feel like overcooked pasta. It would give her nightmares for the rest of her life. When she was a grandmother and time had blessed her with longevity, she would occasionally relive this night in her sleep and wake from a terrifying dream, screaming until her lungs were empty and her nightgown was stuck to her skin with the cold clammy sweat of absolute panic. This night would haunt her until her final breath was drawn, the kind of fear that only death itself could relieve.

Sawyer punched the pedal to the floor and barely held on to the wheel as his car sped away. He was scared shitless; his palms were coated in greasy, cold sweat. It didn't help that Sarah was crying next to him, or that Tammy and Anne were staring at him through the rear-view mirror with eyes that were glassed over with terror.

Sam watched the taillights of the car fade as it made its way back to the road. A part of him was saddened and frustrated, upset that his prey had so easily eluded his grasp. Another part of him was relieved, relieved that he had let them go.

There was an instant when he had known how easily he could strike, how easily they would fall to his intent. They were so helpless, so weak, and so easy to kill.

He had let them go.

Sam collapsed to his knees, trembling. The internal battle had almost been lost, his darker nature nearly prevailing.

He had to learn.

The coyote whined for permission and then trotted forward, smelling the scent of the pizza box on the ground.

The coyote's nose told him everything. The humans had left, but there was still food for its young. The pizza was found easily in the darkness and the coyote filled its mouth and belly with as much food as it could carry before leaving for the den. One more trip would take it all.

Sam felt the coyote leave his side.

As it left with the pizza in its mouth, Sam could feel the coyote's satisfaction that there was still more to bring back to its young. They would not be hungry tonight. Tonight they would be well fed.

Sam watched the coyote go before he finally stood and left, eager to be away from this place.

He had come close to losing control, come close to losing himself.

He had to learn.

No more chances.

He had been stupid, overconfident.

The side of himself that he feared the most was never far away, never too distant to ignore. He had to control his situations and his environment, at least until he was more confident.

He had to learn.

Tonight he had.

He felt that somehow Lamia was aware of him, feeling his torment.

Sam fled the darkness, towards the light of the city.

# Chapter 16

"He lay like a corse 'neath the Demon's force,
And she wrapp'd him in a shroud;
And she fixed her teeth his heart beneath,
And she drank of the warm life-blood."

-Henry Liddell

Sam stood uneasily on the rooftop, staring down two stories to the uncut grass below. A sturdy trellis had gotten him safely to the first level of rooftop; a clenched-fist, pale-faced climb up a stout drain pipe had gotten him to the very top. He had not dared to look down; he didn't have a fear of heights per se, he just had a fear of falling. He was perfectly at ease in a jetliner at thirty thousand feet, enjoying the view from a comfortable seat above the clouds. Ten feet up a ladder, however, his knees knocked like a poorly maintained engine. It was irrational he supposed, but that was the way it was.

The house was at the far end of a cul-de-sac that was still under construction, a collection of new homes that wouldn't be finished until the first glimpse of winter snow. Only this show home was complete, flanked by the rising wooden skeletons of its neighbors. Other lots were still bare; only the markings of where the basements were yet to be dug marked what was yet to come.

The grass seemed to laugh, mocking him.

"Screw you," he mumbled.

He knew the fall wouldn't kill him, but he also knew there would be a certain amount of pain involved, and that wasn't appealing in the slightest.

What if he got it wrong?

He'd end up lying on that mocking grass with two shattered ankles, waiting for them to heal before he could walk, perhaps to try again.

"Do or do not, there is no try. Easy for you to say Yoda, you little green fucker."

Sam sighed with exasperation.

The logical part of his brain told him that he was only twenty feet up.

If he jumped and got it wrong, all he really needed to do was roll and that would absorb the excess energy of the fall, sparing him any broken bones.

If he got this right, he should be able to fly.

A multitude of stories told of the legendary ability of a vampire to transform into a bat, or an array of other hosts. From a rooftop, the option of a bat seemed the most interesting. He just didn't have any idea of how or where to begin.

*You need to learn.*

Yeah well, here he was.

The problem was; there was no textbook, no "How-to" guide. There was no occult section for "How to Fly" in the local bookstore that would help him out.

Lamia was nowhere to be seen, although she was close, still in his vicinity.

He stood on the precarious edge of a rooftop, dangling his toes over white aluminum eavestroughs and rectangular grey asphalt shingles, hoping for a miracle. Or at least a moment of enlightenment.

He doubted that either would come.

Sam extended his arms out to his sides, holding them horizontal to the ground.

He waved his fingers and closed his eyes.

Maybe if he just *thought* about it hard enough, put enough mental grease into it, he would suddenly just transform and fly away.

He thought about his arms becoming wings, his fingers becoming the trailing edges of those wings.

Nothing happened.

He blocked everything out, ignoring the wind and the air and the height, trying to clear his mind of everything but becoming something else. He steadied his breathing, taking in deep slow breaths to calm himself and collect his thoughts.

With his eyes closed, nothing could visually distract him.

All he had to do was think about it; he was sure.

He leaned forward at the knees, thinking that maybe if he was prepared to jump off of the roof, that something would happen.

He wanted to lean forward and let himself fall, to let the support under his feet just vanish and fade away.

And maybe break his legs and hips in the process, he thought bitterly.

*Shut up*, he thought to himself.

*Shutupshutupshutup.*

There was also the possibility that this was impossible, nothing but a myth concocted by Hollywood to sell movie tickets, a trick to sell books. This possibility was the seed of all his doubt; the flaw in the foundation that ate at his confidence.

He might jump off this roof a dozen times or even a hundred times, and each time he would end up breaking his bones and shattering his limbs, all for nothing.

Sam took in another deep breath and squeezed his eyes shut, wondering if he needed to flap his arms.

Was that a part of the trick? Was there a trick?

"Do you understand how foolish you look?" a contemptuously amused voice spoke aloud.

Sam fell back onto the roof with surprise.

Lamia had come upon him unawares again.

*No,* he thought to himself. He had blocked out the feeling. It was his fault, not hers.

"Good," Lamia said calmly, "you see your mistake."

Sam nodded reservedly, still glad to see her.

She had come. He tried to conceal his satisfaction, but sensed she was aware of it.

"I was concentrating," he said, attempting to explain himself.

"You can concentrate and still be aware," she replied, "just focus your thoughts."

He nodded, wishing it was truly as easy as she thought it was.

Sam stood again, opening up the vague channel that sensed her being.

"Good," she answered.

He returned to the side of the roof and extended his arms yet again, closing his eyes. He felt her amusement vaguely, like she was remembering an old joke.

Lamia walked over to him, standing at his side, just slightly behind him on his right.

Sam felt her nearness, could smell her fragrance. She was not at all angry with him. A scent caught his nose, firing his nerves. It was not anger at all.

"You have fed," he stated.

"So have you," she added smugly. "Well done, you allowed yourself to surrender."

"I chose," Sam said.

"The outcome is what matters," she said, not seeming to care at all that he was being particular in how he fed.

Lamia moved and stood behind him.

She traced her hands along his back, trailing upwards from his lower spine up to the base of his neck.

Goosebumps raced along his body.

"What are you doing?" she asked, curious, wondering why he was standing there in the shape of a T.

"I am trying to figure out how to fly," he said finally.

Lamia laughed sincerely, the stark beautiful features of her face lightening up as she enjoyed his comment.

Finally, when she was finished laughing and Sam was feeling partially humiliated, she returned to his side.

"You are open to learning?"

He saw her eyes were darker, more intense. They were sultry and frightening. He felt that if he were to lie to her, her wrath would be immediate and terrible.

He nodded.

She smiled only a little, allowing him to see her restrained satisfaction.

"Good. Your stubbornness is not infinite."

She stood behind him once again.

He felt her warm breath on his neck, the closeness of her presence.

Lamia closed her hands on his arms, pushing them down to his sides with gentle persuasion. She let go when his hands were at his hips.

"You must know where it is you want to go," she said patiently, "do you know where you want to go?"

Sam shook his head.

"If you had been successful, you would have never returned," she scolded him.

"I would have died?" he asked her.

"You would have become a winged creature, with only the smallest part of you remaining within, the part of your mind that is you. From that, you cannot return. The remainder of your short life would be spent trapped within its body, doomed to live out only the creature's natural life span. You would have been aware of it, knowing your fate but unable to escape, unable to take control and return. The creature's mind would have overpowered your own. It is a slow and terrible way to die."

Sam shuddered, feeling her own personal revulsion reach him.

"You must know where you want to go. With that vision in your mind, clearly and strongly, you will be dominant, able to return to yourself when you reach your destination. Only then will you control the body."

"I understand," Sam said.

"Where do you want to go?" she asked.

He looked around, looking for a landmark.

An old birch tree towered over a nearby park where it was now king, a part of the natural landscape that was spared for the housing development.

Sam pointed at the tree.

"There," he said, "the tree. How do I change?"

"Patience," Lamia whispered, pressing herself into his back. Her hands again traced down his back, stopping above his hips and holding there.

"Where is the image of where you want to go?" she asked.

"I am looking at it. It is the tree."

Lamia clenched her teeth and Sam felt her nails dig into his hips.

She was not being gentle.

"NO. It must be in your mind, a thought and an image. What you see is not enough. It must be in your MIND. Now, close your eyes."

Sam reluctantly but obediently closed his eyes.

"What do you see?" she asked, her voice was soft and low, into his ear.

"Nothing," Sam said

His eyes were closed; he couldn't see anything.

"Do you see the tree? In your mind, can you picture the tree?"

Sam nodded.

"Where on the tree will you go?"

"To the top?" Sam guessed, not entirely sure.

"The top of the tree, then," Lamia said, "is it clear? You must be sure."

"Yes."

Lamia violently shoved him from the rooftop, forcefully pushing him by his hips over the edge of the roof.

Sam felt his heart jump into his throat, his stomach clench with fear.

He was going to fall. He was going to hit the ground and he was going to feel his bones snap and puncture his skin; he was going to feel his ribs shatter like a row of delicate icicles. He was too frightened to scream.

Sam waited to feel his legs buckle, the bones in his ankles shattering in all directions.

Except that he wasn't falling.

He could feel air rushing past his face and under his... arms? No, they didn't feel like arms anymore.

Sam opened his eyes.

The house was to his left and below him, slowly spinning as he circled around it with the casual beating of his wings.

*His wings!*

The feathers were speckled gray and brown and white, and he could feel the air whistling through them and under them, giving him lift.

Sam shouted in enjoyment.

*"Whooo!"*

*I'm an owl,* he thought with delight.

He laughed when he heard the hooting sound that he had meant to be a shout. His laughter came out in a series of broken hoots and chirps.

He beat his wings harder, climbing higher into the air. It was effortless and without thought, the graceful manoeuvres were completed by instinct alone.

He was the owl.

Sam understood now what Lamia had meant.

Far below, a mouse squeaked as it ran along its path in the long grass.

Sam instantly banked to the right, dipping his wing to angle aside for the proper descent from which he could strike the mouse.

It was an instinctual reaction, an action that he quickly regained control over.

He evened out his wings and banked left, returning to the proper heading towards the tree. He circled the tree smoothly and saw Lamia watching him. Lamia stood on the rooftop, observing him with her arms crossed under her breasts; an impatient look was etched on her face.

Sam flew down to the roof, catching the draft with his wings as he put out his talons to land on the shingles. He felt his claws scrape against the roof and then suddenly he was there, standing beside her, his back to the yard.

"There you have it," she said calmly.

He was thrilled, like a child having returned from a favorite ride at the carnival.

A moment later he was utterly furious and dumbfounded, all at once.

"You pushed me off the roof!" he screamed at her.

Lamia didn't blink. She actually smiled a little.

"I pushed you off the roof," she agreed. Her open and casual admission left him speechless. "It was necessary, to make you see."

He remained dumbfounded.

"Would you have jumped if I had told you to jump?"

He stared at her, voiceless.

*No*, he thought.

"I didn't think so," she answered his blank look. "Trust will not come easy for you. I chose the fastest way."

"You could have shown me yourself," he stumbled, his voice returning.

"And you would not have suspected I could be withholding some concept that made flight possible? You needed to experience it for yourself, to see that there is no trick."

"Then, how?" he asked, trying to replay the sequence of events in his mind.

He couldn't separate anything. In one moment he was falling and then in the next he was *different*.

"Sometimes there are no answers to questions," Lamia replied. "I don't know how, and I don't believe that any of us do. We just *do*, and then we are. It is instinct, self-preservation."

"Self-preservation?"

"I have already explained that we are not immortal. A fall from this height could surely have killed you, in one way or another. To prevent that, your body reacted and you become the owl. You will not like this, so be warned."

"What?"

"Think of the tree."

"The tree? Wha...?" he began, interrupted when Lamia shoved him on the chest, pushing him backwards over the roof.

He disappeared below the edge of the roof.

A moment later an owl raced away from the spot where he had vanished, eyes wide with terror.

She watched him fly up to the tree, a broad great horned owl that flew almost without effort, its wide wings catching the slightest of breezes. It perched clumsily upon the top and stared back at her with baleful eyes.

It hooted at her angrily.

"You see? It just happens. Now come back."

The owl stared at her with its great yellow eyes, clicking its beak in dismay.

"The lesson is learned; I will not do it again. On that, you have my word."

After several moments the owl finally spread its wings and hopped off the tree, drifting easily down to the house.

When it landed, the owl quickly transformed back into Sam.

"Why?" he demanded angrily.

"It's a good lesson; one you needed to learn. Once, you may have considered good fortune or coincidence. A second time serves to prove the truth of my words."

"I believed you the first time," he countered, still upset.

"A second time does no harm," Lamia said, "it's important that you understand it is a need, not a want. Many gifts are responses to danger, responses you cannot control by thought alone."

Sam walked away from the edge of the roof.

"I will not push you again," Lamia said.

"You might understand my paranoia."

Lamia smiled slightly.

"I'm sorry for what I did. With your thoughts," Sam said quickly, wanting to talk to her before she went away again.

The smile was erased from her face in an instant; her eyes gave him a frigid stare.

"It just happened and I was curious. I won't do it again."

Her composure softened, but only slightly.

"You are fortunate that I am willing to accept your apology. What you did was a violation that not all of us would be so kind as to forgive easily, if at all."

"I am sorry," he repeated.

"You are sincere; I hear the truth in what you say. I accept your apology. Never do it again."

Sam shook his head, "I won't. Can you teach me about it, about what I did?"

Lamia looked at him curiously.

"You don't know how you did it?" she asked.

"I remember wondering what you were thinking, and then it felt like I was reaching out, like with a hand I couldn't see. It was strange, hard to explain."

"That is a suitable explanation. There is a connection made, a union of thoughts. All of us have the same sensation, the feeling of reaching out."

"Can you block it? If someone tried to do it to you?"

"I will do it to you. Try to stop me."

Sam suddenly felt unsure.

The thought of Lamia probing his mind made him feel uneasy.

Lamia seemed to know exactly what he was thinking.

"Not an inviting concept is it?" she said.

Sam shook his head in agreement, now with a better understanding of why she was so angry with him.

"Will you allow me to try?" she asked, seeking his permission.

"Will it hurt?"

"No. I will be there, in your mind and that is all. Think of something pleasant."

Sam took a breath and steeled himself, clenching his fists as his mind raced for a memory to hold onto.

"Do it," Sam muttered.

Lamia stared at him with unblinking eyes.

Sam felt a tickling in his mind, a feeling that he was being watched. There was a peculiar sensation that his mind was pushing back, keeping her at bay through a thin, elastic membrane. It was like she was pushing at it, making it stretch as she searched for a weakness through which to tear an opening.

He felt a moment of fogginess and vertigo as the membrane relented.

Lamia was in his mind; he could feel her clearly.

It was not unpleasant, but it was unsettling.

A moment later she was gone.

Strangely, he found it made him feel lonely.

"Do you see?" she asked him.

"That was…" Sam searched for the word that fit the experience the best. "That was weird," was all he could come up with.

"Unusual," she added.

"Yes," he agreed. He wanted to see if he could stop it from happening. "Try it again."

Lamia looked at him oddly.

"You wish it again?" She asked it as though she thought he was out of his mind.

"I want to see if I can stop you."

She stared at him again, focusing her will on him.

Again, as before, he felt the tickling feeling, like her fingers were inside his skull.

He felt her probing at the strange wall between them, the invisible barrier between their minds.

Sam focused on the feeling, thinking forcibly that he wanted her out.

Wherever she touched, he pushed back, opposing her attempts.

He saw her frown.

*It's working*, he realized, pushing her back yet another time.

He saw her grow angry, her brows furrowing in frustration.

Her eyes became black. She was no longer probing for a space to push at; she was throwing herself against his mind.

Sam gritted his teeth in obstinate concentration.

It was tiring.

He could feel the fatigue settling into his limbs. This was enough. He had proven to himself that it was possible to resist, best to just let her into his mind.

Then he saw the look on her face.

Lamia was sweating profusely and her face was haggard with exhaustion. Rage burned behind her obsidian eyes.

"Enough," he said, raising his hand to her in a motion to stop.

Her attempts to break through were weakening, becoming feeble.

He knew it was becoming dangerous, not for him, but for her.

"Stop, Lamia," he said quietly.

He felt that if she did not stop, there was a risk that somehow this small part of her could become trapped within him, leaving her body with only a slim part of herself remaining. That leftover part would not survive long without the other.

Still she kept trying.

"Lamia, STOP!" he shouted.

If she heard him, she gave no indication of it.

She was scratching at his mind now, clawing at him, no longer able to push.

He felt her there, her mind against his.

Sam felt nauseous.

He summoned the last of his strength and shoved against her presence, wanting to push her away one final time with enough force that she would know she had to give up.

He felt the connection between them snap like a taut cord.

Lamia shuddered and fell to her knees, staring at him blankly before swooning and falling to her side. She crumpled into a heap on the shingles.

"Lamia!" he gasped, holding her by the shoulders, trying to look into her eyes to see if she was conscious.

He was shocked to see her eyes were no longer black; they were ice green and entirely unaware of his presence.

He was suddenly terrified that maybe he had killed her or maimed her in some awful way.

"I am going to try to feel your mind," he whispered into her ear, "I am sorry but I have to see if you are okay."

She didn't make a sound.

Sam closed his eyes and felt for her, fumbling through darkness with invisible hands. He felt a tendril of her thoughts and reached a little further, testing to see where her wall between them began.

The moment he felt it, it shattered like brittle glass.

A thousand crystal shards exploded in his mind.

He was in.

Lamia gasped, not in horror or pain, but like a diver who had swum too deep and had just made it to the surface at the last possible moment before drowning, her lungs burning for fresh air.

She was there.

She had made it back.

He let it go, retreating back as quickly as he could.

The image of the man flashed before him as he left her thoughts, the man in the fields with his beige shirt. The sun was so very warm that day, the fields were filled with the sweet scent of pollen and the trees were bursting with summertime green. There was the laughter of children and then....

Sam sagged on his knees and took deep ragged breaths as he fought to push away the nausea that was a cold lump in his throat. He let himself lie down, not possessing the strength to sit any longer.

Lamia was asleep at his side, her eyes closed and her features erased of all cares as she slept the sleep of the exhausted.

He stared at her with concern, listening to her breathing. It was soft and regular.

Relieved, he laid back and caught his own breath, waiting for hours as he felt strength returning to his limbs.

He was starving.

There was no time left tonight to eat. The thought came to him quickly and innocently, without regret. He was shocked at how simply it was there, the acceptance of having to take a life.

*On my terms*, he said to himself, but not tonight.

He wondered if Lamia would wake before dawn.

*We are not immortal* she had said to him.

He could leave her here, leave her sleeping; leave her for the dawn.

The killing light of dawn would be a small taste of revenge for Lilith.

He was angry at himself for thinking it.

It was NOT Lamia's fault; she was NOT to blame.

She was completely vulnerable. Perhaps for the first time in ages Death had a glimpse of finally being able to claim her rightfully and reap her soul.

*NO* he shouted to himself. He couldn't leave her like this; she was now his responsibility to protect, at least until her strength had returned.

He could smell the hunger upon her.

It made his hunger look like a plaything. His hunger was a mere trifle, a craving in comparison to the dreadful appetite that was within her.

For the first time he also smelled upon her the scent of time, the odor of countless centuries. She was ancient. This young-looking woman that lay before him was an illusion. She was a mistress of Time itself, a being that drifted through the changing seasons, removed from the clutches of age. She had passed through the centuries, her body untouched by the fingers of time, but she bore deep scars within. Wounds that, instead of healing, had come to define her.

Sam bleakly wondered how he was going to get her down to the ground.

He heard her voice in his mind.

*It is a need instead of a want.*

It was instinct; the fall itself would change her as a means of self-preservation.

He had to trust what she said.

Would he be able to carry her if he jumped from the roof with her in his arms? Or would he then change into an owl and be dragged to the ground with her? Or would she then change? There were too many ifs.

"Dammit," he said under his breath. He knew too little. Lamia had to teach him.

Sam lifted her gently to the edge of the roof, one arm under the bend in her knees and the other cradling her back.

The ground stared up at him defiantly.

He rolled her off the edge, watching with dread, expecting to see her hit the ground with a terrible snapping bounce.

She had just started to fall when her body seemed to slip and loosen, coming apart in a billion different places while still holding her basic shape. It was like watching painted sand fall to the ground. Even in a state of unconsciousness her instincts responded to keep her from harm.

She landed not with a thump but with the soft whispering sound of sand cascading over itself. Once there, she came back together, the silent and peacefully sleeping form once more.

Sam stared at her with wonder, partly admiring how beautiful she was.

He imagined the spot on the ground next to her and jumped.

# Chapter 17

"I saw their starved lips in the gloam,
With horrid warning gaped wide,
And I awoke and found me here,
On the cold hill's side."

-John Keats

It was almost dawn before he found the rock fissure again, the narrow granite gap where he had spent the previous night. He had no choice but to carry the unconscious Lamia the entire way. He was sick with exhaustion and he was hungry; hungry enough to wonder if he would be able to sleep at all during the coming day.

He positioned himself belly down and feet first at the widest part of the opening and began to retreat into the earth, dragging Lamia down with him by her arms.

The small gap seemed miraculously wide, wide enough that descending downwards was easy. He pulled Lamia down carefully, catching her so she wouldn't fall, using his weight to counter her expected slide when they reached the most vertical part of the descent into the tiny cavern. Before long they were safe underground. When she was safely down, he laid her in the most comfortable position he could, with her arms crossed on her chest. A narrow swath of her hair crossed over her face and he delicately swept it aside with his fingertips. Sam found himself staring at her, admiring her complexion and the exotic contours of her face. Here was Helen he thought, Helen that mobilized the armies of Menelaus. Helen, whose beauty had brought about the fall of Troy. Miranda had been beautiful in her own right, attractive to many men for many different reasons. Lamia would appeal to all men, another lure that ultimately resulted in her being deadly to many.

He tore his eyes away from her, whispering a quick prayer to Miranda. He was too tired to cry and so he lay upon the cold stone to wait out the day, trying to ignore the pain in his midsection and the part of himself that would try to assert control the following night.

* * *

He was running down the street, running in a blind panic through fog that seemed to pour from the alleys like so many overflowing creeks into a swollen river. Street lights shone like regularly spaced moons above him; their light was diffused and indistinct, their clarity lost in the hazy air. The fog impaired his vision but it did nothing to block the sound coming from behind him. It was the sound of pursuit, the sound of many feet running on the road behind him; driving him forward in terror.

They were running him down and they would kill him once they did.

His legs were growing weak and his chest was aching for air, but the pursuers never relented.

They were gaining on him.

His only hope was to run faster, to run longer, to put some distance between himself and his pursuers so he could find a safe spot to hide and rest, to throw them off and escape into the obscuring mist.

It wasn't working.

When he ran faster they kept up to him. When he turned they followed him perfectly. The fog was no impediment to their pursuit. It was as if they could see him, even though he could not see them.

"What do you want?" he cried out, hoping for an answer, for anything he could bargain with.

It was desperate and likely futile, but he had no options, no cards hidden up his sleeve. He was grasping at straws, hoping beyond hope for anything that might provide salvation. Fear began to gnaw at him.

There was no reply, only the relentless pounding of feet upon the dark wet road.

"Leave me alone!" he pleaded, hoping he sounded dangerous and worthy of being left alone.

The distance closed.

He looked over his shoulder, craning as he ran, trying to see who was behind him.

He should be able to see something, they sounded so close.

There was nothing.

The streetlights overhead disappeared, leaving the fog to close in on him, taking away any ability to gauge his speed.

There was no obvious source of light, yet the fog seemed to shimmer with a faint neon blue, throwing off enough illumination that he could see swirls in the air and his own hot breath.

There was a giggle behind him, a child-like laugh that was full of merriment.

*Oh no!*

A wall loomed out of the darkness suddenly, a barrier of red bricks closing in on all three sides.

He had run into an alley. He was trapped.

There were no sounds except for his thundering heartbeat and his gasping breath.

His arms were outstretched, the palms of his hands pressed against cold bricks.

Sam turned to see a shadow loom out of the fog, facing him defiantly.

The shadow knew he was there and said nothing, confident its quarry was trapped.

It seemed to be only a foot or two away and he still couldn't see who it was.

He didn't dare to move, irrationally hoping that remaining motionlessness would make him invisible.

A sharp stabbing pain pierced his chest, a pain that made him convulse while robbing him of the ability to utter a sound. Pure and exquisite, it was a searing pain that melted away the cold and the fear. There was nothing else; pain became his entire existence.

Sam fell to his knees as the stake slid between his ribs. He felt bones snapping like dry twigs.

"In the heart, children," he heard Miranda say affectionately.

"Mir-anda?" he gasped, "Why?" trying to see her.

She emerged from the fog, her black hair a stark contrast to the white fog.

Her eyes were dark and smoldering, her wide lips were the reddest of red, upturned at the corners with an amused vulpine smirk. Her skin was flawless and light brown, the color she attained after a hot summer of sunbathing.

When she looked down at him he felt despised and loathed; there was no love left in her dark eyes for him.

Two smaller shadows emerged from the fog at her sides, flanking her.

Tommy and Cindy mirrored Miranda's perfect complexion and her look of perfect hatred. Each held a sharpened wooden stake in their fist, clenched tightly in their small perfect hands.

Cindy smiled at him in the same manner her mother had; a look of final victory.

Tommy struck first, driving his stake forward and using his body to add momentum to its impact.

Sam felt it cut cleanly into his skin, finding a space between his ribs and sliding downwards into his guts.

He felt it slide under his heart.

Tommy looked disappointed in himself.

Miranda kissed him warmly on his smooth forehead and whispered, "Almost, my dear, almost."

"Higher," Miranda said to Cindy, "a little higher than your brother, my love."

Cindy screeched and drove her stake upwards in a curving streak that ground under his breastbone. The point pierced his heart and kept going, coming through the other side before she let it go with a look of satisfaction.

"Very good my loves, very good," Miranda cooed warmly, hugging them to her waist, kissing them both.

Sam collapsed to the ground as a spurt of his life's blood gushed up through his throat and past his lips.

Tommy and Cindy were smiling as they watched him die, their eyes shining with an internal light. Miranda alone glared at him, her lips fixed in a joyless line.

"Why?" he croaked, watching his blood gather and pool in front of his face.

He felt his heart stop beating.

"Why?" he asked one more time.

They did not answer and his world faded to black.

*\*\**

Sam opened his eyes, still feeling the stakes buried in his chest. His heart was beating furiously. He gradually became aware that Lamia was sleeping next to him, half draped over him with her head nestled on his chest by the crook of his neck. She was breathing softly, at ease and resting peacefully. Her warmth was soothing, helping him to relax. He had not slept so well as she was now since…he let the thought fade away, not wanting to let it come to its inevitable conclusion. His heart began to slow and his mind cleared. He focused on the immediate present and his surroundings. A thin glow of orange light sparkled on the wall, slowly shifting as the sun went down.

Lamia stretched and opened her eyes slowly, acclimating to her surroundings.

She looked up and smiled faintly, yawning lightly.

Sam looked down at her calmly, satisfied to see her come around. The depth of her exhaustion had frightened him.

He felt a distinct sensation of relief.

"Good morning," he said quietly, "or is it good night?"

Lamia woke fully with a start, quickly pushing herself off of him and backing away to the wall with her eyes wide and alert, staring at him accusatorily.

She said nothing, her chest heaving in sudden exertion.

"What?" he asked her, wondering why she had reacted so fearfully.

"Where are we?" she spat nervously.

"In a cave I found two days ago."

"How did we get here?" She was uneasy, not remembering the previous night.

"I carried you," he replied as casually as he could, not wanting to add to her discomfort.

Her eyes darted around the cave, examining it hastily as though there might be a hidden danger lying in wait.

Sam hadn't moved.

He was still lying on the ground, one ankle crossed over the other and an arm behind his head as a makeshift pillow. He was looking at her with obvious concern. Her eyes looked to him and then flicked away as though she was embarrassed.

"What?" Sam asked, genuinely perplexed at her reaction.

"Why did you let me sleep like that?" she asked him in a demanding tone.

"Like that? What are you talking about?"

"Next to you," she blurted.

"I woke up with you next to me, only a few minutes before you did," he replied.

"And you didn't try to move me?" She seemed surprised, almost shocked.

"It was warm and I didn't want to disturb you," was all he had to say.

She had no reply to his response; the honesty of it was plain to see.

Lamia drew her knees up to her chest and wrapped her arms around her legs, watching him warily.

Sam sat up, feeling the bite of the cooler air now that she was sitting away from him.

"It is cold," he commented, rubbing his own shoulders for the temporary and unsatisfying heat of friction.

Sam moved a little and saw Lamia tense up, her eyes still on him doubtfully.

"I was uncomfortable," he said, brushing away a stone that had been pinned underneath him. "A rock," he explained.

Lamia relaxed, but only slightly.

He felt goose bumps rise on his forearms.

"Can I sit next to you?" he asked.

"Why?" Lamia asked, unsure.

"I'm cold."

She hesitated for a moment, looking him over as though she expected him to suddenly leap at her.

"Yes," she finally replied.

Sam shuffled over to her side until her shoulder and his were touching.

It was still cool, but tolerable.

Sam was certain that he felt her shiver and draw a little closer to him, not wanting to admit that she too was cold.

He almost put his arm around her without thinking about it, but stopped himself, suspecting she might react harshly to his innocent motion.

"Can I put my arm around?" he asked, gesturing partially to help her understand.

She looked at him suspiciously.

"It will be warmer," he added.

Her eyes narrowed for a split second, thinking it over.

*Why is she so paranoid?* He asked himself, almost smiling at her reactions.

"Yes," she finally said, leaning forward to make room for his arm.

Sam put his arm around her cautiously and with a minimum of expenditure.

He felt that any extra motion could be risky in her present state.

"There," he said. "Better."

It was a little warmer; just a little.

"I wish I had a blanket," he mumbled to himself.

Lamia ignored him for a minute in awkward silence before she changed the subject.

"I was showing you about reading thoughts," Lamia suddenly recalled.

Sam nodded. "Yes, last night."

Lamia concentrated, trying to recall the previous events.

"I was trying to read yours," she said at last.

"You did, the first time."

She looked at him questioningly.

"You did enter my mind. Then we tried again, where I tried to stop you."

Her face went pale at the recollection. She remembered.

"And you did," she said softly, sickly.

"Yes. That was how you lost consciousness. It was like I had to push you out, like you were trapped and couldn't stop."

Lamia looked ill, like she was coming down with a bad flu. Her normally bright eyes were dull and glassy and her complexion was subdued and flat, missing its normal vibrant appearance.

"How do you know that?" she asked him.

"That was how it felt," he said, watching her for any improvement.

"Tell me how it felt."

He shrugged.

The experience was suddenly fresh in his mind and easy to recall.

"I felt you were trying to push through into me, only wherever you pushed, I pushed back harder. You were behind a curtain, and I was on the other side. I just felt you getting weaker and weaker. It seemed you were struggling more at the end. That was when I got scared."

"Scared?"

"It was as though I could feel you were starting to panic. Somehow I knew you were trapped. It was sort of like drowning I suppose. I kept thinking that it was like you were tangled in the curtain and getting smothered by it."

Lamia leaned over and retched.

Sam held her as she hunched over, feeling her weakness, and prevented her from falling into the dirt.

When she stopped, he pulled her back up by the shoulders.

"Better?" he asked, the concern etched into his face was unmistakable and Lamia saw it plainly.

"You carried me." It was a statement, not a question.

"Yes."

"Why?"

"I couldn't leave you there to die."

"You could have."

"I could have," he agreed.

"Why didn't you?"

A thousand reasons tumbled through his mind, sifting and sorting through them all was impossible. He chose the closest to the truth.

"You are the closest thing I have to a friend."

"A friend?" Lamia replied, shocked.

"You don't have to help me, but you do. You could easily leave me alone but you haven't. Without you, I would be alone."

Lamia fell silent yet again, chewing her bottom lip absently.

"It did feel like drowning. I thought I was going to die, that you were killing me."

"I don't want to kill you," he said honestly.

She looked at him with eyes that were penetrating, hinting at hidden surprise.

Sam sensed that if there was ever a moment to ask the question that was burning in his mind, this was it.

"Who was he?" Sam asked carefully.

He felt Lamia tense at the question, but she did not pull away.

Instead, she sighed deeply, more from pain than from being tired.

"His name was Adama," Lamia said, her voice was a muted whisper, a sound barely heard through her lips, spoken as though it was precious to her.

"Adama," Sam repeated, wanting to be sure that he heard her correctly.

Lamia nodded once, only slightly. "He was my husband."

Sam was taken aback, made speechless by her admission. She saw his reaction.

"You see, Samuel Maxwell, I was not always what I am. There is a past to everything, even to the terrible Lamia of the *Vardat Lilitu*."

Her voice was bitter and sarcastic.

She lowered her head to her forearms, muffling her voice.

"Perhaps one day you too will have your own legend. Perhaps one day you will be named a child-killer." She laughed condescendingly, mocking her own words.

"What happened to Adama?" he asked her.

She snorted as if it were plain to see.

"He died."

"He was not...?"

"No, he was not a vampire."

She sighed again, her body shivering, not from cold but from an unpleasant memory.

"He was thrown from his horse. I found him, out in our fields. He died there on the ground, his back broken."

"What did you do?"

"I buried him there, next to where I would soon bury our daughters. Afterwards, I burned our home to the ground. I never returned. Never once in all this time have I returned to that cursed spot."

Sam saw her secretly wipe tears from her eyes and as she spoke she was trying to conceal the hoarseness in her voice.

"Your children?" he asked.

"They were taken by a plague that same year." Her voice was thick.

He felt a strange kinship with her, bound by incomprehensible loss.

"I am sorry for how I treated you before," Sam said to Lamia, "You didn't deserve it. I was angry and I wanted someone to blame. I guess you were convenient."

"There is no need for an apology. The transition can be hard to accept, and not everyone that has experienced it has survived."

"I do need to apologize. That was not how I was before, and that is not how I choose to be now."

"Grief comes in many forms," Lamia replied.

"I am sorry."

Lamia looked at him, a smile forming upon her lips as she understood what he was saying.

"You have accepted it."

Sam nodded. "I have."

"I accept your apology, Samuel."

"You offered to help me before, to teach me."

"I did."

"I now accept your offer."

"What brought you to this decision?"

"I realized that I can be who I am, not who she wants me to be."

Lamia nodded, a satisfied look upon her face.

"Then I will teach you."

Sam felt she was done talking.

He was wrong.

"You remind me of him, my Adama. For a moment before I woke, for just a moment, I felt he was by my side once more. It was a sweet sleep and a terrible awakening, to have thought even for that brief moment that he was here. Fate is cruel, you see. I have suffered his senseless loss for all of these long years. Still, for all of this fresh pain I would not take that moment back. For that moment I was Lamia again. Not Lamia the child-killer, not Lamia the serpent. I was Lamia, the beloved mother and wife."

It was an opening into the person she once was, an opening Sam had not thought she would ever reveal.

"When did you…change?"

"I had just lost my last and youngest when my sister appeared late one night. I still remember it perfectly, as though it were last night. I have relived it in my mind too many times to count. It was nearing the end of summer and the fields were full of grain. It was dry and the night air was cool; there were no clouds, just a full moon that was bright and clear, bright enough that you could see in the darkness. The air was still full of that dusty, sweet summer smell. In those days I still loved summer, like I had as a young girl. I got that from my mother, a love of summer. She would braid our hair and lace it with the tiny flowers she found around our village."

She laughed a laugh that was partially a muffled sob. She smiled a haunted smile.

"My father used to say that the bees would come get me and take me back to the hive because of all the flowers in my hair. He was a good man too, a good father."

Lamia drew silent, lost in some memory that she kept to herself, a memory that brought the ghost of a genuine smile to her solemn face.

"That night, my sister found me screaming. I didn't even know she was there at first. I was just screaming at the night and she took me by the shoulders and held me tightly."

Sam saw that her eyes were clamped shut as she relived the moment; her cheeks glistened with fresh tears.

"She didn't let me go until I was done, until I was exhausted by my grief. I remember she picked me up and carried me to my bed. It seemed so easy for her.

She stayed with me until I slept; her fingers brushed my face like they did when I was little, like our mother did for both of us when we were still little. She sang to me quietly and kept the hair from my face. I remember the look in her eyes. They were so full of pain for me that she couldn't stand it. And anger. She was so angry. It took all of her strength to stay there with me. I could see how it hurt her, seeing me like that, but still she stayed. She didn't let me go. When I woke up she had buried my girls next to their father. I didn't even hear her leave, and I don't know when she did, but it was sometime during the night as I slept. I was grateful to her for burying them. Does that make me a terrible mother to be glad that someone else buried my children?"

"No," whispered Sam. He was aghast at the vividness of her memory and the raw emotion that was pouring from her. He felt like he was experiencing it for himself, like her story was reopening the wounds of his own family. His mind had partly connected to hers, adding imagery and memory to her words. It was like participating in her loss. He knew what they had looked like, how they had laughed and how they had smiled.

"I couldn't imagine doing that. I don't think that makes you terrible at all. It makes you human."

"I was, for another night only."

"The next day I spent on their graves, crying and then sleeping, only to wake and cry again. I was burned red by the sun and I cared nothing at all for that pain. That pain was nothing. My heart was broken. I had no other reason left on this earth to live, not even for my sister. I sat there all day, with my hands dug into the soil of the graves of my family. I was happy that Adama was with his daughters again. In his eyes, the entirety of creation had revolved around their every breath. I was the only one left behind, the one left to suffer. I alone was in misery. They were together for eternity."

She wiped her eyes, opening them at last.

"*Az ona faghat khaterehashon beja mimone.*"

"What?" Sam asked curiously.

He had heard what she had said, but didn't understand any of it. It was said softly and quietly, reverently, as though it was something she treasured.

"It is Persian. A very beautiful language, I think. It rolls off the tongue like a song. It means "the only thing that will be left is their memories". I was very young when I heard those words, too young to know what they meant exactly. They are simple words that conceal a very deep meaning. Only age and maturity reveal how deep they go. Or perhaps pain; some great loss that comes when you are at an age to understand it fully. My father said those words to me once and once only, when his brother, my uncle, died. I was young at the time and I don't think he ever knew that I remembered what he said. I think it was because I saw the anguish on his face and so I knew the words were important to him. I often wondered if perhaps his father had said it to him. You would know, if you had ever met my father, that he was never upset. He found joy and beauty in everything. I once found a dead bird and he told me that it was to be respected, for its life was at an end. It had served its purpose in creation and was now returning to the earth to begin anew. Life was a grand mystery to him and he enjoyed every day like it was a secret to be revealed. He was quick to laughter, quick to smile, always the first to help. He spoke those words to me the only time I ever saw him upset, the only time I saw him unable to smile. He bent down and kissed me on the forehead and whispered them into my ear. And so I remembered those words. I only understood them when he died, when I came to realize that he was now only a memory. *Az ona faghat khaterehashon beja mimone*."

"My family is now only a memory," Sam whispered, his own eyes flooded with silent tears.

"They are not forgotten. Their memory is a powerful thing; the last piece of them still lives within you. Treasure it, keep it safe, and do not let it spoil. Find their beauty in your memories."

"My dreams haunt me. They are not beautiful."

"Your dreams are not your memories. Cast them aside. Remember what was."

"Your sister did not see things the same way."

Lamia shook her head.

"When our father died a part of her died too. She became angry and bitter, but that was not what set her on her path. She came to me that night, I think because she knew I was going to join my family. Somehow she knew that I had given up. She offered me a way to help with the pain. In my grief, I accepted."

"Would you take it back now, if you could?"

"The only thing left of my family is my memories. They were taken into the earth so long ago that their bones are dust; their gravesites have been swallowed by time. If I were dead, they would be truly gone. No. I keep them alive in me. You live for your family; I live for mine."

"That is your purpose?"

Lamia nodded. "I am who I want to be," she said quietly.

Sam reflected on what she had said, finding her more similar to himself than he had thought or could have ever believed. No monster sat by his side, only a grieving mother and widow. He wondered if one day he might be in her place, sitting next to another who was still grappling with the problems he was faced with.

"Your myth will come in time, twisted and warped by those that fear us. Stories grow and become ever more complex. The original truth rapidly fades and is corrupted, bent to serve another purpose."

"You called yourself 'the serpent' and a 'child-killer'?"

"It is my legend, my untruths. But useful to instill fear in those willing to listen."

"What is your truth?"

"I take those that no longer have the will to live, who seek peace in what I can offer them."

"In death?"

"In death."

"You said before that is how you play."

"Time to learn, Samuel. Those are words from my darker side. The hungrier we are, the angrier we are, the more our need controls us. We become our more basic primal self. For some, the play is in the hunt, for some it is the kill, for others it is what comes afterward, when we are sated."

"Is our darker side separate from us?"

"No, it is you; not another entity within us. It is you, all of your darkest thoughts and rages and impulses, all of them allowed to surface, allowed to take form in order to survive."

"You called it play."

"In time, it becomes a game. You will see."

Sam doubted her, hoping he would never see it as a game.

"You doubt me. It is easy to judge when one is so young, so untested. Wait. Time is a great teacher. Analyze your own thoughts and memories and you will see that it has already begun. It is in your nature and it will unfold as it will."

Outside, night had fallen. The last prism of daylight had succumbed to the beckoning call of night.

"I must feed. Come with me. You will see." She stood and offered him her hand. Sam felt his insides quake with hunger.

"Choose, while the choice is yours to make." She looked at him warmly.

Sam took her hand and smiled.

# Chapter 18

"But first, on earth as vampire sent,
Thy corpse shall from its tomb be rent:
Then ghastly haunt thy native place,
And suck the blood of all thy race..."

-Lord Byron, *The Giaour*

They walked for some time without a word between them, as though an understanding had been reached, and within that unspoken treaty the need to talk had been erased.

Sam walked patiently by her side, casually leaving her to decide their destination.

It was Lamia who finally broke the silence.

"Did you find…blocking me… easy?"

She was unsatisfied with that word to describe the experience, but it was close enough and so she had finally surrendered.

Sam thought about it for a moment.

"It was strange. But yes, once I got used to it, I guess it was. Can you teach me a better way?"

She looked at him quickly with surprise and then looked away again, suddenly studying to the path before them.

"No," she said, "I cannot."

"Why?" he asked, expecting her to have a better way, thinking that he had only stumbled onto some primitive and basic solution.

She glared at him, not angrily, but with a look of frustration.

"You...don't understand. What you are able to do already I would have said was impossible. It can take decades, if not centuries to learn to use our abilities effectively. Some of us are far stronger in certain talents than others will ever be, no matter how long we live. I can block a reading mind only if I can catch them by surprise, and then it is like I am striking out with a fist. I can't control it and I can barely describe how it feels. The important difference is that it isn't in my control. A second, more determined attempt, I cannot stop at all. From what you said, for you it is different. You said you could control the experience and plan for it. That you could strike back, using whatever strength you deemed necessary."

Sam looked at her dumbfounded.

"You are unusually strong. I said before that you will come into your powers over time and that they will develop and strengthen. If yours continue to grow, you will be formidable."

Sam absorbed what she had said.

"What are the other talents?" he asked after several minutes of walking quietly.

Lamia reflected before answering him.

"Choosing different animals to change into is one. You have shown your preference for the owl, but others can choose from several creatures, depending on their liking."

"How?" he wondered, thinking about it avidly.

Could he be an eagle or a hawk? Was it possible to be even smaller, like an insect?

"I can't say. I do not have that ability."

"What do you change into when you fly?"

"I become the raven. It is a beautiful bird; majestic."

"I suppose," he said, not really confident that he had ever seen a raven before. Crows yes, but not a raven. Weren't they just big crows? He thought better than to ask.

"What else?"

"The next step from reading someone's thoughts is controlling them through their thoughts, encouraging them to act in a certain way, a way that is desirable for the end you wish to achieve."

"Mind control?"

"Yes and no. It is more of an influence, a suggestion as to what you want someone to do. Their mind is theirs alone and can never be controlled, but it can be steered, if they are in the right mind set."

"And what is that? If they are afraid?"

"No. Fear is paralyzing. If the person is afraid they are useless and closed to suggestion. They must be at ease and free from distraction, or at least not concentrating on anything else. A relaxed mind is one that can be influenced."

She pointed ahead.

"We are nearly there."

A stately waist-high black iron fence emerged from the darkness, bordering a well-manicured property, complete with groomed trees and trimmed hedges.

A low fog clung to the grass like a rippling blanket.

Sam paused.

"It's a graveyard," he said, his mouth growing dry. Visions of his nightmares seeped into his mind. Four empty coffins set before seated mourners.

"Yes."

Lamia approached the fence and stepped *through* it, delayed only for a moment by the cold metal.

He barely noticed what she had done.

Lamia looked at him quizzically, waiting for him to follow.

He was frozen in his tracks, looking at the grounds uneasily.

"Well?" she said impatiently.

He looked at her and swallowed the lump in his throat.

"Bad dreams," he replied.

"They are only dreams. Come."

He tried to banish his memories from his mind.

The graveyard seemed to mock him, calling him forward as if as a dare from his dreams. His heart thumped heavily in his chest. The memory of the sod closing in over him flashed in his eyes; the closing darkness above his outstretched hands.

He heard their voices clearly. "Now we are together, forever," Miranda had said to him in that awful darkness. He saw the eyes; the six glowing, yellow eyes.

His mind recoiled as if he had been punched hard in the gut, doubling him over and leaving him painfully gasping for air.

The dream was gone.

Lamia stood before him impassively, watching him recover.

He saw her eyes were black.

"What? Why?" he croaked still feeling the phantom pain in his sides.

"Pain is a powerful motivator and it can be created without causing you physical damage. I played with your mind, nothing more."

"I was distracted. You said mind control works better if the mind is clear."

"I didn't control your mind, nor did I enter your mind. That was entirely different.

Are you ready to come?"

He stood upright with a wince as one last image from the ghastly funeral played through his memory: *"I will fear no evil: For thou art with me."*

The irony almost made him cry.

He would fear no evil for he was in the company of evil. It was his guardian and he was its apprentice.

Lamia walked through the fence again, towards him, giving it scant attention as she did so.

Sam paused at it, pressing his leg to the metal.

It was cold and wet, chilling his flesh.

"Through," Lamia said quietly.

He felt her mind change somewhat as she said the word, like she had changed her perspective momentarily.

*Through* was not a command, it was an explanation.

Sam saw her eyes were still black.

It was her hunger, taking some sort of physical manifestation over her.

He stepped forward, trying to somehow continue.

The fence stopped him easily.

"Look at me," Lamia said.

Sam looked at her.

"Clear your mind. Look behind me, towards the grass and the trees. Think of where you want to be. Think of walking through an open field. No obstruction. There is nothing to impede you. There is nothing to impair your way. You and the fence are made of the same material. Allow it to become you, and allow yourself to become the fence. It is a part of you, for only a moment. The fence is an extension of yourself. *Through.*"

"Through," Sam repeated hesitantly.

He tried to copy how he had felt her mind shift, changing his thinking.

The world swam before his senses, shifting and altering into another state of being altogether.

She was right.

Everything was the same; nothing was different.

He was brethren to everything around him.

The trees, the grass, the very air itself were all intricately connected.

So was he; only his mind had created an artificial barrier between them.

There was no barrier. He was one with everything.

The fence became a part of his leg; its atoms and the vast spaces between them becoming a part of him, moving through him like tiny solar systems in a vast and orderly universe.

He was *through*.

He felt invigorated.

Lamia was looking at him as though she had observed something she had not noticed before. She said nothing, ignoring his elation. Only the look of her face betrayed the appearance of a calm demeanor. Something was troubling her.

"Come," she said finally, smoothing her features.

They wandered the graveyard silently, through the trees and hedges only, never in the wide open spaces between.

Sam felt Lamia change, feeling her enter an open state of awareness.

Was it the same for him? Did he do the same thing?

He felt her hunting and he unknowingly fed off of her energies, becoming attuned to her own senses.

Sam smelled her before he saw her.

Lamia tensed.

"Stay here; I must go alone. It is my game now."

Her eyes were pinpricked with churning yellow cores.

Sam acquiesced, lowering himself near to the base of the tree they were behind.

She strode out into the open graveyard, silently stepping in and amongst the stones and markers towards the grieving woman who was her quarry.

Sam was unable to tear his eyes from them.

The woman's scent was powerful, hanging heavily in the air. It was the odor of grief and pain and silent mindless agony.

Sam relished it, inhaling it deeply. He wanted to follow, to partake in the stalk.

Lamia was different altogether. She smelled of confidence and hunger, of the desperate need to feed. Behind it, under it, was a subtly different scent.

Sam recognized it with difficulty, so weak was its taste.

It was sadness and a terrible understanding. It was cold mercy.

Lamia came in beside the old woman who was stooped low over the granite marker. She was motionless, one curled finger on her right hand sadly tracing the fine carving of the name cut into the freshly engraved stone.

Her weeping was done; the energy spent and exhausted. Only her pain remained, unquenched and visceral.

Lamia knelt by her side, one arm over her back in a kind and reassuring gesture, like a daughter comforting her distraught mother.

Sam knew she was talking to the grieving woman, but what she said was lost to him, somehow undetectable. There was a hint that something was passing between the two of them, something he was not permitted to share. There was a wall there, but this wall was vast and unyielding, a force that scoffed at his tiny attempts to listen.

Time passed indefinitely, and then the old woman nodded, turning to take Lamia into her arms as she would take the most entrusted of companions.

There was no reservation, no reluctance.

In all of that sadness and despair, he caught a scent of welcome relief; of hope.

They embraced and he sensed Lamia begin to feed.

He wanted in, to taste and to drink and to share.

He recoiled backwards, falling into the tall grass behind him, appalled at how easily her feelings had blended into his own, becoming a part of him.

He beat at his head with his fists to get her out, to get her away, to pull back from her invitation to join her.

Sam sensed something strange; a feeling of Lamia and a trickle of energy, that she was doing something to the old woman with it.

He didn't want to know any more.

*"NO, NO! Not her! Not like this!"* he screamed in his mind.

He broke free, panting in the grass, his appetite gripping at his innards and twisting painfully without remorse.

There he waited, not wanting to see any more, fighting to ignore the pain and the need to consume. If he did watch, if he rose to see her, he was afraid he would not be able to resist. He was losing the battle; the scent was too powerful, the energies he could feel from Lamia were too close.

Sam turned and fled, anxious and desperate to be away.

He could not feed on someone like that, that was not something he could tolerate, that was something he could not live with.

The old woman was good and kind.

He could not kill her; he could not feed off of her. If he did that, he would cross a line, a line he was terrified to cross. It might mean that he was no different than that which he despised most.

Sam collapsed under a tree, finally far enough away to be removed from Lamia's emotions or at least far enough that he could suppress them and deny them further strength.

He could feel her motivations but they were faint and removed, only a hint of what they once were.

Sam faced the ground and drew his legs up to his belly, curled up like a turtle with his hands over the back of his neck, clenched tightly while his body convulsed with a vicious energy.

He was not alone.

The presence was there, suddenly, awakening all of his senses like a light switch had suddenly been flicked on.

He had been unaware before, as he had been trying to shut out the powerful emanations from Lamia. Now that he was away and isolated, the other presence finally came through, weak and small in comparison but definitely there.

Sam felt a cold blade press to his neck, the point digging into his skin without breaking it.

"Give me your wallet."

Sam reacted instantly, grabbing the knife hand and pulling it to the ground while rising himself, pushing the owner aside and knocking him off balance.

Sam clenched his fist and felt the arm bones snap beneath his fingers. His would-be assailant cried out before he hit the ground, the scream ending abruptly when the impact winded him.

Sam released the broken arm and gripped the man by his neck, lifting him into the air and pressing him against the rough bark of a pine tree.

He was in his early forties and rough-shaven, heavy set from years of inactivity and excess drinking. Sam winced at his smell; it was that of cheap cigars, stale beer and infrequent bathing.

Sam reached out with his mind, probing for who this person was.

He felt a panicked rush of thoughts and images course through his mind.

*Whatthefuckwhatthefuckwhatthefuck* the man kept repeating, wondering how things had gone so badly so quickly.

"Let me go, man," he hissed, trying to breathe in hitching gasps. "I wasn't gonna hurtcha," he sputtered.

Sam saw a brief flash of the knife sinking into his neck. A moment of what could have been.

"Really?" Sam replied casually.

Sam recognized the tone in his voice; it was the same dark voice as in the alley, and by the campfire with those kids.

The man tried to nod as quickly and as best he could. "Promise."

"Then why the knife?"

Sam could see the terror in the man's eyes, the reflection from his own yellow eyes glistened back to him.

Sam released his grip ever so slightly, enough to let the man speak with a little more clarity.

His fear smelled delectable.

"To…to make you listen. I p-promise."

Sam searched the man's thoughts in a moment, sifting through years of experiences and memories and information. His name.

"What's your name?" Sam asked dreadfully.

"Stephen," he choked, "Steve."

Sam tightened his grip, not stopping until the man began to choke and cough.

Sam laughed in disgust and rising anger.

"You lie, Andrew."

Sam loosened his grip until he could breathe again.

"Jesus Christ man, let me go and I won't tell nobody!" he pleaded, spittle spraying over his lips uncontrollably.

"You beat your wife, Andrew," Sam said coolly.

Another vision came to light. Screams.

"And your children."

Andrew shook his head desperately, trying to deny it.

"Do you know your wife has a suitcase packed up so she can leave you?"

Sam didn't know how he knew it, but he knew it was perfectly true. It was in the basement, hidden behind a couple of blankets. She was waiting to save just a little more money before she caught a Greyhound on whatever run took her and her kids out of town, in any direction, away from this asshole forever.

"She is going to take your kids away from you, Andrew. You're a coward, aren't you, Andrew? A coward that feels stronger by beating on helpless children."

Andrew glared at Sam.

"Fuck you, man. Those little shits deserve it. And so does their bitch of a mother.

Fucking cunt."

Sam could smell his instant anger; it was uncontrollable and all-consuming, a hatred that burned until he beat it out of whoever was closest to him. Sometimes it was the children. Most of the time it was their mother.

To Sam, the emotion exuded a scent that was enticing, even better than Andrew's earlier fear. It was still there, and the two mixed wonderfully, like sugar and cream.

"She won't have to leave you now, Andrew. I'm going to take care of that personally."

Andrew reached out with his legs, trying to kick Sam soundly, to break his grip.

Sam laughed with amusement. It was solemn and echoed deeply through the woods.

"Say good bye, Andrew. This is the last moment of your miserable life."

The air became saturated with fear and anger and blinding white hate. Sam thought it was delightful.

His fingers clenched into the man's neck, tearing into his skin and sinking deeply into the flesh behind his windpipe. When Andrew began to gargle, Sam tore out his throat, throwing the severed flesh over his shoulder.

He drank deeply, like a lost man happening across a clear mountain stream. He drank until his thirst and hunger were slaked, the burning craving within his belly satisfied and put to sleep.

He released the corpse to the ground, letting it crumple unceremoniously. Sam was unconcerned; Andrew didn't deserve any better.

Sam knelt, satisfied.

A pleasant chuckle came from behind him.

"See? You have already begun your game."

Lamia came to his side and knelt beside him, inspecting his kill and looking deeply into Sam's eyes, looking for something that only she would recognize.

Her smile was controlled but genuine, all-knowing.

"Game?" he asked, wiping his mouth clean.

"You play with them, like a cat with a mouse. Don't claim you don't know what I am talking about. The memory is still fresh within you, even I can see that, and I can feel your other feedings. You wondered how this could become a game. You toy with them, taking satisfaction in their terror and fear. To you it is flavorful, like the richest of any spice, a flavor to make any other spice you've known before seem pale and flat, like stale bread. You like to amuse yourself with your prey."

She laid a hand upon his shoulder.

Her touch was soft and gentle, welcoming and approving.

Sam looked at her hand for a moment, not expecting the familiar gesture.

"Dispose of this; it is doubtful he will ever be missed."

She looked at the corpse with disdain, disgusted not by the remains but by the person Andrew was.

"Spread him out, far and wide. He does not deserve a grave. The coyote and the raven and the beetle will take care of the rest. I will help you."

"Don't you need to hide yours?"

"No, there is no need."

She saw the confusion on his face.

"Come see; you will understand."

"I don't want…" he protested, not wanting to see what he expected to see; the torn remains of an old grieving woman.

"Come," she insisted, "come, and you will understand."

\*\*\*

Sam looked down at the body, confused. There was nothing that hinted at any sort of violence, none whatsoever. The woman was just lying there on the grass, a peaceful and rested look on her face.

"I don't understand," Sam said, looking at her neck for any sort of damage.

There was nothing besides what would be expected on the neck of an octogenarian.

Age spots.

Wrinkles.

"So much pain," Lamia said quietly, "and now she is at rest."

Sam looked up at her, seeking an explanation. He was not expecting to see the trace of tears on her face, their marks clear upon her perfect skin.

"How?"

"It is a skill I have had time to hone, a practice that conceals my presence. Before death I return some small part of her life force back to her, healing my marks upon her. There is no trace of my crossing her path. Her family will believe she died in mourning."

"She asked for it," Sam understood, somewhat amazed.

Lamia nodded.

"She wanted an end to her suffering, an end to what could be years of more pain. I granted her final request."

"You are not a killer," Sam marvelled aloud, reanalyzing his perception of her.

"Oh I am a killer," she replied, "of that there is no doubt. I hunger for her blood just as you hungered for his. I took her life and used it to perpetuate my own. To my marrow, I am the dark creature feared in legend."

"I meant it differently," Sam answered her.

"I have a choice of what kind of killer I want to be Samuel. I can be random and cruel, feeding off of fear and enjoying those last moments of mortal recognition. The choice is mine. I choose mercy, to be permitted to end the suffering of those whose suffering I have known all too well. I choose before it is chosen for me."

"Graveyards?" Sam asked.

"Where better to find those who might seek my most tender affection? This is the part of my legend that has remained truthful, the only part that is accurate. They are alone and able to bare their pain to a sympathetic ear."

"Do you force them? Suggest it?"

"I offer a solution. For many, the fear of death is a fear of the unknown. The unknown time of its arrival. Today? Tomorrow? In middle age? I can give that answer."

"I couldn't hear you talking to her. It was all too faded."

"I wasn't always speaking to her in a way that you could hear."

Sam was confused again. What did she mean?

"I was speaking with her through her mind, touching her thoughts."

"You can do that?"

She gave him a look that told him the question was pointless and the answer obvious.

"I start by speaking with them, to get them used to the sound of my voice, so they don't get startled or put on edge. Grief is a very private emotion, one that most people find embarrassing. I must approach softly to keep them open to talking with me."

"And then what?"

"When I feel they are receptive; I speak through their mind."

"And they do it back?"

Sam hadn't heard the old woman talking back to Lamia at all.

"Once I open the way for them, they do it without realizing it."

"I couldn't listen in to what you were thinking to each other."

"No, what is spoken in that fashion remains between the two involved. A third mind cannot become involved."

"What if it does?"

"It cannot. It has never happened, to any of us. There is a wall, a divide that no one has been able to cross. I cannot explain it. It just is."

"Is it mind control, speaking to her like that?"

"It is nothing like that. Speaking within her mind is very intimate, very private. Not only the words are shared, but the feelings as well. The feelings from both of us."

"So she would know if you were being deceitful."

"Yes."

"That's risky," Sam said.

"I do not lie when I make my offer. They know that I understand their pain. That is the great equalizer, to know that someone in that vulnerable moment understands how you feel."

"They understand you mean to take their life."

"And they understand that I mean to give them peace. Through me, they can feel their heart and mind put at ease. I can be salvation."

"There must still be fear from the people you approach."

"There is fear, but it is lessened. When Death stares you in the eyes, its randomness stripped away and revealed to you, that stare can be welcoming. There are worse things in this world than death. I am confirmation of life after death; I can be the Gate into Heaven."

"Or into Hell," Sam added.

Lamia smiled coldly.

"Have you been refused?"

"Yes, and from those, my legend was created."

"You did not kill them anyways? The people you revealed yourself to?"

"No. They are few and far between. I am very good at my game, a skilled player. Some regretted their refusal, and later waited for me to return."

"Did you?"

"Eventually, yes."

"What do you feel, when they accept?" He wondered if it was the same bloodlust and satisfaction that he felt when he decided the time to strike had come.

"It feels like love."

"Love?"

"Peace."

"Is it easy?"

"You would not have opposed me if I had come to you, grieving your wife and children. You would have accepted my offer, and I think you would have given me your neck gratefully."

Sam felt chilled, feeling the truth in her words.

"Yes," he replied. "Yes, I would have."

He would have prayed for the darkness to take him; he would have embraced it.

"Would you now? Think carefully and answer truthfully."

The question confused him and surprised him all at once. For a few brief moments, he couldn't clear his thoughts.

And then, like sand in stirred water, his doubts settled and the water became clear.

"No."

Lamia was watching him with a keen interest, her eyes never breaking from his own. Her stare should have been awkward and unsettling, but it wasn't. When he finally answered her she seemed satisfied.

"When grief clouds your mind again, and it will, remember the answer you gave me today. It is the answer brought forth from a mind at ease, a mind untroubled."

He looked down at the old lady one last time.

Sam found that he didn't pity her; she had lived a good and long life. He also didn't envy her; the time had passed when he wished for death. He had some trouble deciding how he was feeling. It had been a while since he had felt it.

When it came to him, he recognized it at last.

He was content.

# Chapter 19

*"We will go no further.*
*Here begins the land of phantoms."*

-Nosferatu (1922)

Sam sat quietly on the bench in City Park, staring blankly at the mirror-like surface of Duck Lake. He had arrived in Denver the night before, wandering its streets and becoming familiar with its more natural areas, preferring them over the harsh unwelcoming scents of asphalt and concrete.

He had left Lamia asleep in the grotto, careful to not disturb her rest. He had sensed her awaken some time later, aware that she did not follow him, something that simultaneously pleased and displeased him. He was growing comfortable with her company, and now that he was alone he found that he missed her presence.

He cleared his mind. It was better that he was alone. If Lamia were nearby he felt that she might be a distraction. He needed time on his own, if only for a few days, time to think. More importantly, he needed time to just be himself.

No, he thought, he needed time to rediscover himself.

Alone, there was no sense of interference, no mingling of Lamia's thoughts with his. With her, he could feel her appetite grow; he could feel her emotions. In turn, they stimulated his senses.

He did not know to what degree he was being influenced by Lamia, either by accident or by design, and so he had made the decision to leave, if only temporarily.

Sam was gratified to discover that he was much more aware of his surroundings than he once had been.

He was able to discern the activity in the park and to pay attention to what interested him. All other extraneous sights and sounds and smells were no longer confusing.

What he enjoyed most was the anonymity. Sitting on a park bench was an escape in plain sight, somewhere where he could sit out in the open and still be overlooked.

People did not pay attention to a single man sitting on a park bench, so normal was the expectation of a passerby to see just that. Sam sat on the bench and studied those that passed him, learning what he could from them in the few moments when they were close. He discovered that it was easier with people that hadn't noticed him. He also found that in sitting on the bench, just off the path, people came to him. He did not need to seek them out.

There were a few joggers that liked to run in the early evening, in the subdued twilight when the air was still warm from the day. He could tell who ran the path regularly, sensing their comfort in following a path taken many times before. Some of them noticed him, most did not. It was the women that saw him, more often than not. Most of the men that passed by paid him no attention at all, at least nothing more than the recognition of a man sitting on a bench. The women were instantly wary, especially those that frequented the area.

He was unusual, out of place. The feeling triggered a response within him, the recognition of their fear.

He enjoyed it.

It was a predator/prey response, the same feeling that a wolf or a falcon felt when their prey took flight. It was a feeling of power, a sense of enjoyment derived by knowing that he was feared.

*No*, he thought, angry at himself for feeling as he did. He squashed the feeling, not wanting any part of it. He did not want to enjoy the uneasiness of people that had nothing to fear from him.

Sam discovered that by trying to ignore the feeling, he decreased the awareness of his other senses, like he had covered his ears or dimmed the lights. Only by giving in to his instincts was he fully aware of everything around him. He had to allow himself to feel what they felt, if he was to be able to learn as much as he could.

It was then, entirely unexpectedly, that he became aware of something else.

It began as a recognition of the same feeling he had felt, that of a predator stalking its prey, only it wasn't coming from him. Not wanting to be obvious, he refrained from turning around, trusting his other senses to lead him in the right direction.

The feeling grew whenever someone traveled on the path, specifically a woman.

A twig snapped and Sam could hear a bush being pushed aside, slowly and cautiously.

It was a man. A man hunting women on the path.
The man was looking for a victim, someone traveling alone. He wanted someone young, someone fit, and someone that he could enjoy overpowering. It was not the act of rape that satisfied him, it was the pleasure he gleaned in watching the terror fade from their eyes as they took their last breath.

It was his intention to find a victim tonight.

Sam rose from the bench and slipped into the shadows, becoming one with the darkness. Sam followed the scent easily, undisturbed by the foliage in his path.

The small trees and bushes were like the wire of the fence and he allowed them to flow *through*, and so he travelled in silence through the woods, closing the distance to his quarry. Sam could hear the man's heart beating, a droning *thump thump* that was as clear as a drum in the quiet woods.

Sam closed the distance and fell in behind the man quietly, not betraying his presence. Sam smiled darkly and watched him looking out over the path, oblivious to his own danger. A girl came around the bend, her ponytail swinging with each stride as she ran, the exercise her nightly ritual after a long day at work.

Sam reached out with his mind, wanting to know more.
*His name was Jeff.*

Jeff rose, meaning to slip between the narrow gaps of two bushes that grew up to the very edge of the path. Once there, he would wait for her to come within his reach and then he could pull her away, kicking and screaming into the undergrowth.

There he would slowly watch her die. Killing her quickly was no fun at all.

Sam coolly cocked his head to one side, his anger building.

Jeff had done this before, moving from city to city, leaving a path of missing victims across the country.

The girl could be Miranda.

The girl could be Cindy.

He took hold of a nearby branch and purposefully snapped it, letting it drop to the ground.

"What?" Jeff said, startled by the sound behind him.

Jeff turned and saw the outline of someone behind him, an outline that was marked with the burning glow of two hellish eyes. He felt his insides loosen in fear.

Sam smiled. This was a fear that he could savour; a fear to be relished.

Sam detected the change in Jeff's scent, from perverted lust to fright and laughed coldly, taking a hold of the man at the jawline and pushing him down to his knees.

Jeff struggled furiously, trying to break Sam's grip, but he could not. Jeff was six foot two and thickly muscled, unused to be beaten in a physical contest.

Sam lowered himself to Jeff's ear.

"I will not let you," Sam hissed.

"Let me go," Jeff pleaded, still trying to loosen Sam's grip around his throat.

"Let you go?" Sam whispered inquisitively, "Why would I want to do that?"

Sam recalled Lamia's words to him.

*You have already begun your game.*

"I'll leave her alone."

"Yes, you will," Sam agreed, nodding his head ever so slightly, "You will leave them all alone."

Sam did not want to kill him, not just yet, so he was careful, knowing what he needed to do.

Sam carefully snapped his neck with a sharp twist of his hands, feeling Jeff collapse to the ground as a gasp escaped from his mouth.

Jeff looked up at him fearfully, his eyes full of questions.

"Paralyzed," Sam chuckled.

The girl ran past the clearing, oblivious to her good fortune.

"It would be a waste to kill you quickly, don't you think?" Sam asked conversationally. He spoke aloud, in a normal volume, unafraid of being overheard.

There was no one else around.

Sam scooped Jeff up in his arms, careful of his neck, and walked him down to the shoreline.

Once there, he walked out into the water slowly, taking his time.

"I am going to drown you in the lake," Sam told him, "deep enough that you will not easily be found."

Sam was now up to his waist in water and it was getting deeper with each step.

He could feel the sense of terror growing in Jeff.

Jeff was used to violence, acts of sudden aggression to achieve satisfaction.

Sam's casual conversation about his coming death was filling him with dread.

Sam breathed in the scent and relished it.

It was a more satisfying sensation than if he had fed off him.

"The tricky part with drowning is that a body eventually rises to the surface. Do you know how to keep a body from rising?" Sam asked him.

Jeff of course couldn't respond.

"It's very simple. All you have to do is puncture the bowels deeply enough that the gas can escape. Then, the body will never float to the top."

Sam looked into Jeff's eyes, seeing the dawning horror in them.

"Good," Sam laughed whole-heartedly, "I'd hoped you would understand. It would be a waste if you hadn't."

Sam was now up in water to his chest.

"Deep enough, I think," Sam said.

"If you are a praying man, this is your time."'

With that, Sam drove one hand into Jeff's bowels, eviscerating him neatly.

Jeff blinked, the greatest response he could muster.

Sam held Jeff out over the water.

"Time to die," Sam whispered, releasing Jeff into the water.

His eyes wide with fear, Jeff quickly sank to the bottom.

Sam stood there, looking down where Jeff had disappeared.

Jeff was invisible under the black water, but Sam could feel his panic.

It was immensely satisfying, feeling Jeff drown beneath him.

Enjoying the sensation of terror, Sam slipped below the waves and finished Jeff in privacy, rising to the surface a minute later.

Sam was quiet, thinking to himself.

Sam walked out of the lake and along the shore, annoyed by the feel of his wet clothes. He wanted to be dry, to be warm and he crossed his arms over his chest reflexively. Sam thought about being warm and a feeling grew in his belly, a sensation that spread outwards from his core to his extremities.

Sam left the path and walked into the woods, seeking shelter.

Steam rose from his clothing and he smiled, concentrating on feeling warm.

He wondered if Lamia could do this as well.

As his clothes dried he understood the price he paid to do this.

Getting warm took energy, and the sensation turned into something far more pressing.

He was hungry again; hungry enough that he did not want to suffer through a restless sleep.

***

Sam found him walking along East Quincy Avenue in Cherry Hills, a wealthy subdivision where a modest home began at well over a million dollars and the pricier ones ran into eight figures. In the middle of the night the streets were quiet and abandoned; the ideal place to walk unnoticed.

In the summer months Ian scoped out the select neighborhood for an easy mark; a residence whose tenants were away on vacation, usually somewhere foreign and exotic. It took some time to deduce what properties were vacant, but Ian was never in a rush. It was his first rule of business.

Taking short cuts created mistakes.

His second rule was to never use a vehicle. A slow car was easy to notice, especially over the course of several evenings, and so he walked. Walking made things slower, but it had its advantages. It was easier to hide if someone was coming, and it was easier to notice things; things that could be muffled by the noise of a running engine.

Walking also allowed for more flexibility in taking advantage of spontaneous opportunities. If he noticed something, it was easier to react than to have to worry about where he could park his ride and hope that no one saw him. As it was, he dressed as inconspicuously as possible.

Dark jeans and a dark grey shirt made detection more difficult, while being less obvious than if he had been wearing all black.

Ian was twenty-one, white, smart, and fancied himself a modern version of Robin Hood; where he and his fence were the sole recipients of the fruits of his labors. A blend of Robin Hood and Jack the Ripper.

He had learned from his past errors and had gone for nearly two years without an arrest, building up a criminal record that had started in his early teens and was now almost four pages long.

The house on the right promised to enrich him. The owners had taken all of the predictable countermeasures. The lights had been programmed to come on to look like someone was home. The mail was taken in every day, the sprinklers came on and the lawn was mowed.

But the dog was gone.

It was always outside, resting by the front steps and growling at those who passed by.

To Ian, it was a dead ringer.

They had gone away on a trip and had either taken the dog with them or had placed it in a kennel.

Which didn't matter to him; all that mattered was that the absence of the dog was painfully obvious, if you paid attention to routine and detail.

The house may or may not have an alarm; that didn't matter either. It wouldn't take him long to check for that, and he knew his way around most of the alarms on the market. If he triggered an alarm, he would be gone before the police showed up anyways. Sometimes, he did that on purpose. Setting off an alarm for several nights in a row gave the impression of a faulty system, giving him more time before it would generate a response. On occasion, there would be no response at all.

He hadn't come tonight looking to steal from the house.

He had come for the teenage girl that lived here.

She too had a pattern.

Shortly after eleven thirty she would sneak out of her ground floor room, through the window, and go through a large lilac bush to escape her yard unseen. From there, she went to see friends. She was usually back before one.

Ian was not dissuaded.

Tonight, he would take what he could from the house.

He would come back later and take what he wanted from the girl.

He would wait for her in the lilac bush and sedate her there. When she was unconscious, he would do what he wanted and leave her.

They usually didn't survive.

He would have what he wanted, one way or another.

Ian walked to the edge of the property and stopped at the fence line, looking around nonchalantly to see if the coast was clear.

It was dead quiet.

Ian put his hands on the top of the wall in preparation of climbing over it, to disappear behind it and get cover.

He loved walls and bushes; they hid him perfectly while he worked.

He was about to jump up when a figure appeared beside him.

He was lost in the dim shadow of the streetlight; a silhouette under a low tree.

"No," the figure said.

Ian stopped and turned to face him, mildly curious and prepared to run.

"Fuck you, man," Ian replied.

He must have missed someone out on a walk, someone that, against all odds, had seen him.

The figure said nothing and did not move.

Ian took a step towards the shadow, his motion full of swagger, meaning to bluff.

"Run," the figure said.

"What?" Ian replied cockily, wanting to laugh. Just who the hell did this guy think he was, telling him to run? Once he lost his front teeth he would sing a different tune.

"I said run," the figure said.

"Hey man, fu…" Ian began.

He stuttered when two glowing eyes suddenly stared at him out of the darkness.

At first he wanted to discount them as a trick of the light, some reflection, but then he saw them blink.

The hairs on the back of his neck stood on end.

Ian stopped where he stood and his mouth dried up, suddenly unsure.

He inexplicably needed to urinate.

His car was three blocks over; he could be there in less than two minutes, if he ran full out.

The shadow took a step towards him and emerged from the shade into the pale glow cast by the street light.

When Ian saw him fully, his stomach clenched in fear.

"Oh man," he croaked, not believing his eyes.

The figure laughed, a low menacing sound that made Ian feel weak in the knees.

Ian turned and bolted.

He didn't know what the fuck he had just seen but he had seen some scary movies in his day and that had reminded of all of them combined into one.

He was cold with fright, afraid like he had never been afraid before.

Ian ran a hundred yards before he looked over his shoulder, expecting to see the figure in the distance, still standing by the shadow at the wall.

It wasn't.

It was behind him, running just as fast as he was but with a grace and ease that suggested that this pace wasn't very hard at all.

Worst of all, it was grinning, grinning a mouthful of white pointed teeth.

Ian gulped and ran, wetting his pants.

The figure laughed.

Ian knew he was running for his life and he ran as fast as his legs would carry him.

He rounded the corner of the block and looked behind again.

It was closer than before and grinning just as terribly, with a look in its eyes that made him want to vomit.

His lungs were beginning to burn.

He was running at a pace he couldn't keep up for much longer, a pace that was being fueled by terror and adrenaline alone.

Ian didn't look back again; he could hear the figure running behind him, getting ever closer.

He thought he could feel its breath on his neck.

Then he felt its hands grab him by the shoulders and pull him down.

There was no time to scream.

***

Sam knelt in the small clearing of a greenbelt, feeling life and energy beating in his veins. Around him, in the trees and the bushes and the grass, he could feel life encircle him. He was still flush with excitement, recalling the pursuit that had filled him with a satisfaction he had never known. It was almost as satisfying as when had pulled the thief down and tore out his throat, the scream dying in his chest.

Lamia had been right; he had begun his game.

He did not have to be like Lilith.

He could find meaning in how he survived.

He did not regret taking the two lives tonight; both of them deserved far worse than they had received under his care.

Sam looked up at the night sky at the familiar stars.

He would stay here for another night before returning to Loveland, another night to explore.

Then he would return and learn from Lamia.

He had questions.

# Chapter 20

The Reverend Paul Kowalczyk sat at his desk, kneading his temples in a gesture meant to loosen the grip of a headache that refused to budge, despite the four aspirin that he had dry-swallowed thirty minutes earlier. The bitter taste lingered in his mouth, a reminder of their failure. It wasn't a hangover that he was coping with, and oh, how a hangover might be a lovely reason to feel so terrible. At least with a hangover he could have experienced the pleasant drunken stupor that came beforehand and would feel justified in his current condition.

This was insomnia.

He just couldn't sleep.

Up until this point in his life, sleep had been something he had taken for granted. He had never understood insomnia, having no well of experience to draw from for personal reference. Since his earliest moments he recalled how easily he had been able to find sweet comfort in a good night's sleep.

Now that comfort evaded him like a thief in a maze of dark, smoky alleys.

It used to be such a simple thing.

Step one: lay down.

Step two: place head on pillow.

Step three: adjust blanket.

And just like that, sleep would always take him. It was like switching off a light.

He had never tossed and turned for more than five minutes any night of his life.

Until very recently.

To be more precise; until he had faced Lilith down on the street in front of the First United Presbyterian Church in Loveland, Colorado.

He had relived that experience over and over again in his mind, night after night.

He knew they were dreams, he knew what was going to happen, and each time that knowledge made no difference. He still woke screaming, his bedclothes soaked through and clinging to his back. He was covered in a cold clammy sweat that felt dirty and unclean.

*Lilith.*

He rubbed his temples a little more furiously, feeling the pain under his fingertips.

It helped, if only for a moment.

Nothing in his experience had come close to preparing him for what he had encountered, and he had considered himself well exposed to the supernatural.

He had seen ghosts and spirits and phantoms. He had felt their touch; felt them staring at him in dark cold basements and in dusty attics they had claimed as their own. Good and evil were known to him. He thought he knew them intimately.

Until now.

He would be reluctant to admit it to anyone, but he had always felt that the Bible was a collection of pre-historic fables; stories passed down from one generation to another that told a story of some common truth or virtue, with the occasional retelling of a witnessed natural disaster.

A form of Dr. Seuss from 10,000 BC.

One fish two fish, red Samaritan blue Samaritan.

Every major religion shared similar stories, tales woven from common threads that emboldened and verified his personal beliefs.

Christianity tells the story of the Great Flood, and of Noah who built a great ship in which to survive the disaster. Ancient Sumer speaks of a much older tale of Utnapishtim, a man who, like Noah, was warned of a coming flood and who built a ship in preparation of its coming. Science had provided a very possible natural disaster that could have provided inspiration for such a story; the flooding and creation of the Black Sea at the end of the last ice age. Paul felt it was entirely reasonable that some Stone Age civilization or culture could have perceived the steady flooding of that dry basin as a flooding of the world. They knew so little of it. They had been so taken by the event that the memory of it was written down for posterity and embraced as a religious event, as there had been no scientific understanding of the natural world at that time. Everything was controlled and governed by gods of one name or another.

A pile of books sat on the corner of his desk, each book thoroughly scrutinized and dog-eared. He had become somewhat of an expert on Lilith and Lamia over the past several days; at least an expert on what he could find.

Lilith; with whom he had fought in the street.

The very same Lilith mentioned in the Epic of Gilgamesh?

He couldn't discount it out of hand.

Lamia; with whom he had spoken.

The same Lamia feared by the ancient Greeks and Romans?

The mythical Lamia? The *factual* Lamia? The flesh-and-blood Lamia?

His theological education had discounted them out of hand. Their names had arisen in his studies, but only in order to understand their context or hidden meanings. They were manifestations or symbols, sins and fears given names in order that they might be understood and learned from. He had studied their evolution and roles in multiple faiths and cultures over centuries.

Over millennia.

He shivered at the thought.

Millennia. They had already been entrenched in Sumerian lore; how much farther back did it go?

He was interacting with people - no, *creatures* he corrected himself; they were no longer human - *creatures* that had existed seemingly since the dawn of history, interweaving themselves into the lore of the earliest of civilizations.

They were bound to be wise, and in experience they would have no equal.

They would be arrogant.

"Would they?" he pondered, trying to think about it without prejudice or bias.

They might be no more or no less susceptible to the faults of mankind than others; their personalities, strengths and weaknesses ingrained from birth.

But the question was; which birth? The personality born of their living existence, or the personality born at their rising from the clutches of death?

Sam had clearly been upset, so grief still existed for him; that part of his human scope of emotion still existed.

*Or.*

Grief might be confused with anger. Wrath. The line between the two was thin.

Wrath.

Greed.

Sloth.

Pride.

Lust.

Envy.

Gluttony.

The cardinal sins, the seven vices.

The transition from grief to anger was miniscule; Paul might have confused Sam's grief for anger. Sam might be confusing the two as well, deceived by his own nature, confused and trapped between the two.

That was a dangerous confusion.

Perhaps all of their emotions would be confused.

Paul rubbed at his temples.

This bloody headache just refused to lay down and die.

Biblical references to either of the two women were rare, often extrapolated from translations or inferences, or disguised as a description of animals.

The reference most referred to was found in Isaiah.

"There shall the Lilith repose, and find for herself a place to rest," Paul mumbled, his finger tracing along underneath the fine script.

Other references were to be found, but scattered over the ages, almost lost to the amnesia of time. Paul had assembled several pages and sat transfixed, not by any great wisdom imparted by the writers, but instead by the passage of time they represented.

Generation upon generation.

"Whoever sleeps in a house alone is seized by Lilith," came from a Babylonian text. She was hinted at in Arabic, not named precisely but hinted at in a quote taken from an old Hebrew passage. In the Zohar, she was mentioned several times implicitly. In the Dead Sea Scrolls her name was used once clearly. She appeared to the Sumerians as a demon or spirit, and then again to the Hittites and Egyptians as a killer of children. There was precious little else until she resurfaced again in the Middle Ages, and then again in the period of the Renaissance. For a few more centuries she vanished, reappearing finally in the literature of the seventeenth century, slowly ambling down to the present time.

Now they had come to him, not as the theme of a lonely poet nor in the research of a ruminating theological scholar, but in person.

Thousands of years.

It made him feel very small, a tiny cog in a giant wheel.

What was he, in the scope of all this?

His lifetime was short, a quick snap of the fingers to these creatures, a fleeting scent carried on a strong wind from far and barren hills.

In the passing of the previous few days, he felt he knew what he needed to do, and the thought of it terrified him.

He needed to learn so much more than could be gleaned from a few sentences snatched here and there from the hand of history, revealed to him like some trail of dropped breadcrumbs.

There was only one way to learn; he needed to go to the source.

No, he thought with a cold stab of fear, he needed to talk to Lamia. She had come to him revealing a certain degree of trust.

Even if he was only a pawn in a game where she was a master, he felt fairly certain that she would not turn him away. Even a queen had use for pawn now and then. He was useful to her, a piece that might still be in play. Lilith was out of the question; she had come solely for a confrontation in which he had nearly been slain.

Paul had emerged, but not unscathed. The paint had been chipped, a dent driven into the bodywork. His right hand trembled involuntarily when he recalled her coming to speak with him, demanding of him something which he was powerless to give.

He was damaged; but also strengthened.

He had won.

Paul softly closed the scrapbook that held the pages of information he had so painstakingly gathered together, watching the cover slowly fall as the last of the air was squeezed out from between the pages.

He didn't know where he might find Lamia.

Paul shook his head. That wasn't the problem; the problem was whether she would allow herself to be found, revealing herself to him. The choice of a meeting wasn't his to make. He had to hope that she might yet have a need for him.

If not, it would be a fool's gambit.

He would start tonight, when the last of the light of day had faded from the sky.

When night came, he would strike out into the streets, anything but boldly.

\*\*\*

The Reverend would have no luck on his first night, nor would it be any better on his second, wandering the street where he had met with her once before. He refined his search, trusting in her mythos to hold some degree of truth.

He began to stroll through the few cemeteries in the area trusting in blind luck, or perhaps fate, to cross their paths.

On the third and fourth night he returned to the church empty handed and exhausted, dizzy with fatigue and shivering with cold. The following nights passed miserably, a blur of discomfort that became indistinguishable. Unless he referred to a calendar he could not know it, but it was on the tenth night that the hands of fate finally came together.

*\*\*\**

Paul was standing amidst a field of polished gravestones, staring up at the sky and the shining glow of the moon, when his watch silently ticked over into the witching hour. The chill of the night settled into his bones and he drew the zipper of his fleece jacket all the way up, the cold steel of the clasp pressed to his stubbly chin.

He stood, a dark sentinel brooding over the resting spots of both the damned and the deceased, when he suddenly became aware that he was no longer alone.

A deeper cold fastened to his joints, a cold that was altogether different than a touch of fatigue and the night air. It was the cold of those that lay dying; the cold hand of mortality felt by those in the presence of the Reaper come to collect another soul.

Paul stopped in his tracks and did not move; hesitant and afraid to turn and face his fear.

There was no sound, no sound at all.

The owl and the cricket fell silent.

Paul closed his eyes and silently prayed for strength.

*Be careful what you wish for.*

In this very moment there were no truer words.

"I will fear no evil: for thou art with me," he prayed, gripping the crucifix tucked in his undercoat with a hand that had become clammy.

"I am with you Reverend, and none other," Lamia said calmly, the level tone of her voice daring him to turn around.

Turn around, or flee.

Paul turned around to face her, his limbs trembling.

He was taken aback by her appearance; her skin was a pallid white, contrasting starkly with her dark eyes and mouth.

She looked…regal. And fearsomely beautiful.

"You still fear me," she said, appraising him confidently. "You are covered in the scent of it."

"As should anyone be, knowing you for what you are," he replied.

"If I had wanted to take your life I would have drunk from you the last time we met. If I had wanted to take your life, you would not be speaking to me now."

Paul wanted to believe her. He wanted to believe her very badly.

This was not at all like being approached unaware on the street; he was in her element now, and he had thrown himself on her mercy, flung himself into her web.

She looked him over from head to toe with cool curiosity.

"Why have you come? I do not think it is for my bitter kiss."

"I was looking for you."

"That I already know. It is the 'why' that interests me. Very few have sought my company, especially on land put aside for the dead."

"I have questions."

"I may have answers for you. I may not. You interest me, Reverend. You are rare. You have seen with your own eyes what many consider to be myth, and it has not broken you; nor shaken your resolve. The weak of faith scoff at my name and that of my sister and our kind. They stand behind their gods like hucksters selling snake oil, bending the holy written word to suit their needs; to line their pockets like a common whore. You know what I am and I can see in your mind that you have studied me. You know I am old, but you cannot grasp how old. I am primeval, Reverend."

She stepped closer to him, until he could feel her hot breath upon his face.

Her eyes stared deep into his. Her eyes sparkled like polished jade.

"The men and the places I have known have come to dust. I have witnessed the rise and fall of empires lost. You know I am dangerous, and yet you come to find me. Your faith has been strengthened by the revelation that I walk this earth. Many would have instead turned to a bottle to find false courage. That bottle would have led them astray; consumed them. You did not. You fear me, and your fear makes you no less wise. But I am not so unkind that I would turn you away. Tonight, I can entertain. Shall we stand here like old friends and converse? Or perhaps find somewhere to sit? I can feel your discomfort. The ache in your bones sings to me clearly."

He was intrigued.

"You have played with me," he accused her boldly.

Lamia laughed.

"I have used your empathy to further a personal interest. Is that so unreasonable?"

Paul studied her, not knowing what to say. She was completely at ease with him.

Her green eyes were glistening with amusement; her mouth upturned in the hint of a playful smile.

"Besides; you would be a poor representative of the Church if you were to deny comfort to a troubled man, even though he might be one of my own kind. Now, shall we sit?"

Paul sat reluctantly, feeling that he was somehow more vulnerable on the ground.

The ground was cool but dry, and he ruefully admitted to himself that it was much more comfortable than standing. His lower back has started cramping.

"Better?"

Paul nodded.

Lamia joined him, sitting across from him with her legs crossed comfortably, her hands resting in her lap.

He was having a difficult time seeing her for what she was. She was not disfigured or hideous, loathsome or hateful. Sitting across from him was a beautiful woman in her prime, a woman that every man might appreciate with at least a second look.

"I confuse you."

"Yes," he admitted.

"Prejudice?"

"Possibly. As well as a lack of experience. I have been taught that you represent my enemy. You are my enemy."

"Best to keep your enemies close," she replied, her eyes not turning away from his.

"I am unsure how close is safe."

"That is for you to determine."

Paul could lean forward and touch her knee, if he wanted to do so.

"Why are you confused?"

"You represent my opposite, but I am not sure you are my enemy."

"I am not your enemy. And you still fear me."

"I fear you for what you are, *Striga*."

Her eyes widened to a degree in surprise. A hint of anger touched them, but only for the briefest moment. A moment later she chuckled deep in her throat, a fond laugh of appreciation.

"I have not been called that name for a great many years, Reverend. I appreciate the unexpected reference. Why do you choose to use it?"

"I wondered if it was your original name."

"The Greeks and the Romans called me Striga, but it is not my name." She sat upright in a correct and precise posture, as if in study.

"Where is Sam?" Paul asked, looking about as though he expected him to emerge from the forest shadows.

Lamia smiled. "Samuel is not with us tonight. He is hungry."

Lamia saw that Paul appeared disappointed.

"You do not approve?" she asked him, watching his expression closely.

"I had hoped he might find another way."

"He has found his way; do you know of another, Reverend? Tell me, for I would be keen to learn from your vast knowledge on the matter."

The condescension in her voice was thick. She leaned forward over her lap to speak with him more intimately.

"Throw away your misconceptions and foolish ideals, Reverend. You judge him with only the slightest understanding into the nature of his being. You have no concept of what you say. He is doing what he must."

"He is a murderer," Paul replied.

"A murderer?" Lamia scoffed. "You have given him advice and he has taken it; he has found his motivation and direction. You should be thankful that he followed your encouragement."

"I did not encourage him to kill!"

"And what did you expect him to do? You had some concept of his potential, were you really so naïve as to think he might do otherwise?"

"I would have killed myself, rather than become a monster."

"Easy for you to say what you would have done. You are not in his place. You are not Samuel."

"What he is doing is wrong."

Lamia sighed in soft frustration.

"Again, you expose your prejudice. So sad to live life through such a narrow window. I could turn you Reverend, expose you to our world. Then, and only then, would you have any right to express an opinion on our matters. Only then could you state with any degree of privilege what you might have done."

Paul heard the threat in her words, the anger that simmered just below her surface.

He wanted to turn and flee.

"Run away if you must," she said, again somehow reading his mind, "but if you run, I will never again seek you out, you will take all of your questions to the grave."

"You won't kill me?"

"You are not what I seek."

Paul remembered what he had read.

Lamia, the killer of children.

"Children?"

Her face went flat with barely controlled rage and she reached out for him with a single hand, gripping him tightly by the throat, her fingertips dug into the recess that outlined his windpipe.

She had moved so quickly that he hadn't seen it coming.

Paul watched her emerald eyes fade quickly to black, like an oily bottomless pit.

This was not mere anger, he recognized, it was unadulterated, hot fury. A yellow spot churned within the center of each black pool.

He was frozen to the ground, not daring to move.

He expected to feel her tear his throat out.

"Do not speak of that lie to me ever again," she hissed through pointed teeth.

Her other hand was clenching her knee viciously, her knuckles turned white as her fingertips dug into her own flesh.

"It is what I read," Paul tried to explain; very afraid of the transformation she had made.

He thought he might wet himself.

"It is a lie," she whispered coarsely, "a lie put forth by the foolish and the ignorant. I have never harmed a child and I never will. Never, in all of my days. That I swear to you."

She let him go swiftly, as if she was revolted by his touch.

Slowly, gradually, she returned to a calmer state. Her eyes were the last to change.

"I understand how you see me, but you must understand that you are wrong. I forgive your ignorance. You have been taught by the ignorant, and so it is not your blame to accept."

"You can read my mind?" he asked her, needing to understand how she knew certain things.

"If you want to call it that. In your mind I can taste your fear and also your wonderment. You never expected me to be real, and now you feel your life is all the richer for it. You admire my longevity. My experience."

"I am a student of history and you have lived what I have only read."

"Ancient."

"Pardon me?"

"It is the word I get from you, the feeling you link with me. With us. Ancient."

Paul nodded.

"You are envious."

"I am," he admitted. "What you have seen, I can only imagine."

"Have you travelled the world?" Lamia asked him quietly, her eyes momentarily casting upwards to the night sky.

"A little. Not as much as I would have liked."

"Have you been to Rome?"

"Yes."

"What did you think of it?"

"Amazing. My fondest memory is of the Coliseum, the feel of those bricks under my hands. It was like I could feel the history under my fingertips, like I could feel a connection with that time."

She nodded faintly, her expression softening as her mind wandered away ever so slightly.

"I was there when it was new. Did you know that?"

He was helplessly transfixed. What wine was to a connoisseur, history was for Paul.

"I watched as it rose ever upwards, brick by brick, built by slaves and craftsmen brought in from all reaches of the Roman Empire. What I remember most is not how it looked, but how it smelled in that time, and that is something you cannot experience.

You can touch the same stones I saw set into place, but you cannot know the scents that were in the air. The sweetness of jasmine and orange blossom in the spring; the smell of the bakeries and their freshly risen bread. The smell of the sea carried on the wind. The dry dust in the street and the stink of the blood and fear of the slaves that were worked to death in its construction."

"What else have you seen?" he asked her. "Where else have you been?"

Paul saw her smile and in her smile he saw that her memories were not entirely happy. Her memories also brought sadness.

"I have travelled the world, Reverend. I gazed over the desert as the Egyptians built their pyramids. I smelled the sweet smoke from the fires of Troy. I followed the great armies of Alexander to the east and danced with his soldiers in Persia. I listened to Socrates preach to the young in Greece. I was there when Xerxes pitched battle against Leonidas. I watched as Byzantine burned and the Roman Empire was lost. I have seen the cities of Europe rise and fall and seen them emptied by plague. I watched as the Chinese built their wall, the wall paid for in blood, suffering and lives. I saw Tenochtitlan fall under horse and sword and saw the survivors suffer from pestilence. You might envy me for the things that I have seen, but only for those rare moments; there are many more you would wish you had not. You name me a murderer. You name Samuel as a killer. The numbers of men I have taken pale next to the kindest of generals. You think of me as evil, and yet men have killed throughout their history in the name of their gods. Women and children have fallen by the millions under the touch of fire and sword. You dare to call me evil? Do not look upon me as a villain. Look into the reflection of the mirror and you will see the true face of evil staring back at you. The Devil is hidden in there somewhere, safely in the masks of men."

Lamia fell silent at last, looking down towards the ground.

Paul had nothing to say. He sat before a creature that had seen history birthed before her very eyes, and instead of wonder, she had come away with a feeling of senselessness. She did not sit before him proudly or arrogantly. She appeared crestfallen, almost broken by tragedy.

A feeling arose in him that he did not expect to feel in her presence.

It was pity.

"History is cold, Reverénd. It is the writing of an event, maybe memorable, maybe not, but in the end it is always the same. It is impersonal. The names are there and so are the places, but never the part that makes it tangible. I have told you of the places I have been, of the things that I have seen, but there is so much more, and only in what has been forgotten, can you find that which is important."

"What is that?"

"I will share with you a lullaby. It is a lullaby that you likely have never heard, for it is very old and very few have heard it aloud. I will first repeat it to you as it was originally sung, to honor the memory of he who sang it. Then I will translate it for you." Her words were solemn and reverent.

"I would be honored," he replied, sensing to her it was very personal, a very real link to her past.

When she spoke the words, they were soft and respectful.

Her eyes faded away, lost to a memory buried by time.

"Usa ŋanu usa ŋanu
usa ŋanu ki dumuŋaše
usa kulu ki dumuŋaše
igi badbadani u kunib
igi gunani šuzu ŋarbi
u eme za malilikani
za mallilil u nagule."

When she was finished, she wiped a tear from the corner of one eye. She was silent for a moment longer.

Paul could see she was collecting herself, regaining her composure. It was a look he had seen many times, the look of the grief-stricken as they prepared to speak.

"What you heard was Sumerian."

"It was beautiful."

"Now, once more, in your English;

Sleep come, sleep come,
Sleep come to my son,

Sleep hasten to my son!
Put to sleep his open eyes,
Settle your hand upon his sparkling eyes –
As for his murmuring tongue,
Let the murmuring not spoil his sleep."

She spoke it softly, as a mother would to her infant child tucked warmly into its bed.

When she finished, she sighed.

"*That* is history," Lamia said, "the part that gets lost, the part that is not recorded in books and libraries.

"When did you hear it?"

"On a battlefield Reverend, in the midst of a mindless battle, many centuries ago."

Paul did not understand her explanation.

Lamia sighed sadly and gathered the strength to clarify her words.

Another tear ran slowly over her ivory cheek, a tear that this time she ignored.

She allowed it to gather on her jawline where it finally fell, lost in the grass, glittering like a cut diamond as it fell.

"History is cold, Reverend. It lacks the tragedy and loss that marks the passing of time. I heard that lullaby sung softly on a battlefield by a grieving father over the body of his dying son. Night had not yet fallen and the cries of the dying and the wounded had not yet ceased. The place and the names of those who fought are unimportant. The generals who fought, the empires that clashed, the acts of heroism have all been forgotten. What is important is the comfort that was offered and the pain that marked those words, sung by a man over his dying child."

"A vampire, talking to me about loss and grief," Paul said, quietly humbled.

"I told you. You did not understand. You have not heard me. You have not experienced the conflict Samuel has endured. You cannot comprehend the cost he has paid in making his decision. We appreciate better than anyone the final price of death and its touch on those left behind. In that awareness we come to recognize better than all others, the value of life. Perhaps now, the window in your world is open a little wider. At least, I hope it is so."

Paul swallowed, thinking of the nameless man from her memory singing over his child as he died.

"What happened to him?" Paul asked.

Lamia wiped away the last of her tears.

"Do you really wish to know?"

"Yes," he said sincerely.

"Why?" Her eyes burned with a need to know.

"So I might pray for him."

Her eyes softened.

"He buried his son and then he fell weeping onto his sword. Life for him had lost all meaning, and so he ended it. Ultimately Reverend, not all of us fear death. To some it can be a merciful friend."

# Chapter 21

*"A lily in a twilight place?*
*A moonflow'r in the lonely night?—*
*Strange beauty of a woman's face*
*Of wildflow'r-white!"*

*The Vampire*
-Madison Julius Cawein

"You said that Sam needed to learn."

"He is, and quickly. He has learned much, but does not yet understand the significance of everything that he has studied. Samuel does things without knowing how he does them. He is a new child, coming into his own."

"Why is it so important that he learn so quickly?"

"They are coming."

"They?"

"Others of our kind."

"Here? Now?"

"Yes."

"Why?"

"Samuel," she said, as if that explained everything.

He sensed a great foreboding in that one word, like a dark undercurrent prepared to drown the unwary.

"I don't understand. Does he know?"

"He doesn't yet sense it. He will soon enough, when they are closer. He has been distracted."

"Is he in danger?"

"Yes."

"Why?"

"Long ago, it was decided that we should remain very few in number. It is easier to remain hidden and stay concealed when there are very few of us to be found."

"Then why gather in one place, all together?"

"In order to determine if Samuel poses a risk to our survival."

"By whom?"

"By us. He will be tested."

"And if he fails?"

"He will die."

"Have you all been tested?"

"No."

"Why not?"

"His creation was an event not intended. It has been over a millennium since a new vampire was born to us. The existence of Samuel exceeds our agreed upon number."

"Which is?"

"Twelve."

"He is thirteen."

"Yes."

"Is that significant?"

"It comes after twelve."

"I see."

"He might yet be killed for his number, regardless of his ability or his willingness to remain concealed."

"Does he know this?"

"He suspects danger. He knows he is not safe. He does not know the full extent of his peril."

"Will you tell him?"

"No. He cannot be afraid. It would impair his ability to learn."

"Lilith created him."

"Yes."

"Why does she want him? Why doesn't she deal with him herself?"

"She already tried."

Paul frowned.

"She tried? What did she do?"

"My sister discovered that he survived her attentions, and came to fix her error the next night. She was thwarted by his good fortune it would seem. She found him and moved to strike moments after his first kill."

"She attacked him?"

"Yes."

"And he survived." Paul wondered how Sam had defeated her, knowing that without his cross he himself would have fallen. Her attack on him had been horrific.

"He survived. I came to him after she had left him in order to see for myself. I could feel that he was not dead and yet I did not believe it to be true."

"What would have happened if she had found him first; before he had killed?"

"Then he would be dead and we would not be here. She did not intend to create him and so she would not have left him alive."

"How did he survive?" Paul asked, appalled.

She fixed her eyes on him in a level glare, the weight of what she was about to share was evident.

"Samuel is unusually strong."

"Stronger than you? Could you resist her?"

"No. She is the strongest of us."

"Then how could he fight her off?"

"He is unusually strong. He was able to fight her to a draw; a stalemate in which, if she were to press any further, they both would have been killed."

"What? Why would they both die if she continued? He wouldn't be able to kill her?"

"She is the Master, the Mother of Demons. We cannot kill her; she gave us life but we are not as strong. Samuel was strong enough to stop her. If she attacked with enough fury to kill him, she opened herself to the risk that he would be able to kill her."

"So she was forced to stop."

"Yes; he could not kill her unless she tried to kill him."

"The same wouldn't work for you?"

"No, I am not strong enough. None of us are. She could kill any of us. Only he could resist her to the point where she herself became vulnerable."

Paul tried to absorb the implications of what she was saying. "Could he be killed if he was attacked by several of you?"

"Perhaps."

"Is that what Lilith wants?"

"She doesn't want him dead. She tried to kill him before he completed his change, to correct her mistake. She was too late for that. Now she wants him to submit to her, to accept her as his Master."

"And if he doesn't?"

"If he doesn't swear fealty to her I fear she will be tempted to end him. She will not permit disobedience."

"Would she be prepared for that?"

"Lilith does not bluff. She will do what she thinks must be done."

"Would you try to stop her?"

Lamia frowned. "That would be dangerous. I am not as strong as he is. There is little I could do, especially once the Others come. They do her bidding."

"None will refuse?"

"She is the Master," Lamia reminded him. "She is the mother of all of us; without her, we would all be dead. You need to remember something Reverend; he will not be dealing with people sympathetic to his plight. We have been named demons, and for good reason. We have grown our reputations over time, thriving on catastrophe and the suffering of others. We do not fear death, we are its soldiers. Pity is a trait we have learned to ignore. It is not in our nature."

"You are one of their number, and yet you do not agree."

Lamia clenched her jaw. "I have different motivations."

"It is your actions I find the most interesting, not your words. You have shown him pity, you have shown him compassion. You are here, talking to me. The Others may be as you say, but you are not."

Lamia stared at him coldly.

Paul continued, "My entire life revolves around observing others. As a Reverend, I need to be aware if someone is feeling down or if they may need my help. You are very interesting, Lamia. You are torn. I can see it. You help Sam even though you know Lilith would not agree. You have been pushing him to learn in the

303

face of the danger coming his way. You may serve a dark purpose, but there is kindness in you yet. Your actions speak it clearly, even if your words try to deny it."

Paul finished what he had to say and watched her, looking for hints she might unconsciously reveal to him.

She didn't move. She just stared at him. The intensity of her gaze increased. Her cold appraisal of him became more intense.

Paul saw the look upon her face and recognized it for what it was: an air of supremacy.

She pitied him. He was small, something of little or no consequence.

Lamia was not sitting across from someone she considered an equal to her. She looked at Paul as though he were insignificant, something she could play with to pass the time. She was here because she was curious. But still, he felt there was something more to her than what he could see or what she was telling him. He sensed there was something she was protecting. Was it herself? Her emotions seemed to swing widely, changing as quickly as their conversation. Paul realized it was her emotions that frightened him. She was a slave to her emotions; they changed as quickly as the clouds in a summer sky. He had seen Sam shift in the same way. Reacting; rising and falling like the crest of a wave.

The Lamia he was talking to right now might be a completely different one a moment from now. The Lamia that had wept while reciting an ancient lullaby was gone for the moment, replaced by a version that was arrogant and disdainful of him.

It was fascinating to behold, and more than a little disturbing.

He understood he was sitting with her because she allowed it. If she was no longer interested in him, or bored, she would leave him. There might be more to it; the thought that he might serve a purpose to her own ends, some purpose she would not share willingly with him. He thought she was merely being methodical, covering all of the variables. She needed to be prepared in case Sam came to see him again, to know what Sam might discuss with this tie from his previous life. She would leave nothing to chance.

He was a variable in her equation.

Compared to Sam, he was a variable that was easier to control. Or manipulate?

He did not know her entire agenda; he was navigating blind through her maze, hoping to find his own answers while making moves in a game in which he didn't know the rules.

And there were others.

*Ten* others.

Might each of them also have a stake in what was to come, a part that he was utterly unaware of?

These were ten other personalities he did not know; ten personalities that could be just as unpredictable and cunning as Lamia was.

Would they all tolerate him? Would they want to remove him from whatever equation was being written on their chalkboard?

Sam was in danger, and Paul understood for the first time that he was also at risk.

Lilith had come for him and he had won, but what if she had not come alone? What if she had not come at him openly as she had? What if she had sought to outnumber or surprise him?

His involvement with Sam kept him at least partially safe with Lamia. It might not be so with the Others. He might be seen as a meddler, someone to remove.

The woman sitting in front of him now was not the same as the one that had first come to him.

He shivered at the memory of her fingers upon his neck.

When she spoke to him at last, her voice was scolding, as though she were reprimanding a spoiled child.

"The Others are coming to test him, as many before have been tested. I prepare him for that challenge because it will be harsh and he will be given no leeway, no ounce of mercy. If he fails, he will likely die. I have my own motivations Reverend, but I am not being selfish. He deserves a fighting chance and so I will give it to him. My sister thinks I am wasting my time, but she does not oppose my actions as you might think. So long as he might serve her, she will tolerate his presence. He might yet be useful to her. My sister does not waste. We are all tools and if he can be used, she will be patient. Time is not the hindrance to us that it is for you. You have perhaps another twenty years to live? Thirty, if you are fortunate. Time. That is nothing to me. It is nothing to any of us. A decade is an amusement. A century can pass in contemplation. Long after you are laid in the ground I will be here. You don't understand fully, for your mind is constricted by the short timeline of your existence. You can have a sense of our motivations, but your limited perception only touches the surface. You are pitifully ignorant of the depth of our desires."

"You are afraid again, Reverend," Lamia noted quietly. "Is it me?"

"No," he answered truthfully.

She was changing again; he saw that his answer pleased her. "It is the Others," he replied.

Lamia nodded once as though he was wise to feel the way he did.

"You wonder if they know of you?"

"Maybe. Do they?"

"Perhaps in time. You are concerned that they will take an interest in you?"

"It crossed my mind," he admitted.

Lamia snorted as though the fear was unreasonable.

"They come for Samuel."

Her confidence did not reach him.

For some, Sam might be the sole purpose of their interest. For others, if they had more investigative personalities, they might want to explore his story a little deeper. Some - and this was his largest concern - might begrudge a priest who involved himself in their personal interests. They might perceive him as a loose end, a dangling string that needed to be cut.

"How will he be tested?"

"They will want to test his abilities."

"You already said he was strong."

"He is," she agreed.

"Can't they feel that?"

Lamia chuckled.

"When dormant, our abilities cannot be felt, nor can they be implied. It is not until they have been activated that we can even guess at how talented one actually is. The one being tested reveals the extent of his talent to us. Otherwise, we can only assume. We can only be prepared as best we can, to expect more from the initiate."

"Will he be warned?"

"No. His abilities must adapt to the moment; to the unexpected. It is not easy. I do not expect him to fail, but I have been surprised before. Others have come before him, others that failed."

"What became of them?"

"They are dead."

"All of them?"

Lamia returned with question with a look that chilled him.

He saw no compassion for them in her eyes; no regret or remorse.

"There is no room for the weak," was all she would say.

"Will you be with him?"

"I must attend. We will all be witness."

"Where?"

"That will be determined when the time is right. We have never before met in the new world; most of us have never been to this land."

"Why?"

"It is not our home. We were born in distant lands in distant times. The ties that bind us to certain areas are within the roots of the earth herself."

"Memories?" Paul offered.

"Memories can be foul things, Reverend. I have never once returned to my home. Memories can be awash with pain."

"But for the Others…"

"The Others may have fond memories of certain places, but memories are the weakest tie. It may be the scent of the soil, the taste on the wind or the subtle light of daybreak or nightfall. Each place is unique and cannot be replaced. Perhaps it is the sense that the place of our creation binds us, our reverence for the dust from whence we came."

"Sam is the first then, from here."

"He is."

*He might also be the last.* Paul thought to himself.

"Who are the Others? I know three. Who are the other ten?" he asked, wanting to know more.

"Why do you wish to know their names? Names are not important. If I were *Striga* or Lamia, to you it would change nothing."

"Curiosity. I wish to study them."

"Books reveal very little, Reverend. What have you learned of me from my name? You have only learned that tales can be false."

"Entertain an old man's interest," he gently pleaded softly, refusing to be so casually dissuaded.

"I will share one name with you and one name only. Some of us have the ability to know where our names are spoken. You would not appreciate their interest."

"Why the one name in particular?"

"His name is still so often spoken that he has no interest in pursuing such matters. With the Others, it is not so. Their names have largely been forgotten, seldom referred to. It is they who would be intrigued to know who spoke of them. They might come looking, to learn why they were of interest."

"One name only, then," Paul agreed.

"Cain," said Lamia.

"Cain?" repeated Paul, surprised.

A passage popped into his mind, a series he had often read. He recited it aloud, the words coming to his mind clearly.

*"What hast thou done? The voice of thy brother's blood crieth unto me from the ground. And now art thou cursed from the earth, which hath opened her mouth to receive thy brother's blood from thy hand; when thou tillest the ground, it shall not henceforth yield unto thee her strength; a fugitive and a vagabond shalt thou be in the earth... And the Lord said unto him, Therefore whosoever slayeth Cain, vengeance shall be taken on him sevenfold. And the Lord set a mark on Cain, lest any finding him should smite him."*

"Yes," said Lamia calmly, "the very same."

She then quoted Paul a passage of her own.

*"God the first garden made, and the first city Cain."*

"How can that be?" he asked, perplexed and shocked. He knew the story of Cain and Abel well; it was one his favorites. "Cain was cast away to live out the rest of his days; he was not made immortal as a consequence to his punishment. He was sent out to live his life, to eventually die."

"You are correct," Lamia agreed, "He is not immortal, just as Samuel is not, just as I am not. Lilith found him, as the Hebrews have written. She found him by the Red Sea, and there she showed him the power of blood. Lilith provided him with a very long life, a life that to this day has not been quenched."

"Are you saying he made the first city *after* he met Lilith? *After* he was changed?"

"The city was Enoch," Lamia said, "named after his son."

Paul's mind reeled.

"He is one of us, but he is not evil, just as I am not evil. Not your perception of evil, a prejudice of your faith. He was taught the power of blood. In that lesson he grew his mission. He passed his wisdom on to humanity. With it, the first city was built. From it, civilization was birthed."

Paul was speechless.

"We serve a purpose," Lamia said, "We are not aimless creatures. We are not random instruments of demise. We have existed from the very beginning. We will exist unto the end of days."

# Chapter 22

―――――――――――――――〜―――――――――――――――

*"Left to herself, the serpent now began*
*To change; her elfin blood in madness ran,*
*Her mouth foam'd, and the grass, therewith besprent,*
*Wither'd at dew so sweet and virulent."*

-John Keats

"They are coming," Sam said quietly, in a voice that was hushed and muted.

Through the narrow crack of stone, the sunset had faded into shades of orange and pink, a splash of colors that slowly slid across the face of grey stone.

He turned his head to look at her.

"They are coming for me."

Lamia was surprised that there was no doubt in his voice, no question in his statement. When he said it, the words were calm and sure.

"Yes," she said.

"You knew they were coming," he said to her.

"I felt them earlier," she replied.

"Why didn't I feel them?"

"I have known them longer. I am more aware of their presence, the subtlety of their nature."

Sam turned away and nodded, sensing the truth in her words.

"They are all coming. Every one."

"Yes," she said. "They must."

She pressed closer to him, feeling the tension in his flesh.

She could not tell if he was afraid or merely uncertain. He was difficult to read. She was still surprised at how easily things came to him. Very seldom did anyone know when the vampires were converging in one place, especially a vampire that was still so young.

"Why didn't you tell me?" He wasn't accusing her of anything, he just wanted to know.

"I didn't want to frighten you. Fear can be a weakness."

He felt her heat against his side, enjoying the extra warmth. They had spent the last several days like this, sleeping in the daylight hours next to one another. Sometimes he woke early, for just long enough that he was able to watch her sleep. It was never for very long; it was like she could feel his eyes on her. Not long afterwards, she would always wake up.

He liked to watch her sleep; it reminded him of better days.

"I believe you," he said.

She watched him look outside, thinking to herself how much like Adama he was. Adama had been young then too, like Samuel was now. Young and confident, so certain in the path of his life. The unknown had not scared him, not in the slightest. Adama saw every day as a gift, every event as a hidden meaning, a guide to follow and learn from.

"They are thinking of me," he said to her, "I can feel their thoughts sometimes come to me. I have heard them speak my name."

"How does it make you feel?" she asked, wanting to know if he was only hiding his fear.

"Some of them hate me already," he answered, "and some of them fear me."

"That is normal," she assured him. "They are coming to meet a new member of the *Lilitu;* they do not know what to expect either."

"You will be there. To test me."

Lamia felt a moment of surprise. She suppressed the feeling, to deny it any strength. *How had he known?*

"Yes."

"Will you test me?"

"I have been teaching you. I will not test you, but I will observe."

"Are you afraid?" he asked her.

"Afraid?"

"Afraid I will fail?"

"You are strong, Samuel. You will prove your worth. I am not afraid."

"But you are," he said, "I can feel it in you. You hide it well."

Lamia bit her lip and observed the fading spot of light.

"That is exactly why I am not afraid. If you can sense that, you have nothing to fear from the Others."

"Some of them don't want to come."

Lamia looked at him sharply, questioningly.

"How do you know?" she asked pointedly. She could sense nothing of what he was saying. She could feel them coming, feel them approaching, but it was only a sense of their presence; a proximity and nothing more. Samuel was saying that he could feel their minds? It couldn't be possible. She had never heard of anything like it.

"Cain is coming, but he is coming out of a desire to see her, to see Lilith. Not me."

"How do you know this?" Lamia asked, shocked. He could not know this, it wasn't possible.

"I just do. I can feel where he is. Through that, I can feel why he is coming. It's thin, but it's there."

She had never told him of their names, how had he known about Cain? Had he spoken to the Reverend? Yes, that must be it! No, it couldn't be. She would smell the Reverend on Sam if he had. He had not spoken with the Reverend since the cemetery. How? How?!

"You can't know this!" she said, "it's impossible."

Sam looked at her unconcerned.

"I know what I am feeling. Samael wants to test me, Ashmodai as well. They are looking forward to it."

"Don't say their names! Don't!" Lamia blurted quickly, wanting him to stop. They would know! They would know!

"Selene and Nega' are curious. They are coming only because they must."

Lamia backhanded him strongly across the face.

"Fool! Shut your mouth when I tell you. Didn't you hear a word of what I just said? Don't say their names! They will know you spoke of them; they will know you are aware."

Sam felt his cheek, feeling the tingling pain subside. The pain was good; it kept him focused.

"Let them know. They can't think I am afraid of them. I want them to know.

Rahab. Mahalath. Naamah. Ambrogio. Igrat. Let them come. I want to meet them."

Lamia stumbled back, almost crumbling against the stone at her back.

She stared at him with stunned eyes.

"You have no idea what you have done. None at all. It will be different now, because of this. You fool." Her voice was a whisper, a gasp of dismay.

Her mind began to tingle. A confused and outraged blend of thoughts reached her.

Sam smiled with satisfaction.

"Do you feel it, too?" he asked her.

Lamia shook her head, her eyes wide with disbelief.

"They have heard," she groaned.

"Yes," Sam replied.

Lamia couldn't comprehend how he was so calm and unruffled. He seemed to be pleased. If he was afraid, she couldn't smell any of it. Didn't he know? Didn't he understand? No; of course not. He had no idea.

Not only did they know exactly where he was, they knew he was not going to be surprised. It would be harder now, their test. Someone that expected to be tested needed to be tested harder. Before, they would likely have come by surprise, giving him credit for being caught unexpectedly. Now they knew he was prepared. They would push him harder.

He should be afraid.

Instead, he only sat there against the wall, blank and emotionless, looking at everything while seeing nothing.

"What else can you feel?" she asked him, unsure what he was able to sense.

"There are more women than there are men."

"That surprises you?"

"I didn't expect it. A bias, I suppose. They are closer than I thought. I could tell before that they were getting near, but now it is clearer, more set in my mind."

"Because they heard their names."

"Yes. It's interesting. Some of them expected this. They weren't surprised to hear me say their name."

"Samuel, you…"

He cut her off casually.

"Some of them were. Those are the ones that are angry. They don't like to be surprised."

"They will test you harder now," she finished, not wasting a moment before he might begin to speak again. "When you live a long life such as we have, there are seldom any surprises left. To show them this, that you know their names, makes them curious, it makes them want to know what else you can do. They will be less forgiving."

"I am not seeking their approval. I want this done."

"For what reason? So you can belong?"

"No, that is what Lilith wants of me. She wants a new puppet."

Lamia scowled at him. "We are not puppets. We are not her toys."

"She is your Master," Sam said to her.

"And she is yours!" Lamia retorted.

"No. That is where we are different. She made me, but I will not yield to her."

"You misjudge her strength. She will press you."

"And I will resist her. My life is my own."

Lamia shook her head, thinking him foolish and naïve. He did not know what he was talking about. Lilith would bore into his mind and overpower him, bending him to her will. Before she was done with him he would gladly submit, with or without the Others to face him.

But he had said that some did not want to come.

Were they a united front against him, committed to seeing him taken within their number? If they were not together, it could prove difficult. Sam needed to sense that they accepted him, that he was to be added into their fold. If he perceived a threat he was much more likely to resist, to rebel against their will. Such a scenario was more dangerous, not only to Sam, but to the rest of them.

"Then what?" she asked, "Why are you so eager to run their gauntlet?"

"To get it over with. To start fresh. I can't do that fully until this is done."

"You think they will let you go."

"They will have no choice."

"A long road awaits you," Lamia said.

"And that is why I want to start. The road isn't getting any shorter."

They were silent for a few minutes, listening to the fading sounds of the last of the day.

"What is wrong with me?" Sam asked sullenly.

"Wrong with you?"

"I am sitting here watching the last light of day and I feel normal. My wife and my children are lost to me forever, and I can sit here as though all is well. I have no more tears left for them. Did I love them so little that I can forget them so easily?"

Lamia sat upright to look at him.

He continued to look away, to stare at the sunset. His gaze was unfocused.

Lamia grabbed him by the chin and forced him to look at her, to look into her eyes.

"We are not creatures of regret, Samuel. It is not in our nature to mourn like we once did. What we are… changes us."

"So I am cold then? Destined to forget them?"

Lamia frowned angrily.

"How can you say such things? You have seen me shed tears for my children and husband. Did you forget that?"

Sam tried to look away; she forced him to look at her, her fingers digging into his jaw.

"Forget how you once mourned. Time has passed and with the passing of every day you will lose your connection to how you were. You will feel things differently. When you were a child you felt things differently than you do as a man. It is the same. You will know things differently. You will mourn things differently. Before, you felt loss like a passing whim in comparison to how it feels for me. How it will for you. It hurt you and you wept; then it passed.

Life was too short for you to spend any more time on it than you did. Now it is different. You will harbor grief, and it will age within you like a spiced wine. It will not fade so easily and it will not so easily be relieved. Your grief will stab at you like a dagger in the heart, a dagger that you cannot remove. You will feel its pain just as surely as you feel hunger. It is so very real, far richer than any grief you have known before. That is how you will mourn them."

"Through pain?"

"Pain like you have never known. You will experience moments like now, where you feel numb and uncaring, but these times are in opposition to the suffering you will experience. It will come upon you and you will feel how real it is. The loss experienced because of death can only be truly appreciated by the long-lived. What sense does a child have of death when a grandparent dies? To them, the whole of life has yet to be unfurled before them. They have no concept of what has been lost, the life experiences that are now gone. They have no understanding of the fate that awaits them, no idea of the wisdom turned to dust. The whole of earth is a grave and nothing escapes the cold touch of death. Nothing. Even you and I will one day be taken into its fold. Before you changed, you were that child, touching upon the shallowest grasp of death. As real as it felt, it was still thin and weak. Now, with a long life ahead of you, that grief will grow and it will mature. As the years pass each tear will become more bitter. Every memory will become more treasured. Time does not heal every wound; only death brings that ultimate grace. Grief is a wound that will not fade. Its roots will sink into your bones."

"When?"

"You didn't know when you would grieve before, and that has not changed. It will come over you. It will come when it needs to. Even after all this time I can't say when I will feel their loss. It just happens."

The last light upon the stone wall vanished.

"The sun has set," he said to her.

Together they emerged into the darkness, listening as other creatures that walked the night began to rise.

***

"You must go through," she instructed him.

They had come across an old hunting cabin tucked in the woods, crafted along the stony bank of a thin, fast-flowing stream that gurgled merrily.

The front of the cabin was adorned with a simple deck, which - along with the cabin itself - had begun to lean backwards ever so slightly, like a lumbering giant had strolled past and given it a gentle nudge.

One more heavy snowfall might be its last.

Sam stared at the grey wooden door jamb.

It was speckled and slivered, the ravages of time showing plainly upon it.

Moss had settled on the roof like a green blanket and lichen was taking root upon its walls, dotting the surface here and there. A plank in the sagging deck creaked ominously, complaining as Lamia shifted her weight over it. Two rusty nails had popped free of the warped joist beneath, giving the plank room to move.

He could see plainly into the interior of the cabin through the gap in the jamb. It was musty and streaked with cobwebs; empty save for a plain wooden table in its center.

Somehow she expected him to just go in.

"Why don't I just open the door?" he asked, thinking that was perfectly acceptable way of entering a building.

"It might be locked," she said.

Sam pushed at the door with his left hand.

It rattled against its hinges.

A screw was nearly out, ready to fall to the floor.

"It would break easily," he said.

Lamia sighed in exasperation.

"Stealth can be preferable to strength," she chided him, "especially when you are seeking a place to rest."

"Is it like the fence?"

"It is similar, but still different. Forget the fence. It will only confuse you."

"Forget the fence," he mumbled to himself, trying to forget about just going *through*. It seemed like the same thing to him. Instead of letting the wire fence pass through him, he somehow needed to pass himself through this gap.

He guessed it was maybe a quarter inch at its widest. Where the wood wasn't warped, it was much tighter.

Sam cleared his mind and focused on the gap, hoping a resolution would just come to him.

He stepped forward.

The door, as decrepit as it was, refused to grant him passage.

He bumped into it soundly.

"Ouch," he muttered, rubbing the point of his nose.

"You can show me now," he suggested, showing her the way with his arm.

Lamia didn't move.

"Again," she said obstinately.

"Why don't you just show me?" he asked.

"Why don't you just listen?" she answered him.

Sam sighed. "Fine," he replied obstinately.

Sam stepped up to the door once again and took a breath.

He felt like the entire cabin was mocking him.

It was old and rotten, but it could still keep him out. It seemed to taunt him.

"Humph," he grunted as he stepped forward, looking directly into the narrow crack, thinking that maybe looking *in* might be the key to the riddle.

He stepped forward tentatively, expecting to feel his nose hit the wall again.

He wasn't disappointed.

"Ahh," he complained, fighting the watery feeling that had welled in his eyes. He was glad that there weren't any slivers poking out of his nose, like misshapen porcupine quills. He saw that Lamia was clearly unimpressed, looking at him with a bored and sarcastic expression.

"Move," she ordered him, waving him aside.

"Be my guest," he welcomed, grateful to be spared another painful attempt.

Lamia stood against the wall, very nearly touching it.

"It is easier, if there is danger," she began, "a need, not a want."

Sam instantly had a vision of her pushing him into the door, like she had pushed him off of the roof.

She knew what he was thinking.

"If I pushed you into the wall, you would run into the wall. You will not pass through to save your life in that way; you know my intent is not to kill, and so, the attempt would fail. Pushing someone into a door is seldom fatal. Off a roof, frequently. Since this cannot kill you or harm you, you will not change. This requires thought."

"Like the fence," he said.

"Only in that fact that you actually have to think about it, but nothing else is similar. In that instance you allowed the fence to pass through you, to flow between you as you passed. The fence was thin, and passed easily through your flesh. The wood is thicker. Broader. More substantial. It cannot pass through you."

Sam paid attention and forgot about his nose; he now followed her train of thought.

"In this case, you must be the fence. You must find the gap that will allow you to pass."

Sam could feel her thinking about the wall, thinking about getting past the door and into the room beyond. She was ignoring the door and she was ignoring the wall. It was like she was standing in an open field with nothing at all in her way.

The cabin was not there.

She wanted to go from once space into another, from the space she occupied into the space beyond the door.

She didn't move.

He expected her to close her eyes as her breathing eased and her mind focused.

She looked at him one last time and her lips turned upwards into a hint of a smile.

Then, as he watched, she seemed to pour into the narrow space, her body losing its solidity and becoming like thick smoke.

The cabin seemed to draw her inwards ever faster, inhaling her form between whatever gaps existed. As Sam stood dumbfounded, she slipped out of sight, gone from view.

A moment later, he heard her footsteps on the old rough-cut floor boards.

They creaked under her weight as she walked around the room in a slow meandering route.

"Coming?" she called out patiently.

Sam could hear the smugness in her voice.

He frowned and stood before the door. She was just beyond it, along the back wall, facing him. She was still smiling; her eyes alight with her challenge to him.

He took a deep breath and let it out slowly, seeking relaxation in that controlled exhale. When it was spent, he inhaled again, once more exhaling calmly. It helped him to concentrate, and at that moment his attention was fixed on how he had 'seen' her mind adjust to what needed to be done.

The door wasn't there.

The wall wasn't there.

He was standing before a wall of empty space; the solid door between himself and Lamia was an illusion, a trickery of light and shadow.

The wood was inconsequential; the nails that fastened it together were nebulous.

He wanted to be elsewhere; not here, but just beyond in a different space.

Sam felt something change, an alteration in his perception of the world.

He could feel he was surrounded by empty space; not the empty space of the outside air, but the empty space that occupied everything.

The unimaginable distance between the electron and the neutron that made up the atoms that were all around him. They were vast solar systems unto themselves, small pieces of matter occupying a cold and immense empty space.

The atoms of the wood.

The atoms of his body.

Empty space.

Solidity was an illusion, a fabrication of his narrow perception.

Sam felt cold. He was the fence.

Sam felt thin and loose, like he was evaporating before the door.

He felt himself drawn forwards, like he was falling; only he was falling through the door. He felt it around him, his own vaporous body passing through the spaces within the wood.

The door. It was freezing.

The sensation was abrupt and frightening, akin to the fear and discomfort of vertigo. Before he could react, he realized his surroundings had changed.

He blinked twice quickly.

Lamia stood before him, a confused collection of expressions upon her face. He could see she was surprised, maybe a little angry. And shocked. Mixed with these, he detected a scent of satisfaction that was stronger than the look upon her face.

Her arms were at her sides, and when he finally felt normal she took a step towards him, keeping an arms-length between them.

She said nothing to him; her forehead was creased into a frown of intense thought. Her eyes were wide and clear, staring into his own.

"What?" he asked her, trying to break the silence.

He felt a little dizzy from the experience, trying to forget the cold, empty sensation of falling that had gripped him.

Lamia blinked after a few moments and exhaled quickly, looking him over from head to toe. When she was done she looked him sternly in the face.

"How did you do it?" she asked.

"Like you showed me," he answered. "I just remembered what you were thinking and I tried to copy it. Like with the other things you've shown me. Like the fence."

"You copied what I was thinking?" she replied uneasily.

Sam nodded; he could see she was not at all pleased.

"How," she demanded him, "tell me how."

"I don't know. I could just see how your mind was working, how you were thinking in order to do what you did."

She brought a hand up to her forehead and Sam flinched, thinking that she was going to slap him. Afterwards he felt badly that he had expected her to hit him.

Instead, she rubbed her forehead, mulling over what he had explained to her.

"What?" he asked her. "What have I done?"

She dropped her hand back to her side in exasperation.

"Only something that you shouldn't be able to do. How can you feel what I'm doing without me knowing you're doing it? You're reading my mind without me knowing it. That is what has me confused. You have learned by copying my thoughts. I thought that's what you were doing, but I couldn't be sure."

"I'm not reading your mind. I can just see how you're thinking about something. It's like I'm watching you, only differently."

He could see she was trying to understand him.

"It's hard to explain," he finally added, hoping it helped.

Lamia shook her head. "Hard to explain," she exhaled, flustered. "You can somehow see how I'm thinking, without me feeling anything. You copy an action that is in no way easy to perform, on your first try at that, and you tell me it's hard to explain?!"

Sam blinked.

"Do you know how much practice that particular skill usually needs before finally finding success? The fence is one thing; this is entirely more difficult!"

Lamia saw him staring at her without the faintest idea, and she threw up her arms in disbelief.

She turned and paced, running her hands through her hair, shaking her head.

"What?" Sam asked, wondering what he could say to calm her down.

"Nothing. Just... nothing," she replied, agitated by his naiveté. "You don't know, so what's the point of my asking? None!"

Sam had nothing to say to that; it was undeniably true.

"You wanted to teach me. I'm learning."

She stopped pacing and stared at him. "You think I'm upset that you're learning?"

"I don't know. Maybe."

"Oh I swear," Lamia groaned.

Lamia strode towards him with purpose, her eyes burning.

"The only thing that keeps me from striking you is that I know you honestly have no idea how you're doing the things you're doing."

Sam unconsciously leaned back, ever so slightly, thinking she might just strike him once for good measure anyways.

"You're strong Samuel, very strong. Skills come to you easily. You learn fast. I fear you are much stronger than I think you are. You know what to do without knowing why. Or how."

"Is that dangerous?"

"Yes!" she shouted at him, wanting to shriek instead.

"The Others are coming to test you, to measure your worth, and you don't know the depth of your own abilities yet. Already, you surpass several of mine. You have beaten Lilith. You have scorned her. You think they come to make friends? They come to see if you are worthy to live! You sensed I was afraid? That is why!"

"I…," Sam began, interrupted quickly by Lamia.

"And then you speak their names aloud, so they know that you know of them! When my sister speaks to them of you, you will have no friends there. None. They are coming and before you meet a single one of them she will have told them about you. They will be prepared for you. They will want justice for you defying her, scorning her; for resisting the Master!"

"That is no one's fault but her own," Sam replied, his voice like steel. When it came to Lilith, he had no care. "I will not submit to her, even if it means my end. They will see. All of them; they will see that I will not surrender."

"Lilith and our kind will not see it as a fault, they will only see insubordination. They might want you dead for that."

"Then they can try to kill me. You think I am strong. Maybe we'll see how strong."

Lamia looked at him, her frustration evaporating.

She could feel his eagerness to confront Lilith, his confidence in meeting her again.

"I will have one friend there," Sam said to her.

Lamia sighed, her ranting forgotten.

"Yes," she said. "One."

"When?" he asked.

"Soon.

# Chapter 23

———————⌒—————

*"What shape was this who came to us,*
*With basilisk eyes so ominous,*
*With mouth so sweet, so poisonous,*
*And tortured hands so pale?*
*We saw her wavering to and fro,*
*Through dark and wind we saw her go;*
*Yet what her name was did not know;*
*And felt our spirits fail."*

–Conrad Aiken, *The Vampire*

"Speak to me!" Sam cried, clawing at his family with fingers that were unable to find a hold. His hands slipped away from them as though they were behind impenetrable glass. If they saw him, they gave no hint of it at all. Their eyes stared forward unseeing and unblinking, their arms at their sides. He couldn't even see if they were breathing. They were entirely motionless. Frozen.

Miranda was standing in the middle, flanked by Cynthia and Tommy. Baxter was sitting; the ever-present guardian at their feet.

They were all dressed in white, standing in a world where the sky was white and the ground was white. Not snow, just flat and featureless and white.

Sam had seen them in the distance and had run to them quickly, only to despair that upon reaching them, they were silent figurines.

He had screamed each of their names countless times.

His throat was raw and his voice was hoarse, strained and exhausted from yelling.

He collapsed to his knees and wept, understanding for the very first time what Lamia had explained to him.

The grief he had experienced before paled in comparison to what he felt now.

When he had first grieved for them, it had flowed like a wave, growing and building before cresting; finally breaking upon the shore, leaving him feeling thin and tired.

What he had felt was only a parody of what he felt now.

His grief had suddenly come over him and dragged him under, threatening to drown him in a deep, vicious undercurrent. There was no buildup of loss, no gradual developing of despair; no foreplay so to speak. It just fell upon him, the complete and matured sensation from the bottom of a pit of senseless loss. He cried viciously, he wept angrily. His body shook as though seized by death spasms. It was a thorough and complete cleansing of the mind and body, an experience that left him feeling hollow.

"This is a dream," he croaked, still kneeling on the smooth white ground. It was glossy and cool, like melamine.

If he could grieve like this in his dreams, he dreaded what it would be like when he was awake.

For all of his crying, his wife and children had not moved. They were like wax statues set in this strange alabaster realm.

Slowly his strength returned, enough that he could finally kneel and look at them, grateful that he could see them and that, in this dream at least, they were not trying to kill him or chase him through some dark and foggy forest.

"I might see you soon," he said to them, staring and hoping to see their eyes move, to surrender some form of acknowledgement.

"They are coming for me. I don't know whether I should be afraid. If they fail, I've beat them. I beat them for you. I want to defeat her, the one who stole you from me. She needs to know she made a mistake."

Sam sighed and pressed his right hand to Miranda's hip, as close as he could come to touching her. The invisible barrier kept him away, pushing at him like a wall of invisible hands.

"If I fail, I will be with you. Is that so wrong? To hope to die? To see you again? To hold you and feel you? I need to know what you want me to do. Should I let them kill me? Do you want me to be with you?"

He waited in vain for an answer, for a hint of what they wanted him to do. If they told him to die he would welcome death like a long-lost lover. If they told him to live; he would, driven forward by their desire.

But they gave him no answer, no clue as to what they wanted him to do, and after countless minutes he lowered his hand and just stared at them, trying to remember everything.

They were flawless, each of them, and somehow in each of them he could see what they would have become, had they lived to see the fruition of their years. In Miranda he saw a doting grandmother, a family matriarch that was the cornerstone of generations. Tommy he saw as a grown man; Cynthia as a striking woman.

Outcomes denied to them all; the strings of their futures cut far too early.

His grief spent, he just looked at them. He eventually had a sense that this - just as everything else - must pass. The time had come, he must go.

He stood on cramped legs and took one last look at them, waving at them silently.

"I love you forever," he whispered.

Sam turned and walked away, towards the silent white horizon from which he had originally come. It was the way back to reality, the way out of this world of dreams. Behind him, at some great distance, the three motionless figures finally stirred. He never saw them wave back, nor the tears that fell from their eyes.

# Chapter 24

*"I had just fallen asleep
When suddenly the door was burst open with
Violence too great for one to believe
That it was robbers;
Nay, the hinges being entirely broken and wrenched,
It was thrown to the ground..."*

-Lucius Apuleius, *The Tale of Aristomenes*

Sam woke, and for a moment he felt disoriented, surrounded by darkness. The blinding white nimbus of light had been instantly replaced by shadows in the refuge where he and Lamia rested, tinting everything in shades of grey and black.

A half-moon hung in the sky.

He felt strangely at peace.

A foreboding feeling draped itself over his shoulders, quenching his contentment.

"What is it?" he asked Lamia, never having felt this level of dread before.

It was like being caught in the eye of a storm when the air was charged with electricity, and etched into the dark and troubled sky, was the certainty that there worse yet to come.

Lamia sat staring hollowly towards the outside world. She seemed calm, sitting in the shadows with her hands folded in her lap, one over the other. Her color however, had turned a pale ghastly white and the gaze that was cast from her eyes was as black as the night that surrounded them. Her mouth was grim; a straight dark line scratched across her face. A cold chill dug into his stomach and the small hairs on the back of his neck stood on end.

"They've come, haven't they?"

Lamia only nodded, a motion that was slight and collected.

"We need to leave, before they find us here." Her voice was gritty under the weight of great pain and duress.

"Where will they meet us?" he asked.

"Where they choose to. We must part for this. You must be alone when they find you. I cannot be with you."

"Will you be there?"

"I must." Her gaze fell to the ground, vacant. "Be careful, Samuel. Do not underestimate them. They will show you no mercy."

"I will," he replied quietly. His voice was not low in fear; it was clear and steady, hushed so as not to disturb the serenity of the moment.

Lamia looked up at him and her eyes searched his face for something.

Then, she was gone.

Lamia fled from the small cave, flowing out through the opening the same way she had at the abandoned cabin, seeming to evaporate like a mist through the stones.

Sam saw her standing on the ground above.

"Leave. Now," she said, and then she left him alone.

Sam followed her direction, pausing to take a look at the moon overhead when he reached the open ground.

"Tonight," he said to himself. "One way or another, it will be over tonight."

# Chapter 25

―――――∽―――――

*"...and what seemed to be a woman*
*— From her face — came to me,*
*Veiling her body and limbs with the hair she had loosened.*
*And I, Solomon, said to the demon:*
*Who are you? She said:*
*...seat yourself on your throne again and ask me.*
*Then you will learn, o king, who I am."*

-The Testament of Solomon

Standing between the dark woods and the light of the city, he decided to turn towards the city. He'd had enough bad dreams in the forest; he didn't want to be met in the woods if he could help it.

He found that his senses were overcome. There was so much detail available to him that he was unable to focus on much. He felt overwhelmed and did his best to turn down his awareness, like trying not to listen to a bad but catchy song on the radio. It didn't get any better or worse as he neared town. He wondered if what he was feeling was a result of his proximity to the Others. He couldn't even touch the familiar sense of Lamia. She was lost amongst the fuzzy static in his mind.

The tickle of hunger played at his mind.

"Later," he mumbled.

If there was a later.

What were they going to do to him? Was he going to have any allies? Could he count on any support? Or were they all going to be as cruel and ruthless with him as Lamia suggested they would be? He didn't know, and would have no way of knowing until it began.

Another sensation pulled at him, heightening his senses.

It was fear. Not the vague fleeting fear of the unknown, but the gnawing unsettled grip of the onset of terror.

Sam wanted to run. He wanted to run away from all of this, to leave it all behind him. He had never wanted any part of it, and now it had caught up with him, seeking to drag him under dark and sweltering covers.

Lamia had become a welcome acquaintance, a friend with whom he could learn to adjust and pass the time; someone to help him explore his new hidden talents. There was no one else. He didn't want to meet the Others.

He didn't care if he never met any of them.

But they wanted to meet him. They had come from all corners of the world for him. Not to meet him; to test him. To see if he was worthy of walking this earth.

The pervasive fear that crept into him and settled in his flesh confirmed something important.

He wanted to live.

His fear was a mortal one; the fear of death. He very much wanted to live. Maybe not like they did, but he had been finding his own way.

He had stumbled more than once, but for the first time in a while, he no longer felt aimless. He felt sure of his purpose, a purpose that he had chosen for himself. A purpose that he could justify.

He would feed on those that preyed on others. He could strike against those that served misery and pain to others. He could be a brand of justice. Justice that was removed from the courtroom; a justice that was cruel and vicious and as cold as biting steel.

An eye for an eye.

He could protect what was good, from that which was evil. Sam savored the irony and it brought a smile to his lips.

He was a creature of evil, a creature of darkness, and through his horrid gift he meant to dispense pain to those that deserved it most. He meant to feed terror to those that spread its fruit. He meant to bring death to those that had every reason to fear its cold judgement.

Sam wandered west and was ever watchful of places that were solitary and poorly lit, trying to be mindful of ambush. He would try to avoid them if he could. If they would come for him, he would at least try to hold the advantage of deciding the place where they would meet.

It might be small, but it was something.

Highway 34 became his path, a well-lit stretch of asphalt that still exuded the baking heat of day from its hard, pitted surface.

He walked, ever to the west, his mind clear.

The scents of summer preoccupied his mind, a pleasant reminder of days gone by.

Young people drove past him, oblivious to his shadow on the side of the road. He could smell their energy and their zest as they left him behind. It was the scent of exuberant life; a youthful energy so ripe that it seemed as though it might burst from their skin like an overfilled balloon. Life had not yet ingrained any deep disappointments; no great tragedies or any of the painful aches that were sure to occur in the years to come. Some people carried the scent of maturity, the enjoyment of the summer air and of years gone by, feelings not so different than the ones Sam felt, rejuvenated by the summer fragrances. Others still were old. Some of these were pleasant and thoughtful; others were fearful, trying to enjoy the pleasures of summer while aware that this might be the last, or one of only a few remaining. The young felt timeless; the old felt the cold stare of mortality upon them.

After some time, Sam decided to veer away from the highway, content to turn north.

The confusion in his mind still reigned supreme; the Others were indeterminate and vague, no closer yet no farther away.

There was no odor on the wind that might give them away, no sound that might betray their presence, only the feeling that they were here. Waiting.

The city lights fell behind him and he found that he did not care.

Let them come, he decided. He was still wary, still watchful, but he decided not to be afraid of something that was inevitable. If it was to be tonight, then better to accept it. Perhaps that was a part of what was expected of him, a part of the test that he was to endure.

And so he walked onward.

The asphalt failed and yielded to dry dirt and gravel, flanked by the thin grasses and bushes that thrived at the side of gravel roads.

In the distance, hills rose into the air, providing dark voids set against the backdrop of evening stars and a moon that had already reached its zenith in the sky.

An owl crossed his path, its beating wings almost perfectly silent in the warm air.

It flew in front of him and then veered east, steering towards a promising field in the distance.

He could feel its confidence and its determination. It had young and its mate was waiting for him to return.

Sam grinned, pleased to have seen such a solitary bird of prey cross his path.

The steady drone of insects rose as he walked, all of them burrowing and foraging and searching for mates. Bats filled the night air with countless chirps and squeaks; their hunting chatter was all around him.

He pressed forward as the night drew on, walking and watching as the low hills in the distance rose to dominate his view, towering before him. Thin trees clung to life in those barren hills. Vast piles of scree formed treacherous slopes amongst spires of oddly-shaped spires of stone.

It was desolate and beautiful.

Without reason he turned again and followed a thin and scarcely travelled path that passed between two rising hills that widened sharply at their base, unfolding into a broad and open plain between them. The clearing before him was flat and desolate; the dry earth was pockmarked with stones of every shape and size. There was a variety of thin stubby plants that had managed to find enough moisture to survive in the arid hills.

The stones crunched underfoot as he walked, grinding under the soles of his shoes.

Sam walked through the tapering part of the path with his eyes downcast, seeking to avoid larger stones, before he reached an area that was open and free of larger obstacles.

The chaos in his head continued to rumble and distract, nothing in particular was any less random or confusing.

Then, without warning - it vanished.

It was like a summer cloudburst had expended itself and surrendered suddenly to a bright clear sky.

The noise and confusion fell away, replaced by the very pointed and precise sensation of people.

"He has come," a voice said suddenly, shattering the calm silence of the evening.

Unfamiliar voices, male and female, repeated the statement. Some overlapped; some were distinct.

*"He has come."*

A single figure emerged from the darkness in front of him. It was Lilith.

Not Lilith by the lakeside, the killer and the stalker. Not the shrieking Lilith who had attacked him in the alley. This was a different Lilith, the Lilith of ancient myth and tale, surrounded by her offspring on the mountainside.

This was Lilith of the *Vardat Lilitu*, the Mother and Queen of them all, surrounded by her children in the high desert.

She was serene and majestic, fully beautiful and terrifying all in one instant.

Sam felt them all close in to surround him, sealing off the path he had travelled.

"Welcome, Samuel," said Lilith.

Her arms rose from her sides, her palms facing up to the night sky.

Her eyes were as dark and shimmering as volcanic glass.

It sounded ceremonial to him, as though it was how she was meant to begin.

"Welcome to the Devil's Backbone. We have gathered here to await your coming. Come and meet them, come to them and see them revealed to you, your Brothers and Sisters of the *Lilitu*."

Sam looked about, turning to see everyone around him.

There was no pattern to how they stood around him, no obvious plan. Although he had never before seen their faces, he knew at once which name belonged to which face.

None of them moved.

All of them seemed to be waiting, but for what, he had no idea.

Not wanting to wait, he turned and slowly walked to the one that had blocked the path behind him.

He felt pulled forward, constrained by an unspoken ritual he had to obey.

The man appraised him boldly, keenly observant.

Sam stopped when he faced him directly, within an arm's length.

"Ambrogio," Sam said to him.

His hair was dark and slightly curled; his frame youthful and strong.

Although his eyes were dark, they contained an inexplicable merriment as well as a festered, corrupted ego.

Sam saw a series of images and memories flow through his mind as he looked upon him. A particular phrase gathered itself in his mind. The words and images coalesced.

"The curse. The moon. Blood will run."

Ambrogio blinked unexpectedly and the surety in his eyes faltered.

Sam ignored his reaction and approached the woman to Ambrogio's left, stopping before her at the same proximity.

She was dressed in white robes and seemed to shine from within. Her hair was the darkest black; her skin was like ivory. Everything about her seemed to be a study in contrasts. While her figure was supple, the line of her neck was sharp and angular. Her hands appeared soft; the hands of nobility, while her arms and shoulders hinted at unspoken strength. She was an enigma.

She stared at him boldly; a slight smile touched her lips as she watched him look upon her.

As with Ambrogio, images flooded his mind.

In a moment she was clear to him.

"Selene. Goddess of Moonlight."

The smile was erased from her lips in an instant, replaced by a smoldering look.

Sam left her and stood before the next of them, interested to see what images would come to him.

She was dressed plainly and scrutinized his every motion, eager to see him closely. She appeared to be intrigued.

"Mahalath."

"How is it you know my name?" she asked him curiously.

He did not answer her, for he himself did not know how he knew. He just did.

"Mahalath, daughter of Ishmael."

She nodded subtly and seemed pleased to be recognized, willing to forgive that her question drew no answer. Her eyes narrowed in interest. He felt a thousand unasked questions burst into her mind. Sam moved on.

A broad shouldered man glared at Sam as he came to him.

He seemed to be of middle age, mature, and possessed of a look that was ill-tempered and quick to anger. His mind was filled with hatred and loathing; his visage was broad with nurtured conceit.

His name came quickly, for which Sam was grateful.

"Ashmodai."

An image of crowns and a fiery throne swirled into his thoughts.

"King of the Nine Hells."

Sam felt Ashmodai's anger grow at the identification, not at all pleased for being known. He was resentful for having been drawn here, to be compelled to a land that, for him, held no beauty.

Sam pressed onward, feeling drawn to complete a task.

The next woman was dark-skinned, elegantly dressed in pale robes that fluttered gently and caught the slightest breeze, tugging at a slender and athletic frame. Like her skin, her eyes were dark and they held a glittering depth, like a precious stone that glinted from some deep internal flaw.

He saw dunes, great rolling waves of sand inexorably creeping over the land. He saw the baking heat of the day and the freezing grip of night. Behind all of this, a reclusive Being dwelt, bathed in stark beauty, revelling in its own harshness and its precious islands of life. This Being was her father, and loved her above all else. She was as close as It would come to being a part of the wider world.

"Igrat, the Daughter of the Desert Spirit."

Her dark eyes spoke of the countless questions she had for him but her mouth remained fixed, twisted as though she had tasted the bitterest of fruit.

A man stood at her side, a man that was at once healthy and sickly. He was no taller than Sam was, with shoulder-length brown hair and the thin wiry build of a long distance runner. His eyes sparkled with vitality and yet were stained bloodshot as though he was infinitely fatigued. His musculature was lean and Apollonian, yet Sam sensed his limbs were weak and exhausted.

"Nega'."

The man bowed his head to him slightly in acknowledgement.

Sam saw a vision of locusts and pestilence, a vast array of lesions and illness, coughing and drought. His mouth grew dry.

"Lord of Plagues."

Nega' remained motionless, solemn and silent.

The next in line was dressed more daringly, her hair tied into an intricate braid and held at the end with a knotted scarlet ribbon. Her figure-hugging dress revealed a plunging, open neckline that exposed a great deal of flesh. She held the composure and grace of haughty femininity.

Sam saw great halls of travellers and merchants, vagabonds and wanderers filling cramped rooms and bustling kitchens, of maidens serving drinks and food, of coin changing hand. He saw trade and smuggling, both in goods and in people.

Everything coalesced at once.

"The Innkeeper," he said, "Rahab, the Harlot."

He felt embarrassed at her second title, seeing it only in the final moment of his revelation.

Rahab watched him pass onto the next of the Lilitu, casting her gaze upon him calmly as he left her as she was.

Sam almost stumbled as he came upon her, momentarily confusing her with either Lamia or Lilith. She looked so similar to them that she could be mistaken for family. As his mind revealed her to him he saw that this was not the case, although she too was ancient, older than most of those that had collected here tonight around him. She was somehow even more stunning than the others, and none of them would be considered anything less than beautiful. Besides her appearance and figure, she was also confident and collected. The way she looked at him was as though he was being deciphered, read like a book. Her mannerisms were regal, her posture flawless. He saw an ancient city, a center of commerce and trade, an exciting center where new possibilities had begun to take root and would spread to all the four corners of the world. Like Rahab, her hair was intricately weaved into a classical style, but her clothing was finer and more colorful, an ensemble that spoke of taste and great attention to detail. She left no stone unturned, no avenue unexplored. She smelled of history and antiquity.

"The Great Lady of Ur," he finally said, blinking as he recollected his concentration.

Her face was unmoving and she looked upon on him with studious attention.

"What else am I called?" she asked him directly, pointedly. It was not a question.

It was a command.

She wanted to know the depths of his ability to see her, to know her.

It came to him easily.

"The Bright Lady."

She remained still, save a small narrowing of her eyes at his answer. "And my name?"

"Naamah."

Her mouth betrayed the smallest of smiles; the rest of her features were set like stone. She was pleased but would reveal no more.

He left Naamah and came to an older red-haired man with a build that had been developed over a lifetime of hard labor. His musculature was not that of youth, instead it was that of maturity and great hidden strength, a frame that was densely set and difficult to truly discern. It was a trait that a young man could easily miss; a mistake that could cost him dearly in an altercation. It was not the man's stature that held Sam fast; it was the unrestricted sadness beneath his skin. His regret scented the air around him, like the fragrance permeating a rancid apple. Murder was behind those sullen eyes, murder that could not be taken back.

Sam saw the killing of a brother and the onset of a terrible curse; being set on a vagrant's path everlasting.

"Cain, the Fugitive."

Sam saw the man flinch when he spoke the words.

The next in line was tall, a good head taller than all the rest. His eyes were piercing and what came through to Sam was a feeling of a dread and irrevocable closure. From him there was no escape.

"Who takes the soul away from Man. Samael."

Sam saw that he had nearly completed the circle.

He came next to Lamia.

She was so like Naamah; she held a similar bearing of the great passage of time, another being who was, in many ways, a manifestation of history itself. Unlike the others, she was not reserved at his approach. She held the faint scent of fear, a scent that Sam was certain the Others could also detect, as faint and diffuse as it was. The question was, what was she afraid of? Afraid of him? Afraid of what was to come? Or was she afraid of something else?

Like Naamah, she was terribly beautiful.

Here, amongst the Others, that beauty seemed to intensify; become more pure. She held rank here. Authority.

Her images flooded into his mind and seized him, briefly taking him out of himself into a state where he was catatonic and helpless.

He saw civilizations come and go; cities and empires rise and fall. He saw great men weep; he saw weak men conquer. He saw children die. He saw sorrow and grief, he felt despair and hopelessness. He saw her as a young woman; he saw her as a mother. He saw her bury her children. He saw Lilith come and take her. He felt the sting of her eternal bite and the grace that she bestowed on those who welcomed her. He saw the cunning of the beast that she was. He saw the lust and the satiation.

He saw the tenderness.

She was a great many things, too many for him to individualize within a time that he sensed was meant to be short.

He saw the Others yield unquestioningly to her. She was the sister of Lilith; blood kin to the Master.

"The Queen of Demons," he finally said, summarizing everything he could absorb.

Sam moved on to his final experience; to Lilith who stood before them all - an Imperial Empress before her royal court.

She seemed pleased with him, as though he had handled himself well.

Horrified, Sam realized that he desired that of her; something within him wanted to kneel before her.

He was standing before the root of his misery; the core of his cancer.

If she had never come, he would not be here. He would be with his family, home with Miranda and his children, free to watch as they grew old for as long as nature permitted.

She had taken that from him; had stolen that from him forever.

Her vision took him and he felt as though he was drowning, pulled feet-first to an ocean floor that lay somewhere below a great, dark maw of water; a silent and frigid tomb.

Naamah and Lamia had given him an impression of the ancient; Lilith was a casting of eternity, where what was ancient was nothing but a blink of Time's eye. The weight of her antiquity draped over him like a waterlogged cloak, heavy and omnipresent.

She was the manifestation of vengeance itself, a creature whose sole purpose was revenge and retribution.

She was deep like the sea and, like the sea, she was dark and cold, untouched by the warmth of the sun. Terrible currents raged beneath, crashing waves surged above, malevolent forces joining to drag whatever floated above down to the eternal night below, to be consumed by blind toothsome horrors.

She meant to break him; an endless series of waves that would eventually erode a granite cliff into coarse sand, to claim him into her fathomless depths.

"Lilith, the Mother of Demons," he finally said, breaking out of his hypnosis.

She smiled broadly, her eyes alight with a wicked gleam. Jagged teeth clenched together and she burned with a dreadful ferocity.

"Bow, Samuel. Bow to me and be taken into my fold as one of the *Lilitu*."

# Chapter 26

*"Better to light a candle*
*Than to curse the Darkness."*

- Chinese Proverb

Lilith's voice was cool and commanding; not at all welcoming.

She sought his subservience, his recognition of her as his Master. If he were to bow, to submit to her, Sam realized it would mean his ultimate surrender.

He remembered Miranda, Cindy and Tommy standing before him in that world of white, in that last bitter dream where he could not touch them.

If he surrendered, he cast them aside forever. If he yielded, he turned his back on them. He would repudiate everything he had lost.

The air was filled with the static charge of expectation. All of them waited for him to submit, to yield to her for eternity.

Their expectation was stoking the charge that hung over them all, a self-feeding cycle that was only intensifying and growing stronger. The longer he waited the more electric it became.

He felt like that small and fearful rabbit cowering under the beech roots of Watership Down awaiting the onset of a summer thunderstorm; feeling the weight of the clouds on approach and dreading the inevitable clap of bellowing thunder.

The longer he took, the greater their outrage grew.

Sam understood that there was no turning back, that his delay only fed the danger.

*But if he surrendered...*

Sam clenched his fists as he made his choice.

"I will not yield to you. I have never bowed to you, nor will I ever."

Lilith's composure crumbled.

Her eyes dimmed to the darkest black and her lips drew back in a taut rage, rigid over her teeth.

"You will yield to me," she whispered darkly, a clawed finger pointed at him like the point of a sword.

Sam took a deep breath.

"I will not."

His senses suddenly peaked and he could feel everyone around him, all at once.

It was a murderous outrage, shared and amplified by those who had harbored and sharpened hatred over centuries. Almost hidden in that great wave of rage, was a slim thread of underlying fear. It was Lamia, barely discernible in the inferno of the Others' fury.

"You will yield to me or you will die," Lilith spat, her pale skin was red with fury and her teeth were like eager white daggers.

"If I am to die, I will do my best not to go alone," Sam replied.

She hissed at him like a giant enraged serpent.

The words were unspoken, but he felt her desire for violence, a mental blessing which allowed the Others to unleash their fury and do as they saw fit. If her presence alone would not sway him, perhaps the fear of pain and death would.

She would no longer hold them back, letting slip the hounds of hell.

Sam backed himself quickly into the center, giving himself room to move; to react.

He expected a move from Samael or Ashmodai, someone who had felt naturally violent to him as he had passed by them earlier.

Mahalath suddenly leapt at him, her hands held out to claw and tear at his skin, her mouth open expectantly to bite.

He had not expected it to be her; he had felt so little from her, and nothing overly aggressive.

His martial arts training allowed him to react instinctively, as a thoughtless reflex.

Sam moved at the last moment, pivoting on the balls of his feet and striking out with his palm. His extra reach caught her squarely on the chin, connecting soundly and driving her aside to the ground.

She collapsed into a crumpled heap and was slow to rise. She grinned darkly at him, her eyes glistening with amusement.

"I only want to be left alone," he said to them. "I don't want to fight any of you."

Mahalath rejoined the circle and watched him, biding her time.

"That is not your choice. You will be one of us, or you will be left here to rot upon the ground." The voice was as smooth as silk and cultured. It was Naamah.

She approached him steadily, her features smooth and unconcerned.

Two large incisors had grown over her lower lip, exacerbating the gleeful smile that suddenly developed.

"I shall enjoy this game."

She quickly reached out with a clawed hand, meaning to catch him on the side of the head with a raking strike.

Sam sensed it and ducked, catching her hand as it passed over him.

He seized her by the wrist and he saw her smile drop, replaced by shock and disbelief.

He spun and threw her down harshly, driving her to the ground face first.

There was the unmistakeable sound of cracking ribs and a scream broke from her mouth as she smashed into the earth.

Sam backed away from her, re-establishing his distance and ready stance.

Blood oozed from her mouth as Naamah rose, a flow that stopped even as he watched.

She wiped her blood from her face with her forearm, never dropping her eyes from his.

Her expression had changed.

She was furious.

*Creatures of emotion.*

Sam inhaled deeply, catching his breath, waiting for the next attempt.

He could feel their minds thinking about how to strike him.

Was he reading their minds? Was he doing what had so offended Lamia? No, he wasn't reading their minds, at least not as she had explained it. He was doing something different, something she hadn't been able to predict or sense.

They came at him individually, less and less tentatively as he was steadily able to repel them. Only Lilith and Lamia refrained from becoming involved, observing each encounter as they came at him in turn.

Sam had expected a tougher challenge when one of the males attacked him, but his training and the sense of what they were thinking gave him a supreme advantage.

They struck harder and they fell faster, committing more of their own energy to be turned against them.

Cain had simply come at him too eagerly and Sam had sidestepped him, sticking out a leg that caught Cain and sent him to the dirt.

Ashmodai was more cautious, striding up to him at a walking speed and choosing to engage in more of a pugilistic display. Sam dodged his first swing and grabbed his arm, turning to spin and dropping one knee as he turned. Ashmodai tumbled ungraciously, rolling away with only his pride wounded.

Nega' was defensive, standing his ground and waiting for Sam to strike first.

Sam refused to make the first move and eventually Nega' impatiently struck out, leaning forward excessively as he hoped one strong strike would end the contest.

Sam deftly avoided the swing and pushed Nega's strike down, bringing his own elbow up and over the redirected punch.

His elbow landed on Nega's chin squarely.

He saw Nega's eyes roll back as he fell limply at Sam's feet.

He was unconscious only for a moment, struggling to his feet and staggering away a few moments later, confused and irate.

Igrat was the last to face him.

She fared no better with her attempted kick, although she managed to dodge his counter.

She was lithe and moved quickly, more so than the others had.

He finally beat her with a punch to the solar plexus.

She collapsed to her knees, gasping for breath.

Once they had all come at him, it changed.

Again, he knew before it came.

A rage emanated from Lilith, a rage that coated the ground like oil, a rage that spread, encouraging them to press.

Unsuccessful in a one-on-one challenge, they were going to attack him in groups.

Sam felt what Lamia felt. It was unheard of, a test coming to this. Lamia was privately outraged.

It was going to be Nega' and Selene, from opposite sides, thinking he would be unable to defend against two of them.

He felt them commit to the attack and rush simultaneously.

Sam faked attention to Selene only to pivot out of her way when Nega' was nearly upon him, ready to bite down on his neck.

He allowed Nega' to continue but he caught Selene by the neck and pulled her into his former position, holding her there as Nega' violently collided into her.

Their skulls connected with a sharp crack and they both fell to the ground, blood trickling from their ears.

They did not rise, although Sam knew they were alive. It would take them some time to heal before they would awaken.

The group held a collective breath of disbelief.

He had resisted all of them successfully, in defiance of Lilith, and now he had beaten two at once; handily.

Their anger only intensified; Lilith's most of all.

He could feel her anger permeating the air, driving the Others forward with more and more abandon.

He saw Lamia watching him closely. She was not angry; she was shocked and fearful. He understood; she was afraid they would all turn on him. Against so many there was no way he could prevail. If he continued to defeat them, whatever rational they still possessed would vanish. Her hope had been for a truce. Those chances were rapidly fading.

Another pair rushed him.

Naamah and Igrat circled him and then came forward together, trying to overwhelm him by immediately joining forces headlong into him.

They moved like serpents. Sam caught and deflected their strikes, concentrating intently, waiting for an opening.

Finally, Igrat left herself exposed and Sam punched her in the throat. She fell and crawled away, struggling for breath. Naamah broke her concentration for a moment as she watched Igrat fall, her expression one of concern and dismay.

Sam swept her legs out from underneath her, pushing forward with both hands as she lost her balance to add force to her fall.

She rolled away unhurt but furious, scowling at him.

No sooner was she away, than Cain and Rahab came at him, Cain trying to punch him, swinging with both hands. Rahab appeared to be waiting for Sam to fall, to gain the upper hand when he was at a disadvantage.

Cain stumbled on a loose stone as he came forward and Sam grabbed him by the back of the head, driving him down into his own rising knee.

There was a distinct crunch and scream as Cain's nose was broken. Cain dropped to his knees and covered his face, trying to stem the flow of crimson blood.

Rahab just stared, unwilling to face Sam alone. She backed away. Sam sensed all of them gathering for an onslaught. He could see small portions of what each planned to do, of how they meant to reach him, but not the sequence. They had been unsuccessful alone and in pairs. They now meant to use their greater numbers to bring him down. Sam tried to organize the feelings that came to him, the thoughts and visions muddled together, clouded by many different perspectives and personalities.

It was too many images to sort through, too much to piece together.

He seemed on the verge of being able to clear away the clutter and see what would come, but it remained intangible and fleeting. It was almost there. Almost.

And then they were on him.

He ducked and dodged as best he could, striking out as best he could when he saw an opportunity.

Rahab successfully bit into his arm and Ashmodai was able to temporarily hold one arm back, restricting his ability to fight back for just a moment.

He was kicked in the midsection and then he struck out, catching a blood-soaked Cain in the groin. The effect was what he had hoped; Cain rose up into the air and then came back down, bent over in a fetal position and helpless with pain. Selene returned, her hair caked with matted blood.

Her glare was fearsome and full of loathing.

Lilith watched the tide rise against him, a satisfied grin rising to her lips.

"Are you going to just stand there and watch?" she asked Lamia, her voice like ice.

"This is a travesty," Lamia replied, keeping her concerned eyes on Sam as he lost ground.

"A travesty? He is being tested," Lilith rebutted easily, her eyes alight with amusement.

"This is no longer a test, this is personal for you. You mean to see him fail."

"Perhaps this is too personal for you," Lilith whispered, her voice tainted with displeasure.

Then Lilith grinned, prepared to surprise even her sister. "He looks like Adama, doesn't he?"

Lamia was shocked to hear it said aloud.

"Don't deny it. I saw it plainly the first time I saw him. Is that why you took an interest in helping him? Do old feelings for Adama cloud your judgement?"

Lilith gauged the reaction to her words, watching with avid eyes. Then she grinned; cold and evil.

She saw Lamia struggle.

"Yes," Lilith chuckled. "I can smell it on you." She grabbed Lamia by the throat and brought her face close, wanting to see her torment.

"Adama is dead. His bones are dust. Clear your mind."

Lamia broke the grip and moved away, gnashing her teeth.

"NO! He needed my help to prepare for this. You have no intention of letting him be! No intention. It's your mind that is clouded. YOU can't admit your mistake. YOU can't let him live."

She turned and saw Sam falling under a swarm of the Lilitu. There were just too many of them.

"There were to be twelve. Not thirteen. He must falter," Lilith said evenly.

This was no longer a fair test; this was Lilith ensuring her own desire would come to fruition under the guise of ceremony. If he would not yield to her, she would kill him.

Sam managed to grip Igrat by the throat, crushing her windpipe and forcing her to withdraw. He knew it wouldn't kill her. She would slowly heal, but she was out of the fight for the moment.

He punched Nega' desperately, driving him backwards by breaking his orbital bone before kicking Samael soundly in the chest, sending him onto the lower slope of the hillside behind them. But they kept coming, and with every strike he managed to deflect or inflict, several more reached him. He tried to keep his mind on whoever was nearest; to counter the closest threat first.

He fell slowly to the ground, unable to resist, forced downwards where they could tear at him with leisure.

Lilith laughed bitterly, her dark eyes absorbing the maelstrom before her.

Her bloodlust was driving the frenzy, driving the Others to continue.

No test had ever decayed to this point, had regressed to such an unbalanced affair.

"There is room for another!" Lamia cried to her sister, her voice rising in concern and outrage. Based on what she had seen, Sam had passed the test. He had fared better than anyone. He had correctly named them all and he had known about them, known things that only having the talent to probe another mind would reveal. He had done so, and flawlessly. Then he had repelled them all when they had come for him singly, never mind that he had been able to do so when they had come in pairs.

He was strong. She was proud of how he had fared. He made the Others nervous; she could feel their hesitation, even with their greater numbers.

Only his strength had kept him alive this long.

She sensed he was not tapping into his full ability; something was holding him back. His strength was flowing into him slowly, like a cup being filled by a trickling faucet. There was something deeper behind it, something he was not aware of.

She could smell his desperation growing.

In his desperation, he was becoming confused.

"There cannot be another," Lilith replied with a sinister voice.

"Another that refuses you!" Lamia retorted.

Lilith only smiled, a callous smile that spoke volumes of the fate she had in mind for Sam. "Correct," Lilith said.

Lamia understood at once, and it solidified her resolve.

She ran into the fray.

Lilith remained where she stood, her face freezing into a vicious look of disgust and anger.

"STOP!" Lamia screeched, pulling Ambrogio off of Sam and throwing him to the dirt. A few of them released Sam in surprise, not expecting this turn of events. Others she had to remove forcibly, making them release their grip on him.

Her raging black and yellow eyes were enough to make some let go willingly, fearful of her wrath.

She was not Lilith, but she had birthed her own legend and they had reason to fear her.

Selene glared at her furiously, nursing a broken arm that was almost healed.

"Enough! He is one of us! He has passed the test!"

Lamia placed herself in front of Sam, between him and the Others.

"He saw through each of you! He named you. He saw into your past when you tried to deceive him. You could not block him. He bested all of you in single combat. Have any of you managed to defeat four in your test? To defeat pairs?"

"He will not yield to the Master," Naamah said coldly.

Lamia stood over him protectively, keeping the Others at bay.

Lilith's raw hatred was still strong in the air; still enticing the Others to resume the attack, to end him. They had been in a frenzy and only Lamia's immediate presence kept them from rejoining the fight.

"He will not yield to my sister. He is young. He may yet, if he is given time.

Time enough to heal from the wounds inflicted while he was still mortal."

"He must bow to our Mother," Nega' muttered angrily.

"He beat you, Nega'. I say he be given time. Time to adjust. It has been many centuries since any were added to our number."

"He is more than our agreed upon number. There was to be only twelve," Ashmodai replied.

"He is one more. The world has room for thirteen if it has room for twelve. You all remain in the Old World. The New World has room for one! He can hide easily enough. I have taught him. I have watched him hunt. He is learning."

"Yes he is," a voice agreed.

It was Lilith.

She came to them quietly, surprising them all with her stealth.

Her voice was like death upon the air.

"And who has been his teacher?"

Lamia met her cold gaze and then dropped her eyes, not willing to defy her sister.

"Yes, you have been his teacher. We have all felt it. He is learning, but I wonder if your mind is clear, dear sister? We have listened and sensed as you aided him. We have all sensed as he learned. Learned from *you*."

Sam lay back and gasped for breath, not bothering to rise.

He lay back and listened, letting himself heal as Lilith spoke, feeling a strength return to his body. He felt blood trickling from a dozen wounds, a trickle that slowed and then ceased as he rested.

"You question my motives?" Lamia screamed defiantly. "I taught him as I would have any of you! As I have taught you! This is no test and you all know it. This is personal and you are doing as she bids!"

Lamia hoped this would lower the veil from their eyes, to show them how far they had strayed.

"She is our Master," Mahalath replied calmly.

Lamia looked around, staring at their faces, seeing that none of them disagreed.

"You all disgust me," Lamia spat.

"Leave him, Sister. Let us finish this," Selene said calmly. Her eyes betrayed the bloodlust that coursed through her. She was nearly trembling. She needed to kill. Lamia stood fast, setting her feet firmly into the ground, challenging them to get through her.

Sam slowly stood beside her, renewed.

"Stay on the ground where you belong," Lilith barked at him, disappointed to see him rise.

"I do nothing to please you," Sam said to her, "if you want me on the ground, come and try your hand with me. Coward."

There was a collective gasp from the Others, all of them shocked to hear him talk to her in such a way.

"She is a coward," Sam shouted at them.

Lilith went the purest white with rage, her eyes as black as the void above.

"She could not kill me before and now she fetches you like loyal dogs to face me.

How does it feel, to be her pack of hounds? The dogs of a coward?"

Sam was no longer just renewed, he was trembling with anger.

He had understood there was to be a test, but in learning that there was a vendetta against him, his patience ceased. The test was a farce. He would participate no longer. If they had been shocked at how he addressed Lilith, they were appalled to hear themselves named dogs.

The insolence! The disrespect! The gall!

Sam could feel everything they thought, their collective disbelief at his words.

Instead of feeling them singly or in select pairs as he had when they had fought him, he could feel them all. The blindfold had been removed; a roadside barrier exploding into a myriad of jagged splinters.

He smiled, a look he meant them all to see.

He was not afraid of them and he wanted them all to know it.

"Poor Sister," Lilith whispered to Lamia, placing a hand upon her shoulder, turning Lamia to face her. "Perhaps it was too much for you."

With a slashing motion, Lilith raked her fingertips deeply across her sisters' throat.

Lamia's eyes went wide and she stared at Lilith in disbelief.

With her free hand, Lilith held Sam at bay even though at the moment, he was stunned beyond action.

"Why?" Lamia mouthed just as a gout of blood flowed over her lips, trying to grip Lilith by the shoulders as she quickly weakened.

"To keep you from meddling."

Lamia slipped awkwardly to the ground, her hands moving to clutch her slashed throat.

Blood was matting her shirt and her hands were red, soaked and slippery.

Air bubbles frothed between the arterial spurts pumping through her frantic fingers.

"No!" screamed Sam, prying at the hand that held him back, slowly peeling back the fingers that held him captive.

Lilith fought him and then let him go, using the last of her grip to push him towards Lamia and away from her.

He ignored her entirely, focused only on Lamia.

She was looking at him regretfully through sorrow-filled eyes.

He didn't know if she was going to survive, if she could live through such a terrible and vicious cut.

He bent down to her, kneeling.

"Lamia," he begged, "LAMIA!"

She was conscious but did not reply.

She only smiled at him a little, one side of her lips turning upwards as her fading gaze shifted elsewhere. He saw the memory of a farm enter her mind, a man working in a golden field of wheat and the laughter of daughters.

He suddenly felt the Others begin to move, seeking to capitalize on his distraction.

Sam ignored his compulsion to seek out those nearest to him, those that would strike at him first. He remembered how it felt to sense them all and he opened himself as a conduit to them, able to see all of them, able to know what they were thinking.

He stood and braced himself to meet the first of them.

It was Igrat. She charged him impulsively, overconfident with hands outstretched like talons, meaning to rake and claw at his flesh and bite wherever she could.

Selene came from the other direction. She meant to go for his neck, seeking to bleed him and weaken him for the Others that were not far behind. They meant to overwhelm him like before, to press and to assault him until he was driven down. There, pinned to the earth they could kill him, spreading his entrails across the ground and quartering him, rending him limb from limb. This was no test.

That ploy was over; this was meant to end him.

There was to be no mercy, no respite from this onslaught.

Sam felt his anger rise like an air bubble; no mere emotion that gave him courage or a clear mind. This was an expanding sphere of hatred and strength, and it released within him a vast store of energy. He recalled his night in the alley, the night when he had first turned.

He felt the instinct of violence rise within him, the instinct for self-preservation that had enabled him to viciously attack his assailant and to feed. Within that memory was a dam, a mental barrier that, when breached, allowed him to fight as he once had, unaware of the potential lurking within him. The dam had loosened when he had fought Lilith in the alley; he knew now where that strength had come from, how he had managed to hold her at bay.

The anger and fury of the Others filled the air and he absorbed it, drinking it in and allowing it to fill him.

And now he knew how to let it go.

The barrier dissolved, opening a well of power that seemed to have no bottom.

He didn't smile.

He leered at them all.

Behind his lips, two white canines protruded, their points gleamed like ivory daggers.

"Come then," he said to Igrat.

She faltered as she met him, seeing something that unnerved her.

He caught her by one arm, gripping her above and below the elbow.

He snapped her joint, bending the elbow to an unnatural angle before throwing her, shrieking with pain, at Selene.

Selene ducked and threw herself at him.

Sam knelt and caught her by the throat, squeezing her windpipe shut within his fingers. He felt cartilage crack like dried twigs under his fingertips; heard her gasp of shock and pain as she was suddenly unable to breathe. He didn't let her go; he held her on her knees as she struggled, meeting her desperate gaze with eyes that were flat and emotionless.

He tossed her aside like garbage.

Ambrogio and Ashmodai came at next, full of outrage over Selene. Naamah was at Sam's side and Rahab came behind him. He could smell the shock under their anger.

What he had done to Selene and Igrat fueled their desire for retribution.

No matter.

Ambrogio fell like a candlestick, hoarse and desperate to hold in the intestines that now flowed through his fingers. Sam had slashed at him quickly, disemboweling him neatly. He spun and caught Ashmodai still unprepared for his attack. He drove his hand forward and ran him through with his arm just below the heart, letting him fall limply to the earth.

Ashmodai gasped silently and folded to the ground, not comprehending the hole in his chest. Sam turned to face Naamah. He tripped her with an outstretched leg and then he was on her, twisting her left foot with both hands, not stopping until he heard her knee crack like a rifle shot.

Naamah screamed for mercy.

He shoved her head into the ground to mute her and then caught Rahab by the neck, seeing her eyes grow wide with terror.

No matter how much she struggled, she could not break free.

He held her there for a moment, enjoying her terror.

"Do you understand?" he asked her coldly, seeing her eyes flicker from person to person around him, seeing the carnage that fell before him.

She nodded in fear and then screamed as he knelt and broke her back over his knee, letting her slide to the ground weeping and paralyzed.

He stood and waited for the rest of them, turning to see who was going to come next.

His mind was clear; none of them had committed to another attack.

They simply stood there, mute and unbelieving.

"COME ON!" he shouted at them, taunting those that were left.

His blood was boiling.

He took a step towards Mahalath.

She stepped back, her face pale. He could see his yellow eyes reflected in her own. They burned like torches. "This is what you wanted! This is what you came for! Obey your Master like the spineless dogs you are!"

"Enough!" snarled Samael.

He boldly stepped forward to meet Sam, sneering with contempt.

Sam smiled and met him half way, not content to wait.

Samael clenched a fist and swung at him; his entire weight behind him.

Sam caught his punch smoothly, squeezing his own hand over Samael's fist, adding pressure until he felt knuckles snap in his palm.

Samael held in a stifled shout of pain, but he refused to surrender.

"Yield," Sam ordered him.

Samael clenched his teeth in refusal. "No," he muttered, dropping to his knees as Sam forced him down.

Sam looked up and saw Lilith watching him; her face was ashen.

Under Samael's denial, cloaked behind anger and rage; was the faint odor of fear.

Sam grinned.

"Yield or I will break your neck," he hissed to Samael.

Samael gaped at him in disbelief.

Then Sam glared. "So be it."

Sam gripped him by the neck and head and held Samael close, preparing for the final jerk that would snap his vertebra.

At the last moment Samael screamed into his shirt, "I yield! No! I yield, I yield!"

Sam held him tight for a moment before releasing him, shoving him to ground with his knee. He allowed Samael to crawl away, defeated.

Of those that remained, none other came to him.

Cain had backed away, nervously watching him.

Seeing there were no other challenges, Sam returned to Lamia.

She was barely conscious, her eyes flittering and unable to focus. The flow of blood from her neck had slowed to barely a trickle, but she was surrounded by a pool of it, far too much blood loss to survive.

"Lamia," he whispered into her ear, looking for a response.

Her eyes seemed to try to look for him for the scantest of moments before rolling back in her head to show their whites.

Lilith was glaring at him, caught between her own fury and a fear that she would not prevail.

"You are even worse than I imagined," Sam said to her, wondering how she could do this to her own sister.

"You are weak," she sneered at him, looking to the wounded that lay on the ground around him, listening to the moans and cries of pain.

"Even in victory you could not kill them."

"I chose not to!" he retorted, "I will not be like you. You would kill your own sister to satisfy your petty ego."

Her demeanour became even more frozen and detached, more rigid at his denial of her.

"I never want to see you again. Leave." With that, he dismissed her and lowered himself to the ground to help Lamia, kneeling behind her and raising her upper body up off the ground, resting her against his own chest.

Sam remembered something Lamia had said to him before, a night not too long ago in a graveyard. To hide her own marks on her victims she infused them with a little of herself, enough to hide the evidence. He had fled when he had first experienced that feeling, thinking she was doing something repugnant to the old woman. He recalled carefully how that had felt, how her thoughts had felt as she had done exactly that.

He gently moved a trestle of hair away from her neck and lowered his mouth to her skin, feeling with his mind where he needed to bite her.

"What are you doing?" Lilith barked, her voice filled with outrage.

She took a step towards him, her face livid. He sensed she was considering interfering, seeking a moment of weakness.

She might still be able to kill him if she attacked quickly, before he was able to defend himself. If she managed to do that, they would either fight to a horrific stalemate or, ultimately, to the death of them both.

If he focused on Lilith, Lamia was likely to die.

If he focused on Lamia, they both might.

He was content with the outcome of the night; he had denied Lilith and he had defeated her legion.

If he were still to die tonight, he might at least save Lamia.

Sam ignored Lilith, pushing everything but Lamia out of his mind, focusing everything on her. A mistake would kill her. This was not so different from another type of bite. He was aware that Lilith continued to protest and howl, and that she was coming closer.

He knew she was able to see that he was distracted, not focusing on her at all.

For a moment, what he saw in her mind was clear and precise. She would come, to mete whatever justice she felt was due to be served.

Sam resigned himself to saving Lamia.

He had only a moment to spare and that was all he needed; one moment and then he could fall into the sweet arms of death and all of this would be done, forgotten and washed away by a cleansing river.

Then suddenly, it was quiet.

He paused over her neck, his teeth ready to deliver her salvation.

Something was different.

He was not alone.

Lilith came no closer; her voice was strangely muted, like a faint and twisted echo.

"Save her," a familiar voice said beside him.

Sam looked up to see that a brilliant blue light was around him, over *them*, dropped like some nebulous curtain. A silhouette stood between him and that cold blue barrier, a silhouette that held aloft a cross that glowed with a burning golden flame.

The Reverend.

Sam had ignored everything around him while he concentrated on Lamia, not even noticing the faint steps of the Reverend's soft shoes on the loose stones as he had approached undetected into their very midst. None of them had noticed him enter their fray. Sam saw the Reverend's face, filled with conviction and raw strength; he stood there determined and unafraid.

In that face he saw forgiving eyes, warm grandfatherly eyes that meant to help.

Sam lowered his head to her neck and bit her softly, penetrating her skin and focusing, not on taking life, but on giving it.

He felt dizzy, his thoughts were confused and perilously unbalanced. The world swam before his eyes. He saw her thoughts. He felt her thoughts. He was her. She was him. He felt her awareness of him; he sensed her acceptance of inevitable death. He saw that although she fought against her own death, a part of her awaited its sweet final kiss. He saw her lowering her children into a black and fertile earth millennia ago, vowing to never forget them. He felt her body reach out to connect with him, her wound seeking the energy it so desperately needed to heal.

He released himself to that connection, feeling it draw from him. It flowed from him willingly, a tingle of small electrical sparks.

Lamia's eyes flew open and he recoiled from a feeling of surprise; the connection was severed instantly, and the release drove him backwards as though he had been pushed.

Sam fell back and sat queasy on the ground, trying to drive the vertigo from his mind. Lamia sat up and felt her neck gingerly, looking at Sam and then up at the Reverend with a confused and scattered look.

There was no mark upon her neck; no slash marred her fair skin.

Her fingertips traced where the wound had been and then dropped to her side. Only the blemish of dried blood sullied her appearance.

"How?" she asked.

The Reverend offered her his hand with a smile.

His attention never wavered from its point of focus somewhere beyond them, just outside of the dome of light.

She took it warmly and he pulled her up to his side.

"He saved you, Child."

She squinted at the harsh light that hovered over them, seeing Sam trying to rise. He shook wearily on unsteady feet, like a newborn calf testing untried legs.

She helped him to his feet, each helping to steady the other.

Lamia noticed a figure standing in the night, a shape that was gazing upon them with a deep loathing.

It was Lilith, standing just beyond the strange light.

Her black eyes were bottomless, staring equally at them all.

Her lips were dark and straight, cold and thin.

Pointed teeth marred that perfect line.

"You live," she said from between those dark lips.

From the shadows other shapes came and gathered around her, barred from approaching any closer than she herself stood.

They hissed at the light and would not dare to look upon the cross, averting their eyes instead to other things that lay within the dome, beyond their reach.

"You are beaten," Lamia said to her sister, her own voice flat and without emotion.

Lilith's brow momentarily creased with anger, then smoothed and she was still.

"For today," she replied.

Her eyes shifted to Sam, fixating upon him with a brutal fascination.

Sam faced her, looking down upon her face, only inches away.

"I renounce you. To you, I will never submit. You, I will never follow. You will leave me be."

Lilith sneered, revealing the full extent of her vicious mouth, filled with dagger-like teeth.

Sam's hand shot out through that blue light and gripped her by the neck, his nails digging into her eternal flesh.

She tried to resist and touched the light, instantly repulsed by a crackle of electricity and a burst of black smoke. Her flesh was charred.

The Others around her stepped back, appalled and afraid of the terrible glow.

He pulled her towards the light, near enough that she could move no further.

He stood closer to her, almost touching, eye to eye.

"If I pulled you through, you would die."

Her eyes grew wide with fear and loathing, seeing the truth in what he said.

It was not him she resisted; it was not him that could kill her, it was something else, the power behind the light that burned her. To that she was not immune. She saw that it did not harm him and that to him it was no impediment.

"Do it then," she snarled at him.

"No. I'm not like you. I will never be like you."

Unexpectedly, she laughed, her sharp teeth snapped in the night air.

"You are like me, you fool! You are one of us!"

Lamia's eyes sparkled.

A moment later, Lilith saw her mistake.

Her laughter vanished and her razor-filled mouth clamped shut.

"The Master has judged. He is one of us. Samuel has passed the Test and he is welcomed into the Lilitu," Lamia announced formally.

Sam released her easily, glad to be rid of her foul touch, removing his hand from her throat and pulling his arm back through the barrier.

All of them had heard Lilith say it. All of them understood at once the weight and formality behind those words.

The hatred in the air broke and was replaced by the sweet smell of summer blossoms carried on dry breezes.

It was over.

# Chapter 27

*"They sacrificed to demons that were no gods,*
*to gods they had never known,*
*to new gods that had come recently,*
*whom your fathers had never dreaded."*

-Deuteronomy 32:17

The gathering around Lilith began to disperse, none of them taking the same path.

Only Lilith stayed where she was, alone and sullen, staring blankly at them.

"He is safe now," Lamia said to the Reverend, "the Others will not harm him. You saw to that personally."

"He will not be welcome among us," Lilith hissed to Lamia, ignoring Sam and the Reverend for the moment.

"I don't seek your welcome. I want to be left alone," Sam said, intruding on what was meant to be a private conversation.

"That remains to be seen," she said coldly.

"I can feel where everyone is. Even when they are trying to hide themselves, I will know where they are. I will know if they try to surprise me or if they mean me harm."

"And what then? What will you do? Wound them like you did tonight and then flee howling into the woods?" Lilith asked mockingly, trying to belittle him.

"No," Sam said, "I will kill them."

His words were flat and calm, without hate, carrying with it the burden of truth.

"Our paths will cross again," Lilith said, "Perhaps in ten years; perhaps a hundred. I will always be."

"Perhaps," Sam said, "Now leave us."

Lilith gave each of them one final glance, lingering for a moment longer on her sister; her sister who somehow stood beside the Reverend. A question crossed her face and then, like her, was gone.

They stood alone, alone under a million stars and the ghostly web of the Milky Way.

The dome faded and then abruptly ceased to be, allowing the dark of night to close in on them.

Lamia heard a labored breath.

"Reverend," Lamia said, catching him just as he fell into her arms. Sam helped lower the Reverend to the ground as he slumped over. Lamia felt his forehead and Sam felt her reach out with her mind.

"He is exhausted," she said.

Sam nodded. "He just needs sleep. Sleep and something to eat. He'll be fine."

Sam looked up at her, glad to see she was well.

A thin white line was all that was left of her near-fatal wound. Within the hour it would be gone.

She smiled back at him, understanding how he felt without a word being spoken.

He looked back down at the Reverend, seeing the many years of life that had been etched into his skin like delicate tree rings.

"How did he come here? How did he know?"

"I told him," Lamia replied.

"Told him what?"

"Told him what was happening."

"You knew it was going to happen here?"

"Not everything is a mystery Samuel. Lilith has a flair for the dramatic and I knew she would be drawn to a place with such a name. The Devil's Backbone. It was almost too obvious."

"And how did I get here?"

"You were summoned by all of us to come. It can never happen again, as it can only happen for this one rite."

"Why did he come?"

Lamia looked at the Reverend with soft eyes.

"You will need to ask him that when he wakes. I hoped he would come. He is a good man."

"We can ask him."

Lamia shook her head.

"I can't. I must leave you now," she explained.

Sam looked pained.

"I must leave for a while. You must find yourself and make peace with this. You have taken your first step, the first step on a long journey. That takes preparation. You have the abilities, now you have to be at peace with them." She looked down at the Reverend like a mother looking down upon her child. "Thank him for me, when he wakes. Tell him I will see him again."

"You will come back?"

"Or you will find me, eventually. Will you stay here?"

Sam looked about, admiring the low hills and jagged rocks. It was beautiful, but it wasn't home.

"I don't know. Maybe for a while. I have some ties to this place now."

From here he didn't know where else he might go.

They looked at each other without speaking, an unusual silence between them.

"Thank you," he said finally.

"I have a final question for you," Lamia replied, "Why?"

"Why what?" asked Sam, confused.

"Why did you help me?" she explained, "you could have left me to die. It was risky, doing what you did. It made you vulnerable. It was what Lilith wanted; to distract you."

"She wanted to kill you."

"No, if she wanted me dead I would be. I was bait, and you took it."

"I owed you at least that much."

It wasn't the full breadth of what he wanted to say, but he didn't have the words to explain himself. He was relieved when she seemed to understand.

She fondly placed her hands on his face, making him pay attention to her.

"Remember what you are, and make it your own. You are not cast into a mold. You are what you choose to be. You have shown them that tonight, and they will not forget. You are a beautiful creature, a very rare creature."

"And what is that?" he wondered.

Lamia smiled warmly.

"*Ina akhkharu.*"

He gave her the same puzzled look he always did when she spoke to him in a foreign language.

"Are you going to tell me what that means?"

"It is Sumerian, and you have earned the title, *Vampire*. Your journey begins tonight and the road is long. It leads but one way. The rest; *ana harrani sa alaktasa la tarat.*"

She gave him once last glance and let him go. Then she was gone, the soft kiss on his cheek planted before he even knew that she was no longer there.

He felt her leave, following a path that led her to the southeast. Seeing that she was not returning he let the feeling slip away, focusing on his immediate surroundings.

The Reverend was still fast asleep, breathing slowly and deeply in a dreamless sleep. His mind was clear and without worry.

"I envy you," Sam said in a hushed tone.

He wished he could sleep that peacefully again, a sleep untouched by night terrors and tormented thoughts.

Maybe tonight, he hoped.

Maybe tonight.

# Chapter 28

———— ⌒ ————

Sam finally arrived at the steps of the church early in the morning, at the point where the sky was brightening quickly and early risers were already well into their morning routines enjoying their coffee, or their eggs, or whatever got them going for the day. There was maybe an hour left before the sun crested the horizon.

He stood at the foot of the steps with apprehension; reluctant to proceed.

This was a place of pain for him, a place that was forbidden.

The church was aware of him and, if it were a person, he would say it was biding its time with him; smug and reassured.

His memories of this place were uncomfortable.

Sam climbed the steps, the Reverend still sleeping soundly in his arms.

But it was different than the last time he was here. The compulsion to be away from this place was gone. He didn't feel repulsed.

All the same, he was cautious, feeling that the building was watching him warily; like a wrecking yard dog watching someone walk along the fence line of its territory.

He expected it was the presence of the Reverend, warding off some of the effects he expected to feel.

With care, he placed the Reverend against the wall near to the doors; cautious he wouldn't fall over and hurt himself, careful to not touch the doors himself.

He vividly remembered how they had thrown him aside before and the pain that had burned through him like liquid fire.

He was not eager to relive that experience.

Sam was satisfied that Paul would wake soon and find himself in a place where he was safe. He might have some questions about how he had made it back here and what else he might have missed, but he would understand that things must have turned out alright in the end. He could feel Paul's mind stirring, responding unconsciously to the brightening sky.

"How unalike we now are," Sam whispered.

He was beginning to sweat, to feel an uncomfortable dread with every passing moment. His body was screaming for him to find safety, to find shelter, and quickly.

A dog barked somewhere nearby, relieved to have been let outside for its morning pee.

"Sleep well."

Sam left the church, glad to be away. The small hairs on his neck slowly settled as the distance between him and the building widened.

He looked anxiously over at the sunrise.

The sky was pink and blurred, like a paintbrush had spread the colors across it.

The horizon was uncomfortably bright.

Daylight was flooding over the land as he reached his small cave, breaking into the dark places into which he had been ducking and weaving to reach safety.

He settled into the corner and, for a while, was reluctant to let sleep take him.

The sky brightened and slowly shifted into the full glory of summer.

For all that, it was not the glorious blue that he thought about as he gazed out at the world above.

It was the emptiness of the cave.

***

He was sitting alone on a dark basalt cliff in his dream, a cliff backed by a mature, deep green forest. He was overlooking a stream that was far below, little more than ankle deep but fast flowing, cascading over rounded glossy stones. Vibrant mosses and ferns lined its banks and neon dragonflies hovered over its surface. Far beyond, the emerald-colored forest extended to the horizon, bordered by hazy blue mountains in the far off distance. It was late in the afternoon and the sky was clear, marked only by a few high patches of thin wispy clouds. It was still warm, but the growing evening breeze promised cool air to come.

He was completely alone.

Alone, except for his thoughts.

He was waiting for the dream to take a turn for the worse, for something to emerge that would torment him.

Somehow, he expected a cold dense fog to emerge from the woods, like an amoeba crawling around the trees, seeking to envelop him, to obscure his vision, to block his path. He expected the glorious sunlight to fade away, to be replaced by familiar darkness. Worst of all, he expected to be pursued, to be chased relentlessly down a thin forest path, cut at by branches, swatting at insolent insects, fearful of the growling or the cold laughter that would be pursuing him, drawing ever closer. Then he might feel the raking of claws on his back, or of fingers. Or he might find it was Miranda that had been chasing him, or his children, and they would show him no mercy. In fact, they would relish in his panic and pain. They would delight in his misery.

In spite of the almost idyllic surroundings, he was filled with dread, expecting the worst to begin. Any minute now this serene wilderness would dissolve, replaced by an unfolding nightmare.

He was sure of it.

When he heard footsteps in the distance, the crackling of dry twigs and the rustling of leafy branches, he felt sure it had come for him at last.

He made a mental decision not to run.

Running only made it worse, prolonged the terror.

If he stayed put here on the cliff, he would be killed quickly and he could wake up. Maybe he could jump off the ledge and he would wake up before he hit the ground. That had always seemed to happen before. Then he could be spared the worst of it. The only thing left for him to fear would be the unpleasant feeling of falling. It wasn't good, but it was a lot better than the usual assortment of alternatives, a box of chocolates, each flavorful tidbit ending in a different frightful experience.

The footsteps came closer, no longer in the thickest part of the woods where the undergrowth had been dense. It was now in the clear spaces between the trees where a thick blanket of fallen needles littered the ground. They looked deceptively soft and they were quiet to walk on, but he had learned one summer as a youth that they were anything but soft. He had reached for a thick clot of them, intending to throw them at a friend. He came away with a hand suffering from a dozen puncture wounds. Sam couldn't tell precisely how many; it had hurt so frickin' bad. He never tried to throw pine needles again. Lesson learned, A+ on that test.

The footsteps now padded on the basalt.

Sam tensed, waiting for the inevitable growl, or creepy laughter.

The only thing missing was the fog and the darkness. Other than that, the mood was set.

The footsteps stopped.

Whatever it was, it was now behind him.

Ignoring the little voice inside him that was screaming in a terribly high-pitched squeal - *'don't look don't look don't look'* - he looked.

A man was looking back at him with kind, pleasant eyes and a smile that was warm and friendly. His eyes seemed to be filled to the brim with merriment and joy.

Sam blinked, expecting something to change.

The stranger's fine brown hair was stirring in the faint wind, something that clearly didn't bother him in the slightest. He was wearing a button up cotton shirt with the top two buttons undone, faded blue jeans, and smooth dark leather sandals. If Sam had to guess, he would say the man was in his late twenties. His bright white teeth really did look like Chiclet's. They were flawless.

"Hi," Sam said reflexively; he just couldn't help it. The stranger was perfectly inviting on a day that was also perfectly inviting.

"Hello," the man replied warmly, like he was answering an old friend. His face was flushed faintly; the look of a man who had just beat his way through the bush. Other than that, he sported a light tan. A few brambles were stuck to his jeans.

"May I sit with you for a while?"

Sam offered him a spot on the basalt with a flourish of his hand.

The man smiled warmly and took a spot, sighing when he was finally seated and comfortable. He looked out to the horizon, taking in the scenery from their vantage point.

"It is a beautiful view," he said.

It was a comment, not a question, but Sam felt helpless to resist answering, the man was intensely amicable.

"It is," Sam agreed. Some nightmare this was turning out to be.

"I am named Semangelof," the man said, offering his hand.

Sam shook it twice and released. "Sam."

Then his full name. The abbreviated version didn't seem appropriate.

"Samuel."

Semangelof nodded politely and grinned, leaning back on his hands, completely relaxed and enjoying himself.

For several minutes they didn't speak a word to each other.

They gazed out over the forest like two friends out on a hike, taking a well-deserved rest on a spot made just for that purpose.

"Have you decided what you are going to do?" Semangelof finally asked.

He sounded like an older brother, a concerned and helpful older brother, one eager to give advice.

Sam looked at him without answering, wondering exactly what he meant. *Does he mean what I am going to do today? What?*

Semangelof chuckled, the grin never fading for an instant.

"You have some decisions to make," he said, sitting up and folding his hands in his lap. He didn't look at Sam; he kept his eyes out on the scenery.

"I know what I am not going to do," Sam said, testing the waters of the conversation. He didn't know how reserved he wanted to be.

"What is that?" Semangelof asked politely.

"I'm not going to be like *her*," Sam replied.

Semangelof nodded.

"If you were, I would not be here."

Sam looked at him sharply, seeking answers. This man knew more than he was letting on. Much more, and he was revealing very little.

"I can't change back, can I?" Sam asked.

Semangelof shook his head.

"No. You are what you are. Some things cannot be undone. Some things are not meant to be undone, even if they could be changed. For everything, there is a purpose. The question is: what purpose will you choose? What you will see done by your own hand?"

"I know what I can live with," Sam answered him, "I can try to do some good."

"You already have," Semangelof replied. "A man is judged by his actions, not by his words. You have stood against those that very few have resisted and even less has survived."

Sam flashed back to the previous night, remembering Lilith and her brood gathered around him, seeking blood and vengeance. He remembered refusing them; how they stared at him through that blue veil.

"I will not harm the innocent," Sam said, recalling those that he had fed on. Those that had victimized others; those had thrived on pain and suffering. He remembered his children. He was going to have to feed again, and soon. He had to make the choice before his choice was made for him.

"I will do it for them, to make the world a safer place."

Sam noticed that Semangelof was staring at him intently, as though he was measuring the sincerity and truth of his words. The eyes that had been filled with merriment had taken on a serious and penetrating appearance.

"Then I will call you my brother for as long as your actions remain true to your words. You will be our Dark Brother, although you walk in the Blessed Light. May that be for a very long time."

Sam didn't understand.

Semangelof saw his confusion.

"Before you slept in the cave where you are now, you felt alone."

Sam blinked.

"What?" he asked. There were too many questions that suddenly needing answering. *How did he know I was sleeping in a cave?*

Semangelof smiled in understanding but did not explain.

"You need to know that you are not alone. We will help you on your path if you seek our aid. Know that you are not alone. You will never be alone again."

"You will help me?"

"Myself, or my Brothers. Senoy and Sansenoy. You will meet them in time. This has been our task almost from the very beginning. We have sought to undo *her* work, to deny her free reign upon Mankind. Today, we add you to our number."

Semangelof took him softly by the shoulder.

"Your sins are forgiven. Do our work. Do not worry or fret for your wife and children, for they walk in the Kingdom and are at peace."

Tears rose to Sam's eyes and quickly ran down his cheeks.

"Miranda? Cindy and Tommy? Can I see them?"

"You cannot, for they are in a different place than we are. They are well and they have watched over you. They have guided you. They are content with your Purpose. They are proud of you and how you have honored their sacrifice. They love you, as you love them."

Semangelof comforted Sam as he suddenly wept, a grief that cleansed away all of the doubts and worries he'd had about them. All of his fears were washed away.

When at last he was done, he felt purified and stripped bare. He wiped his face dry.

"I must go now," Semangelof said tenderly. "Visit the Reverend. He has done our work and needs to be told that He is pleased. Tell him my name, and he will know you speak the truth."

Sam nodded.

"When you wake you will find a token in your resting place. It will serve to remind you of this dream. Although it is a dream, what I have told you is real. Do Our Fathers' work with us, my Dark Brother. You serve His purpose in the night, and He is pleased with you. Walk with us in His Light."

Semangelof smiled and then stood, stretching.

"It is a good day for a walk in the woods. Remember my words, and farewell."

Sam watched Semangelof walk into the trees, taking the open path back to the forest. Before long he disappeared from sight, lost amidst the lush greenery.

\*\*\*

Sam woke comfortably; curled into the corner where he had originally lay down, warm in a fetal position. He was surrounded by darkness, the moon already high and bright in the sky. He was ravenous and needed to feed, but for the moment that could wait. The dream replayed vividly in his mind.

"Semangelof," he said aloud, recalling the name he was to give the Reverend. He didn't know how he was going to get into the church to see him; he supposed he could just wait for him to eventually come out.

Sam sat up and saw a bright white feather resting on the ground. He picked it up carefully, not wanting to damage it. It was totally clean and perfect, not a speck of dirt or dust marred its appearance. It was large, like from a goose or maybe from a swan; easily as long as his forearm.

He left his cave, still holding the feather, and began the walk to the church, content just to stroll and observe whatever crossed his path. He felt different, in a way he could not put his finger on.

Everything seemed easier.

He logically suspected that a part of it was experience; he was getting used to reaching out with his mind, feeling people and their thoughts. It was a skill, and like all skills, it improved with practice.

There was no one near him, none of *them*. Even Lamia was a considerable distance away, far enough for him to reason that she had spent whatever remained of last night and this night travelling at a good speed. He wondered where she had spent the day. He wondered where she was headed. She was further to the south than she was to the east.

He came to Fourth Street and soon after was standing at the bottom of the staircase in front of the church. He had not expected to find the Reverend waiting for him on the steps, and so he was not

371

disappointed to find them empty. A single brown moth hung from the rise of the second step, fluttering its wings in a steady vibration.

The twin red doors stood closed before him.

As before, he could feel that the building itself, or perhaps it was the ground, was aware of his proximity. Instead of standing in plain sight on the sidewalk he decided to climb the stairs to reduce his visibility.

Semangelof had told him he was his Brother; that he walked in the Light.

His 'Dark Brother'.

He wondered who Semangelof really was.

It was an unusual name, as were Senoy and Sansenoy, for that matter.

He doubted that if he had asked Semangelof about himself, he would have been answered directly. It didn't seem to be the sort of meeting where those details were going to be discussed.

The Reverend could explain it to him, if and when he finally saw him.

Sam felt odd.

The church felt different. It was difficult to put a name to the sensation. He supposed that he didn't feel *opposed*. The feeling that he was going to crawl out of his skin never came. The hairs on his neck hadn't stood on end.

The last time he had stood on the stairs like this, without the Reverend, he recalled that he had wanted to puke. He had wanted to be anywhere else other than on these steps. Now, his palms were dry and cool.

He felt… well, now that he thought about it, he felt normal.

An experimental idea entered his mind.

What if?

Feeling emboldened, he reached his hand out to the polished brass handle on the door, his thumb ready to depress the button that would release the latch.

He took a deep breath, recalling how the last time he had done this, he had recoiled as though he had just grabbed onto the most powerful electrical wires ever built.

He began to sweat.

Semangelof told him that he was doing Gods' work.

Semangelof hadn't said anything about being able to enter a church.

His palm closed around the handle, feeling the cool metal on his skin.

There was no sudden shocking pain, no mindless explosion of repulsive energy.

He depressed the button and heard the distinctive click of the door mechanism.

Sam pushed the door open and stepped inside.

Another feeling came to him, one that was easier to recognize.

He felt welcome.

He felt at home.

Made in the USA
Columbia, SC
25 April 2017